**Ruth Ozeki** is an award-winning novelist and filmmaker. Her third novel, *A Tale for the Time Being,* won the Independent Booksellers Book Award and the Kitschies Red [...] listed for the Man Booker Prize and [...] for Fiction. She is also the author o[...] *Creation.* Ozeki was born and raised [...] father and Japanese mother. In June [...] Buddhist priest. She divides her time between British Columbia and New York.

ruthozeki.com
@ozekiland

'Ingenious and touching'
Philip Pullman

'*A Tale for the Time Being* is a timeless story. Ruth Ozeki beautifully renders not only the devastation of the collision between man and the natural world, but also the often miraculous results of it. She is a deeply intelligent and humane writer who offers her insights with a grace that beguiles. I truly love this novel'
Alice Sebold

'This is one of the most deeply moving and thought-provoking novels I have read in a long time. In precise and luminous prose, Ozeki captures both the sweep and detail of our shared humanity, moving seamlessly between Nao's story and our own'
Madeline Miller

'Packed with philosophical asides about time, and is unexpectedly moving'
*The Times*

'A beautifully interwoven novel about magic and loss and the incomprehensible threads that connect our lives'
Elizabeth Gilbert

# A TALE
## FOR THE
# TIME
# BEING

# RUTH OZEKI

CANONGATE

This Canons edition published in Great Britain in 2019 by Canongate Books

First published in Great Britain in 2013 by Canongate Books Ltd,
14 High Street, Edinburgh EH1 1TE

First published in the United States of America in 2013 by Viking,
an imprint of Penguin Group (USA)

canongate.co.uk

2

*British Cataloguing-in-Publication Data*
A catalogue record for this book is available on
request from the British Library

ISBN 978 1 78689 390 1

Printed and bound in Great Britain by Clays Ltd, Elcograf S.p.A.

*For Masako,*
*for now and forever*

# Part I

An ancient buddha once said:

*For the time being, standing on the tallest mountaintop,*
*For the time being, moving on the deepest ocean floor,*
*For the time being, a demon with three heads and eight arms,*
*For the time being, the golden sixteen-foot body of a buddha,*
*For the time being, a monk's staff or a master's fly-swatter,*[1]
*For the time being, a pillar or a lantern,*
*For the time being, any Dick or Jane,*[2]
*For the time being, the entire earth and the boundless sky.*

—Dōgen Zenji, "For the Time Being"[3]

1. Jpn. *hossu*—a whisk made of horse tails, carried by a Zen Buddhist priest.
2. Jpn. *chōsan rishi*—lit. third son of Zhang and fourth son of Li; an idiom meaning "any ordinary person." I've translated this as "any Dick or Jane," but it could just as well be "any Tom, Dick, or Harry."
3. Eihei Dōgen Zenji (1200–1253)—Japanese Zen master and author of the *Shōbōgenzō* (*The Treasury of the True Dharma Eye*). "For the Time Being" (Uji) is the eleventh chapter.

# *Nao*

## 1.

Hi!

My name is Nao, and I am a time being. Do you know what a time being is? Well, if you give me a moment, I will tell you.

A time being is someone who lives in time, and that means you, and me, and every one of us who is, or was, or ever will be. As for me, right now I am sitting in a French maid café in Akiba Electricity Town, listening to a sad chanson that is playing sometime in your past, which is also my present, writing this and wondering about you, somewhere in my future. And if you're reading this, then maybe by now you're wondering about me, too.

You wonder about me.

I wonder about you.

Who are you and what are you doing?

Are you in a New York subway car hanging from a strap, or soaking in your hot tub in Sunnyvale?

Are you sunbathing on a sandy beach in Phuket, or having your toenails buffed in Brighton?

Are you a male or a female or somewhere in between?

Is your girlfriend cooking you a yummy dinner, or are you eating cold Chinese noodles from a box?

Are you curled up with your back turned coldly toward your snoring wife, or are you eagerly waiting for your beautiful lover to finish his bath so you can make passionate love to him?

Do you have a cat and is she sitting on your lap? Does her forehead smell like cedar trees and fresh sweet air?

Actually, it doesn't matter very much, because by the time you read this, everything will be different, and you will be nowhere in particular, flipping idly through the pages of this book, which happens to be the diary of my last days on earth, wondering if you should keep on reading.

And if you decide not to read any more, hey, no problem, because you're not the one I was waiting for anyway. But if you do decide to read on, then guess what? You're my kind of time being and together we'll make magic!

## 2.

Ugh. That was dumb. I'll have to do better. I bet you're wondering what kind of stupid girl would write words like that.

Well, I would.

Nao would.

Nao is me, Naoko Yasutani, which is my full name, but you can call me Nao because everyone else does. And I better tell you a little more about myself if we're going to keep on meeting like this . . . !☺

Actually, not much has changed. I'm still sitting in this French maid café in Akiba Electricity Town, and Edith Pilaf is singing another sad chanson, and Babette just brought me a coffee and I've taken a sip. Babette is my maid and also my new friend, and my coffee is Blue Mountain and I drink it black, which is unusual for a teenage girl, but it's definitely the way good coffee should be drunk if you have any respect for the bitter bean.

I have pulled up my sock and scratched behind my knee.

I have straightened my pleats so that they line up neatly on the tops of my thighs.

I have tucked my shoulder-length hair behind my right ear, which is pierced with five holes, but now I'm letting it fall modestly across my face again because the otaku[4] salaryman who's sitting at the table next to me is staring, and it's creeping me out even though I find it amusing,

---

4. *otaku* (お宅)—obsessive fan or fanatic, a computer geek, a nerd.

too. I'm wearing my junior high school uniform and I can tell by the way he's looking at my body that he's got a major schoolgirl fetish, and if that's the case, then how come he's hanging out in a French maid café? I mean, what a dope!

But you can never tell. Everything changes, and anything is possible, so maybe I'll change my mind about him, too. Maybe in the next few minutes, he will lean awkwardly in my direction and say something surprisingly beautiful to me, and I will be overcome with a fondness for him in spite of his greasy hair and bad complexion, and I'll actually condescend to converse with him a little bit, and eventually he will invite me to go shopping, and if he can convince me that he's madly in love with me, I'll go to a department store with him and let him buy me a cute cardigan sweater or a keitai[5] or handbag, even though he obviously doesn't have a lot of money. Then after, maybe we'll go to a club and drink some cocktails, and zip into a love hotel with a big Jacuzzi, and after we bathe, just as I begin to feel comfortable with him, suddenly his true inner nature will emerge, and he'll tie me up and put the plastic shopping bag from my new cardigan over my head and rape me, and hours later the police will find my lifeless naked body bent at odd angles on the floor, next to the big round zebra-skin bed.

Or maybe he will just ask me to strangle him a little with my panties while he gets off on their beautiful aroma.

Or maybe none of these things will happen except in my mind and yours, because, like I told you, together we're making magic, at least for the time being.

## 3.

Are you still there? I just reread what I wrote about the otaku salaryman, and I want to apologize. That was nasty. That was not a nice way to start.

I don't want to give you the wrong impression. I'm not a stupid girl. I know Edith Pilaf's name isn't really Pilaf. And I'm not a nasty girl or

5. *keitai* (携帯)—mobile phone.

6

a hentai,[6] either. I'm actually not a big fan of hentai, so if you are one, then please just put this book down immediately and don't read any further, okay? You will only be disappointed and wasting your time, because this book is not going to be some kinky girl's secret diary, filled with pink fantasies and nasty fetishes. It's not what you think, since my purpose for writing it before I die is to tell someone the fascinating life story of my hundred-and-four-year-old great-grandmother, who is a Zen Buddhist nun.

You probably don't think nuns are all that fascinating, but my great-grandmother is, and not in a kinky way at all. I am sure there are lots of kinky nuns out there . . . well, maybe not so many kinky nuns, but kinky priests, for sure, kinky priests are everywhere . . . but my diary will not concern itself with them or their freaky behaviors.

This diary will tell the real life story of my great-grandmother Yasutani Jiko. She was a nun and a novelist and New Woman[7] of the Taishō era.[8] She was also an anarchist and a feminist who had plenty of lovers, both males and females, but she was never kinky or nasty. And even though I may end up mentioning some of her love affairs, everything I write will be historically true and empowering to women, and not a lot of foolish geisha crap. So if kinky nasty things are your pleasure, please close this book and give it to your wife or co-worker and save yourself a lot of time and trouble.

4.

I think it's important to have clearly defined goals in life, don't you? Especially if you don't have a lot of life left. Because if you don't have clear goals, you might run out of time, and when the day comes, you'll

---

6. *hentai* (変態)—pervert, a sexual deviant.
7. New Woman—a term used in Japan in the early 1900s to describe progressive, educated women who rejected the limitations of traditional gender-assigned roles.
8. Taishō era, 1912–1926, named for the Taishō emperor, also called Taishō Democracy; a short-lived period of social and political liberalization, which ended with the right-wing military takeover that led to World War II.

find yourself standing on the parapet of a tall building, or sitting on your bed with a bottle of pills in your hand, thinking, Shit! I blew it. If only I'd set clearer goals for myself!

I'm telling you this because I'm actually not going to be around for long, and you might as well know this up front so you don't make assumptions. Assumptions suck. They're like expectations. Assumptions and expectations will kill any relationship, so let's you and me not go there, okay?

The truth is that very soon I'm going to graduate from time, or maybe I shouldn't say graduate because that makes it sound as if I've actually met my goals and deserve to move on, when the fact is that I just turned sixteen and I've accomplished nothing at all. Zilch. Nada. Do I sound pathetic? I don't mean to. I just want to be accurate. Maybe instead of graduate, I should say I'm going to drop out of time. Drop out. Time out. Exit my existence. I'm counting the moments.

One . . .

Two . . .

Three . . .

Four . . .

Hey, I know! Let's count the moments together![9]

---

9. For more thoughts on Zen moments, see Appendix A.

# *Ruth*

## I.

A tiny sparkle caught Ruth's eye, a small glint of refracted sunlight angling out from beneath a massive tangle of drying bull kelp, which the sea had heaved up onto the sand at full tide. She mistook it for the sheen of a dying jellyfish and almost walked right by it. The beaches were overrun with jellyfish these days, the monstrous red stinging kind that looked like wounds along the shoreline.

But something made her stop. She leaned over and nudged the heap of kelp with the toe of her sneaker then poked it with a stick. Untangling the whiplike fronds, she dislodged enough to see that what glistened underneath was not a dying sea jelly, but something plastic, a bag. Not surprising. The ocean was full of plastic. She dug a bit more, until she could lift the bag up by its corner. It was heavier than she expected, a scarred plastic freezer bag, encrusted with barnacles that spread across its surface like a rash. It must have been in the ocean for a long time, she thought. Inside the bag, she could see a hint of something red, someone's garbage, no doubt, tossed overboard or left behind after a picnic or a rave. The sea was always heaving things up and hurling them back: fishing lines, floats, beer cans, plastic toys, tampons, Nike sneakers. A few years earlier it was severed feet. People were finding them up and down Vancouver Island, washed up on the sand. One had been found on this very beach. No one could explain what had happened to the rest of the bodies. Ruth didn't want to think about what might be rotting inside the bag. She flung it farther up the beach. She would finish her walk and then pick it up on the way back, take it home, and throw it out.

## 2.

"What's this?" her husband called from the mud room.

Ruth was cooking dinner, chopping carrots and concentrating.

"This," Oliver repeated when she didn't answer.

She looked up. He was standing in the doorway of the kitchen, dangling the large scarred freezer bag in his fingers. She'd left it out on the porch, intending to deposit it in the trash, but she'd gotten distracted.

"Oh, leave it," she said. "It's garbage. Something I picked up on the beach. Please don't bring it in the house." Why did she have to explain?

"But there's something in it," he said. "Don't you want to know what's inside?"

"No," she said. "Dinner's almost ready."

He brought it in anyway and laid it on the kitchen table, scattering sand. He couldn't help it. It was his nature to need to know, to take things apart and sometimes put them back together. Their freezer was filled with plastic shrouds containing the tiny carcasses of birds, shrews, and other small animals that their cat had brought in, waiting to be dissected and stuffed.

"It's not just one bag," he reported, carefully unzipping the first and laying it aside. "It's bags within bags."

The cat, attracted by all the activity, jumped up onto the table to help. He wasn't allowed on the table. The cat had a name, Schrödinger, but they never used it. Oliver called him the Pest, which sometimes morphed into Pesto. He was always doing bad things, disemboweling squirrels in the middle of the kitchen, leaving small shiny organs, kidneys and intestines, right outside their bedroom door where Ruth would step on them with her bare feet on her way to the bathroom at night. They were a team, Oliver and the cat. When Oliver went upstairs, the cat went upstairs. When Oliver came downstairs to eat, the cat came downstairs to eat. When Oliver went outside to pee, the cat went outside to pee. Now Ruth watched the two of them as they examined the contents of the plastic bags. She winced, anticipating the stench of someone's rotting picnic, or worse, that would ruin the fragrance of their meal. Lentil soup.

They were having lentil soup and salad for dinner, and she'd just put in the rosemary. "Do you think you could dissect your garbage out on the porch?"

"You picked it up," he said. "And anyway, I don't think it's garbage. It's too neatly wrapped." He continued his forensic unpeeling.

Ruth sniffed, but all she could smell was sand and salt and sea.

Suddenly he started laughing. "Look, Pesto!" he said. "It's for you! It's a Hello Kitty lunchbox!"

"Please!" Ruth said, feeling desperate now.

"And there's something inside . . ."

"I'm serious! I don't want you to open it in here. Just take it out—"

But it was too late.

## 3.

He had smoothed the bags flat, laid them out on top of one another in descending order of size, and then sorted the contents into three neat collections: a small stack of handwritten letters; a pudgy bound book with a faded red cover; a sturdy antique wristwatch with a matte black face and a luminous dial. Next to these sat the Hello Kitty lunchbox that had protected the contents from the corrosive effects of the sea. The cat was sniffing at the lunchbox. Ruth picked him up and dropped him on the floor, and then turned her attention to the items on the table.

The letters appeared to be written in Japanese. The cover of the red book was printed in French. The watch had markings etched onto the back that were difficult to decipher, so Oliver had taken out his iPhone and was using the microscope app to examine the engraving. "I think this is Japanese, too," he said.

Ruth flipped through the letters, trying to make out the characters that were written in faded blue ink. "The handwriting's old and cursive. Beautiful, but I can't read a word of it." She put the letters down and took the watch from him. "Yes," she said. "They're Japanese numbers. Not a date, though. Yon, nana, san, hachi, nana. Four, seven, three, eight, seven. Maybe a serial number?"

She held the watch up to her ear and listened for the ticking, but it was broken. She put it down and picked up the bright red lunchbox. The red color showing through the scarred plastic was what had led her to mistake the freezer bag for a stinging jellyfish. How long had it been floating out there in the ocean before washing up? The lunchbox lid had a rubber gasket around the rim. She picked up the book, which was surprisingly dry; the cloth cover was soft and worn, its corners blunt from rough handling. She put the edge to her nose and inhaled the musty scent of mildewed pages and dust. She looked at the title.

"*À la recherche du temps perdu*," she read. "Par Marcel Proust."

### 4.

They liked books, all books, but especially old ones, and their house was overflowing with them. There were books everywhere, stacked on shelves and piled on the floor, on chairs, on the stairway treads, but neither Ruth nor Oliver minded. Ruth was a novelist, and novelists, Oliver asserted, should have cats and books. And indeed, buying books was her consolation for moving to a remote island in the middle of Desolation Sound, where the public library was one small humid room above the community hall, overrun with children. In addition to the extensive and dog-eared juvenile literature section and some popular adult titles, the library's collection seemed largely to comprise books on gardening, canning, food security, alternative energy, alternative healing, and alternative schooling. Ruth missed the abundance and diversity of urban libraries, their quiet spaciousness, and when she and Oliver moved to the small island, they agreed that she should be able to order any book she wanted, which she did. Research, she called it, although in the end he'd read most of them, while she'd read only a few. She just liked having them around. Recently, however, she had started to notice that the damp sea air had swollen their pages and the silverfish had taken up residence in their spines. When she opened the covers, they smelled of mold. This made her sad.

"In search of lost time," she said, translating the tarnished gilt title, embossed on the red cloth spine. "I've never read it."

"I haven't, either," said Oliver. "I don't think I'll be trying it in French, though."

"Mm," she said, agreeing, but then she opened the cover, anyway, curious to see if she could understand just the first few lines. She was expecting to see an age-stained folio, printed in an antique font, so she was entirely unprepared for the adolescent purple handwriting that sprawled across the page. It felt like a desecration, and it shocked her so much she almost dropped the book.

## 5.

Print is predictable and impersonal, conveying information in a mechanical transaction with the reader's eye.

Handwriting, by contrast, resists the eye, reveals its meaning slowly, and is as intimate as skin.

Ruth stared at the page. The purple words were mostly in English, with some Japanese characters scattered here and there, but her eye wasn't really taking in their meaning as much as a *felt* sense, murky and emotional, of the writer's presence. The fingers that had gripped the purple gel ink pen must have belonged to a girl, a teenager. Her handwriting, these loopy purple marks impressed onto the page, retained her moods and anxieties, and the moment Ruth laid eyes on the page, she knew without a doubt that the girl's fingertips were pink and moist, and that she had bitten her nails down to the quick.

Ruth looked more closely at the letters. They were round and a little bit sloppy (as she now imagined the girl must be, too), but they stood more or less upright and marched gamely across the page at a good clip, not in a hurry, but not dawdling, either. Sometimes at the end of a line, they crowded each other a little, like people jostling to get onto an elevator or into a subway car, just as the doors were closing. Ruth's curiosity was piqued. It was clearly a diary of some kind. She examined the cover again. Should she read it? Deliberately now, she turned to the first page, feeling vaguely prurient, like an eavesdropper or a peeping tom. Novelists spend a lot of time poking their noses into other people's business. Ruth was not unfamiliar with this feeling.

*Hi!*, she read. *My name is Nao, and I am a time being. Do you know what a time being is? . . .*

## 6.

"Flotsam," Oliver said. He was examining the barnacles that had grown onto the surface of the outer plastic bag. "I can't believe it."

Ruth glanced up from the page. "Of course it's flotsam," she said. "Or jetsam." The book felt warm in her hands, and she wanted to continue reading but heard herself asking, instead, "What's the difference, anyway?"

"Flotsam is accidental, stuff found floating at sea. Jetsam's been jettisoned. It's a matter of intent. So you're right, maybe this is jetsam." He laid the bag back down onto the table. "I think it's starting."

"What's starting?"

"Drifters," he said. "Escaping the orbit of the Pacific Gyre . . ."

His eyes were sparkling and she could tell he was excited. She rested the book in her lap. "What's a gyre?"

"There are eleven great planetary gyres," he said. "Two of them flow directly toward us from Japan and diverge just off the BC coastline. The smaller one, the Aleut Gyre, goes north toward the Aleutian Islands. The larger one goes south. It's sometimes called the Turtle Gyre, because the sea turtles ride it when they migrate from Japan to Baja."

He held up his hands to describe a big circle. The cat, who had fallen asleep on the table, must have sensed his excitement, because he opened a green eye to watch.

"Imagine the Pacific," Oliver said. "The Turtle Gyre goes clockwise, and the Aleut Gyre goes counterclockwise." His hands moved in the great arcs and spirals of the ocean's flow.

"Isn't this the same as the Kuroshio?"

He'd told her about the Kuroshio already. It was also called the Black

Current, and it brought warm tropical water up from Asia and over to the Pacific Northwest coast.

But now he shook his head. "Not quite," he said. "Gyres are bigger. Like a string of currents. Imagine a ring of snakes, each biting the tail of the one ahead of it. The Kuroshio is one of four or five currents that make up the Turtle Gyre."

She nodded. She closed her eyes and pictured the snakes.

"Each gyre orbits at its own speed," he continued. "And the length of an orbit is called a tone. Isn't that beautiful? Like the music of the spheres. The longest orbital period is thirteen years, which establishes the fundamental tone. The Turtle Gyre has a half tone of six and a half years. The Aleut Gyre, a quarter tone of three. The flotsam that rides the gyres is called drift. Drift that stays in the orbit of the gyre is considered to be part of the gyre memory. The rate of escape from the gyre determines the half-life of drift . . ."

He picked up the Hello Kitty lunchbox and turned it over in his hands. "All that stuff from people's homes in Japan that the tsunami swept out to sea? They've been tracking it and predicting it will wash up on our coastline. I think it's just happening sooner than anyone expected."

# *Nao*

### I.

There's so much to write. Where should I start?

I texted my old Jiko this question, and she wrote back this: 現在地
で始まるべき.[10]

Okay, my dear old Jiko. I'll start right here at Fifi's Lovely Apron. Fifi's
is one of a bunch of maid cafés that popped up all over Akiba Electricity
Town[11] a couple of years ago, but what makes Fifi's a little bit special is
the French salon theme. The interior is decorated mostly in pink and red,
with accents of gold and ebony and ivory. The tables are round and cozy,
with marblelike tops and legs that look like carved mahogany, and the
matching chairs have pink puff tapestry seats. Dark red velvet roses curl
up the wallpaper, and the windows are draped in satin. The ceiling is gilded
and hung with crystal chandeliers, and little naked Kewpie dolls float like
clouds in the corners. There's an entryway and coatroom with a trickling
fountain and a statue of a nude lady lit by a throbbing red spot.

I don't know if this decor is authentic or not as I've never visited
France, but I'm going to guess that probably there aren't many French
maid cafés like this in Paris. It doesn't matter. The feeling at Fifi's Lovely
Apron is very chic and intimate, like being stuffed inside a great big
claustrophobic valentine, and the maids, with their pushed-up breasts
and frilly uniforms, look like cute little valentines, too.

---

10. *Genzaichi de hajimarubeki*—"You should start where you are." *Genzaichi* is
used on maps: You Are Here.
11. Akihabara (秋葉原)—area of Tokyo famous for electronics; the heart of
Japanese manga fan culture.

Unfortunately, it's pretty empty in here right now, except for some otaku[12] types at the corner table, and two bug-eyed American tourists. The maids are standing in a sulky line, picking at the lace on their petticoats and looking bored and disappointed with us, like they're hoping for some new and better customers to come in and liven things up. There was a little bit of excitement a while ago when one otaku ordered omurice[13] with a big red Hello Kitty face painted in ketchup on top. A maid whose name tag says she's Mimi knelt down before him to feed him, blowing on each bite before spooning it into his mouth. The Americans got a real kick out of that, which was hilarious. I wish you could have seen it. But then he finished, and Mimi took his dirty plate away, and now it's boring again. The Americans are just drinking coffees. The husband is trying to get his wife to let him order a Hello Kitty omurice, too, but she's way too uptight. I heard her whispering that the omurice is too expensive, and she's got a point. The food here is a total rip-off, but I get my coffee for free because Babette is my friend. I'll let you know if the wife loosens up and changes her mind.

It didn't used to be this way. Back when maid cafés were ninki #1![14] Babette told me that the customers used to line up and wait for hours just to get a table, and the maids were all the prettiest girls in Tokyo, and you could hear them over the noise of Electricity Town calling out, Okaerinasaimase, dannasama!,[15] which makes men feel rich and important. But now the fad is over and maids are no longer *it*, and the only

---

12. *otaku* (お宅)—also a formal way of saying "you." 宅 means "house," and with the honorific お, it literally means "your honorable house," implying that *you* are less of a person and more of a place, fixed in space and contained under a roof. Makes sense that the stereotype of the modern otaku is a shut-in, an obsessed loner and social isolate who rarely leaves his house.

13. *omuraisu* (オム・ライス)—omelet filled with pilaf rice, seasoned with tomato ketchup and butter.

14. *ninki nanba wan!*—most popular, number one in popularity.

15. *Okaerinasaimase, dannasama!*—Welcome home, my master!

customers are tourists from abroad, and otaku[16] from the countryside, or sad hentai with out-of-date fetishes for maids. And the maids, too, are not so pretty or cute anymore, since you can make a lot more money being a nurse at a medical café or a fuzzy plushy in Bedtown.[17] French maids are downward trending for sure, and everyone knows this, so nobody's bothering to try very hard. You could say it's a depressing ambience, but personally, I find it relaxing exactly because nobody's trying too hard. What's depressing is when everyone is trying too hard, and the most depressing thing of all is when they're trying too hard and actually thinking that they're making it. I'm sure that's what it used to be like around here, with all the cheerful jangle of bells and laughing, and lines of customers around the block, and cute little maids sucking up to the café owners, who slouched around in their designer sunglasses and vintage Levi's like dark princes or game-empire moguls. Those dudes had a long, long way to fall.

So I don't mind this at all. I kind of like it because I know I can always get a table here at Fifi's Lovely Apron, and the music is okay, and the maids know me now and usually leave me alone. Maybe it should be called Fifi's Lonely Apron. Hey, that's good! I like that!

## 2.

My old Jiko really likes it when I tell her lots of details about modern life. She doesn't get out very much anymore because she lives in a temple in the mountains in the middle of nowhere and has renounced the world, and also there's the fact of her being a hundred and four years old. I keep saying that's her age, but actually I'm just guessing. We don't really know for sure how old she is, and she claims she doesn't remember, either. When you ask her, she says,

---

16. . . . also, because the word *otaku* is honorific, when it's used as a second-person pronoun, it creates a kind of formal social distance between the speaker and the *you* being addressed. This distance is conventionally respectful, but it can also be ironic and mocking.

17. Can't find references to medical cafés or Bedtown. Is she making this up?

"Zuibun nagaku ikasarete itadaite orimasu ne."[18]

Which is not an answer, so you ask her again, and she says,

"Soo desu ne.[19] I haven't counted for so long . . ."

So then you ask her when her birthday is, and she says,

"Hmm, I don't really remember being born . . ."

And if you pester her some more and ask her how long she's been alive, she says,

"I've always been here as far as I remember."

Well, duh, Granny!

All we know for sure is that there's nobody older than her who remembers, and the family register at the ward office got burned up in a firebombing during World War II, so basically we have to take her word for it. A couple of years ago, she kind of got fixated on a hundred and four, and that's what it's been ever since.

And as I was saying, my old Jiko really likes detail, and she likes it when I tell her about all the little sounds and smells and colors and lights and advertising and people and fashions and newspaper headlines that make up the noisy ocean of Tokyo, which is why I've trained myself to notice and remember. I tell her everything, about cultural trends and news items I read about high school girls who get raped and suffocated

---

18. *Zuibun nagaku ikasarete itadaite orimasu ne* —"I have been alive for a very long time, haven't I?" Totally impossible to translate, but the nuance is something like: *I have been caused to live by the deep conditions of the universe to which I am humbly and deeply grateful.* P. Arai calls it the "gratitude tense," and says the beauty of this grammatical construction is that "there is no finger pointing to a source." She also says, "It is impossible to feel angry when using this tense."
19. *Sō desu ne . . .*—Hmm, yes, I suppose that's so . . .

with plastic bags in love hotels. You can tell Granny all that kind of stuff and she doesn't mind. I don't mean it makes her happy. She's not a hentai. But she understands that shit happens, and she just sits there and listens and nods her head and counts the beads on her juzu,[20] saying blessings for those poor high school girls and the perverts and all the beings who are suffering in the world. She's a nun, so that's her job. I swear, sometimes I think the main reason she's still alive is because of all the stuff I give her to pray about.

I asked her once why she liked to hear stories like this, and she explained to me that when she got ordained, she shaved her head and took some vows to be a bosatsu.[21] One of her vows was to save all beings, which basically means that she agreed not to become enlightened until all the other beings in this world get enlightened first. It's kind of like letting everybody else get into the elevator ahead of you. When you calculate all the beings on this earth at any time, and then add in the ones that are getting born every second and the ones that have already died—and not just human beings, either, but all the animals and other life-forms like amoebas and viruses and maybe even plants that have ever lived or ever will live, as well as all the extinct species—well, you can see that enlightenment will take a very long time. And what if the elevator gets full and the doors slam shut and you're still standing outside?

When I asked Granny about this, she rubbed her shiny bald head and said, "Soo desu ne. It is a very big elevator . . ."

"But Granny, it's going to take forever!"

"Well, we must try even harder, then."

"*We?!*"

"Of course, dear Nao. You must help me."

"No way!" I told Granny. "Forget it! I'm no fucking bosatsu . . ."

But she just smacked her lips and clicked her juzu beads, and the way she looked at me through those thick black-framed glasses of hers, I think maybe she was saying a blessing for me just then, too. I didn't mind. It

---

20. *juzu* (数珠)—a Buddhist rosary.
21. *bosatsu* (菩薩)—bodhisattva, awakened being, Buddhist saint.

made me feel safe, like I knew no matter what happened, Granny was going to make sure I got onto that elevator.

You know what? Just this second, as I was writing this, I realized something. I never asked her where that elevator is going. I'm going to text her now and ask. I'll let you know what she says.

## 3.

Okay, so now I really am going to tell you about the fascinating life of Yasutani Jiko, the famous anarchist-feminist-novelist-turned-Buddhist-nun of the Taishō era, but first I need to explain about this book you're holding.[22] You've probably noticed that it doesn't look like an ordinary schoolgirl's pure diary with puffy marshmallow animals on a shiny pink cover, and a heart-shaped lock, and a little golden key. And when you first picked it up, you probably didn't think, Oh, here's a nice pure diary written by an interesting Japanese schoolgirl. Gee, I think I'll read that! because when you picked it up, you thought it was a philosophical master-piece called *À la recherche du temps perdu* by the famous French author named Marcel Proust, and not an insignificant diary by a nobody named Nao Yasutani. So it just goes to show that it's true what they say: You can't tell a book by its cover![23]

I hope you're not too disappointed. What happened is that Marcel Proust's book got hacked, only I didn't do it. I bought it this way, prehacked, at a little handicraft boutique over in Harajuku[24] where they sell one-of-a-kind DIY goods like crochet scarves and keitai pouches and beaded cuffs and other cool stuff. Handicraft is a superbig fad in Japan, and everyone is knitting and beading and crocheting and making pepa-kura,[25] but I'm quite clumsy so I have to buy my DIY goods if I want to

22. A stout, compact tome, perhaps a crown octavo, measuring approx. 5 x 7½ inches.
23. Cover is worn, made of reddish cloth. Title is embossed in tarnished gold letters on the front and again on the spine.
24. Harajuku (原宿)—area in Tokyo famous for youth culture and street fashion.
25. *peipaakura* (ペーパー・クラ)—papercrafts, from the English *paper + craft*.

keep up with the trend. The girl who makes these diaries is a superfamous crafter, who buys containerloads of old books from all over the world, and then neatly cuts out all the printed pages and puts in blank paper instead. She does it so authentically you don't even notice the hack, and you almost think that the letters just slipped off the pages and fell to the floor like a pile of dead ants.

Recently some nasty stuff has been happening in my life, and the day I bought the diary, I was skipping school and feeling especially blue, so I decided to go shopping in Harajuku to cheer myself up. When I saw these old books on the shelf, I thought they were a shop display so I didn't pay any attention to them, but when the salesgirl pointed out the hack to me, of course I had to have one immediately. And they weren't cheap, either, but I loved the worn feeling of the cover, and I could tell it would feel so good to write inside, like a real published book. But best of all, I knew it would be an excellent security feature.

I don't know if you've ever had this problem of people beating you up and stealing things from you and using them against you, but if you have, then you'll understand that this book was total genius, in case one of my stupid classmates decided to casually pick up my diary and read it and post it to the Internet or something. But who would pick up an old book called *À la recherche du temps perdu*, right? My stupid classmates would just think it was homework for juku.[26] They wouldn't even know what it meant.

Actually, I didn't know what it meant either, since my ability to speak French is nonexistent. There were a bunch of books with different titles for sale. Some of them were in English, like *Great Expectations* and *Gulliver's Travels*, which were okay, but I thought it would be better to buy a title I couldn't read, since knowing the meaning might possibly interfere with my own creative expression. There were others in different languages, too, like German and Russian and even Chinese, but I ended up choosing *À la recherche du temps perdu* because I figured it was probably French, and French is cool and has a sophisticated feeling, and besides, this book is exactly the right size to fit into my handbag.

---

26. *juku* (塾)—cram school.

# 4.

The minute I bought the book, of course, I wanted to start writing in it, so I went to a nearby kissa[27] and ordered a Blue Mountain, then I took out my favorite purple gel ink pen and opened the book to the first creamy page. I took a bitter sip and waited for the words to come. I waited and waited, and sipped some more coffee, and waited some more. Nothing. I'm pretty chatty, as you can probably tell, and usually I don't have any trouble coming up with stuff to say. But this time, even though I had a lot on my mind, the words didn't come. It was weird, but I figured I was just feeling intimidated by the new-old book and would eventually get over it. So I drank the rest of my coffee and read a couple of manga, and when it was time for school to let out, I went home.

But the next day I tried again, and the same thing happened. And after that, every time I took out the book, I'd stare at the title and start to wonder. I mean, Marcel Proust must be pretty important if even someone like me had heard of him, even if I didn't know who he was at first and thought he was a celebrity chef or a French fashion designer. What if his ghost was still clinging to the inside of the covers and was pissed off at the hack the crafty girl had done, cutting out his words and pages? And what if now the ghost was preventing me from using his famous book to write about typical dumb schoolgirl stuff, like my crushes on boys (not that I have any), or new fashions I want (my desires are endless), or my fat thighs (actually my thighs are fine, it's my knees I hate). You really can't blame old Marcel's ghost for getting righteously pissed off, thinking I might be dumb enough to write this kind of stupid crap inside his important book.

And even if his ghost didn't mind, I still wouldn't want to use his book for such trivial stuff, even if these weren't my last days on earth. But since these *are* my last days on earth, I want to write something important, too. Well, maybe not important, because I don't know

27. *kissa* (喫茶)—coffee shop.

anything important, but something worthwhile. I want to leave something real behind.

But what can I write about that's real? Sure, I can write about all the bad shit that's happened to me, and my feelings about my dad and my mom and my so-called friends, but I don't particularly want to. Whenever I think about my stupid empty life, I come to the conclusion that I'm just wasting my time, and I'm not the only one. Everybody I know is the same, except for old Jiko. Just wasting time, killing time, feeling crappy.

And what does it mean to waste time anyway? If you waste time is it lost forever?

And if time is lost forever, what does that mean? It's not like you get to die any sooner, right? I mean, if you want to die sooner, you have to take matters into your own hands.

## 5.

So anyway, these distracting thoughts about ghosts and time kept drifting through my mind every time I tried to write in old Marcel's book, until finally I decided that I had to know what the title meant. I asked Babette, but she couldn't help me because of course she's not a real French maid, just a high school dropout from Chiba prefecture, and the only French she knows is a couple of sexy phrases she picked up from this farty old French professor she was dating for a while. So when I got home that night, I googled Marcel Proust and learned that *À la recherche du temps perdu* means "In search of lost time."

Weird, right? I mean, there I was, sitting in a French maid café in Akiba, thinking about lost time, and old Marcel Proust was sitting in France a hundred years ago, writing a whole book about the exact same subject. So maybe his ghost was lingering between the covers and hacking into my mind, or maybe it was just a crazy coincidence, but either way, how cool is that? I think coincidences are cool, even if they don't mean anything, and who knows? Maybe they do! I'm not saying everything happens for a reason. It was more just that it felt as if me and old Marcel were on the same wavelength.

24

The next day I went back to Fifi's and ordered a small pot of lapsang souchong, which I drink sometimes as a break from Blue Mountain, and as I sat there, sipping the smoky tea and nibbling a French pastry, waiting for Babette to set me up on a date, I started to wonder.

How do you search for lost time, anyway? It's an interesting question, so I texted it to old Jiko, which is what I always do when I have a philosophical dilemma. And then I had to wait for a really, really long time, but finally my keitai gave a little ping that tells me she's texted me back. And what she wrote was this:

あるときや
ことのはもちり
おちばかな[28]

which means something like this:

*For the time being,*
*Words scatter . . .*
*Are they fallen leaves?*

I'm not very good at poetry, but when I read old Jiko's poem, I saw an image in my mind of this big old ginkgo tree on the grounds of her temple.[29] The leaves are shaped like little green fans, and in the autumn they turn bright yellow and fall off and cover the ground, painting everything pure golden. And it occurred to me that the big old tree is a

---

28. *Aru toki ya / Koto no ha mo chiri / Ochiba ka na*
*aru toki ya*—that time, sometime, for the time being (有る時や). Same kanji used for *Uji* (有時).
*koto no ha*—lit., "leaves of speech" (言 の 葉). Same kanji used for *kotoba* (言葉), meaning "word."
*ochiba*—fallen leaves, with a pun on *ha* (葉), implying *fallen words*.
*ka na*—an interrogative particle that imparts a sense of wonder.
29. Ginkgo leaves are used in tea to enhance memory. Ginkgo trees were often planted on Buddhist temple grounds to help monks memorize sutras.

time being, and Jiko is a time being, too, and I could imagine myself searching for lost time under the tree, sifting through the fallen leaves that are her scattered golden words.

The idea of the time being comes from a book called *Shōbōgenzō* that an ancient Zen master named Dōgen Zenji wrote about eight hundred years ago, which makes him even older than old Jiko or even Marcel Proust. Dōgen Zenji is one of Jiko's favorite authors, and he's lucky because his books are important and still kicking around. Unfortunately, everything Jiko wrote is out of print so I've actually never read her words, but she's told me lots of stories, and I started to think about how words and stories are time beings, too, and that's when the idea popped into my mind of using Marcel Proust's important book to write down my old Jiko's life.

It's not just because Jiko is the most important person I know, although that's part of it. And it's not just because she is incredibly old and was alive back when Marcel Proust was writing his book about time. Maybe she was, but that's not why, either. The reason I decided to write about her in *À la recherche du temps perdu* is because she is the only person I know who really understands time.

Old Jiko is supercareful with her time. She does everything really really slowly, even when she's just sitting on the veranda, looking out at the dragonflies spinning lazily around the garden pond. She says that she does everything really really slowly in order to spread time out so that she'll have more of it and live longer, and then she laughs so you know she is telling you a joke. I mean, she understands perfectly well that time isn't something you can spread out like butter or jam, and death isn't going to hang around and wait for you to finish whatever you happen to be doing before it zaps you. That's the joke, and she laughs because she knows it.

But actually, I don't think it's very funny. Even though I don't know old Jiko's exact age, I do know for sure that pretty soon she'll be dead even if she hasn't finished sweeping out the temple kitchen or weeding the daikon patch or arranging fresh flowers on the altar, and once she's dead, that will be the end of her, timewise. This doesn't bother her at all, but it bothers me a lot. These are old Jiko's last days on earth, and there's nothing I can do about that, and there's nothing I can do to stop time from passing or even to slow it down, and every second of the day is another second lost. She probably wouldn't agree with me, but that's how I see it.

I don't mind thinking of the world without me because I'm unexceptional, but I hate the idea of the world without old Jiko. She's totally unique and special, like the last Galapagos tortoise or some other ancient animal hobbling around on the scorched earth, who is the only one left of its kind. But please don't get me going on the topic of species extinction because it's totally depressing, and I'll have to commit suicide right this second.

## 6.

Okay, Nao. Why are you doing this? Like, what's the point?

This is a problem. The only reason I can think of for writing Jiko's life story in this book is because I love her and want to remember her, but I'm not planning on sticking around for long, and I can't remember her stories if I'm dead, right?

And apart from me, who else would care? I mean, if I thought the world would want to know about old Jiko, I'd post her stories on a blog, but actually I stopped doing that a while ago. It made me sad when I caught myself pretending that everybody out there in cyberspace cared about what I thought, when really nobody gives a shit.[30] And when I multiplied that sad feeling by all the millions of people in their lonely little rooms, furiously writing and posting to their lonely little pages that nobody has time to read because they're all so busy writing and posting,[31] it kind of broke my heart.

---

30. "I never think anyone gives a shit," Oliver said. "Is that sad? I don't think it's sad."

31. "Once the writer in every individual comes to life (and that time is not far off ), we are in for an age of universal deafness and lack of understanding."—Milan Kundera, *The Book of Laughter and Forgetting*, 1980.

The fact is, I don't have much of a social network these days, and the people I hang out with aren't the kind who care about a hundred-and-four-year-old Buddhist nun, even if she is a bosatsu who can use email and texting, and that's only because I made her buy a computer so she could stay in touch with me when I'm in Tokyo and she's at her falling-down old temple on a mountain in the middle of nowhere. She's not crazy about new technology, but she does pretty well for a time being with cataracts and arthritis in both her thumbs. Old Jiko and Marcel Proust come from a prewired world, which is a time that's totally lost these days.

So here I am, at Fifi's Lonely Apron, staring at all these blank pages and asking myself why I'm bothering, when suddenly an amazing idea knocks me over. Ready? Here it is:

*I will write down everything I know about Jiko's life in Marcel's book, and when I'm done, I'll just leave it somewhere, and you will find it!*

How cool is that? It feels like I'm reaching forward through time to touch you, and now that you've found it, you're reaching back to touch me!

If you ask me, it's fantastically cool and beautiful. It's like a message in a bottle, cast out onto the ocean of time and space. Totally personal, and real, too, right out of old Jiko's and Marcel's prewired world. It's the opposite of a blog. It's an antiblog, because it's meant for only one special person, and that person is *you*. And if you've read this far, you probably understand what I mean. Do you understand? Do you feel special yet?

I'll just wait here for a while to see if you answer . . .

## 7.

Just kidding. I know you can't answer, and now I feel stupid, because what if you don't feel special? I'm making an assumption, right? What if you just think I'm a jerk and toss me into the garbage, like all those young girls I tell old Jiko about, who get killed by perverts and chopped up and thrown into dumpsters, just because they've made the mistake of dating the wrong guy? That would be really sad and scary.

Or, here's another scary thought, what if you're not reading this at all? What if you never even found this book, because somebody chucked it in the trash or recycled it before it got to you? Then old Jiko's stories truly will be lost forever, and I'm just sitting here wasting time talking to the inside of a dumpster.

Hey, answer me! Am I stuck inside of a garbage can, or not?

Just kidding. Again. ☺

Okay, here's what I've decided. I don't mind the risk, because the risk makes it more interesting. And I don't think old Jiko will mind, either, because being a Buddhist, she really understands impermanence and that everything changes and nothing lasts forever. Old Jiko really isn't going to care if her life stories get written or lost, and maybe I've picked up a little of that laissez-faire attitude from her. When the time comes, I can just let it all go.

Or not. I don't know. Maybe by the time I've written the last page, I'll be too embarrassed or ashamed to leave it lying around, and I'll wimp out and destroy it instead.

Hey, if you're not reading this, you'll know I'm a wimp! Ha-ha.

And as for that business about old Marcel's ghost being pissed off, I've decided not to worry about it. When I was googling Marcel Proust, I happened to look up his sales ranking on Amazon, and I couldn't believe it but his books are all still in print, and depending on which edition of *À la recherche du temps perdu* you're talking about, his ranking is somewhere between 13,695 and 79,324, which is no best seller, but it's not so bad for a dead guy. Just so you know. You don't have to feel too sorry for old Marcel.

I don't know how long this whole project is going to take me. Probably months. There are lots of blank pages, and Jiko's got lots of stories, and I write pretty slow, but I'm going to work really hard, and probably by the time I'm done filling in the last page, old Jiko will be dead, and it will be my time, too.

And I know I can't possibly write down every detail about Jiko's life, so if you want to learn more, you'll have to read her books, if you can find them. Like I said before, her stuff is all out of print, and it's possible that some crafty girl has already hacked her pages and tossed all her golden words into the recycling bin next to Proust's. That would be really sad, because it's not like old Jiko has any ranking on Amazon at all. I know because I checked and she isn't even there. Hmm. I'm going to have to rethink this hacking concept. Maybe it's not so cool after all.

# Ruth

## 1.

The cat had climbed up onto Ruth's desk and was preparing to make a strategic incursion onto her lap. She'd been reading the diary when he approached from the side, placing his forepaws on her knees and nudging his nose underneath the spine of the book, pushing it up and out of his way. Once that was done, he settled himself on her lap and started kneading, butting his head into her hand. He was so annoying. Always looking for attention.

She closed the diary and placed it on the desk as she stroked the cat's forehead, but even after putting the book aside, she was aware of an odd and lingering sense of urgency to . . . what? To help the girl? To save her? Ridiculous.

Her first impulse when she'd started the diary was to read quickly to the end, but the girl's handwriting was often hard to decipher, and her sentences were peppered with slang and intriguing colloquialisms. It had been years since Ruth had lived in Japan, and while she still had a reasonable command of the spoken language, her vocabulary was out of date. In university, Ruth had studied the Japanese classics—*The Tale of Genji*, Noh drama, *The Pillow Book*—literature going back hundreds and even thousands of years, but she was only vaguely familiar with Japanese pop culture. Sometimes the girl made an effort to explain, but often she didn't bother, so Ruth found herself logging on to the Internet to investigate and verify the girl's references, and before long, she had dragged out her old kanji dictionary, and was translating and annotating and scribbling notes about Akiba and maid cafés, otaku and hentai. And then there was the anarchist feminist Zen Buddhist novelist nun.

She leaned forward and did an Amazon search for Jiko Yasutani but, as Nao had warned, found nothing. She googled Nao Yasutani and again came up with nothing. The cat, irked by her restlessness and inattention, abandoned her lap. He didn't like it when she went on the computer and used her fingers to type and scroll instead of to scratch his head. It was a waste of two perfectly good hands as far as he was concerned, and so he went in search of Oliver.

She had better luck with Dōgen, whose masterwork, *Shōbōgenzō*, or *The Treasury of the True Dharma Eye*, did have an Amazon ranking, albeit nowhere near Proust's. Of course, he'd lived in the early thirteenth century, so he was older than Proust by almost seven hundred years. When she searched for "time being," she learned that the phrase was used in the English title of Chapter 11 of the *Shōbōgenzō*, and she was able to locate several translations, along with commentaries, online. The ancient Zen master had a nuanced and complex notion of time that she found poetic but somewhat opaque. *Time itself is being*, he wrote, *and all being is time . . . In essence, everything in the entire universe is intimately linked with each other as moments in time, continuous and separate.*

Ruth took off her glasses and rubbed her eyes. She took a sip of tea, her head so full of questions she barely noticed the tea had long grown cold. Who was this Nao Yasutani, and where was she now? While the girl hadn't come right out and said she was going to commit suicide, she'd certainly implied as much. Was she sitting on the edge of a mattress somewhere, fingering a bottle of pills and a tall glass of water? Or had that *hentai* gotten to her first? Or perhaps she had decided *not* to kill herself, only to fall victim to the earthquake and tsunami instead, although that didn't make a lot of sense. The tsunami was in Tohoku, in northern Japan. Nao was writing in a maid café in Tokyo. What was she doing at that maid café in the first place? Fifi's? It sounded like a brothel.

She sat back in her chair and gazed out the window at the tiny stretch of horizon that she could see through a gap in the tall trees. *A pine tree is time,* Dōgen had written, *and bamboo is time. Mountains are time.*

*Oceans are time . . .* Dark clouds hung low in the sky, forming an almost indiscernible line where they met the still, dull sheen of the ocean. Gunmetal grey. On the far side of the Pacific lay the battered Japanese coastline. Entire towns had been crushed and dragged out to sea. *If time is annihilated, mountains and oceans are annihilated.* Was the girl out there somewhere in all that water, her body decomposed by now, redistributed by the waves?

Ruth looked at the sturdy red book with its tarnished gilt title embossed on the cover. It was lying on top of a tall messy stack of notes and manuscript pages, bristling with Post-its and wound with cramped marginalia, which represented the memoir that she'd been working on for close to a decade. À la recherche du temps perdu, indeed. Unable to complete another novel, she had decided instead to write about the years she had spent taking care of her mother, who'd suffered from Alzheimer's. Now, looking at the pile of pages, she felt a quickening flush of panic at the thought of all her own lost time, the confused mess she'd made of this draft, and the work that still needed to be done to sort it all out. What was she doing wasting precious hours on someone else's story?

She picked up the diary and, using the side of her thumb, started riffling through the pages. She wasn't reading, in fact she was trying not to. She only wanted to ascertain whether the handwriting continued all the way to the end, or if it petered out partway through. How many diaries and journals had she herself started and then abandoned? How many aborted novels languished in folders on her hard drive? But to her surprise, although the color of the ink occasionally bled from purple to pink to black to blue and back to purple again, the writing itself never faltered, growing smaller and if anything even denser, straight through to the very last, tightly packed page. The girl had run out of paper before she ran out of words.

And then?

Ruth snapped the book shut and closed her eyes for good measure to keep herself from cheating and reading the final sentence, but the question lingered, floating like a retinal burn in the darkness of her mind: *What happens in the end?*

## 2.

Muriel examined the barnacle growth on the outer freezer bag through the reading glasses she kept perched on her nose. "If I were you, I'd get Callie to take a look. Maybe she can figure out how old these critters are, and from that you can calculate how long the bag's been in the water."

"Oliver thinks it's the leading edge of drift from the tsunami," Ruth said.

Muriel frowned. "I suppose it's possible. Seems too quick, though. They're starting to see the lighter stuff washing up in Alaska and Tofino, but we're tucked back pretty far inland here. Where did you say you found it?"

"At the south end of the beach, below Jap Ranch."

No one on the island called it by that name anymore, but Muriel was an old-timer and knew the reference. The old homestead, one of the most beautiful places on the island, had once belonged to a Japanese family, who were forced to sell when they were interned during the war. The property had changed hands several times since then, and now was owned by elderly Germans. Once Ruth heard the nickname, she stubbornly persisted in using it. As a person of Japanese ancestry, she said, she had the right, and it was important not to let New Age correctness erase the history of the island.

"Fine for you," Oliver said. His family had emigrated from Germany. "Not so fine if I use it. It's hardly fair."

"Exactly," Ruth said. "It wasn't fair. My mom's family were interned, too. Maybe I could lodge a land claim on behalf of my people. That property was stolen from them. I could just go there and sit in their driveway and refuse to leave. Repossess the land and kick out the Germans."

"What do you have against my people?" Oliver asked.

Their marriage was like this, an axial alliance—her people interned, his firebombed in Stuttgart—a small accidental consequence of a war fought before either of them was born.

"We're by-products of the mid-twentieth century," Oliver said.

"Who isn't?"

"I doubt it's from the tsunami," Muriel said, placing the freezer bag back down on the table and turning her attention to the Hello Kitty lunchbox. "More likely from a cruise ship, going up the Inside Passage, or maybe Japanese tourists."

Pesto, who had been twining himself around Muriel's legs, now jumped up onto her lap and took a swat at her thick grey braid, which hung over her shoulder like a snake. The end of the braid was secured with a colorful beaded elastic, which Pesto found irresistible. He also liked her dangling earrings.

"I like the tsunami narrative," Ruth said, frowning at the cat.

Muriel flicked the braid behind her back, out of the cat's reach, and then rubbed the white patch between his ears to distract him. She peered at Ruth over the top of her glasses. "Bad idea. Shouldn't let your narrative preferences interfere with your forensic work."

Muriel was a retired anthropologist, who studied middens. She knew a lot about garbage. She was also an avid beachcomber and was the person who'd found the severed foot. She prided herself on her finds: bone fish hooks and lures, flint spearheads and arrowheads, and an assortment of stone tools for pounding and cutting. Most were First Nations artifacts, but she also had a collection of old Japanese fishing floats that had detached from nets across the Pacific and washed up on the island's shore. The floats were the size of large beach balls, murky globes blown from thick tinted glass. They were beautiful, like escaped worlds.

"I'm a novelist," Ruth said. "I can't help it. My narrative preferences are all I've got."

"Fair enough," Muriel said. "But facts are facts, and establishing the provenance is important." She scooped up the cat and dropped him onto the floor, then rested her fingers on the latches on the sides of the lunchbox. Her fingers were decorated with heavy silver and turquoise rings, which looked incongruous next to Hello Kitty. "May I?" she asked.

"Be my guest."

On the phone, Muriel had asked to inspect the find, so Ruth had repacked the box as best she could. Now she felt a kind of tension in the air, but she wasn't sure where it was coming from. Something in the formality of Muriel's request. The solemnity of her attitude as she removed the lid. The way she paused, almost ceremonially, before lifting the watch from the box, turning it over and holding it to her ear.

"It's broken," Ruth said.

Muriel picked up the diary. She inspected the spine and then the cover. "Here's where you'll find your clues," she said, opening it to a section somewhere in the middle. "Have you started reading it?"

Watching Muriel handle the book, Ruth felt her uneasiness grow. "Well, yes. Only the first couple of pages. It's not that interesting." She took the letters from the box and held them out. "These seem more promising. They're older and may be more historically important, don't you think?" Muriel laid down the diary and took the letters from Ruth's hand. "Unfortunately, I can't read them," Ruth added.

"The handwriting looks beautiful," Muriel said, turning over the pages. "Have you shown them to Ayako?" Ayako was the young Japanese wife of an oyster farmer who lived on the island.

"Yes," Ruth said, slipping the diary below the table and out of sight. "But she said the handwriting's hard even for her to read, and besides her English isn't so good. She did decipher the dates, though. She said they were written in 1944 and '45, and I should try to find someone older, who was alive during the war."

"Good luck," Muriel said. "Has the language really changed that much?"

"Not the language. The people. Ayako said young people can't read complex characters or write by hand anymore. They've grown up with computers." Under the table, she fingered the blunt edges of the diary. One corner was broken, and the cloth-encased cardboard wiggled like a loose tooth. Had Nao worried this corner between her fingertips, too?

Muriel shook her head. "Right," she said. "It's the same everywhere. Kids have terrible handwriting these days. They're not even teaching it in schools anymore." She placed the letters next to the watch and the freezer bags on the table and looked over the collection. If she noticed the missing diary, she didn't mention it. "Well, thanks for showing me," she said.

She heaved herself to her feet, brushed the cat hair from her lap, and then limped off toward the mud room. She'd gained some weight since her hip replacement and still found it hard to get up and down. She was wearing an old Cowichan sweater and a long skirt, made out of some rough peasant fabric that covered the tops of her gum boots when she put them back on. She stomped her feet in the boots and then looked up at Ruth, who had come to the door to see her off.

"I still say this should have been my find," she said, pulling a rain parka on over the sweater. "But maybe it's better you got it, since at least you can read some of the Japanese. Good luck. Don't let yourself get too distracted now . . ."

Ruth braced herself.

". . . How's the new book coming, anyway?" Muriel asked.

### 3.

At night, in bed, Ruth would often read to Oliver. It used to be that when she'd had a good writing day, she would read aloud what she'd just written, finding that if she fell asleep thinking about the scene she was working on, she would often wake with a sense of where to go next. It had been a long while, however, since she'd had a day like that or shared anything new.

That night, she read the first few entries of Nao's diary. When she came to the passage about perverts and panties and the zebra-skin bed, she felt a sudden flush of discomfort. It wasn't embarrassment. She was never shy about this kind of thing, herself. Rather, her discomfort was more on behalf of the girl. She was feeling protective. But she needn't have worried.

"The nun sounds interesting," Oliver said, as he fiddled with the broken watch.

"Yes," she said, relieved. "The Taishō Democracy was an interesting time for Japanese women."

"Do you think she's still alive?"

"The nun? I doubt it. She was a hundred and four—"

"I meant the girl."

"I don't know," Ruth said. "It's crazy, but I'm kind of worried about her. I guess I'll have to keep on reading to find out."

## 4.

*Do you feel special yet?*

The girl's question lingered.

"It's an interesting thought," Oliver said, still tinkering with the watch. "Do you?"

"Do I what?"

"She says she's writing it for you. So do you feel special?"

"That's ridiculous," Ruth said.

*What if you just think I'm a jerk and toss me into the garbage?*

"Speaking about garbage," Oliver said. "I've been thinking about the Great Garbage Patches recently . . ."

"The what?"

"The Great Eastern and Great Western Garbage Patches? Enormous masses of garbage and debris floating in the oceans? You must have heard about them . . ."

"Yes," she said. "No. I mean, sort of." It didn't matter, since he clearly wanted to tell her about them. She put down the diary, letting it rest on the white bedcovers. She took off her glasses and laid them on top of the book. The glasses were retro, with thick black frames that looked nice against the worn red cloth cover.

"There are at least eight of them in the world's oceans," he said. "According to this book I've been reading, two of them, the Great Eastern Patch and Great Western Patch, are in the Turtle Gyre, and converge at the southern tip of Hawaii. The Great Eastern Patch is the size of Texas. The Great Western is even larger, half the size of the continental USA."

"What's in them?"

"Plastic mostly. Like your freezer bag. Soda bottles, styrofoam, take-out food containers, disposable razors, industrial waste. Anything we throw away that floats."

"That's horrible. Why are you telling me this?"

He shook the watch and held it up to his ear. "No reason. Just that they're there, and anything that doesn't sink or escape from the gyre gets sucked up into the middle of a garbage patch. That's what would have happened to your freezer bag if it hadn't escaped. Sucked up and becalmed, slowly eddying around. The plastic ground into particles for the fish and zooplankton to eat. The diary and letters disintegrating, unread. But instead it got washed up on the beach below Jap Ranch, where you could find it . . ."

"What are you saying?" Ruth asked.

"Nothing. Just that it's amazing, is all."

"As in the-universe-provides kind of amazing?"

"Maybe." He looked up with an astonished expression on his face. "Hey, look!" he said, holding out the watch. "It's working!"

The second hand was making its way around the large luminescent numbers on the face. She took it from him and slipped it on her wrist. It was a man's watch, but it fit her. "What did you do?"

"I don't know," he said, shrugging. "I guess I wound it."

### 5.

She listened to the watch ticking softly in the dark, and the sound of Oliver's mechanical breathing. She reached over to the bedside table and felt for the diary. Running her fingertips across the soft cloth cover, she noted the faint impression of the tarnished letters. They still retained the shape of *À la recherche du temps perdu*, but they had evolved—no, that word implied a gradual unfolding, and this was sudden, a mutation or a rift, pages ripped from their cover by some Tokyo crafter who'd retooled Proust into something altogether new.

In her mind's eye, she could see the purple ink scripting sinuous lines into solid blocks of colored paragraphs. She couldn't help but notice and admire the uninhibited flow of the girl's language. Rarely had she succumbed to second thoughts. Rarely did she doubt a word, or pause to consider or replace it with another. There were only a few crossed-out lines and phrases, and this, too, filled Ruth with something like awe. It had been years since she'd approached the page with such certainty.

*I am reaching through time to touch you.*

The diary once again felt warm in her hands, which she knew had less to do with any spooky quality in the book and everything to do with the climate changes in her own body. She was growing accustomed to sudden temperature shifts. The steering wheel of the car that grew sticky and hot in her grip. The smoldering pillow, which she often woke to find on the floor beside the bed where she'd flung it in her sleep, along with the covers, as though to punish them all for making her hot.

The watch, by contrast, felt cool against her wrist.

*I'm reaching forward through time to touch you . . . you're reaching back to touch me.*

She held the diary to her nose again and sniffed, identifying the smells one by one: the mustiness of an old book tickling her nostrils, the acrid tang of glue and paper, and then something else that she realized must be Nao, bitter like coffee beans and sweetly fruity like shampoo. She inhaled again, deeply this time, and then put the book—no, not a schoolgirl's nice pure diary—back on the bedside table, still pondering how best to read this improbable text. Nao claimed to have written it just for her, and while Ruth knew this was absurd, she decided she would go along with the conceit. As the girl's reader, it was the least she could do.

The steady ticking of the old watch seemed to grow louder. How do you search for lost time, anyway? As she thought about this question, it occurred to her that perhaps a clue lay in the pacing. Nao had written her diary in real time, living her days, moment by moment. Perhaps if Ruth paced herself by slowing down and not reading faster than the girl had written, she could more closely replicate Nao's experience. Of course, the entries were undated, so there was no way of really knowing how slow or fast that might have been, but there were clues: the changing hues of ink, as well as shifts in the density or angle of the handwriting, which seemed to indicate breaks in time or mood. If she studied these, she might be able to break up the diary into hypothetical intervals, and even assign numbers to them, and then pace her reading accordingly. If she sensed the girl was on a roll, she could allow herself to read further and more quickly, but if it felt like the pace of the writing was slowing down, then she would slow her reading down, too, or stop altogether. This way she wouldn't end up with an overly compressed or accelerated sense of the girl's life and its unfolding, nor would she run the risk of wasting too much time. She would be able to balance her reading of the diary with all the work she still needed to do on her own memoir.

It seemed like a very reasonable plan. Satisfied, Ruth groped for the book on the night table and slipped it under her pillow. The girl was right, she thought as she drifted off to sleep. It was real and totally personal.

### 6.

That night she dreamed about a nun.

The dream took place on a mountainside, somewhere in Japan, where the shrill cries of insects broke the silence, and the nighttime breezes in the tall cypress trees were fresh and restless.

Amid the trees, the graceful curve of a tiled temple roof gleamed dully in the moonlight, and even though it was dark, Ruth could see that the building was falling down and close to ruin. The only illumination inside the temple came from a single room adjoining the garden, where the old nun knelt on the floor in front of a low table, leaning in toward a glowing computer screen, which seemed to float in the darkness, casting its silver square of light onto the ancient planes of her face. The rest of her body receded into the darkness of the room, but Ruth could see that her back was curved like a question mark as she bent toward the screen, and that her faded black robes were old and worn. A square of patchwork fabric hung around her neck, like the bib an infant might wear to protect it from spills. Outside in the temple garden, the moon shone through the sliding doors that opened onto the veranda. The curve of the nun's shaved head gleamed faintly in the moonlight, and when she turned her face,

Ruth could see the light from the monitor reflected in the lenses of the glasses she was wearing, which had thick, squarish black frames, not unlike Ruth's own. The nun's face looked oddly young in the pixelated glow. She was typing something, carefully, with arthritic forefingers.

"*S o m e t i m e s u p . . .*" she typed. Her wrists were bent like broken branches, and her fingers curled like crooked sticks, tapping out each letter on the keyboard.

"*S o m e t i m e s d o w n . . .*"

It was the answer to Nao's elevator question. She hit RETURN and sat back on her heels, closing her eyes as though dozing. After a few minutes, a little icon on the side of the screen flashed and a digitized bell sounded an alert. She sat up, adjusted her glasses, and leaned forward to read. Then she began to type her reply.

*Up down, same thing. And also different, too.*

She entered her text and sat back again to wait. When the bell sounded, she read the incoming message and nodded. She thought for a moment, running her hand over her smooth head, and then she started typing again.

*When up looks up, up is down.*
*When down looks down, down is up.*
*Not-one, not-two. Not same. Not different.*
*Now do you see?*

It took her a while to type all this, and at last when she hit ENTER to send her message, she looked tired. She took off her glasses, placing them on the edge of the low table, and rubbed her eyes with her crooked fingers. Putting her glasses back on, she slowly uncurled her body and stood, taking her time. When her feet were steady underneath her, she shuffled across the room toward the sliding paper doors and the wooden veranda. Her white socks glowed brightly against the dark luster of the wood that many feet, many socks, had polished until it gleamed in the moonlight. She stood on the edge and looked out at the garden, where old rocks cast long shadows and the bamboo whispered. The smell of wet moss mixed with the scent of incense burned earlier in the day. She took a deep breath, and then another, and raised her arms out to her sides, spreading the wide black sleeves of her robes like a crow stretching its wings and preparing to fly. She stood like this for a moment, perfectly still, then brought her arms together in front of her body and started swinging them back and forth. Her sleeves flapped and filled with air, and just when it looked like she might take off, she appeared to change her mind, and instead reached around and clasped her fingers behind her, pressing them into the small of her back and attempting to arch her spine. Chin tilted upward, she examined the moon.

Up, down.

The smooth skin on her shorn head caught the light. From a distance, where Ruth stood, it looked like two moons, talking.

# *Nao*

## I.

Timing is everything. Somewhere I read that men born between April and June are more likely to commit suicide than men born at other times of the year. My dad was born in May, so maybe that explains it. Not that he's succeeded in killing himself yet. He hasn't. But he's still trying. It's just a matter of time.

I know I said I would write about old Jiko, but my dad and I are having a fight and so I'm kind of preoccupied. It's not really a huge fight, but we're not talking to each other, which actually means that I'm not talking to him. He probably hasn't even noticed because he's pretty oblivious to other people's feelings these days, and I don't want to upset him by telling him, "Hey, Dad, in case you hadn't noticed, we're having a fight, okay?" He's got a lot on his mind and I don't want to make him even more depressed.

What we're not really fighting about is me not really going to school. The problem is that I screwed up my high school entrance exams, so I can't get in anywhere good, so my only option is to go to some kind of trade school where the stupid kids go, which is so <u>not</u> an option. I don't particularly care about getting an education. I'd much rather become a nun and go live with old Jiko at her temple on the mountain, but my mom and dad say I have to graduate from high school first.

So right now, I'm a ronin, which is an old word for a samurai warrior who doesn't have a master. Back in feudal times, samurai warriors had to have lords or masters. The whole point of being a samurai was to serve a master, and when your master got killed or commited seppuku[32] or lost

---

32. *seppuku* (切腹)—ritual suicide by disembowelment; lit. "stomach" + "cutting." The same kanji are used in *harakiri* (腹切り).

his castles in a war or something, that was it. *Snap!* Your raison d'être was gone, and you had to become a ronin and wander around having sword fights and getting into trouble. These ronin were scary dudes, kind of like what the homeless guys living under tarps in Ueno Park might turn into if you gave them really sharp swords.

Obviously I'm not a samurai warrior, and nowadays ronin just means a dummy who screws up her entrance exams and has to take extra classes at cram school and study at home while she works up enough enthusiasm and self-confidence to take the test again. Usually ronin have graduated from high school and are living with their parents while they try to get into university. It's pretty unusual to be a junior high school ronin like me, but I'm old for my grade, and actually now that I'm sixteen, I don't have to go to school if I don't want to. That's what the law says, anyway.

The way you write ronin is 浪人 with the character for wave and the character for person, which is pretty much how I feel, like a little wave person, floating around on the stormy sea of life.

## 2.

It's really not my fault that I screwed up my entrance exams. With my educational background, I couldn't get into a good Japanese school no matter how much I crammed. My dad wants me to apply to an international high school. He wants me to go to Canada. He's got this thing about Canada. He says it's like America only with health care and no guns, and you can live up to your potential there and not have to worry about what society thinks or about getting sick or getting shot. I told him not to sweat it, because I already don't give a rat's ass what society thinks, and I don't have enough potential to waste time worrying about. He's right about the getting-sick or getting-shot part, though. I'm pretty healthy and I don't mind the idea of dying, but I also don't want to get mowed down by some freaky high school kid in a trench coat who's high on Zoloft and has traded in his Xbox for a semiautomatic.

My dad used to be in love with America. I'm not kidding. It was like America was his lover, and he loved her so much that I swear Mom was jealous. We used to live there, in a town called Sunnyvale, which is in California. My dad used to be this hotshot computer programmer, and he was headhunted when I was three and got this great job in Silicon Valley, and we all moved there. My mom wasn't too thrilled, but back then she went along with anything Dad said, and as for me, I don't have any memory of Japan from when I was a baby. As far as I'm concerned, my whole life started and ended in Sunnyvale, which makes me American. Mom says I didn't speak any English at first, but they stuck me in day care with a nice lady named Mrs. Delgado, and I took to it like a fish to water. That's just the way kids are. My mom had a tougher time. She never got the hang of English or made many friends, but she was okay with it because Dad was making tons of money and she could buy really nice clothes.

So, everything was great and we were just cruising along, except for the fact that we were living in a total dreamland called the Dot-Com Bubble, and when it burst, Dad's company went bankrupt, and he got sacked, and we lost our visas and had to come back to Japan, which totally sucked because not only did Dad not have a job, but he'd also taken a big percentage of his big fat salary in stock options so suddenly we didn't have any savings either, and Tokyo's not cheap. It was a complete bust. Dad was sulking around like a jilted lover, and Mom was grim and tight and righteous, but at least they identified as Japanese and still spoke the language fluently. I, on the other hand, was totally fucked, because I identified as American, and even though we always spoke Japanese at home, my conversational skills were limited to basic, daily-life stuff like where's my allowance, and pass the jam, and oh please please please don't make me leave Sunnyvale.

In Japan, they have special private catch-up schools for kikokushijo[33] kids like me, who get behind in their schoolwork after spending a bunch of years at stupid American schools while their dads are on company

---

33. *kikokushijo* (帰国子女)—repatriated children.

assignments, and then have to catch up with their Japanese grade level when their dads get transferred back. Only my dad wasn't on a company assignment, and he wasn't getting transferred back. He got laid off. And it wasn't like I'd gotten behind my grade level—I'd only ever been to American schools, so I'd never <u>not</u> been behind. And my parents couldn't afford a fancy private catch-up school, so they ended up sticking me in a public junior high school, and I had to repeat half of eighth grade because I was entering in September, which is the middle of the Japanese school year.

It's probably been a while since you were in junior high school, but if you can remember the poor loser foreign kid who entered your eighth-grade class halfway through the year, then maybe you will feel some sympathy for me. I was totally clueless about how you're supposed to act in a Japanese classroom, and my Japanese sucked, and at the time I was almost fifteen and older than the other kids and big for my age, too, from eating so much American food. Also, we were broke so I didn't have an allowance or any nice stuff, so basically I got tortured. In Japan they call it ijime,[34] but that word doesn't begin to describe what the kids used to do to me. I would probably already be dead if Jiko hadn't taught me how to develop my superpower. Ijime is why it's not an option for me to go to a stupid kids' school, because in my experience, stupid kids can be even meaner than smart kids because they don't have as much to lose. School just isn't safe.

But Canada is safe. My dad says that's the difference between Canada and America. America is fast and sexy and dangerous and thrilling, and you can easily get burned, but Canada is safe, and my dad really wants me to be safe, which makes him sound like a pretty typical dad, which he would be if he had a job and didn't keep trying to kill himself all the time. Sometimes I wonder if he wants me to be safe so he'll feel less guilty when he finally succeeds.

---

34. *ijime* (いじめ)—bullying.

## 3.

The first time he tried was about a year ago. We'd been back from Sunnyvale for about six months, and we were living in this tiny two-room apartment on the west side of Tokyo, which was the only thing we could afford because the rents were so crazy high, and the only reason we could even afford that place was because the landlord was supposedly a friend of Dad's from his university days and gave us a break on the key money.

It was truly a disgusting apartment, and all of our neighbors were bar hostesses who never sorted their recycling and ate take-out bento[35] from 7-Eleven and came home drunk with their dates at five or six in the morning. We used to eat breakfast and listen to them having sex. At first we thought it was tomcats in the alley, and sometimes it was tomcats in the alley, but mostly it was the hostesses, although you could never be certain because they sounded so much alike. Scary.

I don't know how to write it, but it was like *ooo . . . ooo . . . ooooh . . .* or *ow . . . ow . . . owwww . . .* or *no . . . no . . . noooo . . .* like a young girl getting tortured by a sadist who was kind of mechanical and a little bit bored, but wasn't ready to stop yet, either.

My mom always pretended not to hear it, but you could see by the way the skin around her lips got really pale and tight, and she ate her toast in tiny bites that got tinier and tinier until finally she just put down the half-eaten crust and stared at it, that she could hear everything. Of course she could! You'd have to be deaf not to hear those stupid girls, moaning and groaning and squealing like boiled kittens, with the sounds of their bare bottoms slapping up against our walls and bumping on our ceiling. Sometimes little clumps of dust and dead insects would drop from the fluorescent light fixture and land in my milk and, like, I wasn't supposed to say anything? My dad pretty much ignored it all, too, except when there was a particularly enormous THUMP! and then he would lower his newspaper and look at me and kind of roll his eyes, and quickly put the paper back up before

---

35. *bentō* (弁当)—lunchbox.

Mom noticed and got mad at him for making me lose it and snort milk out my nose.

In those days Dad was going out every day to try to find a job, so he and I would leave the apartment together in the morning. We used to leave early so we could take the long route. It was something we never had to talk about or plan. As soon as we were done with breakfast, we'd dump our dishes in the sink and brush our teeth, grab our stuff, and then head for the door. I think we just wanted to get away from my mom, who was emanating a pretty toxic vibe at that time in our lives. Not that Dad and I ever discussed it. We didn't, but we didn't want to be around it, either.

There was always this moment, leaving the safety of our apartment building and stepping out onto the street, when we kind of glanced at each other, then looked away. I'm pretty sure we were both feeling the same things—guilty about leaving Mom at home alone, and helpless about going out into a world we were unprepared for—that felt totally unreal. We both looked ridiculous and we knew it. Back in Sunnyvale, Dad was cool. He used to bike to work in jeans and Adidas sneakers and carry this stylish messenger bag, and now he was dressing in an ugly polyester blue suit and slip-on loafers and carrying a cheap briefcase that made him look conservative and old. And I had to wear this dumb school uniform that was way too small, and no matter how hard I tried, I couldn't figure out how to make it look cute on me. The other girls in my eighth-grade class were petite and managed to look supercute and sexy in their uniforms, but I just looked like a big old stinky lump, and I felt like one, too. So when we left the apartment, it was this doomed unreal feeling I remember more than anything else, like we were bad actors in terrible costumes in a play that was guaranteed to tank, but we had to go out on stage anyhow.

The long route took us through all these old neighborhoods and shopping streets and finally past a tiny little temple in the middle of a bunch of ugly concrete office buildings. The temple was a special place. There was the smell of moss and incense, and sounds, too—you could actually hear the insects and birds and even some frogs—and you could almost feel the plants and other things growing. We were right in the middle of Tokyo, but when you got close to the temple, it was like stepping into a pocket of ancient humid air, which had somehow gotten preserved like a bubble in ice, with all the sounds and smells still trapped inside it. I read about how the scientists in the Arctic, or the Antarctic, or somewhere really cold, can drill way down and take ice core samples of the ancient atmosphere that are hundreds of thousands or even millions of years old. And even though this is totally cool, it makes me sad to think of those plugs of ice, melting and releasing their ancient bubbles like tiny sighs into our polluted twenty-first-century air. Stupid, I know, but that's the way the temple felt to me, like a core sample from another time, and I really liked it, and I told my dad so, and this was way before I even knew Jiko, or had spent the summer at her temple on the mountainside, or anything like that. I didn't even know she existed.

"You don't remember visiting her when you were a baby?"

"No."

"We visited her at her temple before we went to America."

"I don't remember anything about before we went to America."

We walked up the path through the wooden gate. A cat was sleeping in the sun by a stone lantern. We climbed some worn steps to where Shaka-sama, the Lord Buddha, was sitting in a shadowy altar. We stood side by side, looking up at him. He looked peaceful, with his eyes half-closed, like maybe he was taking a nap.

"Your great-grandmother is a nun. Did you know that?"

"Dad, I told you. I didn't even know I had one."

I clapped my hands together twice and bowed and made a wish, like Dad had showed me. I always wished the same things: that he would find a job, that we could go back to Sunnyvale, and if neither of those wishes panned out, then at least that the kids at school would stop torturing me. I wasn't interested in great-grandmothers who were nuns back then. I was just trying to survive on a day-to-day basis.

After the temple, Dad would walk me to school and we'd talk about stuff. I don't remember exactly what, and it didn't matter. The important thing was that we were being polite and not saying all the things that were making us unhappy, which was the only way we knew how to love each other.

When we got near the gates of the junior high school, he'd slow down a little, and I'd slow down, too, and he would look around to make sure nobody was looking, and then he would give me a quick little hug and a kiss on the top of my head. It was the most ordinary thing in the world, but it felt like we were doing something illegal, like we were lovers or something, because in Japan dads don't generally hug and kiss their kids. Don't ask me why. They just don't. But we kissed and hugged because we were American, at least in our hearts, and then we'd both step away really fast in case anyone was watching.

"You look real nice, Nao," he'd say, staring over my head.

And I'd study my shoes and say, "Yeah, you're looking good, too, Dad."

We were totally lying, but it was okay, and we walked the rest of the way not saying anything, because if we even opened our mouths after telling such big lies, the truth might come pouring out, so we had to keep our lips shut. But even if we couldn't talk frankly to each other, I still liked it that my Dad walked me to school every morning, because it meant that the kids couldn't start picking on me until after he'd waved goodbye and turned the corner.

But they were waiting. I could feel their eyes on us as we stood by the gate, and the hairs on my arms and the back of my neck started to prickle, and my heart started beating real fast, and my armpits were like rivers flooding. I wanted to cling to my dad and beg him not to go, but I knew I couldn't do that.

"Ja, ne," my dad would say, brightly. "Study hard, okay?"

And I'd just nod because I knew that if I tried to speak I would start crying.

**4.**

The minute he turned his back, they would start to move in. Have you ever seen those nature documentaries where they show a pack of wild hyenas moving in to kill a wildebeest or a baby gazelle? They come in from all sides and cut the most pathetic animal off from the herd and surround it, getting closer and closer and staying real tight, and if Dad had happened to turn around to wave to me, it would have looked like good-natured fun, like I had lots of fun friends, gathering around me, singing out greetings in terrible English—Guddo moningu, dear Transfer Student Yasutani! Hello! Hello!—and Dad would have been reassured to see me so popular and everyone making an effort to be nice to me. And it's usually one hyena, not always the biggest one, but one that's small and quick and mean, who lunges first, breaking flesh and drawing blood, which is the signal for the rest of the pack to attack, so that by the time we got through the doors of the school, I was usually covered with fresh cuts and pinching bruises, and my uniform was all untucked with new little tears in it made by the sharp points of nail scissors that the girls kept in their pencil cases to trim their split ends. Hyenas don't kill their prey. They cripple them and then eat them alive.

Basically, it went on like that all day. They would walk by my desk and pretend to gag or sniff the air and say Iyada! Gaijin kusai![36] or Bimbo kusai![37] Sometimes they practiced their idiomatic English on me, repeating stuff they learned from American rap lyrics: Yo, big fat-ass ho, puleezu show me some juicy coochie, ain't you a slutto, you even take it in the butto, come lick on my nutto, oh hell yeah. Etc. You get the idea. My strategy was basically just to ignore them or play dead or pretend I didn't exist. I thought that maybe if I just pretended hard enough it would actually come true, and I would either die or disappear. Or at least it would come true enough for my classmates to believe it and stop tormenting me, but they didn't. They didn't stop until they'd chased me home to our apartment, and I ran up the stairs and locked the door behind me, panting and bleeding from lots of little places like under my arms or between my legs where the cuts wouldn't show.

Mom was almost never at home at the time. She was into her jellyfish phase, and she used to spend all day at the invertebrate tank in the city

---

36. *Iyada! Gaijin kusai*—Gross! She stinks like a foreigner!
37. *Bimbo kusai*—She stinks like a poor person!

aquarium, where she would sit, clutching her old Gucci handbag, watching kurage[38] through the glass. I know this because she took me there once. It was the only thing that relaxed her. She had read somewhere that watching kurage was beneficial to your health because it reduces stress levels, only the problem was that a lot of other housewives had read the same article, so it was always crowded in front of the tank, and the aquarium had to set out folding chairs, and you had to get there really early in order to get a good spot, all of which was very stressful. Now that I think about it, I'm pretty sure she was having a nervous breakdown at the time, but I remember how pale and beautiful she looked with her delicate profile against the watery blue tank, and her bloodshot eyes following the drift of the pink and yellow jellyfish as they floated by like pulsing pastel-colored moons, trailing their long tentacles behind them.

## 5.

This was our life right after Sunnyvale, and it seemed to go on forever, although actually it was only a couple of months. And then one evening, Dad came home and announced he'd been hired at this new start-up that was developing a line of empathic productivity software, and he was going to be their chief programmer, and even though his salary was a tiny fraction of what he'd made in Silicon Valley, at least it was a job. It was a miracle! I remember Mom was so happy, she started to cry, and Dad got all shy and gruff and took us out to eat sweet grilled eel on top of rice, which is my favorite dish in the whole world.

After that, Dad would still leave with me in the morning and come home late at night, and even though I was still getting bullied at school, and we still didn't seem to have any money, it was okay because we were all feeling optimistic about our family's future again. Mom stopped going to the aquarium and started fixing up our two-room apartment. She cleaned the tatami and organized our bookshelves and she even confronted the bar hostesses, ambushing them in the corridor on their way to the

38. *kurage* (水母)—jellyfish; lit. "water" + "mother."

clubs to yell at them about the recycling and the noise they made.

"I've got a teenage daughter!" I heard her say, which made me feel embarrassed—like, hello, I was almost fifteen and I knew what sex was—but also proud that she considered me a daughter worth fighting for.

That year was my first Christmas and New Year's in Japan that I could remember, and my mom and dad were trying to believe that everything was fine and this whole disaster of our life was just one big adventure, and I went along with them because I was just a kid, and what did I know? We gave each other Christmas presents, and Mom made osechi,[39] and we sat around in front of the television eating candied shrimp and tiny dried fishes and salted roe and pickled lotus roots and sweet beans while Dad drank saké, and during the commercial breaks he told us stories about the line of productivity software he was developing, and how computers were going to experience empathy and anticipate our needs and feelings even better than other human beings, and how soon human beings wouldn't need each other in the same way anymore. Given what was going on at school, I thought this all sounded very promising.

I can't imagine what Dad was thinking. I can't believe he thought he was going to get away with it. Maybe he didn't. Maybe he didn't think at all, or maybe he was already so crazy he really believed his own stories. Or maybe he just got tired of feeling like a loser, so he invented this job to give himself a break and make us all feel happy, at least for a little while. And it worked. For a little while. But soon, he and my mom started arguing at night, first gently, and then more and more intensely.

It was always about money. Mom wanted him to hand over his weekly pay to her so she could manage it. That's the way it's done in Japan. The husband gives the wife all the money, and she gives him an allowance that he can spend on beer and pachinko or whatever he wants, while she hangs on to the rest of it to keep it safe. And Mom had a good reason for wanting to do it the Japanese way. When they went to America, Dad insisted on doing it the American way, where the Man of the House

---

39. *osechi ryōri* (おせち料理)—special cold New Year's dinner, made in advance and served in a multitiered lunchbox.

makes all the Big Financial Decisions, but as it turned out, what with the business of the stock options, the manly American way turned into a disaster. Mom wasn't about to let anything like that happen again, so she was insisting he turn over his pay, and he was insisting that he'd deposited it all into a high-yield blah blah account. Occasionally he'd hand her a stack of ten-thousand-yen bills, but that was it. And they would have gone on like this for longer, only Dad got careless, and a couple of days before my fifteenth birthday, Mom found the stubs from the OTB in his pocket and confronted him, and instead of confessing he'd been lying, he went out and sat in a park, getting smashed on vending machine saké, and then he went to the train station and bought a platform ticket and jumped in front of the 12:37 Shinjuku-bound Chuo Rapid Express.

Luckily for him, the train had already started slowing down as it approached the station, and the conductor saw him wobbling on the edge of the platform and was able to slam on the emergency brakes in time. It just missed him. It ran over that stupid briefcase of his. The station police came and hauled Dad up off the tracks and arrested him for causing a disturbance and interfering with the timely operations of the transit system, but since it was unclear if he jumped or if he was just drunk and stumbled, instead of putting him in jail, they released him into Mom's custody.

Mom went to pick him up at the police station, brought him home in a cab, and put him into the bathtub, and when he came out, damp and a little bit more sober, he said he was ready to confess everything. Mom told me to go into the bedroom, but Dad said I was old enough to know what kind of man my father was. He sat in front of us at the kitchen table, with his fingers white and clenched together, and admitted that he had made the whole thing up. Instead of going to work as a chief programmer, he had been spending his days on a bench in Ueno Park, studying the racing form and feeding the crows. He had sold his old computer peripherals to raise some cash, which he used to bet on the horses. Occasionally he would win, and he would hold back some of the cash to bet again, and the rest he brought home to Mom, but recently he had been losing more than winning, until finally his cash was all gone. There was no high-yield blah blah account. There was no empathic productivity software. There was no start-up at all. There was only the five-million-yen fine from the transit company that they make you pay for causing a "human incident," which is a nice way of saying when you try to use one of their trains to kill yourself. He bowed until his forehead almost touched the kitchen table and said he was sorry he had no money to buy me a present for my birthday. I'm pretty sure he was crying.

The Chuo Rapid Express Incident was the first time and he was drunk, so you could almost believe it was an accident. In the end, that's what Mom decided to do, and Dad went along with her, even though his eyes told me that it wasn't true.

## 6.

My old Jiko says that everything happens because of your karma, which is a kind of subtle energy that you cause by the stuff you do or say or even just think, which means you have to watch yourself and not think too many perverted thoughts or they'll come back and bite you. And not just in this lifetime, either, but in all your lifetimes going way back in your past and into your future. So maybe it's just my dad's karma to end up on a park bench feeding crows in this lifetime, and really you can't blame him for causing a human incident and wanting to move along to the next lifetime pretty quick. Anyway, Jiko says that as long as you keep trying to be a good person and making an effort to change, then finally one day all the good stuff you do will cancel out all the bad stuff that you've done, and you can become enlightened and hop on that elevator and never come back—unless, as I said, you're like Jiko and you've taken a vow not to ride on the elevator until everyone else gets on first. That's the great thing about my great granny. You can really count on her. She might be a hundred and four and say some pretty wack things, but my old Jiko is totally dependable.

# *Ruth*

## I.

"Interesting, about the crows," Oliver said, tentatively.

Ruth closed the diary and looked over at her husband. He lay on his back in bed, head propped up against the pillow, staring down at his toes. She studied his clean, chiseled profile and marveled. After everything she'd just read—about Nao's life, the girl's father, her situation at school—that his mind would alight upon the crows! There were so many other more pressing things she would have preferred to discuss, and she was about to say so, when the slight hesitation in his words made her pause; he was aware that his responses were often irregular, and she knew this worried him. He wasn't trying to annoy her, quite the opposite. She took a deep breath.

"Crows," she repeated. "Yes. What about them?"

"Well," he said, sounding relieved. "It's just funny that she should mention them, because I've been doing some reading about Japanese crows. The native species there is *Corvus japonensis*, which is a subspecies of *Corvus macrorhynchos*, the Large-billed or Jungle Crow. It's quite different from the American Crow—"

"This is Canada," she said, interrupting him even as her mind drifted elsewhere. "We should have Canadian crows." She was imagining Nao's father, sitting on his bench. Every morning he woke, got dressed in his cheap blue suit, ate his breakfast, walked his daughter to school. Maybe he'd fish a copy of the morning newspaper out of the recycling on his way to the park, to read on the bench.

"Well, yes," Oliver said. "As I was about to say, the crow native to these parts is *Corvus caurinus*, the Northwestern Crow. Almost identical to the American Crow, only smaller."

"Figures," she said. Did he have a special bench he liked more than others? He'd sit down and read the paper and study the racing form. Maybe in the afternoon he'd feed the crows crumbs from his sandwich or grains of rice from his rice ball before taking a nap, stretched out on his bench with the newspaper covering his face. Did he really think he could get away with it?

Oliver had fallen silent.

"I didn't know we had crows at all," she said, quickly, to show she was still listening. "I thought we just had ravens."

"We do," he said. "We have both crows and ravens. Same genus. Different birds. And that's the weird part of it."

He sat up in bed and waited until he had her full attention before continuing. "The other day, when you came back with the freezer bag? I was out in the garden and I heard the ravens talking. They were up in a fir, making a lot of noise, flapping around, all excited. I looked up and saw that they were harassing a smaller bird. The smaller bird kept trying to approach them, but they kept picking on it, until finally it flew over to the fence near where I was working. It looked like a crow, only it was bigger than *Corvus caurinus*, with a hump on its forehead and a big thick curved beak."

"So it wasn't a crow, then?"

"No, it was. I think it was a Jungle Crow. It sat there for a long time, studying me, so I got a really good look at it, too. I could swear it was *Corvus japonensis*. But what's it doing here?"

He was leaning forward now, his pale blue eyes fixed intently on the bedcovers, as though he were trying to locate in the sheets an answer to the mystery of this geographical displacement. "The only thing I can think of is that it rode over on the flotsam. That it's part of the drift."

"Is that possible?"

He ran his hands across the blanket, smoothing out the mountains and valleys. "Anything's possible. People made it here in hollowed-out logs. Why not crows? They can ride on the drift, plus they have the advantage of being able to fly. It's not impossible. It's an anomaly, is all."

## 2.

He was an anomaly, a sport, a deviation from the mean. "Fries his fish in a different pan" was the way people sometimes described him on the island. But Ruth had always been fascinated by the meandering currents of his mind, and even though she often grew impatient, trying to follow its flow, in the end, she was glad she did. His observations, like those concerning the crow, were often the most interesting.

They'd met in the early 1990s at an artists' colony in the Canadian Rockies, where he was leading a thematic residency called End of the Nation-State. She had been invited to the colony to do postproduction on a film she was making at the time, and he was a passionate devotee of midcentury Japanese cinema, so they soon became friends. He used to visit her in the editing room with a six-pack, and they would drink beer, and he would talk about montage and assemblage and borders and time while she carefully pieced together the frames of her movie. He was an environmental artist, doing public installations (botanical interventions into urban landscapes, he called them) on the fringes of the art establishment, and she was drawn to the unbridled and fertile anarchy of his thinking. In the flickering darkness of the editing room, she listened to him talk, and soon she had moved into his room in the dormitory.

After the residency ended, they parted ways and went in opposite directions: she, back to New York City, and he, to the island farm in British Columbia where he taught permaculture. Had they met even a year earlier, their affair would probably have ended then and there, but these were the early days of the Internet, and they both had dial-up email accounts, which allowed them to keep the immediacy of their friendship alive. He shared a party line with three other island households, but he would wait until the middle of the night, when no one else was using the telephone, to send daily dispatches with the subject line *missives from the mossy margins*. In the summer, as the heavy moths beat their powdery wings against his window screen, he wrote to her about the island, describing how the berry bushes were laden with fruit, and where the most succulent oysters could be found, and the way the bioluminescence lit the lapping waves and filled the ocean with twinkling planktonic forms that mirrored the stars in the sky. He translated the vast, wild, Pacific Rim ecosystem into poetry and pixels, transmitting them all the way to her small monitor in Manhattan, where she waited, leaning into the screen, eagerly reading each word with her heart in her throat, because by then she was deeply in love.

That winter, they tried living together in New York, but by spring, she had again yielded to the tug and tide of his mind, allowing its currents to carry her back across the continent and wash them up on the remote shores of his evergreen island, surrounded by the fjords and snowcapped peaks of Desolation Sound—the tug of his mind and of the Canadian health care system, because he'd been stricken with a mysterious flulike illness, and they were broke and in need of affordable health insurance.

And if she was perfectly honest, she would have to acknowledge the role she played in their drift. She wanted what was best for him, wanted him to be happy and safe, but she was searching for a refugium for herself and for her mother, too. At the time, her mother was suffering from Alzheimer's disease. She had been diagnosed just a few months before Ruth's father had died, and on his deathbed, Ruth had promised him that she would care for her mother after he was gone, but then her first novel was published, and she embarked on a book tour that took her around the world twice. Caring for a demented mother in Connecticut and a chronically ill husband in Canada was clearly impossible. The only option was to consolidate her remaining family and move her mother to the island.

It seemed like a good plan, so when moving day came, Ruth was content to exchange the tiny one-bedroom apartment that had been her home in lower Manhattan for twenty acres of rain forest and two houses in Whaletown. "I'm just trading one island for another," she told her New York friends. "How different could it be?"

## 3.

It could, she learned, be very different. Whaletown was not really a town, per se, but rather a "locality," defined by the province of British Columbia as "a named place or area, generally with a scattered population of 50 or less." Even so, it was the second-largest population center on the island.

It had once been a whaling station, from whence it derived its name, although whales were rarely seen in nearby waters anymore. Most of them had been hunted out back in 1869, when a Scotsman named James Dawson and his American partner, Abel Douglass, established the Whaletown station and started killing whales with a new and extremely efficient weapon called a bomb lance. The bomb lance was a heavyweight shoulder rifle that fired a special harpoon, fitted with a bomb and time-delay fuse, which exploded inside the whale just seconds after penetrating its skin. By mid-September of that year, Dawson and Douglass had shipped more than 450 barrels of oil, 20,000 gallons, south to the United States.

The primary source of oil in those days was blubber, and the only way to obtain it was to mine it from the bodies of living whales. When the technology for extracting kerosene and petroleum from the prehistoric dead was commercialized in the latter part of the century, the order Cetacea stood a fighting chance of survival. You could say that fossil fuels arrived just in time to save the whales, but not in time to save the whales of Whaletown. By June of 1870, a year after the station was established, the last whales in the area either had been slaughtered or had fled, and Dawson and Douglass closed up shop and moved on, too.

Whales are time beings. In May 2007, a fifty-ton bowhead whale, killed by Eskimo whalers off the Alaskan coast, was found to have a three-and-a-half-inch arrow-shaped projectile from a bomb lance embedded in the blubber on its neck. By dating the fragment, researchers were able to estimate the whale's age: between 115 and 130 years old. Creatures who survive and live that long presumably have long memories. The waters around Whaletown were once treacherous for whales, but the ones that managed to escape learned to stay away. You can imagine them chirping and cooing to each other in their beautiful subaquatic voices.

*Stay away! Stay away!*

Every now and then, there's a whale sighting from the ferry that services the island. The captain cuts the engine and comes on the PA system to announce that a pod of orcas or a humpback has been spotted on the port side at two o'clock, and all the passengers flow to that side of the ship to scan the waves for a glimpse of a fin or a fluke or a sleek dark back, rising up from the water. The tourists raise their cameras and mobile phones, hoping to capture a breach or a spout, and even the locals get excited. But mostly the whales still stay away from Whaletown, leaving only their name behind.

## 4.

A name, Ruth thought, could be either a ghost or a portent depending upon which side of time you were standing. The name Whaletown had become a mere specter of the past, a crepuscular Pacific shimmer, but the name Desolation Sound still hovered in a liminal space and felt to her both oracular and haunted.

Her own name, Ruth, had often functioned like an omen, casting a complex shadow forward across her life. The word *ruth* is derived from the Middle English *rue*, meaning remorse or regret. Ruth's Japanese mother wasn't thinking of the English etymology when she chose the name, nor did she intend to curse her daughter with it—Ruth was simply the name of an old family friend. But even so, Ruth often felt oppressed by the sense of her name, and not just in English. In Japanese, the name was equally problematic. Japanese people can't pronounce "r" or "th." In Japanese, Ruth is either pronounced *rutsu*, meaning "roots," or *rusu*, meaning "not at home" or "absent."

The home they bought in Whaletown was built in a meadowlike clearing that had been hacked from the middle of the dense temperate rain forest. A smaller cottage stood at the foot of the drive where her mother would live. On all sides, massive Douglas firs, red cedars, and bigleaf maples surrounded them, dwarfing everything human. When Ruth first saw these giant trees, she wept. They rose up around her, ancient time beings, towering a hundred or two hundred feet overhead. At five feet, five inches, she had never felt so puny in all her life.

"We're nothing," she said, wiping her eyes. "We're barely here at all."

"Yes," Oliver said. "Isn't it great? And they can live to be a thousand years old."

She leaned against him, tilting her head all the way back so she could see the treetops, piercing the sky.

"They're impossibly tall," she said.

"Not impossibly," Oliver said, holding her so she wouldn't fall. "It's just a matter of perspective. If you were that tree, I wouldn't even reach the bottom of your anklebone."

Oliver was overjoyed. He was a tree guy and had no use for tidy vegetable gardens or shallow-rooted annuals, like lettuce. When they first moved in, he was still quite ill, prone to dizzy spells and easily tired, but he started a daily regimen of walking and soon he was running the trails, and it seemed to Ruth as if the forest were healing him, as if he were absorbing its inexorable life force. As he ran through the dense understory, he could read the signs of arboreal intrigue, the drama and power struggles as species vied for control over a patch of sunlight, or giant firs and fungal spores opted to work together for their mutual benefit. He could see time unfolding here, and history, embedded in the whorls and fractal forms of nature, and he would come home, sweating and breathless, and tell her what he'd seen.

Their house was made of cedar from the forest. It was a whimsical two-story structure built by hippies in the 1970s, with a shake roof, deep eaves, and a sprawling front porch overlooking the small meadow and encircled by the tall trees. The real estate agent had listed the house as having an ocean view, but the only glimpse of water it afforded was from a single window in Ruth's office, where she could see a tiny patch of sea and sky though a U-shaped notch in the treetops, which looked like an inverted tunnel. The real estate agent pointed out that they could cut down the trees that were blocking their view, but they never did. Instead, they planted more.

In a futile attempt to domesticate the landscape, Ruth planted European climbing roses around the house. Oliver planted bamboo. The two species quickly grew up into a densely tangled thicket, so that soon it was almost impossible to find the entrance to the house if you didn't already know where it was. The house seemed in danger of disappearing, and by then, the meadow was beginning to shrink, too, as the forest encroached like a slow-moving coniferous wave, threatening to swallow them completely.

Oliver wasn't worried. He took the long view. Anticipating the effects of global warming on the native trees, he was working to create a climate-change forest on a hundred acres of clear-cut, owned by a botanist friend. He planted groves of ancient natives—metasequoia, giant sequoia, coast redwoods, *Juglans, Ulmus,* and ginkgo—species that had been indigenous to the area during the Eocene Thermal Maximum, some 55 million years ago.

"Imagine," he said. "Palms and alligators flourishing once again as far north as Alaska!"

This was his latest artwork, a botanical intervention he called the NeoEocene. He described it as a collaboration with time and place, whose outcome neither he nor any of his contemporaries would ever live to witness, but he was okay with not knowing. Patience was part of his nature, and he accepted his lot as a short-lived mammal, scurrying in and out amid the roots of the giants.

But Ruth was neither patient nor accepting, and she really liked to know. After a few short years (fifteen, to be exact—brief by his count, interminable by hers), surrounded by all this vegetative rampancy, she was feeling increasingly unsure of herself. She missed the built environment of New York City. It was only in an urban landscape, amid straight lines and architecture, that she could situate herself in human time and history. As a novelist she needed this. She missed people. She missed human intrigue, drama and power struggles. She needed her own species, not to talk to, necessarily, but just to be among, as a bystander in a crowd or an anonymous witness.

But here, on the sparsely populated island, human culture barely existed and then only as the thinnest veneer. Engulfed by the thorny roses and massing bamboo, she stared out the window and felt like she'd stepped into a malevolent fairy tale. She'd been bewitched. She'd pricked her finger and had fallen into a deep, comalike sleep. The years had passed, and she was not getting any younger. She had fulfilled her promise to her father, and cared for her mother. Now that her mother was dead, Ruth felt that her own life was passing her by. Maybe it was time to leave this place she'd hoped would be home forever. Maybe it was time to break the spell.

## 5.

Home-leaving is a Buddhist euphemism for leaving the secular world and entering the monastic path, which was pretty much the opposite of what Ruth was contemplating when she pondered her return to the city. Zen Master Dōgen uses the phrase in "The Merits of Home-Leaving," which is the title of Chapter 86 of his *Shōbōgenzō*. This is the chapter in which he praises his young monks for their commitment to a path of awakening and explicates the granular nature of time: the 6,400,099,980 moments[40] that constitute a single day. His point is that every single one of those moments provides an opportunity to reestablish our will. Even the snap of a finger, he says, provides us with sixty-five opportunities to wake up and to choose actions that will produce beneficial karma and turn our lives around.

"The Merits of Home-Leaving" was originally delivered as a lecture to the monks at Eiheiji, the monastery that Dōgen founded, deep in the mountains of Fukui prefecture, far away from the decadence and corruption of the city. In the *Shōbōgenzō*, the text of the lecture is followed by the date of its delivery: *A day of the summer retreat in the seventh year of Kenchō.*

All well and good. You can imagine the pure summer heat enfolding the mountain, and the cicadas' shrill cry piercing the torpid air; the monks sitting in zazen for hour upon hour, immobile on their damp cushions, while mosquitoes circle their shiny bald heads and rivulets of sweat run

---

40. Jpn. *setsuna* (利那), from the Sanskrit *ksāna* (Appendix A).

like tears down their young faces. Time must have seemed interminable to them.

All well and good, except that the seventh year of Kenchō corresponds with 1255 in the Gregorian calendar, and during the summer retreat that year, Zen Master Dōgen, who was purportedly delivering his lecture on the merits of home-leaving, was dead. He had died in 1253, two years and many moments earlier.

There are several explanations for this discrepancy. The most probable is that Dōgen wrote a draft of the talk several years prior to his death and, intending to revise it, had left notes and commentary to that effect, and these were later incorporated into a final version and delivered to the monks by his dharma heir, Master Koun Ejō.

There's another possibility, however, which is that on that day in the summer of the seventh year of Kenchō, Zen Master Dōgen wasn't entirely dead. Of course, he wouldn't have been entirely alive, either. Like Schrödinger's cat, in the quantum thought experiment, he would have been both alive and dead. [41]

The great matter of life and death is the real subject of "The Merits of Home-Leaving." When Dōgen exhorts his young forest monks to continue, moment by moment, to summon their resolve and stay true to their commitment to enlightenment, what he means is simply this: *Life is fleeting! Don't waste a single moment of your precious life!*

*Wake up now!*
*And now!*
*And now!*

## 6.

Ruth dozed in her chair in her second-floor office. The bristling tower of pages that represented the last ten years of her life sat squarely on the desk in front of her. Letter by letter, page by page, she had built this edifice, but now every time she contemplated the memoir, her mind

---

41. For some thoughts on Dōgen and quantum mechanics, see Appendix B.

contracted and she felt inexplicably sleepy. It had been months, possibly even a year, since she'd added anything to it. New words just refused to come, and she could barely remember the old ones she'd written. And she was afraid to look. She knew she needed to read through the draft again, to consolidate the structure, and then to start editing and filling in the gaps, but it was too much for her foggy brain to process. The world inside the pages was as dim as a dream.

Outside, Oliver was chopping firewood and she could hear the rhythmic thunk of the ax splitting wood. The exercise was good for him. He had been out there for hours.

She summoned her resolve and sat up resolutely in her chair. The stout red diary lay on top of the memoir, and she picked it up to move it aside. The book felt like a box in her hands. She turned it over. When she was little, she was always surprised to pick up a book in the morning, and open it, and find the letters aligned neatly in their places. Somehow she expected them to be all jumbled up, having fallen to the bottom when the covers were shut. Nao had described something similar, seeing the blank pages of Proust and wondering if the letters had fallen off like dead ants. When Ruth had read this, she'd felt a jolt of recognition.

She placed the diary on the far edge of the desk, out of the way, and then glowered at the manuscript. Perhaps the same sort of thing had happened to her pages. Perhaps she would start reading only to find her words had vanished. Perhaps this would be a good thing. Perhaps it would be a relief. The battered memoir stared balefully back at her. While her mother was still alive, the project had seemed like a good idea. During the long period of decline, Ruth had recorded the gradual erosion of her mother's mind, and she had observed herself, too, making copious notes of her own feelings and reactions. The result was this ungainly heap on the desk in front of her. She scanned the first page and immediately pushed it away. The tone of the writing bugged her— cloying, elegiac. It made her cringe. She was a novelist. She was interested in the lives of others. What had gotten into her, to think she could write a memoir?

There was no denying that Nao's diary was a distraction, and even though she was determined to pace herself, she had still managed to spend the better part of the day online, looking through lists of names of the victims of the earthquake and tsunami. She'd located a People Finder site and run a search for Yasutani. There were several, but no Jikos or Naokos. She didn't know the names of the parents, so she browsed through the files that people had posted of the missing, looking for likely matches. The information was sparse: basic facts about age and sex and residence, where the victims worked, where they'd last been seen, and what they'd been wearing. Often there were pictures, taken in happier times. A grinning boy in his school cap. A young woman, waving at the camera in front of a shrine. A father at an amusement park, holding his child. Below this spare layer of data lay the fullness of the tragedy. All these lives, but none were the lives she was looking for. Finally, she gave up. She needed more information about her Yasutanis, and the only way to find it was to read further in the diary.

Ruth closed her eyes. In her mind, she could picture Nao, sitting by herself in the darkened kitchen, waiting for her mother to bring her father home from the police station. What had those long moments felt like to her? It was hard to get a sense from the diary of the texture of time passing. No writer, even the most proficient, could re-enact in words the flow of a life lived, and Nao was hardly that skillful. The dingy kitchen was dim and still. The bar hostesses moaned and beat against the flimsy wall. The metallic clank of the key in the lock must have startled her, but she stayed where she was. Feet scuffled in the foyer. Did her parents speak? Probably not. She listened to the sound of running water as her mother filled the tub in the bathroom, and her father undressed in the bedroom. She didn't move. Didn't look up. Kept her eyes fixed on her fingers, which lay in her lap like dead things. She listened to her father bathe, and then, as her mother grimly looked on, she listened to him stumble through his confession. Did she sneak a glance at his pink cheeks and see it as shame or just the heat of the bath? Did she notice the sweat on his forehead? How many moments passed from the time he started talking until her mother stood and left the room? Did the hum of the fluorescent light sound particularly loud in the silence?

And afterward, in the bedroom she shared with her parents, did she pull the covers over her head, or turn on the light and read a book, or cram for a test that she was sure to fail the next day? Perhaps she went online and googled *suicide, men*, while her parents slept, or pretended to sleep, back-to-back, on their separate futons on the floor behind her. If she did, she would have learned, as Ruth had, that suicide surpassed cancer as the leading cause of death for middle-aged men in Japan, so her father was right on target. Was that a consolation? Dressed in her pajamas, she sat in front of the glowing screen in the dark, dimly aware of the sounds of breathing in and out of sync, her father's breath the louder, steady, despite his professed desire for its cessation, her mother's softer, but punctuated from time to time by a sharp panicky nasal intake or an apneic stopping.

What did she feel at that moment?

Ruth opened her eyes. Something was different. She listened. She could hear birds outside, a flock of scoters coming off the water, the tapping of a pileated woodpecker, the liquid plonk and caw of the ravens, but what had caught her attention just now was not a sound, but rather its absence: the rhythmic thunk of Oliver's ax was missing. She felt a quickening of fear. When had it stopped? She stood and walked to the window that overlooked the woodpile. Had he hurt himself? Gotten dizzy and cut off his leg? Rural life was perilous. Every year, someone on the island died or drowned or was seriously injured. Their neighbor died picking apples. He'd fallen off his ladder onto his head, and his wife found his body under the tree, surrounded by spilled fruit. Dangers were rife: ladders, fruit trees, slick moss-covered roofs, rain gutters, axes, splitting mauls, chainsaws, shotguns, skinning knives, wolves, cougars, high winds, falling tree limbs, rogue waves, faulty wiring, drug dealers, drunk drivers, elderly drivers, suicide, and even murder.

She peered out the window. Down below in the driveway, she could see her husband. He looked all right. He was standing on both legs next to the woodpile, with one hand in his pocket and the other on the handle of the ax, staring up into a tree and listening to the ravens.

## 7.

"That Jungle Crow is back again," he said in the bath that night. "It's driving the ravens crazy."

Ruth grunted. She was brushing her teeth with the electric toothbrush and her mouth was full of toothpaste. Oliver was stretched out in the bathtub, flipping through the latest issue of *New Science* magazine, while Pesto perched on the rim of the tub, next to his head.

"I was reading about the Jungle Crows," he said. "Apparently they've become a huge problem in Japan. They're very clever. They memorize the schedules for trash pickups and then wait for the housewives to put out the garbage so they can rip it open and steal what's inside. They eat kittens and use wire coat hangers to make nests on utility poles, which short-circuit the lines and cause power outages. The Tokyo Electric Power Company says crows are responsible for hundreds of blackouts a year, including some major ones that even shut down the bullet trains. They have special crow patrols to hunt them down and dismantle their nests, but the crows outsmart them and build dummy nests. Children have to carry umbrellas to school to ward off attacks and protect themselves from droppings, and ladies have stopped wearing shiny clips in their hair."

Ruth spat. "You sound happy about this," she said into the bowl of the sink.

"I am. I like crows. I like all birds. Do you remember those owl incidents in Stanley Park a couple of years ago? Those joggers that kept showing up in the emergency room with cuts on their heads, complaining about being swooped by owls? The doctors finally put it together. It was fledging season, and the owls were babies, just learning the owling trade. Then someone noticed that the joggers were all balding middle-aged guys with ponytails. Picture it from above, all these shiny pates and flipping rodentlike tails. They must have looked like shiny fishing lures. Irresistible to a baby owl."

Ruth stood and wiped her mouth on a towel. "You're a balding middle-aged guy," she said. "You should be careful."

She tapped her fingers lightly on the top of his head on her way to the door. The cat took a swat at her hand.

"Yes," Oliver said, going back to his issue of *New Science*. "But you'll notice I don't have a ponytail."

# *Nao*

### 1.

Jiko Yasutani is my great-grandmother on my dad's side, and she had three kids: a son named Haruki, and two daughters named Sugako and Ema. Here's a family tree:

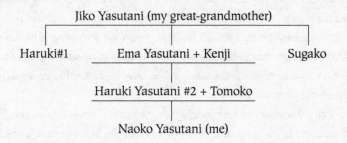

Ema was my grandmother, and when Ema got married, Jiko adopted her husband, Kenji, to take the place of Haruki, who got killed in World War II. Not that anyone could replace Haruki, but the family needed a son to keep the Yasutani name going.

Haruki was my dad's uncle, and Ema named my dad after him. Haruki #1 was a kamikaze pilot, which is kind of weird when you think of it because before he became a suicide bomber he was a student of philosophy at Tokyo University, and my dad, Haruki #2, really likes philosophy and keeps trying to kill himself, so I guess you could say that suicide and philosophy run in the family, at least among the Harukis.

When I said this to Jiko, she told me that Haruki #1 didn't actually want to commit suicide. He was just this young guy who loved books and French poetry, and he didn't even want to fight in the war, but they made him. They made everybody fight in the war back then, whether you wanted to or not. Jiko said that Haruki got bullied a lot in the army because he loved French poetry, so that's something else that runs in the family: an interest in French culture and getting picked on.

Anyway, it was on account of Haruki #1 getting killed in the war that first his sister, Ema, and then my dad got to carry on the Yasutani family name, which is why I'm Nao Yasutani today. And I just want to say that I get kind of freaked out, looking at the family tree, because you can see it's all up to ME. And since I don't intend to get married or have any kids, that's kind of it. Kaput. Finito. Sayonara, Yasutani.

Speaking about names, my grandmother Ema was named after Emma Goldman, who is one of Jiko's heroes. Emma Goldman was a famous anarchist lady a long time ago when Jiko was growing up, and Jiko thinks she was really great. Emma Goldman wrote an autobiography called *Living My Life* that Jiko is always trying to get me to read, but I haven't gotten around to it yet because I'm too busy living my life or trying to figure out how not to.

Jiko named her younger daughter Sugako after Kanno Sugako, another famous anarchist chick and hero of Jiko's and the first woman ever to be hanged for treason in Japan. Nowadays people would call Kanno Sugako a terrorist because she plotted to assassinate the emperor with a bomb, but listening to Jiko talk about her, you can tell she doesn't really buy it. Jiko really adored her. They weren't lovers or anything because Jiko was only a little kid when Sugako was hanged and probably never even got to meet her, but I think she was in love with her the way young girls get crushes on older female pop stars or lady pro wrestlers. Sugako wrote a diary called *Reflections on the Way to the Gallows*, which I'm supposed to read, too. It's a great title, but why did these anarchist women have to write so much?

When my dad was little, Grandma Ema used to take him to old Jiko's temple up north, where she moved after she became a nun, so they got pretty close. Dad said they took me on the train to visit a couple of times when I was a baby, too, but then we moved to Sunnyvale and I didn't see Jiko again until after they found Dad on the tracks and I learned what kind of man he was.

## 2.

The Chuo Rapid Express Incident was a major turning point for us, even though we all pretended it never happened. After the incident, Dad started withdrawing from the world and turning into a hikikomori,[42] and Mom finally got it that someone in our so-called family was going to have to find a job, and it definitely wasn't going to be him. She stopped going to the aquarium to watch the jellyfish, got herself a nice suit and a corporate haircut, called up a bunch of her old classmates from university and managed to land a job as an administrative assistant at a publishing house that published academic journals and textbooks. If you know anything about the way Japanese companies work you'd be pretty impressed, because even though the job was an entry-level position and the pay sucked, it was amazing that she got it at all, since she was thirty-nine years old and nobody hires thirty-nine-year-old OLs.[43]

So now we had Dad hiding out in the apartment, and Mom bringing home the bacon, which left the problem of me. The new school year had started in March, and I had somehow managed to get into the ninth grade, but the ijime was only getting worse. Until then I'd managed to hide all the little scars and pinch-shaped bruises on my arms and legs, but then one night our bathtub broke. It had always leaked and was filled with black mold, but at least we could use it, but when the heating element broke, and the landlord wouldn't fix it even though he was supposed to be a friend of Dad's, we had to start going to sento.[44]

I knew I'd be busted if Mom actually saw me up close and naked, so the first time we went, I was like, No way! Forget it! I'm not taking my clothes off in front of all those old ladies! And I meant it, too. Finally

---

42. *hikikomori* (引きこもり)—recluse, a person who refuses to leave the house.
43. *ō eru*—abbreviation for "office ladies."
44. *sentō* (洗湯)—public baths.

Mom got fed up and left me in the changing room, and eventually I got undressed and followed her in, holding the stupid little crotch towel in front of me and wanting to die. I just remember keeping my eyes on my feet and feeling my face turn bright red when I caught sight of somebody's nipple by mistake. But if there's one thing I've learned from my life, going from being a middle-class techno-yuppie's kid in Sunnyvale, California, to an unemployed loser's kid in Tokyo, Japan, it's that a person can get used to anything.

After that first time, I always tried to go while Mom was at work. The nice part of going to sento early is that the tubs aren't so crowded and you can always find a place at a faucet where you can observe what's going on. In our neighborhood at that hour, it was mostly just really old grannies and the bar hostesses who were getting ready for work, and they were both fun to peek at.

It was kind of amazing, really. In Sunnyvale, California, you don't get a lot of chances to see naked ladies, except for porn stars on magazine covers at truck stops, and they're not exactly what you'd call realistic. And they never show you pictures of really old naked ladies because it's probably illegal or something, so it was interesting to me in a scientific kind of way. What I mean is, the hostesses were slim and smooth-skinned, and even though their breasts and waists and hips were different sizes, they were all young and looked pretty much the same. But the old ladies . . . omg! They were totally different sizes and shapes, some with huge fat boobs and others with just flaps of skin and nipples like drawer knobs, and bellies like the skin on top of boiled milk when you push it to the side of the cup. I used to play this game, matching up the hostesses with the old ladies in my mind, trying to imagine which young body would turn into which aged one, and how this cute breast might wither into that sad old flap, and how a stomach would bloat or sag. It was weird, like seeing time pass, but in a Buddhist instant, you know?

I was especially fascinated with the hostesses and all their beauty routines. I used to follow them into the sauna and study the way they scraped dead skin off their bodies with brushes and sticks and shaved their faces with tiny straight razors on pastel-colored wands. What were they shaving? It wasn't like they had beards or anything. When they walked in, you could tell they'd just woken up, because they yawned a lot and said good morning even though it was late afternoon, but mostly they didn't talk much, and their eyes were all puffy and bloodshot with hangovers. But after an hour in the bath, they were all warmed up and pink and dewy again, and by the time they were dried off and sitting in the dressing room in their lacy underwear and putting on their makeup, they were laughing and talking about their dates from the night before. After they got to know me, they even teased me about my breasts, which had started to grow, and you'd think I would have been ashamed, but I wasn't. I was secretly flattered that they even noticed. I admired them. I thought they were pretty and bold and behaved in a liberated way and did exactly what they wanted, which is probably why Mom decided it wasn't a wholesome environment for me. She started making me wait to go to the baths until after dinner, which is absolutely the worst time because it's all the boring mothers with obnoxious little kids, and nosy middle-aged aunties with metal-colored hair, who stare at you and make comments about things that are none of their business. And sure enough, one of them noticed my bruises, even though I was hanging back and trying to keep myself covered, and she said in a really loud voice,

"Oh! What happened to you, young lady? Do you have a rash?"

At first Mom didn't pay any attention, but then the old bitch actually called to her and said, "Okusan, Okusan![45] What is wrong with your daughter's skin? She's got butsubutsu[46] all over her. I hope she doesn't have a disease!"

Mom came and stood next to me as I hunched over my bucket. She took my wrist and raised my arm and turned it over, looking at the

---

45. *okusan* (奥さん)—wife. The character *oku* (奥) means "interior," or "inside," as of a house. With honorific *-san,* it's a formal way of addressing a married woman.
46. *butsubutsu* (ぶつぶつ)—bumps, a spotty rash.

underside, where the bruises were most dense. Her fingers dug into my wrist bones and it hurt more than when the kids at school pinched me.

"Maybe she shouldn't be going into the water," the old bitch said. "If it's a rash, it could be contagious . . ."

My mom let my arm drop. "Tondemonai,"[47] she said. "Those are just bruises from her gym class. They were playing too roughly. Isn't that right, Naoko?"

I just nodded and concentrated on washing myself and not throwing up or jumping to my feet and running out of there screaming. Mom went back to her basin and didn't say another word while we finished our baths, but then later on, when we were back at the apartment, she made me go into the bedroom and take off all my clothes again. Dad was still at the baths. The sento was the only outside place he would still go, and he liked to take his time and sometimes enjoy a cold can of beer afterward, so Mom had the whole apartment to herself as she laid into me. She pulled a halogen desk lamp over to where I was standing, and she examined me all over, and for the millionth time I thought I was going to die. She found all the bruises and the little scars and scabs made from the scissor points, and she even found the bald patch at the back of my head where the boy who sat at the desk behind me had been pulling out my hairs, one by one. I tried to lie and say it was an allergy, and then I said it was hair loss from stress, and then I said actually it really was from gym class, and then I suggested it might be hemophilia or leukemia or Von Willebrand's disease, but Mom didn't buy any of it, so eventually I had to come clean and tell her what was really going on. I tried not to make a big deal about it, because I didn't want her going to the school and complaining and making a stink.

"It's okay, Mom. Really. It's not personal. You know how kids are. I'm the transfer student. They do the same to everyone."

She shook her head. "Maybe you're not trying hard enough to make new friends," she suggested.

"I have lots of friends, Mom, really. It's fine."

---

47. *tondemonai*—it's nothing.

She wanted to believe me. I know when we first moved back to Tokyo, she was really worried about me fitting in to a new school, but then she got distracted by the jellyfish, and then by the Chuo Rapid Express Incident, and for a while it seemed like I was the most well-adjusted person in our family. And then once Mom went mainstream and started working a real job, she didn't have a lot of time to worry about my situation at school, never mind supervise my after-school activities. She didn't want me hanging out with the hostesses at the baths, but she didn't want me staying in the house alone with Dad, either, since he was depressed and suicidal. I think she was afraid he might do something crazy like those fathers in America who shoot their children and wives with hunting rifles while they're asleep in their bedrooms, then go down to the basement and blow their brains out, except that in Japan because of the strict gun-control laws, they usually do it with tubes and duct tape and charcoal briquettes in the family car. I know this because I was already getting into the habit of reading articles in the newspaper about suicides and violent deaths and suffering. I wanted to know as much as possible so I could prepare myself for my dad's death, but I got kind of addicted to the stories, especially later, when I started reading them out loud to Jiko so she could do that blessing thing with her juzu beads.

Anyway, the point is that compared with what my classmates were doing to me, I knew I'd rather take my chances with Dad after school, especially since we didn't have a family car, never mind a house with a basement. But Mom wasn't so sure.

"What about doing more after-school activities?" she suggested. "It's a new school year. Aren't you supposed to join a club? Have you consulted with your homeroom teacher? Maybe I should have a talk with him . . ."

You know how it is in cartoons, when a character is surprised and his eyes go zooming out of his sockets like they're on springs or rubber bands? I swear that's what happened, and then my jaw hit the floor like the blade of a tractor shovel. I was standing in the middle of our bedroom in my little white cotton underpants and sleeveless undershirt, under the beam of her halogen lamp, and there was this weight in my stomach like a big cold fish was dying just below my heart. I just stared at her, thinking, OMG she's going to get me killed. She had just examined me all over and seen what my classmates were doing to me, and now she was suggesting that I spend even more time with them <u>after</u> school?

I already thought my father was insane, because this was at a time when I still believed that only insane people try to kill themselves, but at the back of my mind, I guess I was hoping that my mom was normal and okay again, now that she had stopped watching jellyfish and had found a job. But at that moment I knew she was as crazy and unreliable as my father, and her question only proved it, which meant there was nobody left in my life I could count on to keep me safe. I don't think I've ever felt as naked or alone. My knees went all soft as I sank, crouching there, cradling my fish. It thrashed one last time, rising up almost into my throat, and then it flopped back down and just lay there, gasping for air. I held it. It was dying in my arms. I gathered up my clothes from the tatami and put them on, turning away from my mom so I wouldn't have to watch her face as she stared at my body.

"I'll be okay, Mom. I'm not really so interested in after-school activities."

But she wasn't hearing me. "No," she said. "You know, I think I will have a talk with your homeroom teacher . . ."

The fish shuddered in the curve of my rib cage. "I don't think that's a good idea, Mom."

"But Nao-chan, this has got to stop."

"It will stop. Really, Mom. Just leave it alone."

But Mom shook her head. "No," she said. "I can't stand by and let this happen to my daughter." There was something new in her voice, an edge of resolve that sounded very American. It went with her new Hillary Clinton can-do attitude and haircut, and it really scared me.

"Mom, please . . ."

"Shimpai shinakute ii no yo," she said, giving my shoulders a little hug.

Don't worry? How stupid is that!

## 3.

Nothing happened at first, and for a couple of days I thought maybe she'd forgotten or changed her mind. Ever since becoming a hikikomori, Dad had stopped walking me to school, so I went alone, and I'd gotten in the habit of arriving at the very last minute, right as the final bell was ringing. I'd also gotten into the habit of killing time at the little temple on the way, smelling the incense and listening to the birds and insects. I didn't pray to Lord Buddha because back then I used to think he was like God, and I don't believe in God, which isn't surprising given the patheticness of the male authority figures in my life. But old Shaka-sama's not like that. He never pretended to be anything more than a wise teacher, and I don't mind praying to him anymore, because it's just like praying to old Jiko.

In the garden behind the temple, there's a small hump of green moss with a stunted maple tree growing on top and a stone bench nearby, and I used to sit there and watch the pale green maple buds uncurl into leafy fingers. In the autumn, when the same leaves turned bronze and fell, a monk used to sweep them from the green carpet of moss with a little bamboo broom, and in the spring, he sometimes came out to pick a few weeds. That small green hump was like his own tiny island that he took care of, and more than anything I wished I could shrink myself until I was small enough to live there under the maple tree. It was so peaceful. I used to sit on the bench fantasizing like this until the very last moment when I had to leave the temple's high walls, where I was safe, and run to school, where I wasn't, slipping through the gates just as the sound of the last bell faded.

This was my habit, but a week after Mom found my scars and bruises, I went to the garden and found a barricade blocking the pathway. They were doing construction work on the temple grounds, and so that day I arrived at school early.

Immediately, I knew that something was different. No one looked up when I approached or even seemed to notice me. I loitered just outside the school gates for a while and then slunk in, but no one was waiting for me, or watching for me, or circling. I listened, but I didn't hear my name being sweetly chanted by kids with glittering eyes. They all just ignored me and continued talking to each other like I wasn't even there.

I felt nervous at first, tingling with something like relief or even excitement, but then I thought, No, wait a minute, maybe they're planning something truly evil. Don't be stupid, Nao! Be cautious. Stay alert! So I kept my eyes open and I waited. The morning classes droned on and on—Japanese history, math, moral education—but still nobody bothered me. Nobody pinched me or spat or poked me with the point of their pen. Nobody held their nose or threatened to rape me or pretended to throw up as they passed by my desk. The boy sitting behind me didn't pull my hair out even once, and by the afternoon, I was beginning to believe that the nightmare was finally over. During lunch hour I was left completely alone at my desk with my lunchbox, and nobody knocked it to the floor or stepped on my rice ball. At recess I stood by myself with my back to the schoolyard fence and watched the other kids laughing and talking. When the bell rang and classes let out for the day, I walked through the crowded hallway like I was invisible, a ghost or a spirit of the dead.

### 4.

I don't know if it was Mom's visit to school that made them stop torturing me physically. I kind of doubt it. Probably they were getting bored and were in the process of stopping anyway, and Mom's complaint just shifted them into this new phase. I don't know who she talked to, but it probably wasn't my new ninth-grade homeroom teacher, Ugawa Sensei, who was just a substitute for the regular teacher, who was on maternity leave. I think Mom must have gone further up, maybe to the vice principal or even the principal himself, and the reason I think that is because Ugawa Sensei was going along with my classmates, ignoring me and pretending he couldn't see me or hear me, either. At first I didn't notice. He'd always ignored me and never called on me, and since I never put my hand up in class to answer questions, you could say the feeling was mutual. But then he started this new thing during roll call in the morning. He would read my name, "Yasutani!" and I would answer, "Hai!" but instead of marking me present, he'd call out again, "Transfer Student Yasutani!" like he hadn't even heard me. Again I'd answer, "*HAI!!!*" in the loudest voice I could, but he would frown and shake his head and mark me absent. This went on for a couple of days, until I happened to notice some of the boys snickering, and I started to catch on. My voice stopped working then. No matter how hard I tried, I couldn't force any sound to come out. It was like the muscles in my throat had turned into a murderer's hands, strangling my voice as it tried to rise. Sometimes one of the kids would answer for me, calling out helpfully, "Yasutani-kun wa rusu desu yo,"[48] until after a while I just sat there when my name was called, staring at the worn-out surface of my desk with my lips pressed tightly together, because I knew they were all in on it, laughing silently.

It was oddly peaceful. I didn't mind the silent laughter so much, because at least it didn't leave scars on my body, and I could almost feel happy to see Ugawa Sensei scoring points and getting in good with the popular kids in our class. Substitute teachers are even lower than transfer students, and Ugawa Sensei was such a loser, even more than me, and so I felt sorry for him. His head was the shape and color of an enoki,[49] and he had bad teeth and thinning hair, and he used to wear polyester turtle-neck sweaters with flakes of dandruff, like spores, on the shoulders. He smelled bad, too, really nasty BO.

I'm telling you all this not to be mean, but so you'll understand exactly what a stretch it was that a loser like Ugawa Sensei would ever become popular with the powerful students in his class, but thanks to me, he was actually achieving this. I could see the excitement in his face when he called out my name and pretended to wait. I could see it in the way he looked at me, and then looked through me, so convincingly I could almost believe I wasn't there. When he marked me absent, it was with a

---

48. *Yasutani-kun wa rusu desu yo*—Yasutani is absent.
49. *enoki* (えのき)—a small white mushroom with a round little cap on a long, threadlike stem that grows in clusters in the dark and never sees the light of day.

triumphant flourish of the pencil in his hand, like he'd really accomplished something great.

I hope you understand that I don't think he was a bad man. I just think he was very insecure and could convince himself of anything, the way insecure people can. Like my dad, for example, who can convince himself that his suicide will not harm me or my mom because actually we'll be better off without him, and at some point in the not-so-distant future we'll realize this and thank him for killing himself. Same with Ugawa Sensei, who probably figured that I, too, would be happier just not being there, and he was actually right about that. In a way, he was just helping me to achieve my goal, and as a result, I could almost feel grateful.

I slipped through my school days like a wisp of cloud, like a drifting patch of humidity, barely there, and after school I walked back to our apartment, usually more or less alone, which was a whole lot better than being chased and tripped and shoved against vending machines or into bicycle racks filled with bicycles. I knew I wasn't completely out of danger yet because sometimes my classmates would follow me, but they always stayed across the street or half a block behind me, and even if they made comments in loud voices about my slummy ghetto neighborhood, at least they never attempted to talk to me or touch me.

Once I got home, my dad usually made me a snack, and I sat with him and did my homework or just surfed around on the Internet, killing time or texting with my best friend in Sunnyvale, Kayla, who still liked me enough to hang out with me online. But even that was kind of stressful, to tell you the truth, because she kept wanting to know what my school was like, and I wasn't going to tell her about the ijime, because then she'd know what a total loser I'd become, so instead I just tried to explain all the funny odd things about Japan to her. Japanese culture is pretty popular among young people in the United States, so mostly we just chatted about manga and J-pop and anime and fashion trends and stuff.

"You seem so far away," Kayla wrote. "It's kind of unreal."

It was true. I was unreal and my life was unreal, and Sunnyvale, which was real, was a jillion miles away in time and space, like the beautiful

Earth from outer space, and me and Dad were astronauts, living in a spaceship, orbiting in the cold blackness.

## 5.

I said that my dad had withdrawn from the world and become a hikikomori, but I don't want you to get the wrong idea. My dad loved me and wanted me to be safe. He wasn't going to flip out and stick both our heads in the oven or anything. And while most hikikomori guys stay indoors all day and night reading porno manga and visiting hentai fetish websites, thank god my dad wasn't that pathetic. He was differently pathetic. He had pretty much quit going online at all, and instead he spent his time reading books on Western philosophy and making insects out of origami, which, as you probably remember from your childhood, is the Japanese art of folding paper.

The whole philosophy thing started because Mom's company used to publish this series of books called The Great Minds of Western Philosophy. As you can probably guess, The Great Minds of Western Philosophy wasn't such a hot seller, so she brought home a remaindered set for Dad, thinking it might help him find the meaning of life, and besides, she got them for free. He started with Socrates and did approximately a philosopher per week. I don't think it was helping him find the meaning of life, but at least it gave him a concrete goal, which counts for something. I believe it doesn't matter what it is, as long as you can find something concrete to keep you busy while you are living your meaningless life.

And whatever you think you know about origami, you can forget about it, because the stuff Dad was folding wasn't your typical cranes and boats and party hats and candy dishes. The stuff he folded was origami on steroids, totally wack and beautiful. Actually, he liked to fold the pages from The Great Minds of Western Philosophy, and after he finished reading them he would cut them out of the book with a box cutter and a steel-edged ruler. As you probably know, there are a lot of great minds in Western philosophy, and the books were printed on superthin paper so they could cram more minds into the series. Dad says thin paper is

84

easier to fold, especially if you're making something complicated like a *Trypoxylus dichotomus*, which is a Japanese rhinoceros beetle, or a *Mantis religiosa*, which is a praying mantis. He only used the minds he didn't like for folding, so we ended up with lots of insects made from Nietzsche and Hobbes.

Dad used to sit on the floor at the kotatsu[50] for hours, reading and folding, and folding and reading, and I'd sit with him and do my homework as long as he promised not to smoke too much. He used to have these fake plastic mint-flavored cigarettes to help with his nicotine craving, and sometimes I'd ask him for one, and we'd sit across from each other, hunched over our books, with our elbows propped on the table, sucking and chewing on our fake cigarettes together. It was kind of sweet, because after a while, he would start getting excited, and when he got excited, he would start to nod. He would nod and nod, and when he really got into it, he'd hold on to the frames of his glasses with both hands like they were binoculars and he was trying to penetrate the pages and see even further into the words to get more meaning out of them. It was hard to concentrate with him across from me, nodding and bobbing his head, especially when he'd start to talk. He'd mutter, "So, so, soooo . . ." or suddenly burst out, "Sore! Yes! Sore da yo!"[51] and sometimes he'd interrupt me and say, "Nao-chan, listen to this!" and then he'd read a page or two out loud from Heidegger.

Like I was going to understand, right? But I didn't care. It was a lot more interesting than the stupid homework I had to do for school. We were doing direct proportions in math, and every time I saw a question like, if a train that travels 3 kilometers per minute goes y kilometers in x minutes, then . . . etc., my mind would go numb and all I could think about was how a body would look at the moment of impact, and the distance a head might be thrown on the tracks, and how far the blood would splatter. Dad's philosophy was a lot drier and not as grotesque as

50. *kotatsu*—a low table with a heating element underneath and a blanket to keep in the warmth.
51. *Sore! Sore da yo!*—That! That's it!

my math, and who knows, even though I didn't understand it all, maybe some of it stuck. Personally, I preferred it that Dad wasn't spending all his time at some stupid job, or polishing his résumé in order to look for some stupid job, or sitting on a park bench in Ueno pretending to be at some stupid job and feeding the crows instead. I liked it that he'd pretty much given up on the idea of jobs altogether, and so he had free time to spend with me, even if I suspected that he would rather be dead.

## 6.

Speaking about free time, do you know about furiitaa?[52] In Japan there's a kind of person called furiitaa, which is someone who works part-time jobs and has a lot of free time because he doesn't have a proper career or full-time position at a company. The reason I thought of it just now is because I'm back at Fifi's Lonely Apron, and I happened to look up and notice that I'm surrounded by all these otaku guys who are probably all furiitaa, which is why they have the free time to sit here in between their part-time jobs, before they go home to their bedrooms in their parents' houses. And the French maids are definitely furiitaa and just working here for the time being, until they find better jobs or sugar daddies. And the waiters and guys in the kitchen are all furiitaa, unless they are immigrants or workers from other countries. You would never call immigrants or workers from other countries furiitaa, because they never had any hope of getting real jobs in Japanese companies in the first place.

But you might be thinking, Who would want a real job in a Japanese company anyway? You've probably heard horror stories about Japanese corporate culture and the long working hours and salarymen who never have time to hang out with their families or hug their children and who drop dead from working too hard, which is a whole other concept.[53] Compared with that, furiitaa probably sounds pretty great, but it isn't.

---

52. *furiitaa*—a freelance worker, from the English *free* + German *arbeiter*.
53. Probably *karōshi* (過労死), "death from overwork"—a phenomenon in the 1980s at the height of the Japanese bubble economy.

# *Ruth*

## I.

A freeter, Ruth thought. That's us. Frittering our lives away.

She closed the diary and let it rest on her stomach. Oliver was sleeping beside her. She'd been reading aloud to him when he'd fallen asleep, and rather than wake him, she continued to read silently. She knew that the hikikomori story made him uneasy. It unsettled her, too.

Their move to the island was a withdrawal. The first New Year's Eve, they'd spent on the couch, with her mother tucked under a blanket between them, drinking cheap sparkling wine and watching the world turn 2000. The BBC was covering the millennial celebrations, tracking the time zones and slowly working its way westward around the planet. Every time a new burst of fireworks lit up the television screen, her mother would lean forward.

"My, isn't that pretty! What are we celebrating?"

"It's the New Year, Mom."

"Really? What year is it?"

"It's the year 2000. It's the new millennium."

"No!" her mother would exclaim, slapping her knees and falling back against the couch. "My goodness. Imagine that." And then she would close her eyes and doze off again until the next burst of fireworks woke her, and she would sit up and lean forward.

"My, isn't that pretty! What are we celebrating?"

By the time the new millennium finally reached their time zone, the rest of the planet had gone to bed, and Ruth had a pounding headache. We're celebrating the End Times, Mom. The collapse of the power grid and the world banking system. The Rapture and the end of the world . . .

My goodness. Imagine that.

It wasn't all the silly Y2K prognostications that worried her. The anxieties that fueled her withdrawal were more diffuse and unnameable, and by the end of that first year, as she sat in front of the television and watched the presidential elections grind to a close, she felt sure something horrible was about to happen. Like a small boat adrift in the fog, she caught glimpses during patches when the mist cleared of a world far away, in which everything was changing.

It was late. She put the diary aside and turned off the light. Next to her, she could hear Oliver's breathing. A light rain pattered on the roof. When she closed her eyes, she could see the image of a bright red Hello Kitty lunchbox bobbing on the dull grey waves.

### 2.

In the morning, armed with a large mug of coffee, she approached her memoir with a renewed sense of resolve. A rapprochement was what was needed. An unfinished book, left unattended, turns feral, and she would need all her focus, will, and ruthless determination to tame it again. She kicked the cat off her chair, cleared her desktop, and centered the stack of manuscript pages in front of her.

The cat, annoyed, jumped back onto her desk, but she swept him up in her hand, dropped him onto the floor, and then gave him a shove in the direction of the corridor.

"Go visit Oliver, Pest. He's the one you love."

The cat turned his back and stalked out of the room, tail in the air, as if leaving had been his intention in the first place.

Sometimes when she was having trouble focusing it helped to do timed sprints, setting short-term achievable goals for herself. Ever since Oliver had gotten the antique watch working, she'd been wearing it every day, and now she unbuckled it and slipped it off her wrist. It was just before nine. Thirty minutes of work, followed by a ten-minute break. She saw that the second hand was moving smoothly around its orbit, but she held the watch up to her ear just to make sure. She found the ticking reassuring. It was a handsome watch, late art deco, with its black face, bold numerals, and luminous dial. The steel backing was pocked with age, but she could make out the kanji numerals—a serial number, or something else? Above the numbers were two other Japanese characters. She recognized the first one. It was the kanji 空, for *sky*. The second kanji, 兵, looked familiar, too, but she couldn't recognize it in the context. She opened up her character dictionary and counted the strokes. Seven. She scanned the long list of seven-stroke kanji until she found it. *Hei*, she read, meaning *soldier*.

Sky soldier?

She woke up her computer and googled *sky soldier Japanese watch*. Hundreds of hits came back for websites where she could watch an anime series called Sky Soldier. Not useful.

She tried *antique watch*, and then *vintage watch*, and then *vintage military watch*. Bingo. There was an entire world of vintage military watch collectors.

Now, making another guess, she added *WWII* and *sky soldier*, but then on a hunch, she changed the latter to *kamikaze* and hit RETURN. The search engine spun, and within moments she was on a community forum for military timepiece enthusiasts, reading about the provenance of the watch that she was holding in her hand, examining pictures of similar watches, learning that they were manufactured by the Seiko Company during World War II, and were favored by the kamikaze troops. For obvious reasons, although they were manufactured in large numbers, only a few survived. The watches were rare and avidly sought after by collectors. The numbers engraved on the back were indeed a serial number, not of the watch, but of the soldier who wore it.

Haruki #1?

### 3.

She searched the Internet for Haruki Yasutani, cross-referencing his name with every search term she could recall from Nao's diary: *sky*, *soldier*, *kamikaze*, *philosophy*, *French poetry*, *Tokyo University*. No luck. She moved on to the second Haruki, inputting new keywords: *computer programmer*, *origami*, *Sunnyvale*, but although she came up with a few Yasutanis, a couple of Harukis, and a handful of tech industry people with one of those names, she found none with both names, and none who appeared to be related to either the kamikaze pilot or his nephew, Nao's father.

Frustrating. She went back to the tsunami People Finder and looked up Haruki and Tomoko, but neither was listed among the missing and dead Yasutanis. That was a relief. She moved on, searching for Zen temples in northern Japan, but she had little to go on, since she didn't know where in the north the temple was located, or even to which sect of Zen it belonged. She tried adding the name Jiko Yasutani to the temple search, along with terms like *anarchist*, *feminist*, *novelist*, and *nun*, in various combinations. Nothing. She looked for temples up north that had been destroyed in the tsunami. There were several of these. Other temples had survived and were spearheading relief efforts.

The hands on the sky soldier watch circled the face, but she ignored them and read on, digging through articles posted back in 2011, in the months just after March 11. Crackpot religious leaders were blaming the earthquake on angry gods who were punishing the Japanese for everything, from their materialism and worship of technology to their dependence on nuclear power and reckless slaughter of whales. Angry parents in Fukushima were demanding to know why the government wasn't doing anything to protect their children from radiation. The government was responding by fiddling with the numbers and raising the levels of permissible exposure; meanwhile, nuclear plant workers, battling the meltdown at Fukushima, were dropping dead. A group calling themselves the Senior Certain Death Squad,[54] made up of retired engineers in their seventies and eighties, volunteered to replace the younger workers. The suicide rate among people displaced by the fallout and tsunami was on the rise. She typed *certain death* and *suicide* and then remembered the train. She entered *Chuo Rapid Express*, and finally *Harryki*, which in her hurry she mistyped, the forefinger of her left hand holding the *r* down too long,

---

54. Shinia Kesshitai (シニア決死隊).

and her right finger overreaching the *u* and striking the *y* instead, but before she could correct her mistakes, her pinky hit ENTER.

She groaned as the wheel on the search engine spun, and then gasped as she stared at the results.

## 4.

The website belonged to a professor of psychology at Stanford University, a Dr. Rongstad Leistiko. Dr. Leistiko was doing research on first-person narratives of suicide and self-killing. He had posted an excerpt from a letter, written to him by one of his informants, a man by the name of "Harry." The excerpt read as follows:

> Suicide is a very deep subject, but since you are interested, I will try to explain my thoughts to you.
>
> Throughout history, we Japanese have always appreciated suicide. For us it is a beautiful thing that gives meaning and shape and honor to our lives forever. It is a method to make our feeling of alive most real. For many thousands of years this is our tradition.
>
> Because, you see, this feeling of alive is not so easy to experience. Even although life is a thing that seems to have some kind of weight and shape, this is only an illusion. Our feeling of alive has no real edge or boundary. So we Japanese people say that our life sometimes feels unreal, just like a dream.
>
> Death is certain. Life is always changing, like a puff of wind in the air, or a wave in the sea, or even a thought in the mind. So making a suicide is finding the edge of life. It stops life in time, so we can grasp

what shape it is and feel it is real, at least for just a moment. It is trying to make some real solid thing from the flow of life that is always changing.

Nowadays, in modern technological culture, sometimes we hear people complain that nothing feels real anymore. Everything in the modern world is plastic or digital or virtual. But I say, that was always life! That is life itself! Even Plato discussed that things in this life are only shadows of forms. So this is what I mean by the changing and unreal feeling of life.

Maybe you would like to ask me how does suicide make life feel real?

Well, by cutting into illusions. By cutting into pixels and finding blood. By entering the cave of mind and walking into fire. By making shadows bleed. You can feel life completely by taking it away.

Suicide feels like One Authentic Thing.
Suicide feels like Meaning of Life.
Suicide feels like having the Last Word.
Suicide feels like stopping Time Forever.

But of course this is all just delusion, too! Suicide is just part of life, so it is part of the delusion.

Nowadays in Japan, because of Economic Recession and downsizing, suicide is very popular, especially for middle-age salarymen like myself. They get downsized from their company and cannot support their family. Sometimes they have much debt. They cannot tell their wife, so they sit on the park bench everyday like gomi. Do you know gomi? It means garbage, the kind to throw away and not even to recycle. Men are scared and feel ashamed like gomi. It is a sad situation.

As for methods, there are many. Hanging is one, and the most popular place for hanging suicide is near Mt. Fuji, in Aokigahara Woods. This place has the nickname "Suicide Forest" because of so many salarymen hanging from the branches in the sea of trees.

Some other methods are:

1. Jumping off train platform in front of the train (Chuo Rapid Express is popular one)
2. Jumping off roof
3. Charcoal briquette method
4. Detergent suicide method

There are many popular suicide movies and also books that teach about how to do these methods. Personally I have tried the train platform method, but I was a failure. Youngsters prefer #2 jumping off roof method, and sometimes they like to do it with each other while holding hands. Unfortunately, suicide is popular with the youngsters, especially elementary and junior high school students, because of academic pressure and bullying. I worry because my daughter is a youngster and not happy in her Japanese school.

Recently there is a fad of suicide clubs as you may have heard. People can find each other on the

Internet and chat about how to make a suicide. They can discuss some method and customize it as they like, for example what kind of music is suited for the soundtrack to their dying? Then, if they can find some friends they feel harmony with, they can make a plan. They will meet somewhere, for example at the train station or in front of a department store or on some park bench. Maybe they will carry something so they will know each other? Or maybe they will wear something special? Then they will text to each other until their eyes meet, and this is how they can recognize each other.

Many club members prefer #3—charcoal briquette method. To do this method, they must rent an automobile together and drive to the countryside. Then they can put some nice music on the CD player and listen to it while dying from $CO_2$ gas.

Most of the time they like to listen to sad songs about love.

Car rental is expensive in Japan, and many suicide people do not have much money because of downsizing and bankruptcy, etc., so it is more economical to have more members. This is why sometimes the police can find five or six bodies in one car.

Every time I read about this method, I remember the day you took me shopping at The Home Depot store. Do you remember this time? You introduced me to the Weber BBQ grill and the mesquite flavor briquette? Sadly, I cannot find the mesquite flavor briquette in Tokyo, and Weber BBQ grill is not so popular here either.

Sometimes I think American people cannot ever understand why a Japanese would like to make a suicide. American people have a strong sense of their own importance. They believe in individual self, and also they have their God to tell them suicide is wrong. This is so simple! It must be nice to believe something simple like that. Recently I am reading some philosophical books written by great Western minds all about the meaning of life. These are very interesting, and I hope I will find some good answers there.

I don't care for myself, but I am afraid my attitude is unhealthy for my daughter. At first I thought I should commit suicide so she will not feel shame on account of my failure to find a good job with big salary, but after I tried #1 method, I could see so much sadness on her face that I changed my mind.

Now I think I must try to stay alive, but I have no confidence to do so. Please teach me a simple American way to love my life so I do not have to think of suicide ever again. I want to find the meaning of my life for my daughter.

Sincerely,

"Harry"

## 5.

Dear Professor Leistiko,

I am writing to you about a matter of some urgency. I am a novelist, and recently, while doing research on the subject of suicide in Japan for a project I'm working on, I happened upon your website and your research on first-person narratives of suicide and self-killing. I read with great interest the very moving letter written by the informant named "Harry," and I am writing to inquire about his identity. By any chance, is this "Harry" a Japanese computer engineer named Haruki Yasutani, who once lived in Sunnyvale, California, and worked in Silicon Valley during the dot-com days?

I realize that this request may sound irregular and there will no doubt be issues of confidentiality involved, but I am trying to get in touch with Mr. Yasutani or his daughter, Naoko. Some items, including letters and a diary, which I believe belong to the daughter, have come into my possession by somewhat mysterious means, and I am concerned about her well-being and would like to return them to her as soon as possible.

If there is any other information I can provide, I will gladly do so. I have been writer-in-residence in the Comparative Literature Department at Stanford in the past, and I am sure that Professor P-L, or any member of that faculty, would be happy to vouch for me. I hope you will contact me at your earliest convenience.

Very sincerely yours,

etc.

She sent off the email, sat back in her chair, and glanced at the sky soldier watch, which was sitting on top of her untouched manuscript where she had abandoned it hours earlier. Her heart sank. It was after one, and the entire morning had vanished. And then, if that wasn't bad enough, she heard the sound of tires, rolling up the driveway.

## 6.

Time interacts with attention in funny ways.

At one extreme, when Ruth was gripped by the compulsive mania and hyperfocus of an Internet search, the hours seemed to aggregate and swell like a wave, swallowing huge chunks of her day.

At the other extreme, when her attention was disengaged and fractured, she experienced time at its most granular, wherein moments hung around like particles, diffused and suspended in standing water.

There used to be a middle way, too, when her attention was focused but vast, and time felt like a limpid pool, ringed by sunlit ferns. An underground spring fed the pool from deep below, creating a gentle current of words that bubbled up, while on the surface, breezes shimmered and played.

This blissful state was one that Ruth seemed to recall enjoying, once upon a time, when she'd been writing well. Now, no matter how hard she tried, that Eden eluded her. The spring had dried up, the pool was clogged and stagnant. She blamed the Internet. She blamed her hormones. She blamed her DNA. She pored over websites, collecting information on ADD, ADHD, bipolar disorder, dissociative identity disorder, parasites, and even sleeping sickness, but her biggest fear was Alzheimer's. She'd watched her mother's mind dwindle, and she was familiar with the corrosive effect that plaque can have on brain function. Like her mother, Ruth often forgot things. She perseverated. Lost words. Slipped in and out of time.

The car belonged to Muriel, and now she and Oliver were sitting in the kitchen, having tea and talking about garbage. Ruth, who had gone downstairs to be polite, sat between them, mildly bored, listening to their conversation and fingering the stack of letters from the Hello Kitty lunchbox. On the table, next to the lunchbox, sat a battered tube of Lion brand Japanese toothpaste, the excuse for Muriel's drop-in. She'd found it on the beach washed up below Jap Ranch and brought it right over.

Ruth disliked drop-ins. When she first moved to the island, she was astonished that people would just drive on in for a visit without calling or emailing first. Oliver found the custom even more unsettling than she did, and once he had even hidden in an old refrigerator box in the basement when he heard the sound of tires coming up the gravel, but the tactic hadn't worked. The guests had just let themselves into the house and sat down at the kitchen table to wait, and when Ruth returned from her errands, she found them there. She offered them tea and wondered out loud where Oliver was.

"Oh, he's not here," they told her.

They chatted and sipped their tea while Ruth tried to ascertain the purpose of the visit. A while later, she heard a furtive sound in the basement, and then Oliver appeared at the door.

"Where have you been?" she asked, suspicious and annoyed that he'd stayed away for so long, leaving her to deal with the situation.

"Oh, out. In the forest," he said, brushing cobwebs from his hair.

Eventually the guests left, and she pressed him, and finally he confessed.

"You mean you were just sitting down there?" she asked.

He nodded, looking a little sheepish.

"In the box? The whole time?"

"It wasn't that long."

"It was hours! What were you doing?"

"Nothing."

"Were you listening to us?"

"A little. I couldn't really hear."

"So what were you doing?"

He shook his head, managing to look both bewildered and a little bit smug. "Nothing," he said. "I was just sitting there. It was nice. And cool. I took a nap."

She really wanted to be mad, but she couldn't be. It was just his nature, and so she laughed instead. Relieved, he laughed, too.

It was his nature, just as drop-ins were a part of the nature of the island. However odd and unnerving the custom might be, when guests showed up, you invited them in for tea.

The discovery of a tube of Lion brand toothpaste was interesting, and it was kind of Muriel to share it, but the conversation had turned to the half-life of plastic in a gyre, which Ruth found tedious, so she turned her attention to the letters. She spread the pages out on the table, unfolding each one and peering at the inscrutable kanji. At the very least, she might be able to decipher an address. Even the name of a prefecture would help. Oliver and Muriel talked on, although it was not quite a conversation they were having, Ruth noticed. Rather, their exchange sounded more like a session at an academic conference, two professors taking turns at the podium presenting information that they both knew, and more or less already agreed with.

"Plastic is like that," Oliver was saying. "It never biodegrades. It gets churned around in the gyre and ground down into particles. Oceanographers call it confetti. In a granular state, it hangs around forever."

"The sea is filled with plastic confetti," Muriel affirmed. "It floats around and gets eaten by the fishes or spat up onto the beach. It's in our food chain. I don't envy the anthropologists, trying to make sense of our material culture from all the bright hard nuggets they'll be digging out of the middens of the future."

The last letter was thicker than the others. It was wrapped in a packet made of several layers of oily waxed paper. Carefully Ruth unpeeled it, laying the sticky paper to one side. Tucked inside and folded into quarters was a thin composition book, the kind a student might once have used in university to write an essay exam. She unfolded it and looked inside, expecting to see more of the cursive Japanese script, but to her surprise, the alphabet was Roman and the language was French.

It was Oliver's turn. "Anthropologists of the future—" he had started to say, when Ruth interrupted.

"Excuse me," she said. "I hate to change the subject, but does anyone read French?"

## 7.

She showed them the composition book and they took turns trying to read it, but they didn't get far.

"So much for bilingual education," Muriel said. She glanced at her watch, put her reading glasses away, and started gathering up her things. "Try calling Benoit."

Ruth didn't know Benoit.

"Benoit LeBec," Muriel said. "He's the dump guy, Québécois, goes to A, drives the forklift . . ."

"A?"

"AA," Muriel said. "But nothing's anonymous on this island, so they just call it A. His wife works at the school, and I know he's a big reader. His parents were literature professors."

She reached for the mangled tube of Lion brand toothpaste that lay next to the barnacle-covered freezer bag.

"Have you called Callie about that yet?" Muriel asked, pointing to the bag, which had begun to off-gas as the barnacles slowly died.

"No," Ruth said, ruefully. She'd meant to, but she was finding it harder and harder to pick up the phone these days. She didn't like talking to people in real time anymore.

"Well, I happen to know she just got back from a cruise and she's on-island for a while. You might want to call her before these guys get too much more dead."

Ruth felt a stab of remorse. "Should we have tried to keep them alive? I never thought . . ."

Muriel shrugged and stood. "Probably doesn't matter, but call her anyway. She might be able to tell you something." She'd changed her mind and left her toothpaste on the table, and now she waved her hand somewhat magisterially in its direction. "I'll leave that with you, then," she said. "Curatorially speaking, I feel it's a collection and should all stay together."

They walked her out to her car. Today Muriel was wearing a ratty men's cardigan sweater over her long skirt and gum boots, and as Ruth watched her struggle to lever her body down the porch steps, she thought about Nao's description of the old ladies in the baths, how they came in so many shapes and sizes. Ruth was feeling her age too, in her knees, in her hips. In New York, she'd walked everywhere and never had a problem getting enough exercise. Here on the island, she mostly drove. She thought about her old neighborhood in the East Village, the coffee shops, the restaurants, the bookstores, the park. Her life in New York still felt so vivid and real. Like Nao's Sunnyvale.

*. . . a jillion miles away in time and space, like the beautiful Earth from outer space, and me and Dad were astronauts, living in a spaceship, orbiting in the cold blackness.*

It was only four o'clock, but outside it was already growing dark. The rain had let up, but the air was still wet and cold. They walked across the sodden grass. Oliver held the car door for Muriel, when a sudden movement overhead caught his attention. He glanced up and then he pointed.

"Look!"

On the bough of the bigleaf maple, in the crepuscular shadows, sat the singular crow. It was glossy black, with a peculiar hump on its forehead and a long, thick curved beak.

"How odd," Muriel said. "It looks like a Jungle Crow."

"A subspecies, I think," said Oliver. "*Corvus japonensis . . .*"

"Also called a Large-billed Crow," Muriel said. "How very odd. Do you think . . . ?"

"I do," Oliver said. "He just showed up one day. I'm guessing he rode over on the drift."

"A drop-in," Muriel said. She knew about their aversion to drop-ins. She thought it was funny.

The crow stretched its wings and then hopped a few feet along the bough.

"How do you know it's a he?" Ruth asked.

Oliver shrugged, as though her question were immaterial, but Muriel nodded.

"Good point," she said. "He could be a she. Grandmother Crow, or T'Ets, in Sliammon. She's one of the magical ancestors who can shape-shift and take animal or human form. She saved the life of her granddaughter when the girl got pregnant and her father ordered the tribe to abandon her. The father told the Raven P'a to extinguish all the fires, but T'Ets hid a glowing coal for her granddaughter in a shell and saved the girl's life. The girl went on to give birth to seven puppies, who later took off their skins and turned into humans and became the Sliammon people, but that's a whole other story."

She braced her arm against the frame of the car and slowly lowered herself into the driver's seat. Ruth offered a hand, supporting her elbow.

The crow watched the proceedings from its branch. When Muriel was safely inside, it stretched its beak and emitted a single harsh caw.

"Goodbye to you, too," Muriel said, starting the engine and waving her hand in its direction.

The crow cocked its head as the car moved slowly down the long, winding driveway, growing smaller and smaller until it disappeared around a bend, amid the towering trees. Oliver went to the garden to pick greens for dinner, but Ruth stood there by the woodpile a while longer, watching the crow.

"Hey, Crow," she said.

The crow cocked its head. *Ke*, it replied. *Ke, ke.*

"What are you doing here?" she asked. "What do you want?"

But the crow didn't answer this time. It just stared back at her with its jet-black eye. Waiting. Ruth felt sure the crow was waiting.

# *Nao*

## I.

It's hard to write about things that happened a long time ago in the past. When Jiko tells me exciting stories from her life, like when her idol, the famous anarchist and anti-imperialist terrorist Kanno Sugako, was hanged for treason, or when my great-uncle Haruki #1 died while carrying out a suicide bomber attack on an American warship, the stories seem so real while she's talking, but later, when I sit down to write them, they slip away and become unreal again. The past is weird. I mean, does it really exist? It feels like it exists, but where is it? And if it did exist but doesn't now, then where did it go?

When old Jiko talks about the past, her eyes get all inward-turning, like she's staring at something buried deep inside her body in the marrow of her bones. Her eyes are milky and blue because of her cataracts, and when she turns them inward, it's like she's moving into another world that's frozen deep inside ice. Jiko calls her cataracts *kuuge* which means "flowers of emptiness."[55] I think that's beautiful.

Old Jiko's past is very far away, but even if the past happened not so long ago, like my own happy life in Sunnyvale, it's still hard to write

---

55. *kūge* (空華)—lit. "emptiness" or "sky" flowers; an idiom for cataracts; also the title of Chapter 43 in Zen Master Dōgen's *Shōbōgenzō*. The kanji *kū* (空) has several meanings, including "sky" or "space," or "emptiness," as in 空兵 (sky soldier). The phrase *sky flowers* refers to the clouding of vision from cataracts, but in traditional Buddhist teaching, *flowers in the sky* refers to delusion brought on by a person's karmic obstructions. Dōgen seems to have reinterpreted it to mean a "flowering of emptiness"; in other words, an enlightened state. All things in the world, he says, are the cosmic flowering of emptiness.

about. That happy life seems realer than my real life now, but at the same time it's like a memory belonging to a totally different Nao Yasutani. Maybe that Nao of the past never really existed, except in the imagination of this Nao of the present, sitting here in a French maid café in Akiba Electricity Town. Or maybe it's the other way around.

If you've ever tried to keep a diary, then you'll know that the problem of trying to write about the past really starts in the present: No matter how fast you write, you're always stuck in the *then* and you can never catch up to what's happening *now*, which means that *now* is pretty much doomed to extinction. It's hopeless, really. Not that now is ever all that interesting. Now is usually just me, sitting in some dumpy maid café or on a stone bench at a temple on the way to school, moving a pen back and forth a hundred billion times across a page, trying to catch up with myself.

When I was a little kid in Sunnyvale, I became obsessed with the word *now*. My mom and dad spoke Japanese at home, but everyone else spoke English, and sometimes I would get caught in between the two languages. When that happened, everyday words and their meanings suddenly became disconnected, and the world became strange and unreal. The word *now* always felt especially strange and unreal to me because it <u>was</u> me, at least the sound of it was. Nao was *now* and had this whole other meaning.

In Japan, some words have kotodama,[56] which are spirits that live inside a word and give it a special power. The kotodama of *now* felt like a slippery fish, a slick fat tuna with a big belly and a smallish head and tail that looked something like this:

---

56. *kotodama* (言霊)—lit. "speech" (*koto*) + "spirit or soul" (*tama*).

*NOW* felt like a big fish swallowing a little fish, and I wanted to catch it and make it stop. I was just a kid, and I thought if I could truly grasp the meaning of the big fish *NOW*, I would be able to save little fish *Naoko*, but the word always slipped away from me.

I guess I was about six or seven by then, and I used to sit in the backseat of our Volvo station wagon, looking out at the golf courses and shopping malls and housing developments and factories and salt ponds streaming by on the Bayshore Freeway, and in the distance the water of San Francisco Bay was all blue and sparkling, and I kept the window open so the hot, dry, smoggy haze could blow on my face while I whispered *Now! . . . Now! . . . Now! . . .* over and over, faster and faster, into the wind as the world whipped by, trying to catch the moment when the word was what it is: when *now* became *NOW*.

But in the time it takes to say *now*, now is already over. It's already *then*.

*Then* is the opposite of *now*. So saying *now* obliterates its meaning, turning it into exactly what it isn't. It's like the word is committing suicide or something. So then I'd start making it shorter . . . *now, ow, oh, o* . . . until it was just a bunch of little grunting sounds and not even a word at all. It was hopeless, like trying to hold a snowflake on your tongue or a soap bubble between your fingertips. Catching it destroys it, and I felt like I was disappearing, too.

Stuff like this can drive you crazy. This is the kind of thing my dad thinks about all the time, reading his Great Minds of Western Philosophy, and after watching him I understand that you have to take care of your mind, even if it's not a great one, because if you don't, you can wind up with your head on the tracks.

## 2.

My dad's birthday was in May, and my funeral was one month later. Dad was feeling pretty optimistic, because he'd made it though another year of life alive, and he'd just come in third place in the Great Bug Wars for his flying *Cyclommatus imperator*,[57] which was a big deal because it's really hard to fold the outstretched wings. So Dad was doing really well for a suicidal person, and I was doing okay, too, for a torture victim. The kids at school were still pretending I was invisible, only now everyone in the whole ninth grade was doing it, not just my homeroom class. I know this sounds pretty extreme, but in Japan it's rather ordinary, and there's even a name for it, which is zen-in shikato.[58] So I was getting some major zen-in shikato action, and when I was in the schoolyard or in the hallway or walking to my desk, I'd hear my classmates saying things like, "Transfer Student Yasutani hasn't been to school in weeks!" They never called me Nao or Naoko. Only Transfer Student Yasutani or just Transfer Student, like I didn't even have a name. "Is Transfer Student sick? Maybe Transfer Student has some disgusting American disease. Maybe the Health Ministry has quarantined her. Transfer Student should be quarantined. She's a baikin.[59] Ew, I hope she's not contagious! She's only contagious if you do it with her. Gross! She's a ho. I wouldn't do it with her! Yeah, that's 'cause you're impo. Shut up!"

Typical. It was the kind of stuff they used to say directly to my face, only now they were saying it to each other, but still in front of me so I could hear. And they did other stuff, too. When you come into a Japanese school, there's this place with lockers where you have to take off your outdoor shoes and put on your indoor slippers. They would wait until I had one shoe off, balancing on one foot, and then they'd walk into me and push me down and step on me like I wasn't there. "Oooh, stinky!" they'd say. "Did someone step in dog shit?"

Before physical education class, you have to change into your gym uniform, but my school here is so pathetic they don't have real locker rooms like in Sunnyvale, so everyone changes in the classroom at their desk. The girls get one classroom and the boys get another, and you have to stand there and take off your clothes and put on these retarded

---

57. Giant staghorn beetle.
58. *zen-in shikato* (全員しかと)—lit. "all-person ostracizing" or "everybody ignoring."
59. *baikin* (ばい菌)—germ.

uniforms, and when I had my clothes off, the girls would cover their noses and mouths and look around and say, "Nanka kusai yo![60] Did something die?" and maybe that's what gave them the idea for the funeral.

### 3.

It was about a week before summer vacation, when I got the creepy feeling that something had changed once again. It's all supersubtle, but you can tell, and if you've ever been the target of military psyops, or been tortured or hunted or stalked, you'll know what I'm saying is true. You can read the signs because your life depends on it, only what was happening this time was basically nothing. I wasn't getting pushed over and stepped on in the genkan[61] anymore, and no one was making comments about me being smelly or sick. Instead, they were all walking around being real quiet and looking very sad, and when one of the nerdy little kids lost it and started giggling when I walked by, he quickly got punched. I knew something was about to go down, and it was making me crazy. Then during lunch I noticed they were passing something around, some kind of folded paper, like cards or something, but of course nobody gave me one, so I had to wait until clubs let out that afternoon to find out.

I went home after school like usual, and I was hanging around the apartment, pretending to do my homework and trying to think of an excuse to go out again, when my dad started rummaging around for something, and then I heard him sigh, which meant that he was looking for his cigarettes and the pack was empty.

"Urusai yo!" I said, grumpily. "Tabako katte koyo ka?"[62]

For me to even offer was a big deal. My dad doesn't like to go outside even though the cigarette vending machine is only a couple of blocks away, but normally I refuse to go buy cigarettes for him because of all

---

60. *Nanka kusai yo!*—something stinks!
61. *genkan* (玄関)—entryway, foyer.
62. *Urusai yo! Tabako katte koyō ka?*—You're so noisy! You want me to get you some cigarettes?

the ways you can commit suicide, smoking has to be the stupidest and also the most expensive. I mean, why make a lot of rich tobacco companies even richer off of killing you, right? But this time his disgusting habit gave me the perfect excuse, and he was grateful, and he gave me a little extra money to buy myself a soda. I put on my running shoes instead of the plastic slippers we usually wear for doing errands in the neighborhood, and on the way out the door, I slipped a small kitchen knife into my pocket. I ran down the alleyway and ducked behind the row of vending machines that sell cigarettes and porno magazines and energy drinks.

I was waiting for Daisuke-kun. He was in my homeroom and lived with his mom in our building. He was younger than me, a little stick insect of a kid, and his mom was a single mom and a bar hostess and poor, so he got picked on almost as much as I did. Daisuke-kun was truly pathetic, and after a while I saw him, holding his book bag up in front of him as he stumbled down the street, keeping his back to the high concrete wall. He was the kind of kid who even in long pants looked like he should be wearing shorts. Just the sight of his little pinhead swiveling around on his skinny neck, and his eyes bugging in all directions even though there was nobody following him, drove me crazy and made me really mad, so when he passed in front of the vending machines, I jumped out and grabbed him and pulled him into the alleyway, and I guess the adrenaline from my anger gave me superhuman strength, because taking him down was about as easy as plucking a sock off a line of laundry. Honestly, it felt great. I felt great. Powerful. Exactly the way I'd hoped I would feel when I fantasized about getting revenge. I knocked his school cap off and grabbed him by the hair and pushed him to his knees in front of me. He crumpled and froze there, the way a baby cockroach does when you turn on the kitchen light, just before you crush it with your slipper. I pulled his head up and held the little kitchen knife to his throat. The knife was sharp, and I could see the vein pulsing in his spindly neck. It would have been no effort at all to cut him. It would have meant nothing.

"Nakami o misero!"[63] I said, kicking his book bag with my toe. "Empty

---

63. *Nakami o misero!*—Show me what's inside!

it!" My voice sounded low and rough, like a sukeban.[64] I even surprised myself.

He opened his book bag and began to dump the stuff inside at my feet. "I don't have any more money," he stammered. "They already took it all."

Of course they did. The powerful kids, led by a real sukeban named Reiko, ran a whole operation fleecing the pathetic kids like me and Daisuke.

"I don't need your stinking money," I said. "I want the card."

"Card?"

"The one they were handing out at school. I know you have it. Give it to me." I kicked his Ultraman pencil case and sent the pens and pencils flying. He scrambled on his hands and knees, searching through his textbooks. Finally he handed me a card made of folded paper, careful not to make eye contact. I took it from him.

"On your knees," I said. "Close your eyes and bow your head. Sit on your hands."

He tucked his hands under his thighs. It was a posture he knew well, and so did I. It comes from a game called kagome kagome[65] that little kids play, sort of a Japanese ring-around-the-rosy. The kid who's It becomes the oni[66] and has to kneel on the ground in the center, blindfolded, and all the other kids hold hands and skip around him in a circle, singing a song that goes,

*Kagome Kagome*
*Kago no naka no tori wa*
*Itsu itsu deyaru? Yoake no ban ni*
*Tsuru to kame ga subetta.*
*Ushiro no shoumen dare?*

---

64. *sukeban* (スケ番)—boss girl, a delinquent girl.
65. *kagome* (籠目)—a style of open bamboo weaving used for baskets or cages.
66. *oni* (鬼)—demon, ogre.

In English it means

> *Kagome, kagome,*
> *Bird in the cage,*
> *When, oh when, will you escape? In the evening of the*
>   *dawn,*
> *Both Crane and Turtle have fallen down.*
> *Who is there, behind you now?*

At the end of the song, everybody stops circling, and the oni tries to guess which kid is standing behind him, and if he's right, they switch places and the new kid becomes the oni.

That's how the game is supposed to be played, only the version we played at school was different. I guess you could say it's kind of an upgraded version, called kagome rinchi,[67] that's very popular among junior high school kids today. In kagome rinchi, if you're the oni, you have to kneel on the ground with your hands under your thighs, while the kids circle around, kicking and punching you and singing the kagome song. When the song is over, even if you could still use your voice, you wouldn't dare guess the name of the kid behind you, because even if you guessed right, you would still be wrong and they'd start all over again. In kagome rinchi, once you're the oni, you're always the oni. The game usually ends when you can't kneel anymore and you fall over.

So Daisuke-kun was on his knees in the alley with his eyes squeezed shut, waiting for me to punch him or kick him or cut him with my kitchen knife, but I was taking my time. It was still early and nobody was in the alley at that hour, since the hostesses can't ever get it together to bring out their recycling before dark. I unfolded the card he'd given me. It was an announcement, written in nice brush calligraphy, for a funeral service. The handwriting was formal and neat, like a grown-up's, and I wondered if maybe Ugawa Sensei had written it. The funeral service was going to be on the following day during the last homeroom period before

---

67. *rinchi*—from English *lynch*.

our midterm summer vacation. The deceased was former transfer student Yasutani Naoko.

Daisuke was still kneeling at my feet, head bowed, eyes closed. I grabbed a fistful of his hair and yanked his head up and shoved the paper in front of his nose.

"Does this make you happy?"

"N-no," he stuttered.

"Usotsuke—!"[68] I said, jerking on his hair. Of course the pathetic insect was lying. When you're a nobody, you're always happy when somebody else is getting tortured instead of you, and I wanted to punish him for that. His hair felt disgusting in my fingers, too coarse for a young kid his age, like old man's hair on a young boy's head, and it was greasy, too, like he'd used some of his mom's boyfriend's styling gel. It creeped me out. I tightened my grip and pulled harder until I could feel the follicles popping from their pores. I took the knife and pressed the blade against his throat. The skin was pale and almost bluish, a girl's throat. The tendons were strung tight and trembling, and the veins throbbed against the thin metal serration. Time slowed down, and each moment unfolded into a future filled with infinite possibilities. It would be so easy. Slice the artery and watch the red blood spurt and stain the ground, draining his stupid nothing life from his stupid nothing body. Or release him. Let the pathetic insect go. It didn't matter which. I pressed the blade a tiny bit harder. How much more pressure would it take? If you've ever examined skin cells under a microscope in biology class, you'll understand how the serrated teeth of the knife could tease the cells apart until the blood started to seep. I thought about my funeral tomorrow, and how this would be a fine way to put a stop to it. Give them a real body. Not mine.

Daisuke moaned. His eyes were closed, but his mouth was slack and his face was strangely relaxed. A small drop of saliva dribbled from the corner of his chapped lips. He looked like he was smiling.

My fist, gripping the knife, looked like it meant business, and my arm

68. *Usotsuke!*—Liar!

felt strong and powerful, too. I liked that. Standing there, we were frozen in time, me and Daisuke-kun, and the future was mine. No matter what I chose to do, for this one moment I owned Daisuke and I owned his future. It was a strange feeling, creepy and a little too intimate, because if I killed him now we would be joined for life, forever, and so I released him. He crumpled at my feet.

I looked at my hands like they belonged to someone else. Strands of his disgusting hair stuck to my fingers by the white blobs of their follicles. I rubbed them off against my skirt.

"Get out of here," I said. "Go home."

Daisuke slowly got to his feet and brushed off his knees. "You should have just done it," he said.

His words surprised me. "Done what?" I asked, stupidly.

He squatted down on the pavement and slowly started putting his books back into his book bag. "Cut me," he said, looking up at me and blinking. "Slit my throat. I want to die."

"You do?" I asked.

He nodded. "Of course," he said, and then he went back to gathering up his papers.

I watched him for a while. I felt sorry for him, because I knew what he meant, and I even thought about offering to do it again, but the moment was gone. Oh well.

"Sorry," I said.

He shook his head. "It's okay," he mumbled.

I watched him for a while longer as he crawled around on his knees, searching under the vending machine for his pencils. I almost wanted to help him, but instead I turned and walked away. I didn't look back. I wasn't worried about him telling anyone. He knew better, like I did. I walked all the way to the station, where they have better vending machines, and I bought my dad a pack of Short Hopes because that was the only brand I would buy for him on account of the name, and then at the drink machine I bought myself a can of Pulpy. It's a kind of orange juice with big bits of pulp in it that I like to pop between my teeth.

## 4.

My funeral was beautiful and very real. All the kids in my class were wearing black armbands, and they had set an altar on my desk with a candle and an incense burner and my school photograph, enlarged and framed and decorated with black and white ribbons. One by one my enemies took turns going up to my desk and paying their respects to me, laying a white paper flower in front of my picture, while the rest of the class stood at their desks with their hands clasped and their eyes fixed on the ground. Maybe they were trying not to laugh, but I don't think so. The atmosphere was very solemn and it felt like a proper funeral. Daisuke-kun was pale when his turn came to go up, but he did it, and he offered his flower and bowed deeply, and I almost felt proud of him, which I know sounds kind of perverse but I think maybe you get a little fond of the people you've tortured and whose future you've owned.

The whole time they were doing this, Ugawa Sensei was chanting a Buddhist hymn. I didn't recognize it at the time because I grew up in Sunnyvale and didn't have much exposure yet to the Buddhist tradition, but later on, when I heard it again at my old Jiko's temple, I asked her about it. She told me it's called the Maka Hanya Haramita Shingyo,[69] which means something like the Great Most Excellent Wisdom Heart Sutra. The only part I remember goes like this: Shiki fu i ku, ku fu i shiki.[70]

It's pretty abstract. Old Jiko tried to explain it to me, and I don't know if I understood it correctly or not, but I think it means that nothing in the world is solid or real, because nothing is permanent, and all things—including trees and animals and pebbles and mountains and rivers and even me and you—are just kind of flowing through for the time being. I think that's true, and it's very reassuring, and I just wish I'd understood that at my funeral when Ugawa Sensei was

---

69. A central text in Mahayana Buddhism.
70. "Form is emptiness and emptiness is form."

chanting because it would have been a great comfort to me, but of course I didn't because these sutras are in an old-fashioned language that nobody understands anymore, unless you're like Jiko and it's your job. But actually it doesn't really matter because even if you can't exactly understand the words, you know they are beautiful and profound, and Ugawa Sensei's voice, which was usually so mumbly and unpleasant, was suddenly soft and sad and gentle, and he was chanting with feeling, like he really meant it. When he walked up to my desk to offer me a flower, the look on his face made me want to cry because it was so twisted up and full of his own particular sorrow. A couple of times I actually did cry—like when I saw my portrait hung with the black and white funeral ribbons, and when I saw how respectful my classmates were being to me, with their bowed heads and their paper flowers. They must have all gotten together in clubs after school to make those flowers and decorate my picture. They were so serious and dignified. I almost loved them.

## 5.

I didn't go to school that day, so I wasn't actually there at my funeral. I saw it later on. After my encounter with Daisuke, I went home and gave Dad his cigarettes and went to bed. When my mom got home that evening, I made myself throw up on the bathroom floor and told her I was sick, and the next morning I threw up again for good measure, and since it was the last day of school before the summer holidays, she let me stay home. I was really happy, figuring I'd escaped the whole thing, but that evening I got an anonymous email with a subject line that said, "The Tragic and Untimely Death of Transfer Student Nao Yasutani." The email was a link to a video-sharing website. Someone had made a video of my funeral with their keitai phone and posted it on the Internet, and over the next couple of hours, I watched the hit counter rise. I don't know who was viewing it, but the video was getting hundreds and then thousands of hits, like it was going viral. Weird, but I was almost proud. It felt kind of good to be popular.

## 6.

I just remembered the last lines of the Heart Sutra, which go like this:

> gaté gaté, para gaté,
> parasam gaté, boji sowa ka . . .

These words are actually in some ancient Indian language[71] and not even Japanese, but Jiko told me they mean something like this:

> gone gone, gone beyond,
> gone completely beyond, awakened, hurray . . .

I keep thinking of Jiko, and how relieved she'll be when all sentient beings, even my stupid horrible classmates, wake up and get enlightened and go away, so she can finally rest. She must be so exhausted.

---

71. Sanskrit.

# Part II

*In reality, every reader, while he is reading, is the reader of his own self. The writer's work is merely a kind of optical instrument, which he offers to the reader to permit him to discern what, without the book, he would perhaps never have seen in himself. The reader's recognition in his own self of what the book says is the proof of its truth.*

—Marcel Proust, *Le temps retrouvé*

# *Ruth*

## I.

The image on the screen shows a man in his late thirties or early forties, standing before a vast field of tsunami debris that stretches into the distance, as far as the eye of the camera can see. The man is wearing a white paper face mask, but he has tugged it down to his chin in order to speak to the reporter. He is wearing tired sweatpants, work gloves, a zippered jacket, boots. He raises his arm to gesture toward the wreckage behind him.

"It's like a dream," he says. "A horrible dream. I keep trying to wake up. I think when I wake up, my daughter will be back."

His voice is flat, his utterances short. "I have lost everything. My daughter, my son, my wife, my mother. Our house, neighbors. Our whole town."

The caption at the bottom of the screen gives the man's name: *T. Nojima, Sanitation Worker, O— Township, Miyagi Prefecture.*

The newscaster, his voice muffled by a face mask, speaks to the camera. He explains that they are standing on the site where Mr. Nojima's house used to be. The scene is one of total devastation, but what the camera cannot pick up is the stench. He pulls the face mask down. The smell, he explains, is unbearable, a choking odor of rotting fish and flesh, buried in the wreckage. Mr. Nojima is searching for his six-year-old daughter. He has little hope of finding her alive. He is looking for the backpack she was wearing on the morning of March 11 when the tsunami hit.

"It's red," Nojima says. "With a picture of Hello Kitty on it. I'd just bought it for her. The school year was starting and she was so proud of it. She wore it in the house. She was going to be entering the first grade."

Nojima and his daughter were at home in the kitchen when the wall of black water and debris smashed through their house. Within seconds, Nojima was crushed up against the ceiling and his daughter was gone. He thought he would drown there, but miraculously the house was ripped from its foundation just as the ceiling gave way, and he was pushed through onto the second floor and into the bedroom, where his wife was crouched in a corner, holding their infant son.

"I tried to catch her hand," he says. "I almost had her, but then the house tipped and split in half."

His wife and son were dragged away. He thought he could still reach them. He managed to scramble onto the roof of a passing concrete building. He could see his wife in the corner of their floating bedroom, holding the baby, but she was being pulled farther and farther away. He called to her. The roar of the water and the crashing debris was deafening.

"It was so loud, but I think she heard me. She looked at me. Her eyes were wide, but she never once screamed. She didn't want to scare the baby. She just kept watching me until the end."

He shakes his head as though to clear further recollection from it. He stares out over the debris field—splintered houses and crumpled cars, cinder block and tangled rebar, boats, furniture parts, smashed appliances, roof tiles, clothing, stuff—a ghastly midden piled several meters deep. He looks down at his feet, poking at a muddy tangle of fabric with the toe of his shoe.

"I will probably never find my family," he says. "I've lost my hope of giving them a proper funeral. But if I can just find something, just one thing that belonged to my daughter, I'll be able to rest my mind and leave this place." He swallows hard and then takes a deep breath.

"That life with my family is the dream," he says. He gestures toward the ruined landscape. "This is the reality. Everything is gone. We need to wake up and understand that."

**2.**

In the days following the earthquake and tsunami, Ruth sat in front of her computer screen, trawling the Internet for news of friends and family.

Within days, she received confirmation that the people she knew were safe, but she couldn't stop watching. The images pouring in from Japan mesmerized her. Every few hours, another horrifying piece of footage would break, and she would play it over and over, studying the wave as it surged over the tops of the seawalls, carrying ships down city streets, picking up cars and trucks and depositing them on the roofs of buildings. She watched whole towns get crushed and swept away in a matter of moments, and she was aware that while these moments were captured online, so many other moments simply vanished.

Most of the footage was shot by panicked people on their mobile phones from hillsides or the roofs of tall buildings, so there was a haphazard quality to the images, as if the photographers didn't quite realize what they were filming, but they knew it was critical, and so they turned on their phones and held them up to the oncoming wave. Sometimes an image would suddenly blur and distort as the photographer fled to higher ground. Sometimes, in the corners and the edges of the frame, tiny cars and people were caught fleeing from the oncoming wall of black water. Sometimes the people looked confused. Sometimes they looked like they were taking their time and even turning back to watch, not understanding the danger they were in. But always, from the vantage point of the camera, you could see how fast the wave was traveling and how immense it was. Those tiny people didn't stand a chance, and the people standing off-screen knew it. *Hurry! Hurry!* their disembodied voices cried, from behind the camera. *Don't stop! Run! Oh, no! Where's Grandma? Oh, no! Look! There! Oh, this is horrible! Hurry! Run! Run!*

### 3.

In the two weeks following the earthquake, tsunami, and meltdown of the Fukushima nuclear reactors, the global bandwidth was flooded with images and reports from Japan, and for that brief period of time, we were all experts on radiation exposure and microsieverts and plate tectonics and subduction. But then the uprising in Libya and the tornado in Joplin superseded the quake, and the keyword cloud shifted to *revolution* and *drought* and *unstable air masses* as the tide of information from Japan receded. Occasionally an article would appear in *The New York Times* about Tepco's mismanagement of the meltdown, or the government's failure to respond and protect its citizens, but this news rarely made the front page anymore. The Business section carried gloomy reports about the cost of Japan's cascading disasters, deemed to be the most expensive in history, and dire projections for the future of the country's economy.

What is the half-life of information? Does its rate of decay correlate with the medium that conveys it? Pixels need power. Paper is unstable in fire and flood. Letters carved in stone are more durable, although not so easily distributed, but inertia can be a good thing. In towns up and down the coast of Japan, stone markers were found on hillsides, engraved with ancient warnings:

## DO NOT BUILD YOUR HOMES BELOW THIS POINT!

Some of the warning stones were more than six centuries old. A few had been shifted by the tsunami, but most had remained safely out of its reach.

"They're the voices of our ancestors," said the mayor of a town destroyed by the wave. "They were speaking to us across time, but we didn't listen."

Does the half-life of information correlate with the decay of our attention? Is the Internet a kind of temporal gyre, sucking up stories, like geodrift, into its orbit? What is its gyre memory? How do we measure the half-life of its drift?

The tidal wave, observed, collapses into tiny particles, each one containing a story:

- a mobile phone, ringing deep inside a mountain of sludge and debris;
- a ring of soldiers, bowing to a body they've flagged;

- a medical worker clad in full radiation hazmat, wanding a bare-faced baby who is squirming in his mother's arms;
- a line of toddlers, waiting quietly for their turn to be tested.

These images, a minuscule few representing the inconceivable many, eddy and grow old, degrading with each orbit around the gyre, slowly breaking down into razor-sharp fragments and brightly colored shards. Like plastic confetti, they're drawn into the gyre's becalmed center, the garbage patch of history and time. The gyre's memory is all the stuff that we've forgotten.

## 4.

Ruth's mind felt like a garbage patch, an undifferentiated mat of becalmed and fractured pixels. She sat back in her chair, away from the glowing screen, and closed her eyes. The pixels lingered, dancing behind her eyelids in the darkness. She'd spent the afternoon watching clips of bullying and harassment on YouTube and other video-sharing sites in both the United States and Japan, but the clip she was looking for, "The Tragic and Untimely Death of Transfer Student Nao Yasutani," which according to Nao had once gone viral, was nowhere to be found.

She rubbed her hands up and down across her face, kneading her temples and pressing her fingers into her eye sockets. She felt like she'd been trying to suck the girl out of the glowing screen with the sheer force of her will and the fixity of her eyeballs. Why did it matter so much? But it did. She needed to know if Nao was dead or alive. She was searching for a body.

She stood and stretched, and then wandered downstairs. The house was empty. Oliver had received a large shipment of dawn redwood seedlings, which he was planting over at the NeoEocene clear-cut. He'd left early that morning, whistling the dwarves' tune from *Snow White*. Hi ho, Hi ho. Nothing made him happier than planting baby trees. The cat was outside on the porch, waiting for him to come home.

It was half past four and time to start thinking about dinner. As she passed by the dining room, she caught a whiff of the fishy odor of barnacle death. The smell was stronger now. She walked to the telephone, picked up the receiver, and dialed Callie's number.

## 5.

"They're goosenecks," Callie said, examining the barnacles on the freezer bag. "*Pollicipes polymerus*. Order Pedunculata. A gregarious pelagic species, not really native, but it's not uncommon to find them on tide-wrack that's drifted in from farther out at sea."

She glanced across the kitchen at Ruth, who was heating water for tea. "Is this the bag you found below Gudrun and Horst's place?"

When she spoke with Callie on the phone, Ruth hadn't mentioned where she'd found the bag, but Callie hadn't sounded at all surprised to hear from her and had offered to come right over. It was almost as if she had been expecting the call, but of course Callie was helpful that way. She was a marine biologist and environmental activist who ran the fore-shore monitoring program on the island and did volunteer work for a marine mammal protection agency. She made her living as a naturalist on the massive cruise liners that plied the sheltered waters of the Inland Passage on their way to and from Alaska.

"The belly of the beast," Callie said. "Those cruisers are the people we have to reach. They're the ones who have the resources to make change happen."

She often told a story about the time she was standing on the deck of a ship bound for Anchorage, pointing out a pod of humpbacks to the excited passengers, who were crowded around the railing, snapping pictures and shooting video. One elderly man stood apart from the rest. When Callie offered him her place at the rail so he could get a better view, he laughed, derisively.

"They're just whales."

Later in the cruise, she gave a lecture about the order Cetacea. She showed video and talked about their complex communities and social behaviors, about their bubble nets and echolocation and the range of their emotions. She played recordings of their vocalizations, illustrating their clicks and songs. To her surprise, the old man was in the audience, listening.

Later, they spotted another pod, which came closer this time, treating them to a spectacular display of surfacing behaviors, breaching, spy-hopping, lobtailing, and slapping. The old man came up on deck to watch.

At the end of the cruise, as they were approaching port in Vancouver, the old man sought her out and handed her an envelope.

"For your whales," he said.

When she thanked him, he shook his head. "Don't."

They disembarked, and Callie forgot about the envelope. When she got home, she found it and opened it. Inside was a check made out to her marine mammal protection agency for half a million dollars. She thought it was a joke. She thought she had miscounted the zeros. She sent it in to the office, and they deposited it. The check cleared.

Using the passenger list, she tracked the old guy down at his home in Bethesda and questioned him. At first, he was reluctant, but finally he explained. He had been a bomber pilot during World War II, he told her, stationed at an air base in the Aleutians. They used to fly out every day, looking for Japanese targets. Often, when they couldn't locate an enemy vessel, or the weather conditions turned bad, they would be forced to abort their mission and fly back to base, but landing with a full payload was dangerous, so they would discharge their bombs into the sea. From the cockpit of the plane, they could see the large shadows of whales, moving below the surface of the water. From so high up, the whales looked small. They used them for target practice.

"It was fun," the old man told Callie over the phone. "What did we know?"

"They're filter feeders," Callie said, about the barnacles. "But they're not very good at moving their cirri around, so they rely on a vigorous move-ment of water to get their nutrition. That's why they prefer more exposed shorelines than ours."

"What's a cirri?" Ruth asked, putting two mugs of tea down and then pouring a third for Oliver, who had just come back from tree planting. He took off his jacket and hung it up, and then he joined them, with the cat following hard on his heels.

"Cheers," Callie said, taking a sip of the tea. "Cirri are the barnacle's arms and legs. Feathery tendrils they use to pull plankton in."

"I don't see any feathery tendrils," Ruth said. She didn't like the barnacles. They were ugly and they gave her the creeps.

"They only extend them when they're underwater," Oliver said, wrapping his reddened fingers around the warm mug. "And anyway, these guys are dead."

Ruth inspected the barnacles, which looked pretty much the same as they had when they were alive. They were attached to the freezer bag by long dark stalks that were tough and rubbery and covered with small bumps. At the free end of each stalk was a hard white cluster of platelike shells that looked like fingernails. Callie used the tip of her pen to point to one of the rubbery stalks. Pesto jumped up onto the counter to watch.

"This is the foot, or the peduncle," she said. "And this hard white part is the capitulum, or the head."

The cat sniffed at the barnacle, and Ruth pushed him away. "Does it have a face?" she asked.

"Not exactly," Callie said. "But it's got a dorsal side, which is up, and a ventral side, which is down."

She took a small plastic box from the pocket of her fishing vest and opened it. Inside was a collection of forensic instruments: a scalpel, a pair of tweezers, forceps, scissors, a small ruler. She selected the largest barnacle and used the scalpel to slice carefully between the plastic bag and the base of the peduncle. She removed the barnacle and laid it on the counter in front of her. She took out the ruler and measured the creature from foot to head.

"Can you tell how old it is?" Oliver asked.

"Hard to say. They reach sexual maturity at about a year, and full maturity at five. They can live up to twenty years or more. This fellow, or gal—actually it doesn't matter because they're hermaphroditic—is a mature adult. They can grow up to twenty centimeters, or about eight inches long, but this one's only just over three inches, which suggests that the colony is fairly young, or the conditions weren't great, or both. Hey, Oliver, can I test-drive that scope on your iPhone?"

He had recently hacked his iPhone by attaching a small 45X digital microscope lens onto the case with superglue. Somehow Callie already knew about this, too. She had just gotten back to the island. How could she know? She held out her hand, and he snapped the case mod onto the phone, opened the app, and passed it over to her. The app activated the iPhone's light as she aimed the lens at the barnacle's head. A close-up image appeared on the small screen. "This is awesome!" she said. "You see these gorgeous calcareous plates?"

Ruth peered over her shoulder at the small screen. The plates looked like toenails on the foot of a prehistoric reptile.

"When they're first secreted, they're shiny and pearlescent, but gradually as they're buffeted about by the waves, they get pitted and dull."

"Like us," Ruth said, sitting back down.

"Exactly," Callie said. "So that's another clue to age. All in all, I'd say that this colony's been floating around for at least a couple years, probably more like three or four."

"Three years puts it before the tsunami," Oliver said.

"Well, like I said, it's hard to be more precise than that. But it seems unlikely that we'd be seeing stuff from the tsunami washing up on our beaches yet. We're tucked in pretty far back here."

She turned off the light on the microscope and admired the lens. "How'd you attach it?"

As Oliver explained the hack, Ruth picked up the severed barnacle between her fingers and studied it. This new information added little support for her tsunami theory. Perhaps Muriel was right after all. Perhaps the freezer bag had been jettisoned from a ship, although Nao didn't seem like the type to take an Alaskan cruise. Maybe she had cast it out to sea, like a message in a bottle, before the tsunami, or maybe it had been in her pocket, along with the rocks, when she walked into the ocean and drowned. Any of these were plausible explanations, but none of them felt right. Ruth didn't like the barnacles to begin with, and now she resented them for failing to provide the evidence she was looking for.

"Why are they called goosenecks, anyway?" she asked. "They don't look anything like geese."

Callie had returned the iPhone to Oliver and was packing up her kit. "Actually, they do. There's a kind of goose called a barnacle goose, which has a long black neck and a white head. Your little friends here were named for it. People used to find these guys attached to a piece of driftwood, which they assumed was a branch from a barnacle tree. They thought the capitula were eggs laid in the tree, and that the barnacle geese hatched from them. It's a reasonable chain of assumptions, but of course they were entirely wrong."

"Assumptions suck," Ruth said. She put the barnacle down on the counter, and Pesto, who was waiting, promptly snatched it and ran off with it. He carried it to the middle of the kitchen floor and dropped it, took another sniff, and then turned up his nose. He wouldn't deign to eat an already dead thing.

"They're a great delicacy in Spain," Callie said. "The peduncle is especially tender. You boil it for a couple minutes, peel off the skin, hold it by the shell, put the foot in your mouth, and . . . *pop!*" She pantomimed this, making the sound with her lips. "Meat slips right out of the shell. Dipped in a little garlic butter and lemon . . . yum!"

It was just before six, and already quite dark outside. Ruth took a headlamp and they walked Callie to her truck. Looking up, she could see that the clouds had parted and a full moon was lighting up the sky. In the moonlight, the treetops were threaded with pale tendrils of mist, but below, the boughs of the cedars were dark and heavy with the rain that had been falling all day. The beam of her headlamp caught a shape in the branches.

"Hey, is that your Jungle Crow?" Callie asked.

Focusing her light, Ruth could see the gleam of black feathers and the glint of a jet-black eye. "Muriel," she said, as though it were the answer to Callie's question.

Callie laughed. "Of course," she said. "But everyone's talking about it. Our local nativists already have their knickers in a twist."

"Why?"

"Why do you think?" Callie said. "Invasive species. Exotics. Black slugs, Scotch broom, Himalayan blackberries, and now Jungle Crows?" She turned to Oliver. "Speaking of exotics, how's the Covenant War going?"

He made a face. The NeoEocene site, where he was planting his climate-change forest, had been clear-cut by a logging company and then placed under a covenant, which stipulated that any subsequent reforestation be limited to species that were native to the extant geoclimatic zone. His trees were deemed to be exotic and thus in violation of the covenant. Neither Oliver nor his botanist friend who owned the property had been aware of this.

"Not good," he said. "The covenant holder wants me to stop planting, but I'm arguing that given the rapid onset of climate change, we need to radically redefine the term *native* and expand it to include formerly, and even prehistorically, native species." He looked discouraged. "Semantics," he said. "So stupid."

As though in agreement, the Jungle Crow gave a harsh caw, and Callie laughed. "See?" she said. "He's acclimating. Don't be surprised if our island xenophobes storm this place, armed with nets and kerosene torches."

Ruth looked up in the tree at the outline of the crow in the darkness. "Did you hear that?" she called. "You better watch out."

The crow flapped its wings and hopped along the branch, sending a shower of water raining down onto Callie's head.

"Hey," she said, wiping the wet from her face. "Cut it out. I'm on your side." She turned to Ruth. "They're very clever. Did you know—"

Ruth held up her hand. "I know," she said, but Callie carried on.

"—that in Sliammon mythology they're magical ancestors who can shape-shift and change into human form?"

"You don't say," Ruth said.

Callie grinned. "You should get Muriel to tell you about it some-time . . ."

## 6.

That night in bed Ruth read the day's allotment out loud from the diary. Pesto lay on Oliver's stomach, purring, while Oliver stared up at the ceiling and rubbed the cat's forehead. She read the part about Nao's funeral and the video that went up on the Internet.

*gone gone, gone beyond,*
*gone completely beyond . . .*

The story of the bullying made him angry. "I hate that," he said. "How could the school allow that to happen? How could that teacher partici-pate?"

Ruth didn't have an answer. Pesto stopped purring and looked uneasily at Oliver.

"But it makes total sense," Oliver said, glumly. "We live in a bully culture. Politicians, corporations, the banks, the military. All bullies and crooks. They steal, they torture people, they make these insane rules and set the tone."

She slipped her hand between the pillow and his head and kneaded the nape of his neck. The cat reached up a paw and laid it on his chin.

"Look at Guantánamo," he said. "Look at Abu Ghraib. America's bad, but Canada's no better. People just going with the program, too scared to speak up. Look at the Tar Sands. Just like Tepco. I fucking hate it."

He turned over on his side, pitching the cat onto the mattress. The cat jumped off the bed and left.

After Oliver fell asleep, Ruth got up and went to the window. Somewhere out there, the crow perched in the boughs. Their crepuscular crow. She couldn't see it, but she liked the thought of the black crow hidden in the shadows. She wondered if it had managed to make friends with the ravens yet. She crawled back into bed and drifted off.

That night, she had the second of her nun dreams. It was the same temple. The same darkened room with the torn paper screen, the same old nun, dressed in long black robes, seated at the desk on the floor. Outside, the same moonlight shimmered softly in the garden, only now in the distance, beyond the garden gate, Ruth could dimly make out what looked like the outline of a cemetery, its jaggedy silhouette of stupas and stones, stark against the pale night sky.

Inside the room, the harsh, cold light from the computer illuminated the old nun's face, making her look haggard and sickly. She looked up from the screen. She was wearing the black glasses that were similar to the ones Ruth wore. She took them off and rubbed her tired eyes, and then she spotted Ruth. Unfurling the wide black wing of her sleeve, she beckoned, calling her closer, and then Ruth was beside her. The nun held out her glasses, and Ruth, realizing that she'd left hers on the bedside table, took them. She knew she had to put them on. She blinked. The lenses were thick and murky. Her eyes would need a moment to adjust.

No, this wouldn't do. The nun's lenses were too thick and strong, smearing and dismantling the whole world as she knew it. She started to panic. She tried to pull the glasses from her face, but they were stuck there, and as she struggled, the smear of the world began to absorb her, swirling and howling like a whirlwind and casting her back into a place or condition that was unformed, that she couldn't find words for. How to describe it? Not a place, but a feeling, of nonbeing, sudden, dark, and prehuman, which filled her with such an inchoate horror that she cried out and brought her hands to her face, only to find that she no longer had one. There was nothing there. No hands, no face, no eyes, no glasses, no Ruth at all. Nothing but a vast and empty ruthlessness.

She screamed but no sound emerged. She strained into the vastness, pressing into a direction that felt like *forward* or even *through*, but without a face there was no forward, or backward, either. No up, no down. No past, no future. There was just this—this eternal sense of merging and dissolving into something unnameable that went on and on in all directions, forever.

And then she felt something, a feather-light touch, and she heard something that sounded like a chuckle and a snap, and in an instant, her dark terror vanished and was replaced by a sense of utter calm and well-being. Not that she had a body to feel, or eyes to see, or ears to hear, but somehow she experienced all these sensations, nevertheless. It was like being cradled in the arms of time itself, and she stayed suspended in this blissful state for an eternity or two. When she awoke to an insipid beam of winter sunlight filtering in through the bamboo outside her window, she felt oddly at peace and well rested.

# *Nao*

## 1.

Have you ever heard of metal-binding?[72] It's something that everyone in Japan knows about, but nobody ever heard of in Sunnyvale. I know because I asked Kayla, so maybe Americans don't have it. I never had it either until we moved to Tokyo.

Metal-binding is what happens when you wake up in the middle of the night and can't move, like some gigantically fat evil spirit is sitting on your chest. It's really scary. After the Chuo Rapid Express Incident, I used to wake up thinking it was Dad on my chest, and if he was sitting there it meant that he was a ghost and therefore he was dead, but then I would hear him snoring across the room and realize it was metal-binding. You open your eyes and stare into the darkness. Sometimes you can hear voices that sound like angry demons, but you can't speak or even make a tiny noise. Sometimes while you're lying there your body feels like it's floating away.

Before my funeral, I was getting metal-bound a lot, but it stopped after my funeral, probably because I became a ghost myself. I ate and slept, I wrote emails to Kayla sometimes, but inside I knew I was dead, even if my parents didn't notice.

Kayla had figured it out, though. We'd pretty much stopped trying to live-chat because of the time difference. Tokyo is sixteen hours ahead, which means that it's daytime in Sunnyvale when it's nighttime here, and since I was living in a two-room apartment the size of Kayla's walk-in closet, it wasn't like I could get up in the middle of the night and turn

---

72. *kanashibari* (金縛り)—lit. "metal" + "binding." A kind of sleep paralysis.

on the computer and start chatting, so mostly me and Kayla were using email, which was a drag. I hate email. It's so slow. On email it's never now. It's always then, which is why it's so easy to get lazy and let your inbox fill up. Not that mine did anymore, but it used to. Right after we left Sunnyvale, everyone was emailing me like crazy and asking me all about Japan, but it took Dad a couple of weeks to get an Internet connection set up, and by then all my friends were involved with their summer vacations, and then school started, and they all kind of dropped me.

I tried to have a blog for a while. My eighth-grade teacher in Sunnyvale, Mr. Ames, told me to start one so that I could write about my impressions and observations and all the interesting stuff that was going to happen to me in Japan. My dad helped me set it up before we moved, and I named it *The Future Is Nao!* because I thought that my future in Japan was going to be one big American-style adventure. How dumb was that?

Actually, it wasn't completely dumb. At the time I was feeling hopeful, which now seems kind of sad and brave. It wasn't my fault that I didn't understand what was happening. My parents weren't exactly being up front with me about our reasons for leaving California. They were saving face and pretending everything was fine, and I didn't actually know we were broke and unemployed until we got here. When I saw the crappiness of our Tokyo apartment, it started to sink in, and I realized that I wasn't going to have any big adventures, and that basically there was nothing I could post on the blog that didn't make me feel like a total loser. My parents were pathetic, my school life was horrible, the future sucked. What could I write about?

"Me and my mom enjoy soaking in the hot tub at the public bath."

"Today at school I had a hilarious time playing kakurenbo with my new friends. Kakurenbo is like hide-and-seek, and I got to be It!"

"My dad applied for a new job as a track inspector on the Chuo Rapid Express Line."

I kept it up for a while, making these cheerful, chirpy postings to *The Future Is Nao!* but I felt like a total fraud. And then one day, a couple of months after I got back, I happened to check my statistics, and I realized that the whole time since I started my blog, only twelve people had ever visited it, for about a minute each, and I hadn't had a single hit in weeks, so that's when I stopped. There's nothing sadder than cyberspace when you're floating around out there, all alone, talking to yourself.

Anyway, it didn't take Kayla long to figure out that maybe I was becoming a pathetic loser and it wasn't cool to be my friend anymore. I swear, even on the Internet people can give off a virtual smell that other people pick up on, although I don't see how that's possible. It's not like a real smell, with molecules and pheromone receptors and so on, but it's just as obvious as the stink of fear in your armpits or the vibe you give off when you're poor and don't have any confidence or nice stuff. Maybe it's something in the way your pixels start behaving, but I was definitely starting to have it, and Kayla was sniffing it out from the opposite side of the ocean.

Kayla is totally the opposite of me. She is superconfident and has lots of money and isn't afraid of anything. Even though we haven't corresponded for a while, and I don't even know what high school she's at, I'm 100 percent sure she is the most popular girl there, because she is the type who will always be the most popular girl wherever she is. Being number two isn't even a possibility for Kayla, and that was the case even in second grade, when she picked me out and allowed me to sit next to her at lunch. Now that I think about it, it was a miracle she was ever my friend.

Things started to go seriously wrong after I emailed her a picture of me in my new school uniform, and she texted me back this superironic email, which went something like, "OMG i luv yr uni4m! its soo manga! u gotta snd me 1 so i cn go as a jap skoolgrl 4 haloween!"

To her, my new life was just cosplay,[73] but to me it was totally real. We had nothing in common anymore. We couldn't talk about fashion, or the kids at school, or who was a loser, or what teachers we liked or hated. Our chats and emails went nowhere, and then she started taking longer and longer to write me back, and after a while she just kind of

---

73. cosplay (コスプレ)—dressing up in costume, especially of favorite manga and anime characters Japanese slang, from "costume" + "play."

disappeared. When I tried to find her online and she was always off even when I knew she had to be on, I realized she had blocked me from her buddy list.

I still wrote her emails sometimes, but she almost never answered. After my funeral, I tried to share my feelings honestly about how much I hated my school and being in Japan, and how much I missed Sunnyvale, but I still couldn't tell her about the ijime or my dad or our whole situation, so to be perfectly fair, she didn't have a whole lot to go on. I can't blame her for not understanding. When she finally wrote me back, it was this tight, bright, cheerful little email that made it clear that she really wasn't interested in me if I was going to be a whiner.

After that, I forwarded her the "Tragic and Untimely Death of Transfer Student Yasutani" link to my funeral. Mostly it was to shock her, but like I said, I was kind of proud of my stats too. I waited and waited for an email to show up from her, but it never did. Maybe this is what it's like when you die. Your inbox stays empty. At first, you just think nobody's answering, so you check your SENT box to make sure your outgoing mail is okay, and then you check your ISP to make sure your account is still active, and eventually you have to conclude that you're dead.

So, you can see why I was feeling like a ghost. Ghosts in Japan are pretty intense. They're not the kind you get in America that go around dressed in sheets. In Japan, they wear white kimonos, and they have long black hair hanging in their faces, and also they have no feet. Usually they're women who are righteously pissed off because someone has done something horrible to them. Sometimes, if a person has been treated really badly, she can even become an ikisudama,[74] and her soul leaves her sleeping body and wanders around the city at night doing tatari[75] and wreaking vengeance on all her shitty classmates who have tortured her by sitting on their chests. That was my goal for the summer vacation. To become a living ghost.

It wasn't so crazy as it sounds, because haunting runs in our family,

---

74. *ikisudama* (生き魑魅)—a living ghost.
75. *tatari* (祟り)—spirit attacks.

although I was only beginning to understand this. My dad had started
acting even weirder. He stayed in the house during the daylight hours,
but every night, after me and Mom were asleep, he would go out walking.
Why was he sneaking out at night? Was he haunting someone, too? Was
he turning into a vampire or a werewolf? Was he having an affair?

I used to lie awake in bed, metal-bound and unable to move, picturing
him in his scuffed plastic slippers, shuffling along the dark and winding
shitamachi[76] streets, through the wards of Arakawa and Senju and the
old neighborhoods of Asakusa and Sumida, where the working-class
people live, which are empty at that time of night because everybody's
sleeping. After a couple of hours, he'd end up at a small park on the banks
of the Sumida River, where a low concrete wall keeps the kids from falling
into the water, and I could imagine him leaning against the wall, watching
the garbage drift by. Sometimes I could even hear him talking to the feral
cats, who slunk in and out of the garbage and the shadows. Sometimes
he'd sit on a swing, smoking the last of his Short Hopes, trying to figure
out how to make a living body sink. When he ran out of cigarettes, he
would walk back again and sneak into the apartment. I always heard the
clank of the bolt on the front door, because I waited for it. The bolt in
the latch broke the spell. I couldn't move until I heard it.

## 2.

One night, maybe a week after my funeral, I had this crazy cosmic dream
about one of my classmates, the sukeban named Reiko. I think I told you
about her earlier. She was supersmart and popular, like a Japanese Kayla.
She never bullied me directly, and what I mean by that is she never
pinched me or pushed me or poked me with her scissors. She didn't have
to, because all the other kids were lining up to do it for her. All she had
to do was look at me with this expression, like she'd just caught sight of
something loathsome or half-dead, and her friends would jump in to do
the job. Most of the time she didn't even bother to watch, but sometimes

76. *shitamachi* (下町)—downtown.

I caught her eye as she turned unhurriedly away, and her eye was the cruelest and most empty thing in the whole world.

And that's what was in my dream, her cruel eye, only it was gigantic, as big as the sky. I don't know how to explain it. It was nighttime, and I was in the schoolyard, metal-bound and lying on my back in a box, but maybe it was a coffin. My classmates were looking down at me, and their eyes were glittering like those of animals in a dark forest. Then they started blinking, and one by one they disappeared, until all that was left was Reiko's eye, staring down at me and emitting this laser beam of light, only it was the opposite of light, because it was cold and black and empty. It grew bigger and bigger, pressing down, enveloping me and the whole world and everything in it, and the only way I could save the world was to plunge my little kitchen knife right into the pupil, and so I did. I closed my eyes and stuck the knife into the dark hole, over and over again, until I felt something tear. A thick liquid as cold as nitrogen started oozing slowly from the rip in the membrane. I knew I had to move but I couldn't, and then the sac burst, and the icy liquid came pouring out, and it was too late, but even though I knew I would die from the cold, the world would be safe from Reiko's horrible eye, thanks to me.

The clank of the bolt in the door woke me up. It was Dad, returning from his nighttime walk, and I realized I had been dreaming. It was July, and hot and humid even at night, but I was shivering so hard my teeth chattered. I hugged myself tightly, pretending to be asleep until I heard my dad come into the bedroom and crawl into his futon. I waited, listening until I could hear the sound of him sleeping. Mom slept silently, but Dad always made little pu-pu-pu noises with his lips as the air went in and out. When I was sure he was asleep, I got up and stood by his side and watched him for a while. The LEDs from the computer in the corner emitted just enough light for me to see the little opening between his lips, and I wondered what would happen if I pressed my thumb against the hole, but I didn't. I tiptoed into the living room instead.

His jacket was hanging on a hook in the hallway, so I slipped it on over my shoulders. It was a jacket he'd gotten from his company in Sunnyvale, a cool, high-quality jacket like they give you on film shoots, made of Gore-Tex with the IT company logo on the back, and he used to wear it with a hoodie underneath, in the days when he was cool and high-quality, too, before the polyester suits. The smooth, silky lining was still warm from his body, but against my bare skin it made me shiver even more. I hugged it around me until I felt warm again.

I went over to the doors that led onto the tiny balcony and pressed my forehead against the glass. There wasn't a great view from the balcony. The neighborhood we lived in wasn't like the image most people have of Tokyo, all slick and modern like Shinjuku or Shibuya, with skyscrapers made of concrete and glass. This neighborhood was more like a slum, old and crowded, with small, ugly apartment buildings made of water-stained cement all crammed together on this crooked street. From our balcony, all I could see was walls and roofs and old roof tiles, meeting at weird angles. It looked like a jagged patchwork of disconnected planes and surfaces, strung together by phone lines and electrical cables that hung down everywhere in loops.

During the day you could see patches of sky, but at night it was all dark except for the pools of light from the streetlamps, and the headlights from taxis slicing up the buildings, and the wobbling beams from bicycles tickling the walls. It was quiet, too. You could hear rats scrabbling in the garbage, and the shrill laughter of the hostesses stumbling home from the bars with their dates. And I remember that everything was especially dark and still that night, as though the entire city had felt the horror of my dream and was metal-bound. Nothing moved, not even the shadow of a cat.

My dream was so real. Maybe the next day I would hear news that Reiko had hanged herself or was murdered in the night. Would it be my fault? And that's when it occurred to me that maybe I had become an ikisudama, and if I hadn't, maybe I could. It would take practice, but summer vacation had just started, and what else did I have to do with my free time? The more I thought about this idea, the more excited I got, and all the next day and the following days, I listened for news of Reiko. I even cornered Daisuke to find out if he'd seen her. Daisuke and Reiko went to the same cram school during summer break. Most of my classmates went to a cram school in order to get ready for the high school entrance exams that you take in the second half of ninth grade. Basically, if you're a Japanese kid, these exams decide your whole future, and the rest of your life, and even your afterlife. What I mean is:

where you go to high school decides where you'll go to
    university,
which decides what company you'll work for,
which decides how much money you'll make,
which decides who you'll marry,
which decides what kind of kids you'll have and how you'll raise
    them,
and where you'll live and where you'll die,
and whether your kids will have enough money to give you a
    classy funeral with high-quality Buddhist priests to perform
    the proper funeral rites to ensure that you make it into the
    Pure Land,
and if not, whether you'll become a hungry vengeful ghost, fated
    to haunt the living on account of all your unsatisfied desires,
which all started because you flunked your entrance exams and
    didn't get into a good high school.

So you can see why, if you care about your life, cram school is pretty important. Most of my classmates and their families took it very seriously, but my parents couldn't afford the extra tuition, and I didn't care, either. I mean, I was already a vengeful ghost, haunting the living, so it didn't really matter if I lived or died, and anyway, I grew up in Sunnyvale, so I have a different attitude about these kinds of things. In my heart, I'm American, and I believe I have a free will and can take charge of my own destiny.

But to get back to Daisuke, I cornered him by the soft drink machines again and pushed him around a little, and then I asked him about Reiko, if anything had happened to her or if she'd been absent, but he told me she was okay and that she'd been in school every day.

I questioned him harder. Perhaps she'd caught a summer cold, I suggested, pinching his arm, or developed an allergy? A runny nose? Watery eyes?

Yes, he told me, now that I mentioned it, she had come to class wearing an eyepatch a couple of days earlier.

My heart pretty much stopped and I released him. When? I demanded, and he counted back on his fingers.

Monday, he said. She wore the patch to school on Monday. I caught my breath. I'd had the dream on Sunday night.

I pinned him up against the soft drink machine and made him tell me the whole story. He said that at first everyone thought she had a sty, which was gross, and one boy even dared to call her a baikin. But Reiko just laughed gorgeously and told him it was cosplay, and she was being Jubei-chan the Samurai Girl in *The Secret of the Lovely Eyepatch*. And it was true, Daisuke told me, that her eyepatch was pink and shaped like a heart, just like Jubei-chan's lovely eyepatch, so when Reiko turned on the boy who'd called her a bacteria and actually beat the crap out of him herself, everyone just figured that the eyepatch had given her the magical and awesome fighting powers of the Samurai Girl. It was the first time anyone had actually seen her fight, so it really was kind of supernatural, Daisuke said.

He told me all this in a whispered rush of words in the alley.

"And you believed her?" I said. "You're so stupid!"

He shrugged his thin shoulders. He wasn't wearing his school uniform, and under the T-shirt, his bones stuck out, making him appear even more insectlike. He truly was pathetic.

"She looks like Jubei-chan," he mumbled. "She's got a nice shape."

It was true that Reiko had a well-developed figure for her age, and this made me mad, plus the fact that Daisuke was saying it gave me the total creeps. It meant that even an insect like him was capable of noticing things like breasts and legs, and so I knocked him down and pinched him a little harder than I needed to, which just goes to show that you don't need a Lovely Eyepatch to have the power to make somebody cry. But when I finished and let him go and was walking back to our apartment, I thought back on what Daisuke had said and felt suddenly overwhelmed by what I'd done. I mean, what do you think was under the eyepatch? At least a sty and possibly even a real injury, which meant that I'd actually accomplished my goal. While I was asleep and dreaming, my spirit had actually escaped from my body to wreak revenge upon my enemy. I was a living ghost, and this realization filled me with an awesome sense of power.

## 3.

A week after I became a living ghost, old Jiko showed up at our apartment. I was in the living room reading manga, and Dad was on the balcony, sitting on a pail next to the washing machine and smoking cigarettes, when the doorbell rang. We usually just ignored the doorbell, since we didn't have any friends and it was usually bill collectors or someone from the neighborhood association, but then it rang a second time and then a third time. I looked out at Dad on the balcony to see what he wanted me to do. He was standing there with a panicky look in his eye, his head half hidden in the wet laundry, with the socks and underpants dangling down around his ears like a wig.

Ever since he had gotten arrested for falling on the train tracks, he was getting more and more paranoid, which is pretty typical of hikikomori people. Like I said, except for the midnight walking, the only place he would go was to the public bath, and that was only after dark and only when he was starting to smell bad and Mom threatened to make him sleep on the balcony if he didn't. He probably would have preferred that.

He liked the balcony because he could smoke, and it was the only fresh air he got during the daylight. He sat there on an upturned bucket and read the old manga that I found in the recycling bins, and when he finished smoking, he came inside and read his Great Minds of Western Philosophy and folded his paper insects. He almost never worked on his computer or surfed the Internet anymore, which was totally weird, because that's all he used to do in Sunnyvale. Now he hardly ever went online, except sometimes to send an email to one of his former Sunnyvale friends. I was starting to think he might be an ikisudama, too, or he might have been possessed by a monster, maybe a suiko, a giant kappa[77] from the dark waters of the Sumida River, who had sucked out his blood and returned his empty body to shore. That's what it seemed like.

Anyway, after the doorbell rang four or five times, I got up to answer. I thought it was probably the landlord's wife or the gas man or the census taker or a pair of shiny-faced Mormons on a mission. Why is it that Mormons on missions always look like identical twins, even when they're different heights or races? That's what I was wondering, which is why I wasn't particularly surprised when I opened the door and saw these two dudes wearing identical light grey pajamas and straw sun hats. They weren't Mormons, but they looked enough like clones and their faces were shiny bright, so I figured they were from some other brand of religion that traveled in pairs. Why is it that religious types all have shiny bright faces? Maybe not all of them, but the inspired ones, like the light of God is just leaking through their pores.

Judging by their brilliance, these two dudes were really inspired even though they were also really short. One of them was old and the other one was young, and I could see that under their hats they were both bald. Their pajamas looked like the kind that the monks wore at the temple on the way to school, so I figured they were Buddhists who had come here begging for money, and if that was the case, boy, were they at the wrong apartment.

They bowed deeply. I kind of nodded back at them. I'm not very polite in the Japanese sense.

"Ojama itashimasu. Tadaima otōsan wa irasshaimasuka?" the young one asked, which means something like "Please pardon this intrusion. Would your honorable father happen to be present at this moment in time?"

---

77. *kappa* (河童)—lit. "river child." Mischievous mythological creature, like a water sprite, with webbed hands and feet, and scaly green, blue, or yellow reptilian skin. It has a carapace like a turtle's shell, and a bowl-shaped indentation on the top of its head, which it must keep filled with water. If the bowl spills, the kappa becomes paralyzed.

"Yo, Dad!" I yelled back into the room, in English. "There's two bald midgets in pajamas here to see you."

I used to get into this thing where I refused to speak Japanese to my mom and dad. I did it a lot when we were at home, and sometimes when we were out shopping or at the sento. Japanese people are pretty lame when it comes to understanding spoken English, so you can make snarky remarks and they usually don't know what you're saying. It used to drive my mom crazy when I did this. I wasn't being really mean, just a little mean, and my dad usually thought it was funny. I liked to make him laugh.

Anyway, this time, the younger monk started to giggle, and I was like, Oh shit, I'm so busted, so I turned around to take another look, and just as it was occurring to me these monks were actually females, the old one slipped by me, taking off her zori[78] and hat and crossing the living room, and the next instant she was out on the balcony next to my dad, who by that time was leaning over the edge, looking down at the sidewalk below like he was going to jump. The old monk lady climbed up on the bucket and leaned way over the railing beside him like a little kid about to do a flip on a jungle gym. She was as small as a kid, too, and maybe that's why Dad reacted the way he did, flinging his arm out to block her from falling. It was an instinctive daddy reflex, the same move that had probably saved me from breaking my neck or hurtling to my death a hundred times, only I'd never seen it in action from this angle before, and I was amazed at its speed and precision. Too bad he didn't have an arm like that he could use to save himself.

The old monk lady said something then. I don't know what it was, but Dad turned and stared at her, and then he stepped back from the railing and sat down on the bucket and put his face in his hands. I could feel myself starting to panic. I don't know if your dad cries a lot, but in my opinion, it's a pretty gruesome thing to have to watch, and I'd sat through it once after the Chuo Rapid Express Incident and I didn't particularly want to repeat the experience, especially in front of strangers. The old lady didn't seem to notice, though, or maybe she was just giving

---

78. *zōri* (草履)—flip-flops.

him some space. She continued to look out over the street below, and when she'd seen enough, she turned and straightened her pajamas and started patting my dad on the head in the slightly absentminded way you pat a little kid when he's fallen and hurt himself but not too badly. As she patted him, she looked carefully around with her slow, cloudy eyes, moving over all the surfaces of the apartment, the overflowing ashtray and stacks of clothes and computer parts and manga and dishes in the sink, until finally they came to rest on me.

"Nao-chan desu ne?"[79] she said. "Ohisashiburi."[80]

I looked away, not wanting to give it up too quick that I was Naoko.

"Ookiku natta ne,"[81] she said.

I really hate it when people point out how big I am, and this old lady was a midget, so what did she know, and besides, who did she think she was, anyway, barging into people's apartments and making personal remarks?

And just as I was thinking this, Dad shifted on his bucket and raised his head and sighed, Obaachama . . . ,[82] and I was like, Duh! because of course she was his dear old granny. He was staring up at her, and now I saw that he wasn't crying exactly, but his cheeks were all flushed, the way they got sometimes when he drank, although I happened to know that there hadn't been any booze in the apartment since the Chuo Rapid Express Incident, so you had to figure it was embarrassment or shame. And honestly, I felt ashamed, too, looking at his blotchy face and his reddened eyes with the crusty bits stuck to the lashes, and the big pieces of dandruff lodged in his greasy hair. He was wearing a sleeveless undershirt that was stained and yellowed around the armpits, and when he stood up, I noticed for the first time how his spine had taken on the shape of an S curve, with his belly slumped out, and his chest caved in, and his shoulders humped all over.

I heard a noise behind me.

---

79. *Nao-chan desu ne?*—You are dear Nao, aren't you?

80. *Ohisashiburi*—It's been a very long time.

81. *Ookiku natta ne*—You've gotten very big, haven't you?

82. *Obāchama*—honorific but intimate way of addressing grandmother.

"Shitsurei itashimasu . . ."[83] It was the younger one. I'd forgotten all about her, but now I turned around and looked at her more carefully and saw that she was not as young as I first thought. It's hard to tell with bald ladies. The only other bald lady I'd ever seen close up was Kayla's mom in Sunnyvale, who had breast cancer, and all her hair fell out, even her eyebrows, but her face wasn't shiny bright like these two. It was dry and dull like construction paper.

They each had a small rolling suitcase, which the younger one was trying to drag into the genkan, but all the floor space was taken up with our shoes and slippers, so she had to roll the bags on top. Then she slipped off her sandals and stepped into the apartment next to me and bowed.

"Please, come in?" she asked, in careful English, as though I was the guest arriving from America. I just nodded, because honestly I felt like a foreigner living in that stupid Tokyo apartment with these strange people who said they were my parents but I barely even knew anymore.

In Sunnyvale, I used to think I was adopted. Some of my friends there were Chinese girls adopted by ordinary California parents, but I felt like the opposite, like an ordinary California girl adopted by Japanese parents, who were strange and different, but tolerable, because in Sunnyvale it was kind of special to be Japanese. The other moms would ask my mom to teach them how to make sushi and flower arrangements, and the dads treated my dad like a small pet that they could take for a run on the golf course and teach new tricks. He was always coming home with brand-new high-end appliances, like Weber grills and composting bins, that my mom didn't know how to use, but it was cool. We had a lifestyle. Here we were barely managing a life.

**4.**

Here's a thought: If I were a Christian, you would be my God.

Don't you see? Because the way I talk to you is the way I think some Christian people talk to God. I don't mean praying exactly, because when

---

83. *Shitsurei itashimasu*—Pardon me for intruding.

you pray you usually want something, or at least that's what Kayla said. She used to pray for stuff and then tell her parents exactly what she'd prayed for, and usually she got what she wanted. They were probably trying to make her believe in God, but I happen to know it wasn't working.

Anyway, I don't really think you're God or expect you to grant me wishes or anything. I just appreciate it that I can talk to you and you're willing to listen. But I better hurry up or I'll never catch up to where I'm supposed to be.

Jiko and my dad were still talking out on the balcony, and the younger one, whose name was Muji, helped me make tea, and then we all made polite Japanese-style conversation about nothing until Mom came home, and I could tell by how surprised she pretended to be to find two Buddhist nuns in her living room that she'd arranged the whole thing, plus she'd gone shopping and gotten take-out sushi for five people, and a big bottle of beer, too, which she never would have done for just me and Dad.

After we ate I escaped into the bedroom and went online to check the stats for "The Tragic and Untimely Death of Transfer Student Nao Yasutani," but the number of hits hadn't increased at all since the last time I'd checked, which was depressing, considering that I'd only been dead for less than two weeks and was already being forgotten. There's nothing sadder than cyberspace . . . but I've already said this.

In the living room I could hear them talking about Jiko's temple needing repairs, and how the danka[84] couldn't pay for the work because all the young people were moving to the cities, and the old people left behind didn't have a lot of money. And then the conversation drifted and their voices dropped, and I heard the words *ijime* and *homushiku*[85] and *nyuugakushiken*,[86] so I put on my headphones so I wouldn't have to listen. The only thing lonelier than cyberspace is being a teenage kid, sitting in the bedroom you have to share with your loser parents because they're too poor to rent a big-enough apartment so you can have a room

---

84. *danka* (檀家)—temple parishioners.
85. *homushiku* (ホームシック)—from English *homesick*.
86. *nyuugakushiken* (入学試験)—entrance exams.

of your own, and then listening to them discussing your so-called problems. I turned up the volume and played a few tracks of some old Nick Drake that Dad had given me, which I was really getting into. "Time Has Told Me." "Day Is Done." Nick Drake's songs are so sad. He committed suicide, too. Finally, I couldn't take it anymore, so I gave up and went out to the living room.

They were still sitting around the table where we'd eaten, only now in place of the sushi there was a small plate of fluorescent green mochi[87] covered with some kind of paste, and a bag of green wasabi peas, and they were drinking beer from little glasses in front of them, all except Mom, who was having tea, and Dad, who had taken his beer out on the balcony so he could smoke.

"Where'd that come from?" I asked in English, pointing at the mochi. I don't particularly care for sweet rice balls, but I like to be asked, you know?

Mom frowned and shook her head, which meant I wasn't supposed to point, and I wasn't supposed to talk in English. "Chotto, osuwari . . . ," she said, patting the cushion, which meant I was supposed to sit down next to her like her trained chihuahua. Her eyes were rimmed with red, as though she'd been crying.

I backed away. "I'm going to bed," I told her, still in English. "I was studying. I'm tired."

They were all watching me, Dad from the balcony, Jiko through half-closed eyes from across the table, and Muji, kneeling at my feet, her face bright red from the beer and even shinier now, if that was possible. She picked up the plate of green rice balls and held it toward me.

"Please! This one is Zunda-mochi. It is some special soybean foods from Sendai regional place."

I nodded politely like I understood what she was talking about, which I didn't. She waited, but when I didn't take her up on the offer, she put down the plate and picked up the bottle of beer, pouring the last of it into old Jiko's glass. She was really into serving.

---

87. *mochi* (もち)—sweet rice balls.

"Jiko Sensei is enjoy very much," she said. "Sensei is strong for drinking o-saké, but I am very weak." She giggled and burped, and then put her hand over her mouth. Her eyes grew round, and her eyeballs rolled like roasted chestnuts in their sockets. I dropped down onto the cushion next to her. She was kind of wacky, and I was beginning to like her. Across the table, Jiko had fallen asleep.

"Nao-chan," Mom said. She was speaking in Japanese, and her voice was bright and phony. "Your great-granny Jiko had a wonderful idea. She has kindly invited you to spend your whole summer vacation at her temple in Miyagi . . ."[88]

Unbelievable! It was a total setup. They were all watching me carefully now, my mom, Muji and Jiko, who I sensed could see me through her closed eyelids, and my dad, who was still on the balcony, pretending to be all nonchalant and casual. I hate it when grown-ups watch you like that. Makes you feel like a malfunctioning cyborg. Not quite human.

"It's so exciting, don't you think?" Mom chirped on. "It's very beautiful on the coastline, and so much cooler than the city. And the ocean is right there for swimming, too. Won't that be fun? I told her you'd love to go . . ."

Sometimes when grown-ups are talking to you, and you stare back at them, they start to look like they're inside one of those old-fashioned TV sets, the kind with the thick dark glass, and you can see their mouths moving, only the exact words get drowned out in a lot of staticky white noise so you can barely understand them, which didn't matter because I wasn't listening anyway. Mom was talking on and on like a breakfast TV show host, and Muji was burping and trilling like a drunken sparrow, and Jiko was pretending to sleep, and Dad was exhaling clouds of cigarette smoke into my clean underpants that were still hanging on the laundry line because in all the excitement I'd forgotten to take them down, but none of this mattered because I was deep inside my mind, which is where I go when things get too intense. It was just a matter of waiting them out, and I'm good at waiting, since I get so much practice at school. One

---

88. Miyagi . . . Sendai is in Miyagi!

trick when you're waiting is to pretend you're underwater, or better yet, frozen in an iceberg, and if you really focus hard on it, you can even see the way your face would look if it was frozen under ice, all blue and dim and ripply.

Dad came back into the room from the balcony and sat down across from me.

I still couldn't hear his voice through the static, but I could read his lips. You. Should. Go.

This was not what I wanted. I made my pulse slow. I refrained from breathing. I stopped moving completely.

Jiko opened her eyes then. I don't know how I knew this, because I wasn't even looking at her, but I could feel a kind of energy coming from her side of the table, and so when she leaned forward and placed her old hand on top of mine, I wasn't surprised. Her hand was so light, like a tickle of warm breath, and my skin began to tingle. She kept watching me, and even though I couldn't see her, I could feel her melting the ice, pulling my mind toward hers through the coldness. I could feel my pulse returning and my blood beginning to flow again. I blinked. Dad was still talking.

"It's just for a little while," he was saying. "Your mom's got it all set up. They have special doctors who can teach me to cope with my problems. By the time you get back, I'll be all better. Really. I promise. You believe me, don't you?"

Now that I could hear him and see how tired and sad he looked, the rest of me melted.

"But . . ." I said, trying to find my voice. Of course I didn't believe him, but what could I say? So I just nodded, and that was that.

# Ruth

## I.

Miyagi prefecture is located in the Tōhoku region, in the northeastern part of Japan. This area was one of the last pieces of tribal land to be taken from the indigenous Emishi, descendants of the Jōmon people, who had lived there from prehistoric times until they were defeated by the Japanese Imperial Army in the eighth century. The Miyagi coastline was also one of the areas hardest hit by the 2011 earthquake and tsunami. Old Jiko's temple was located somewhere along this stretch of coastline.

Fukushima prefecture, located just south of Miyagi, was also part of the ancestral lands of the Emishi. Now Fukushima is the prefectural home to the Fukushima Daiichi Nuclear Power Station. The name Fukushima means "Happy Island." Before the tsunami caused the catastrophic meltdown of the nuclear power station, people believed Fukushima to be a happy place, and the banners stretched across the main streets of the nearby towns reflected this sense of optimism.

### NUCLEAR POWER IS ENERGY
### FOR A BRIGHTER FUTURE!

### THE CORRECT UNDERSTANDING OF
### NUCLEAR POWER LEADS TO A BETTER LIFE!

* * *

## 2.

The island where Ruth and Oliver lived was named for a famous Spanish conquistador, who overthrew the Aztec empire. Although he never made it up as far north as his eponymous isle, his men did, which is why the inlets and sounds of coastal British Columbia are scattered with the names of famous Spanish mass murderers. But in spite of its sanguinary name, theirs was a relatively benign and happy little isle. For two months out of the year, it was a gemlike paradise, overflowing with carefree summer people with yachts and vacation homes, and happy hippie farmers raising organic veggies and bare-bottomed babies. There were yoga teachers, body workers, and healers in every modality, drummers and shamans and gurus galore. For two months out of the year, the sun shone.

But when the tourists and the summer people left, the blue skies clouded over and the island bared its teeth, revealing its churlish side. The days grew short and the nights grew long, and for the next ten months, it rained. The locals who lived there year-round liked it this way.

Their island had a nickname, too, a shadow name that was rarely spoken: the Island of the Dead. Some said the name referred to the bloody intertribal wars, or the smallpox epidemic of 1862 that killed off most of the indigenous Coast Salish population. Other people said no, that the island had always been a tribal burial ground, laced with hidden caves known only to the elders, where they entombed their dead. Still others insisted that the nickname had nothing to do with native lore at all, pointing instead to the aging population of retired white people, who'd come to spend their twilight years on the island, turning it into a kind of gated community, like Boca Raton only with lousy weather and no amenities.

Ruth liked the nickname. It had a certain gravitas, and she'd brought her own mother here to die, after all. Her father's ashes, too, she'd brought with her in a box, and after her mother's cremation, she had interred both parents' remains in the tiny Whaletown Cemetery, in a plot with ample room for her and Oliver, too. When she mentioned this to her New York friends, they told her that rural island living was making her tedious and morbid, but she disagreed. It was true that compared with Manhattan, there wasn't a lot of excitement on their island, but how much excitement did you need if you were dead?

**3.**

The Whaletown Post Office was a tiny wooden shack, clinging to a rocky outcrop on the edge of Whaletown Bay. The mail came over by ferry three times a week, and so three times a week, a representative from each of the households in Whaletown got into a car or a truck or an SUV and drove to the post office to pick up the mail. This reckless squandering of fossil fuel drove Oliver crazy.

"Why can't we have a mailperson?" he would rant. "One person, one vehicle, cuts carbon, delivers all the mail. How hard is that?"

He refused to drive and always rode his bicycle, and when it was Ruth's turn to go, he insisted that she walk, even in the rain. Even when a storm was brewing. It was three miles.

"You need the exercise," he told her.

The wind was beginning to pick up and the rain was coming down hard. Ruth was soaked when she got to the post office. She fished her soggy outgoing letters from her pocket and asked for stamps.

"Sou'easter," Dora said, from behind her wicket. "Wind's picking up. Hydro'll be out by dinner. Good night for writing, eh?"

Dora was the postmistress, a small and deceptively mild-looking woman with a sharp tongue and a reputation for reducing her neighbors to tears for failing to pick up their mail in a timely fashion, or arriving too early before she'd finished the sorting, or simply addressing their envelopes in an illegible hand. She was a retired nurse and she wrote poetry, which she submitted in an orderly rotation to journals and literary magazines. She claimed not to like many people, especially newcomers, but she took an immediate shine to Ruth, and this was only in part due to Ruth's subscription to *The New Yorker*, which, as Muriel had informed her one day when she was complaining about the magazine's slow arrival, Dora was in the habit of siphoning off and taking home to read before delivering, belatedly, into Ruth's mailbox. No, the real reason Dora liked Ruth was because Ruth was a fellow writer, a colleague, and whenever she came to the post office, Dora would give her an update on the status of her poetic submissions. Over the years Ruth had known her, Dora had had several poems accepted for publication in small magazines, but *The New Yorker* remained her holy grail, and she was steadfastly refusing to buy a subscription until they published one of her poems. This arrangement worked as long as Ruth kept her subscription current, and Dora didn't seem to mind. She maintained that collecting rejection slips was a noble and necessary part of a poet's practice, and she was proud of her collection. She was papering her outhouse with them, as she'd heard Charles Bukowski had done with his. Ruth admired her for admiring Bukowski.

Dora knew everything about everyone, and not only because she read people's mail. She had an abiding and unapologetic interest in the business of others, and she was kind, too, in spite of her curmudgeonly affect. She used to dote on Ruth's mother and brought her garish bouquets of variegated roses from her garden. She always asked after her neighbors' health and had a stock of morphine left over from her nursing days which she would dispense when needed, when someone was injured, or dying, or needed to put down a favorite pet. She knitted layettes for the pregnant single moms on the island, and on Halloween she made cookies that looked like severed fingers for the children, with almonds for the fingernails and red icing for blood. The post office was like the village well. People lingered there, and it was where you went if you needed information.

Ruth had overcome her aversion to telephones twice that week, the first time to call Callie, and the second time to call Benoit LeBec. She had left a message, but when he didn't call back, she figured Dora would know why.

"Oh, they've been away," Dora said, hammering the stamps onto Ruth's damp letters with the Whaletown postage canceler. She was very proud of this canceler. It was the oldest continuously used canceler in Canada, dating back to 1892, when Whaletown got its first post office.

"They've gone to Montreal for the niece's wedding. They'll be back tomorrow in time for the A meeting. What do you want with Benoit?"

Ruth took a step back from the wicket and pretended to fumble for change. She felt sure there were clues in the mysterious French composition book that would help her track down the Yasutanis, and she wanted to get it translated as soon as she could, but she wasn't about to tell Dora this. If Muriel was bad about spreading gossip, Dora was worse. As the postmistress, she saw it as part of her job description, and Ruth was feeling oddly protective of Nao and her diary and didn't want everyone to know. There were other people in the small mailroom, too, lingering in front of their postal boxes, pretending to read their mail—an oyster farmer named Blake, a retired schoolteacher from Moose Jaw named Chandini, a young hippie chick who used to be called Karen until she changed her name to Purity. No one was talking and everyone seemed to be waiting for her to answer.

"Oh," Ruth said, handing Dora the money for the stamps. "Nothing, really. Just needed some help with a translation."

"You mean that French notebook you found on the beach?" Dora asked.

Damn, Ruth thought. Muriel. There were no secrets on this goddamn island.

"A diary, too, eh?" Dora asked. "And some letters?"

There was no point in denying it. The others in the mailroom had moved closer to the wicket.

"Did it really drift over from Japan?" Blake, the oyster farmer, asked.

"Possibly," Ruth said. "It's hard to tell."

"Don't you think you should turn it in?" Chandini asked. She was a thin, nervous woman with stringy blond hair, who used to teach math.

"Why?" Ruth asked, squeezing past her and opening her postal box. "Turn it in to whom?"

"Fish and Wildlife?" Chandini said. "The RCMP? I don't know about you, but if stuff's washing up from Japan, I'm worrying about radiation."

Purity's eyes grew wide. "Oh wow," she said. "Nuclear fallout. That would totally suck . . ."

"It'll be a problem for the oysters," Blake said.

156

"Salmon, too," Chandini said. "All our food."

"Totally," Purity said, exhaling and drawing the word out long. "'Cause it's in the air, too, and then it rains down and gets into the aquifer and like the whole, entire food chain, and then into our bodies and stuff."

Dora gave her a look.

"What?" the girl said. "I don't want to get cancer and have deformed babies . . ."

Blake stroked his beard and then shoved his hands into his front pockets. His eyes were bright. "Heard there was a watch, too," he said. "A real kamikaze watch."

Ruth flipped through her mail and tried to ignore him.

"I'm interested in that historical stuff," he said. "You think I could see it sometime?"

It was hopeless. Ruth held out her arm, and Blake and Chandini crowded in to see, but Purity backed away.

"That could be contaminated, too, right?" she said.

"Probably," Ruth said. "Now that you mention it, I'm sure it is."

Dora leaned out through the wicket. "Let me see."

Ruth unbuckled the sky soldier watch and handed it to her, dangling it by the strap. Outside, the wind was starting to howl. Dora took the watch and whistled.

"Neat," she said, strapping it to her wrist.

"Aren't you scared of getting poisoned?" the girl asked.

"Honey," Dora said. "I survived breast cancer. A little more radiation isn't going to hurt." She admired the watch, then unbuckled it and handed it back to Ruth. "Here you go," she said, and then she winked. "Good material, eh? How's the new book coming?"

### 4.

Ruth got a lift back home with Blake in his truck, which smelled of oysters and the sea. He let her off at the foot of her road, and she ran up the long driveway to the house through the pounding rain. Gusts of wind lashed the tall firs, and the boughs of the maple trees groaned.

Maple was a brittle wood. A few years back, another neighbor died when a large branch fell on his head in a storm. Widow-makers, they called them. She kept an eye out overhead as she ran. Where was the crow, she wondered.

The power had already flickered on and off, Oliver told her, so she ran upstairs to check her email. She was trying to be less ob-com about email, but more than forty-eight hours had passed since she'd written to Professor Leistiko and she was impatient for a reply. She quickly scanned her inbox. No word from the professor. What now?

She could hear Oliver in the basement, fiddling with the old gas generator, trying to fire it up. They had a system for outages, which relied on a working generator to power several hundred meters of tangled extension cord that snaked up from the basement, delivering electricity to the freezer and refrigerator before coiling through the kitchen and up the stairs to their offices. The cords were hazardous. You could easily trip on a loop and fall down the stairs. If the generator didn't work, they resorted to candles and flashlights and oil lamps. The generator was noisy. Without it, and without the ambient presence of appliances—the hum and whir of fans and pumps and transformers—the silence in the house was profound. Ruth liked the silence. The problem was you couldn't power a computer or surf the Web with lamp oil.

The Internet was their primary portal onto the world, and a portal that was always slamming shut. Their access was supplied through a 3G cellular network, but the large telecommunications corporation that provided their so-called service was notorious for selling more bandwidth than it could provide. The closest tower was on the next island over, and their connection was achingly slow. In the summer, the problem was compounded by oversubscription and traffic. In the winter, it was the storms. The signal had to travel across miles of churning oceans, through densely saturated air, and then, once it reached their shores, thread its way through the tall, wind-lashed treetops.

But at least for now the Internet was working and she wanted to take advantage of it before the power went out. She consulted her growing list of keywords and clues. She typed in *The Future Is Nao!* The search engine returned a few unhelpful hits: some videos of an autonomous programmable humanoid French robot named NAO; a report by the National Audit Office about the importance of safeguarding the future health of the honeybee.

"Did you mean to search for: The Future Is <u>Now</u>?" the engine asked her, helpfully.

She did not. She knew once the power went out she might not be able to get back on for a few days, so she moved on to the next term on her list. She had already made several exhaustive searches for *Jiko Yasutani*, *anarchist*, *feminist*, *novelist*, *Buddhist*, *Zen*, *nun*, *Taishō*, and even *Modern Woman*, in various combinations. Now she added her new word, gleaned from her reading the night before. *Miyagi*. She sat back and waited.

The room had grown dark, and the glow of the computer screen on her face was the only source of illumination, a small square of light on an island in a storm. She felt small, too. She took off her glasses, closed her eyes and rubbed them.

Outside, the wind was really howling, whipping the rain in circles and making the whole house shudder and groan. Storms on the island were primeval, hurling everything backward in time. She thought of her second nun dream, recalled the old woman's black sleeve as she beckoned, the way her thick-lensed glasses made a smear of the world. The storm did the same. And then that ghastly sensation of being cast back into nothingness, nonbeing, of reaching for her face and not finding it. The dream was so vivid, so horrifying, and yet after it was over she had slept so soundly, woken only by the nun's light touch and the sound of a chuckle and a snap.

She opened her eyes and put her glasses back on. The wheel on her browser was still spinning, which was not a good sign. The signal wasn't getting through, and with winds like this, it was just a matter of time before a tree fell across a power line. She was on the verge of refreshing the page and restarting the search when a bright flash lit up the monitor, or was it lightning in the sky outside? She couldn't tell, but a moment later, the screen went black, plunging the room into darkness. So much for that.

She got to her feet and groped her way around the desk for the headlamp she kept on the shelf nearby, but just as she found it and was about to turn it on, the hard drive whirred and the screen flickered, and the blackness was illuminated by the glowing browser page with the results of the search she'd been running. Odd. She went back to the desk and glanced at the page.

It wasn't much. One item, that was all, but it looked promising. Her heart beat faster as she read:

> Results 1—1 of 1 for "Yasutani Jiko" and "Zen" and
> "nun" and "novelist" and "Taishō" and "Miyagi"

She sat back down, pulled her chair in closer, and quickly followed the link, which took her to the Web page of an online archive of scholarly journals. Access to the archive was restricted to academic libraries and other subscribing institutions. Without a subscription, only the article's title, a short preview, and the publishing information were available. But it was a start.

The title of the article was "Japanese Shishōsetsu and the Instability of the Female 'I.'" Ruth leaned in and read the preview, which started with a quote:

> *"Shōsetsu and Shishōsetsu—they are both very strange. You see, there is no God in the Japanese tradition, no monolithic ordering authority in narrative—and that makes all the difference."*
>
> —Irokawa Budai

> The term *shishōsetsu*, and the more formal *watakushi shōsetsu*, refer to a genre of Japanese autobiographical fiction, commonly translated into English as "I-novel." *Shishōsetsu* flourished during the brief period of sociopolitical liberalization of the Taishō Democracy (1912–1926), and its strong resonances continue to influence literature in Japan today. Much has been

said about the form, about its "confessional" style, its "transparency" of text, and the "sincerity" and "authenticity" of its authorial voice. Too, it has been cited in the blogosphere with reference to issues of truthfulness and fabrication, highlighting the tension between self-revelatory, self-concealing, and self-effacing acts.

It has often been noted that the pioneers of *shishōsetsu* were predominantly male. Early women writers of *shishōsetsu* have been largely ignored, perhaps because, in truth, there were far fewer published women writers then, as now, and perhaps because, as Edward Fowler, in his exemplary study of the genre, *The Rhetoric of Confession*, has written, "the energies of prominent female writers working in the 1910s and 1920s were devoted as much to feminist causes as they were to literary production."[89]

This assertion, that a devotion to feminist causes has deleterious effects on literary production, is one I will address, arguing that at least one early woman author of *shishōsetsu* used the form in a way that was groundbreaking, energetic, and radical. For her, and for the women writers who came after, this literary praxis was nothing short of revolutionary.

This writer is unknown in the West. Born in Miyagi prefecture, she moved to Tokyo, where she became involved with radical left-wing politics. She worked with various feminist groups, including Seitosha[90] and

89. *The Rhetoric of Confession* by Edward Fowler. See Bibliography.
90. Bluestocking Society.

Sekirankai,[91] and she wrote, in addition to political essays, articles, and poems, a single unusual and groundbreaking I-novel, entitled, simply, *I-I*.[92]

In 1945, after the death of her son, who was a student soldier and conscripted pilot in the *tokkōtai* (the Japanese Special Forces, also known as the kamikaze), she took the tonsure and vows of a Zen Buddhist nun.

Her name is Yasutani Jiko, a woman pioneer of the "I-novel," who has erased herself from . . .

<read more . . .>

There it was, the name, Yasutani Jiko, on the computer screen. Ruth hadn't realized just how keenly she'd been waiting for this corroboration from the outside world that the nun of her dreams existed, and that Nao and her diary were real and therefore traceable.

She leaned forward, intent on delving into the deeper strata of information to which the preview was just the gate. She wanted to learn everything she could about Jiko Yasutani, and not just the scraps of information that surfaced so haphazardly in her great-granddaughter's diary. She felt a keen and sudden sense of kinship with this woman from another time and place, engaged in self-revelatory, self-concealing, and self-effacing acts. She was hoping the article itself might contain a translation of at least parts of the I-novel, which she now very much wanted to read. It would be useful to get a taste of Jiko's voice and the style of her writing.

---

91. Red Wave Society.
92. This title seems to come from a poem by Yosano Akiko, titled "Rambling Thoughts," which was published in the first issue of *Seito* magazine. See Appendix C.

She clicked the **<read more . . .>** link at the end of the preview and sat back to wait. The page started to load but then was replaced by a "Server Not Found" message. Annoying. She hit the BACK button, but got the same results. The screen flickered. Quickly, she tried to navigate back and recover the original Web page, but before it could refresh, the screen went blank and the power went out, quietly this time, but definitively. She sat back in her chair. She wanted to weep. From deep in the basement she could hear Oliver cursing, as the smell of gas wafted up the stairs. The generator was broken again, and the engine flooded. Sometimes it took days for BC Hydro to fix the lines and restore service. Until then, they would remain in the dark.

## 5.

The next morning the power was still out, but the wind had died down and the rain had stopped. After breakfast, Oliver wanted to go collect seaweed for the garden. Seaweed made excellent fertilizer, and the beaches would be covered after a big southeaster. They loaded up the pickup with pitchforks and tarps and drove across the island. As they approached the turnoff to Jap Ranch, they started to see the cars, parked along the road.

"Lots of people with the same idea," Oliver said.

It seemed odd, though. There were so many cars. More like a rave or a funeral than a few gardeners gathering seaweed after a storm. "I wonder if there's something else going on," Ruth said. "This sucks. We're going to have to park and walk."

They unloaded the truck and headed toward the beach. As they crested the embankment, they spotted Muriel. She was standing on the edge, looking out toward the shoreline. When she saw Ruth and Oliver approaching, she pointed. "Look," she said.

The beach was dotted with people. This in itself was odd. Even in the summer, at the height of tourist season, the island's beaches were never crowded and you could spend the whole day swimming and picnicking and hunting for relics, and never see more than a handful of others doing the same.

Today, though, people were spread out at intervals all up and down the beach. Some had tarps and were collecting seaweed, but others were just walking, eyes fixed ahead, trudging mechanically back and forth. Ruth recognized a few of them. Others she'd never seen.

"What's going on?" Oliver asked.

"Scavengers," Muriel said. "Looking for stuff from Japan. On *my* turf."

She was twirling the end of her long grey braid around her finger, a sure sign she was agitated. She'd gotten there early, but before long the others had started showing up.

"Amateurs," she scoffed. "It's all your fault, you know. Word got out about your freezer bag, and then someone at the post office started talking about all the money that washed up in Japan."

Ruth remembered reading the story on the *Japan Times* website. Most of the tsunami victims had been old people, who'd kept their savings hidden at home, tucked into closets, or under the tatami floor. When their homes were swept away by the wave, their savings went with them and were sucked out to sea. A few months later, the sea started spitting its spoils back up again, and safes and strongboxes started washing up on the beaches. They were filled with cash and other valuables, but the authorities found it impossible to identify many of the owners, or even to determine if they were alive. Still, the people who found them continued to turn them in.

Ruth scanned the beach. The scavengers looked possessed, like zombies, the walking dead. It was ghoulish. "Has anyone found anything yet?"

"Not that I know of. Honestly, your freezer bag was a fluke, and my toothpaste tube, too. We're too far inland. I keep telling them. The real pickings are on the open ocean, up and down the outer coast. We're not going to see too much good stuff drifting this far back. But our friends here don't seem to listen."

"If they find money, they can't just keep it," Ruth said.

"Why not?"

"Because it belongs to the victims. It was their life savings. Most of them were old . . ."

"Just like here," Muriel said.

"Except nobody here has safes," Oliver said. "Never mind any money."

Muriel laughed. "You're right. The only thing that would wash up here is bags of pot."

Ruth felt her face flush. "It's not a joke," she said. "You're horrible. Both of you."

Muriel raised her eyebrows. "Well, the rule of beachcombing is finders keepers. It's a pretty ancient rule. Besides, I see you're still wearing the watch . . ."

Ruth glared at her and shouldered her pitchfork. "I'm trying to find the owner," she said. "I intend to keep trying until I do." She turned to Oliver. "Are we going to get seaweed or what?"

She headed off toward the beach. From the corner of her eye, she saw Oliver shrug and give Muriel a sheepish smile, which annoyed her even more. She stopped and turned back to Muriel. "And this is not my fault. You didn't have to tell the whole fucking island about my freezer bag."

Muriel nodded. Strands of loose grey hair blew across her face, and she brushed them away. "I know. I'm sorry. Actually, I only told a couple of people, but you know how it is. I couldn't help myself. It's exciting. I live for garbage."

# Nao

## 1.

Old Jiko really loves my dad, in spite of all his problems, and he really loves her, too. She used to say he was her favorite grandson. Of course, he's her only grandson, so she was just being amusing, and anyway I happen to know that nuns aren't supposed to have favorites among sentient beings. Now that I think of it, maybe she loves him because all his problems give her so much to pray about, and when you're as old as she is, and your body is like enough already, you need some pretty powerful reasons to stay alive.

She lives in a tiny temple on the side of a mountain near the coastline, but even though the temple is really small, it still has two names: Hiyuzan Jigenji.[93] The little buildings cling to the steep mountainside and are surrounded by a forest of sugi[94] and bamboo. You can't believe how many steps you have to climb to get to it, and in the summer when it's hot, you think you're going to die of heatstroke or something. This is a place that truly could use an elevator, but Zen Buddhists aren't big on modern conveniences. I swear, getting there is traveling backward about a thousand years in time.

My dad agreed to take me on the train to Sendai, which was a really big deal for him to leave our apartment during the daylight. I could tell

---

93. Searched Google for these names but found nothing. Nao wrote the names in *romaji*, so I knew only the pronunciation. Tried guessing the kanji but wasn't able to come up with a combination that could be located on a map. See Appendix D for some possible kanji for *Hiyuzan* and *Jigenji*, as well as more information about Japanese temple nomenclature.
94. Cryptomeria.

it was stressing him out, and I wasn't helping. I'd gotten this childish idea that we could make a little detour to Tokyo Disneyland so I could shake hands with Mickey-chan. I knew this was unrealistic because Tokyo Disneyland isn't exactly on the way to Sendai, and besides my dad freaks out in crowds, but I really wanted to go. Mickey-chan is from California, and so am I, and I thought maybe he was homesick, too, so I begged and begged my dad, but of course he said no. In a normal family situation, I think my request would have been reasonable. I mean, a couple of hours hanging out with Mickey-chan isn't such a huge price to pay for getting rid of your kid for the whole summer. But our family did not have a normal situation, and I knew Dad was not a Disneylandish kind of person. If I'd made the effort, I could have forgiven him for this, and we might have even enjoyed the train ride together, but instead I sulked and made him feel guilty and miserable the whole way, which honestly didn't make me feel so great, either. In the end, he promised we could go to Disneyland when he came to pick me up and take me home, which cheered me up a little, knowing that at least he intended to survive my summer vacation.

He was really nervous at Tokyo Station, and we had to stand for about an hour underneath the departure board until he could figure out which bullet train we needed to take and what tickets we needed to buy, and then we went to the wrong platform and ended up on the Yamabiko Semi-Local, instead of the Komachi Express, but it didn't matter to him if we stopped at every single station on the way, and actually it didn't matter to me, either. So we rode through the suburbs of Tokyo, which go on and on forever, and then through some industrial areas, past factories with smokestacks and ugly clusters of apartment towers and shopping centers and parking lots, and the train doors kept opening and closing, and people kept getting on and off, and the train ladies in their little uniforms pushed their bento carts up and down the aisles, calling out, "Obento wa ikaga desu ka? Ocha wa ikaga desu ka?"[95] Suddenly I was hungry for a sweet grilled-eel bento, but just as I was about to ask my

---

95. *Obento wa ikaga desu ka? Ocha wa ikaga desu ka?*—Would you care for a lunchbox? Would you care for some tea?

dad I remembered that the last time we'd eaten sweet grilled eel was when we were celebrating his new "job," and when I remembered his lie, my fondness for eel disappeared and I ordered an egg sandwich instead. I ate it, staring out the train window at my reflected face as it skimmed across the landscape like a ghost. Everything outside was dirty grey or cement-colored, but from time to time tiny green rice paddies shone like priceless emeralds, and as we got farther from Tokyo, the world became greener.

When we finally got to Sendai, we transferred to a local train that took us to the town nearest Jiko's temple, and then we humped my wheelie bag onto an ancient bus filled with really old people to take us to her village. On the way out of town, we passed some minimarts and coffee shops and an elementary school, but honestly, there wasn't much else: a fish-processing plant, a pachinko parlor, a gas station, a 7-Eleven, an auto repair shop, a roadside shrine, a bunch of small fields. But then, as we drove, the buildings got farther and farther apart until finally I knew we were in the countryside because it was beautiful. It was like being in an anime movie, with our little bus chugging up and down, winding around the mountains and hugging the cliffs. Below, I could see the waves crashing up on these crazy rocks, and sometimes we would pass a small beach, like a sandy pocket tucked into the rock face.

I used to love going to the northern coast of California, to Marin or Sonoma or Humboldt, and this had a little of the same feeling, only here in Japan everything was greener with a lot more trees and none of the designer homes. Instead, there were these little fishing villages along the coastline, with clusters of boats and nets and oyster rafts bobbing on the waves, and racks of fish hung up to dry like laundry next to the houses. The bus made about a hundred thousand million stops that didn't look like bus stops at all, with just a bench on the side of the road, or a rusty round sign on a post, or sometimes a little hutlike thing that looked like where you'd keep the filtration unit for your hot tub if you lived in California. There were lots of steep hilly places in California, too, but I didn't get the feeling that there were many hot tubs or pools or celebrity mansions around here where Jiko lived.

168

There weren't many passengers left on the bus by then, just me and my dad and a couple of really ancient ladies with tenugui[96] on their heads, and spines that were bent over at right angles. The driver was a skinny young guy with great posture. He wore a smart little cap and white cotton driving gloves, and every time he pulled over onto the shoulder of the road to stop, he bowed and touched the brim of his cap with his gloved fingers. Very kakkoii.[97]

The road was getting narrower and steeper, winding upward along the side of a deep gulch, when, once again, the driver stopped. I looked out the window at the mountainside, covered with trees, expecting to see at least a bench or a rusty signpost, but this time there was nothing, just the mountain on one side and the cliff dropping into the valley on the other. But then I looked toward the mountain again, and this time I saw an ancient stone gate, hidden in the trees and covered with dripping moss, and stone steps that led through the gate and disappeared into the darkness.

The bus door opened and the driver touched his cap. The old ladies looked at us expectantly.

"We have arrived, Naoko," Dad said. "Let us disembark?" For some reason, he was speaking English. His English had never gotten real fluent, but when he spoke it, he sounded so polite and intellectual, you'd never think he was the kind of guy who'd lose all his money at the OTB and lie down on a train track.

"*Here?*" I squeaked. I thought he was kidding.

But he was already on his feet, and the old ladies were grinning and bobbing their heads and saying things to us like they already knew who we were, and my dad was bobbing back at them as I tried to maneuver my wheelie bag down the narrow aisle toward the steps. The driver was watching in the mirror, and when he saw me struggling, he jumped up to help, taking the handle of the bag from me. I climbed down and stood at the side of the road, looking over the gravelly edge of the sheer cliff

---

96. *tenugui* (手ぬぐい)—a thin cotton cloth used as a head covering or a towel.
97. *kakkoii* (かっこいい)—stylish, cool, snappy.

that dropped into the valley and led to the sea. I could just catch a glimpse of the water, sparkling and shimmering like some kind of promise of salvation.

I turned away from the ocean and looked up at the mountainside. No building in sight. Stone gate. Moss. Dark steps leading up to nowhere. My dad had gotten off the bus and was standing next to me, and the driver was handing him my wheelie bag. I looked at the stone steps and started to put it together. I tugged on Dad's sleeve.

"Dad . . . ?"

But the driver was bowing to my dad, and he was bowing back, and now the driver was climbing into his seat and closing the doors and putting the bus in gear, and the tires were crunching in the gravel, and soon me and Dad were alone on the side of the road, watching the taillights of the little bus twinkle and wink as it disappeared around a bend.

Suddenly everything was really quiet, and all we could hear was the wind in the bamboo, which sounded like ghosts. I looked at my wheelie bag in the dirt next to me. It was pink, with a picture of Hello Kitty on it. It looked very lonely and sad.

It hit me then. My dad was going to leave me here. First we were going to drag my wheelie bag up the mountain and then he was going to leave me up there with some really old nun who happened to be my great-grandmother who I barely knew, for my whole summer vacation.

"Okay!" Dad said, striding across the road toward the steep steps. "Come on! Let's challenge!"

My throat got tight and the inside of my nose started to prickle. Out of habit, I clenched my teeth to make the tears stop like I did when the kids kicked me during kagome lynch at school, but then I thought, Screw it, I *should* cry. I should howl and scream and throw a huge tantrum, because maybe if I acted pathetic enough, my dad would feel sorry for me and take me home again. I sniffled a little and then looked to see if he'd noticed, but he wasn't paying any attention to me at all. He was staring at the mountainside, and his face was all lit up like he was excited but didn't want to show it. I hadn't seen him look excited since we lived in Sunnyvale and one of his programmer buddies invited him to go fly-fishing. It was nice to see, so I followed him across the road, dragging my wheelie bag over to the first step and up with a bump behind me.

*Ku . . . lunk.*

The bag was heavy, filled with all the books I was supposed to study over the summer holiday. *Ku . . . lunk.* Ancient Japanese history. *Ku . . . lunk.* Japanese current affairs. *Ku . . . lunk.* Japanese morality and ethics. *Ku . . . lunk. Ku . . . lunk.* I was already sweating and about to give up, but Dad was ahead and waiting for me, staring eagerly up at the steps.

"When I was young boy, I could run all the way to the top," he said. "Maybe I still can do . . ."

But instead he came over and took the handle of the suitcase from me, and this time I let him. He'd tried to help me with it on the subway, and then on the train, and again when we got onto the bus, but I'd told him to forget it. I mean, you can picture it—a middle-aged guy with greasy hair and bloodshot eyes and slumping shoulders, dragging a pink Hello Kitty wheelie bag behind him. Would you let your dad out in public like that? It's just too pathetic. He would have looked like a total *hentai*, which he isn't. He's my dad. Maybe he is a *hikikomori*, but I love him. I couldn't have stood it to see people staring at him.

Here, though, nobody was around to see.

"Come on, Nao-chan!" he said. "Let's go!"

Hauling the bag behind him, he charged up the steps, and I followed, and together we climbed. The higher we went, the denser the forest got. Hotter, too. Sweat dripped from my armpits. The stone was slick, not with rain but with humidity that made everything feel slimy, even the air. It reminded me of the fog in San Francisco, only fog chills the air, and this felt hotter than Kayla's mom's sauna, even with the breeze. Moss crept over everything like a rash, oozing through the cracks in the stone. Dad kept climbing. One step. Another. Higher and higher. We were an army of two, him and me, marching up a mountain, but not to conquer it. We were in retreat, a defeated army on the run.

A shrill, high insect whine pierced the air like a vibrating wire, growing louder and louder. *Me—, meee—, meeeeeee—* I couldn't remember when the sound had started. Maybe it had always been there, inside my head, only now someone had turned up the volume until my skull was throbbing like an amplifier, blasting the whine out into the world. I put my fingers in my ears to see if I could tell whether the noise was inside or out, and Dad saw me.

"Me-me-zemi,"[98] he said. He stopped and took out his handkerchief and used it to wipe the sweat from his eyes, and then he ran it around his neck like he was toweling off at the gym, back when he used to go to a gym, in Sunnyvale. "It is only male ones who cry," he said.

I wanted to ask him why, but I didn't want to hear his answer. He tied the handkerchief around his neck and stood there, looking up into the forest canopy with a strange faraway expression on his face.

"I remember this sound from when I was little boy," he said. "It's natsu no oto."[99]

He was standing a few steps above me, and he looked really tall, and as I watched him, I thought maybe I could understand his faraway expression. Maybe it was happiness. I think my dad was happy.

For me the happy sounds of summer were far away, too. They were the Good Humor truck and the lifeguard's whistle and the automatic sprinkler, spitting in the twilight, and the sizzle of ribs on somebody's Weber, and the clatter of lemonade and ice in tall frosted glasses. It was lawn mowers and weed whackers and kids playing Marco Polo in somebody's pool. My throat clogged up like an old drain with these happy memories.

*Ku . . . lunk. Ku . . . lunk.* Dad was climbing again. I wiped my eyes and followed. What else could I do? I had to look on the bright side and try to make the best of things. At least Dad hadn't hijacked the bus and driven it off the side of the mountain. At least he was still here with me, and maybe—maybe he wouldn't leave. Maybe I could do something to make him stay. Because even though he'd promised to come back and pick me up at the end of my vacation and take me to Disneyland, what

---

98. *minminzemi*? (ミンミンゼミ)—*Oncotympana maculaticollis*, a kind of Japanese cicada.

99. *natsu no oto* (夏の音)—the sound of summer.

if he didn't? What if the special doctors couldn't fix him? Or what if, on the way home, the urge to die got too intense, and he suddenly had to hurl himself onto the tracks in front of the oncoming Disneyland Super Express? He didn't really care about shaking hands with Mickey-chan after all. How much can you really trust the promise of a suicidal father?

## 2.

We climbed up and up, higher and higher, not saying much, each of us busy with our own thoughts. Dad was thinking about his boyhood, and I was thinking about Dad. Do all kids have to worry about their parents' mental health? The way society is set up, parents are supposed to be the grown-up ones and look after the kids, but a lot of times it's the other way around. Honestly, I haven't met very many adults in my life who I could call really grown up, but maybe that's because I lived in California, where all my friends' parents seemed really immature. They were all in therapy, and always going to personal growth seminars and human potential retreats, and they'd come back with these crazy new theories and diets and vitamins and visualizations and rituals and relationship skills that they tried to inflict on their kids in order to build their self-esteem. Being Japanese, my parents didn't really care about self-esteem, and they weren't into all that psychological stuff, even if my dad's friend was a psychology professor. He was nice enough, an old guy who got famous in the 1960s for doing drugs and getting high and calling it research, so you have to figure he was a bit of a flake and probably pretty immature, too. Not that I'm an expert. I'm just a teenager so I'm not supposed to know very much, but in my humble opinion, old Jiko is the only real grown-up I've ever met, and maybe it's because she's a nun, and maybe it's because she's been alive on earth for a really long time. Do you have to live to be a hundred to really grow up? I should ask her this.

Hang on . . .

"Hey, Jiko, how old do you have to be before you're really grown up? Not just your body, but your mind?"

That's what I just texted to her. I'll let you know what she says when she gets back to me. It might be a while because it's zazen time up at the temple. Zazen is the kind of meditating they do there, which seems different from the California kind, or at least it seems different to me, but what do I know? Like I said, I'm just a kid.

Where was I? Oh, right, we were climbing up the steps to the temple. Damn, I really suck at this. Sometimes I think I must have ADD or something. Maybe I caught it in California. Everybody in California has ADD, and they all take meds for it, and they're constantly changing their prescriptions and tweaking their dosages. I used to feel really out of it because I didn't have any meds I could talk about on account of my parents being Japanese and not knowing a whole lot about psychology, so I just kept my mouth shut. But one day at lunch someone noticed that I never took any pills, and Kayla had to jump in and cover for me. Actually, she outed me, but in the nicest way. She gave the kid this really superior look and said, "Nao doesn't *need* medication. She's *Japanese*." I know that sounds kind of harsh, but the way she said it made it sound like being Japanese was a good thing, like being healthy or something, and the kid just shrugged his shoulders and shut up.

It was nice of Kayla to stick up for me, but actually I don't think I'm so healthy at all. I'm pretty sure I have all kinds of syndromes including ADD and ADHD and PTS and manic depression, as well as the suicidal tendencies that run in my family. Jiko said that zazen meditation probably wouldn't cure me of all my syndromes and tendencies but it would teach me how not to be so obsessed with them. I don't know how effective it is, but ever since she taught me how, I try to do it every day—well, maybe every other day, or a couple times a week—and now that I think about it, even though I still intend to kill myself, I actually haven't, yet, and if I'm still alive and not dead, maybe it's working.

### 3.

Where was I? Oh, the temple. Right. So, we're climbing up the steps, and finally we see the main temple gate, which is at the very top, and it looks enormous, like the mouth of some kind of horrible stone monster, all mossy and dripping ferns and looming over us, about to fall on our heads and crush us to death. Exactly the kind of place that ghosts would like to lurk around and haunt the living. Later I realized it's not such a huge gate like they have at really important temples. It's actually pretty small, but from below, that first day, it looked gigantic. I was tired after hauling myself up all those steps, and hallucinating from the heat, and hypnotized by the sound of the cicadas and the *ku . . . lunk, ku . . . lunk* of my wheelie bag wheels, and I was pretty terrified, too, thinking about how my dad was going to abandon me here in this spooky place. The moment I saw the gate I had a strong thought to turn around and throw myself headfirst down the steep stone steps or just let myself free-fall backward into the pillowy softness of eternity, and it wouldn't matter if I bumped and bounced like a cabbage all the way down until I hit bottom and then rolled out to sea, because at least I'd be safe and dead.

My legs were trembling. My kneecaps felt like the moon jellies that my mom used to watch at the City Aquarium, and just then something brushed against my bare shin, and all my hairs stood up on end like I'd been zapped with a taser. *Tatari!*[100] I thought, and I jumped and screeched, and my dad started to laugh, and in the next Buddhist moment I found myself looking down into the moss green eyes of a tiny white-and-black cat. He gave me a quick sideways glance, then turned his back and started doing that thing that cats do, winding himself through my legs, arching his spine and sticking his tail straight up in the air while extending his front paws, not toward me but away from me, offering me his butt to scratch as well as a nice view of his puckered asshole and his giant furry white balls. Basically, when a cat offers you his butt to scratch you have to do it and not mind the rest of the package. His fur was soft and hot, and just then the temple bell began to ring with a sound so deep it made the green blades of the bamboo leaves shiver, and Dad, who was standing just beneath the stone gate, looked toward the temple and whispered to no one,

"Tadaima . . ."

which is what you say when you come home.

---

100. *Tatari!*—Spirit attack!

The tiny cat with the giant balls flicked his tail and led us up the walkway, and just then I heard the sound of sandals slapping against stone, and Muji came running out to meet us. She was wearing her grey pajamas, and she had a white towel tied around her head. She scooped up the cat and tucked him under her arm and then, pressing her palms together without dropping the cat, she bowed deeply from the waist.

"Okaerinasaimase, dannasama!" she said, which is more or less exactly what the French maids say in Fifi's Lonely Apron when their masters come home.

That night they had a party to welcome us, although it wasn't much of a party really since it was just me and Dad and Jiko and Muji and a couple of old ladies from the danka who hung around and helped out with the cooking and the garden and the religious services and stuff. Before we ate, we all took turns having a bath in the ofuro,[101] which was fed by the sulfurous hot springs. Dad went first because he's the man, which would be so totally un-PC in Sunnyvale but here nobody even thinks about it. When he came out, all pink and damp, he was in yukata[102] with geta[103] on his feet and a small terry cloth towel on his head. Muji offered him a glass of beer, and he looked happier than I'd ever seen him in my life, even in Sunnyvale, and my hope returned that maybe he would decide to stay with us at the temple for the summer. I just knew this would be way better for him than seeing a bunch of psychological doctors. It wasn't like he had a job or anything, and Mom was busy at work and could take care of herself, and the Great Minds of Western Philosophy had gotten on fine without him for thousands of years and could probably wait until the end of August.

We were sitting on the wooden veranda, overlooking the little temple garden, and an evening wind was rustling the bamboo leaves. I was watching him enjoy his beer, and was just about to ask him if he would stay, when Jiko got to her feet and said, "Nattchan, issho ni

---

101. *ofuro* (お風呂)—bathtub.
102. *yukata* (浴衣)—cotton kimono.
103. *geta* (下駄)—wooden sandals.

ofuro ni hairou ka?"[104] It would have been rude to refuse, so I got up and followed her to the bath, hoping that her cataracts would keep her from seeing all the little scars and bruises and cigarette burns, which were mostly healed up except for some that would probably never go away.

Outside the bathhouse, there was a little altar, and Jiko lit a candle and a stick of incense, and then she did three full-body bows, getting all the way down on her knees and touching her forehead to the floor, which took her a while, but not as long as you might imagine, given that she's so old. She made me do it, too, and I felt really clumsy and dumb, but she didn't seem to notice, because the whole time she was mumbling a little Japanese prayer under her breath that in English would go something like this:

> As I bathe myself
> I pray with all beings
> that we can purify body and mind
> and clean ourselves inside and out.

It seemed like a big deal to go through, but then I thought about the bar hostesses at the sento and how clean and pure they seemed after their baths. It wasn't like they were leading wholesome lifestyles or anything, so maybe Jiko's prayer was really working for them.

The bathhouse is basically a big wooden box with a smaller wooden box inside. The smaller box is the soaking tub, and it gets filled with superhot water that is sulfury and steaming and smells like boiled eggs, which is to say that it takes a while to get used to. Inside the bathhouse is really dark, except for these shafts of intense sunlight that pierce through the dark air like sharp swords and fall upon your naked skin. Next to the tub are a couple of little wooden stools and some plastic basins for dipping into the bathtub to get hot water for rinsing.

---

104. *Nattchan, issho ni ofuro ni hairou ka?*—Nattchan, shall we take a bath together? (*Nattchan*—an intimate and affectionate contraction of Nao-chan.)

The way you take a bath in Japan is first you rinse your body really well with hot water to get the sweat and dirt off so you don't make the bathwater gross, and then you climb into the bathtub and soak for a while to kind of soften things up. Then you get out again and sit on your stool, and that's when you really wash yourself all over with soap and a scrubby cloth, and if you're going to shampoo your hair or shave your legs or brush your teeth or something, you can do it then. And after you're all clean, you rinse off all the soapy suds and get back into the tub to finish things off. You can really hang out there for a long time if you're into it and can stand the smell of rotten eggs.

It was pretty crowded in the bathhouse, because even though Jiko's body is really tiny, mine isn't, and next to her, I felt like a naked hippopotamus, and I was worried that I might knock her over or crush her every time I moved. But Jiko didn't even seem to notice, and after a while I calmed down about it, too. That's the thing about Jiko, one of her superpowers, is that just by being in the same room with you, she can make you feel okay about yourself. And it's not just me. She does this with everyone. I've seen her.

Maybe this is a good time to describe how old Jiko looks, because actually I was totally shocked that first day in the bath. You have to remember that she is a hundred and four years old, and if you've never hung out with an extremely old person before, well, I'm telling you, it's intense. What I mean is that even though they still have arms and legs and tits and crotches like other human beings, extremely old people look more like aliens or beings from outer space. I know that's probably not very PC to say, but it's true. They look like ET or something, ancient and young all at the same time, and the way they move, slow and careful but also kind of spastic, is like extraterrestrials, too.

And then there's the fact that because she's a nun she is totally bald. The top of her head is shiny and smooth, and so are her round cheeks, but everywhere else her skin is covered with the finest and most delicate wrinkles, like a spiderweb with dew in the morning. She probably only weighs fifty pounds, and maybe she's four feet tall and as skinny as bones, so that when you hold her arm or leg, your thumb overlaps your fingers on the other side. Her little ribs are like pencils under her skin, but her hip bones are enormous and bowl-shaped, and way out of proportion to the rest of her. You'd think her body would have lots of loose skin hanging like folds of fabric from her skeleton, but actually the skin on her body is surprisingly young-looking. I think it's because she's always been thin and never developed any excess flaps. Her breasts are small and flat, so her chest looks like a young girl's, who has just started developing, with nipples that are small and pink and fresh.

And then there's another thing, and maybe I shouldn't mention it but I will because I trust you not to take this in a perverted hentai way, which is that between her legs she's also pretty bald and you can see her sex pretty clearly, so that this part of her gives the impression of being quite young, too, until you happen to notice the few wisps of long grey hair hanging down like an old man's beard. In the shadows of the bathhouse, watching her pale, crooked body rise from the steam in the dark wooden tub, I thought she looked ghostly—part ghost, part child, part young girl, part sexy woman, and part yamamba,[105] all at once. All the ages and stages, combined into a single female time being.

I didn't have all these thoughts that first night. What I'm describing is the overall impression after a couple of weeks, watching her climb in and out of the tub and washing her back and even helping her shave her head with a razor. The bathhouse is just big enough for three people to bathe in at once if you really squeeze, and sometimes Muji came with us, and then we did our bows and little prayer together. When you live at a temple, there are all these rules, like for example, you're not supposed to talk in the bath, and mostly we didn't, but sometimes Jiko broke the rule and then it was okay for us to have a quiet conversation, which felt really peaceful.

And talking about rules, the two of them had all these crazy routines they did for every different kind of thing you can imagine, like washing their faces or brushing their teeth, or spitting out their toothpaste, or even going for a crap. I'm not kidding. They bowed and thanked the

---

105. *yamamba* (山姥)—mountain witch, mountain hag.

toilet and offered a prayer to save all beings. That one is kind of hilarious and goes like this:

> *As I go for a dump,*
> *I pray with all beings*
> *that we can remove all filth and destroy*
> *the poisons of greed, anger, and foolishness.*

At first I was like, No way am I saying that, but when you hang out with people who are always being supergrateful and appreciating things and saying thank you, in the end it kind of rubs off, and one day after I'd flushed, I turned to the toilet and said, "Thanks, toilet," and it felt pretty natural. I mean, it's the kind of thing that's okay to do if you're in a temple on the side of a mountain, but you'd better not try it in your junior high school washroom, because if your classmates catch you bowing and thanking the toilet they'll try to drown you in it. I explained this to Jiko, and she agreed it wasn't such a good idea, but that it was okay just to feel grateful sometimes, even if you don't say anything. Feeling is the important part. You don't have to make a big deal about it.

I didn't talk to Jiko about this kind of thing right away. At first I felt shy and didn't want to talk to her or anyone at all, especially after Dad snuck off early in the morning, while I was still sleeping, without even bothering to say goodbye. He left a note, which I found when I woke up. He wrote it in English and it said, "Nao-chan, you look so peaceful as Sleeping Beauty. I will return at summer's end. Please do not worry about me. Be a good girl and take care of your dear Great-Grandmother."

I tore up the note. I thought it sucked that he'd just ditched me there and split before I even had a chance to beg him to stay and make him feel guilty. He didn't say anything about his promise to take me to Disneyland, and he left without buying me an AC adapter for my Game Boy, which he'd also promised to do, so now I was stuck with nothing to play except for Tetris on my keitai, which was not so thrilling. Back then, the temple didn't even have a computer, so I couldn't email Kayla in Sunnyvale, and of course I didn't have any friends in Tokyo I could text or call. The long, hot days of my summer vacation stretched out in front of me, and I thought I was going to die of boredom.

## 4.

"Are you very angry?" old Jiko asked one night, in the bath, as I scrubbed her back.

I was moving the rough washcloth around in circles, being careful not to press too hard because by then I understood how fragile her old skin was, as thin as rice paper. At first, not realizing this, my roughness in scrubbing left dark red marks on her skin, but she never complained, and I realized I had to pay more attention, especially in the places where her bones poked out. So when she asked me if I was angry, I thought maybe I was scrubbing too hard and hurting her, and I apologized.

"No," she said. "It feels good. Don't stop."

I put some more soap on the washcloth and started moving it down the knobby curve of her spine. Like most old people, her spine was pretty stiff and twisted, but when she sat zazen, her posture was perfectly upright. She didn't say any more, and when I finished, I scooped a couple of basins of hot water from the tub and poured them over her back to rinse off the suds, and then I swiveled around so she could start on mine. We took turns like that.

I waited. Old Jiko liked to take her time, and she was really good at it because she'd been practicing for so many years, so as a result, I was always waiting for her, and you'd think that waiting would be annoying for a young person like me, but for some reason I didn't mind. It wasn't like I had anything better to do that summer. I sat there on my little wooden stool, naked and hugging my knees and shivering, not from the cold but in anticipation of the scalding heat of the water, so when, instead, I felt her fingertip touch a small scar in the middle of my back, I was startled. My body stiffened. The light was so dim, how could she see my scars with her bad eyes? I figured she couldn't, but then I felt her finger move across my skin in a pattern, hesitant, pausing here and there to connect the dots.

"You must be very angry," she said. She spoke so quietly, it was like she was talking to herself, and maybe she was. Or maybe she hadn't said anything at all, and I'd just imagined it. Either way, my throat squeezed shut and I couldn't answer, so I shook my head. I was so ashamed, but at the same time, this enormous feeling of sadness brimmed up inside me, and I had to hold my breath to stop from crying.

She didn't say anything else. She washed me gently, and for the first time I just wanted her to hurry up and finish. After we were done, I got dressed quickly and said good night and left her there. I thought I was going to throw up. I didn't want to go back to my room, so I ran halfway down the mountainside and hid in the bamboo forest until it got dark and the fireflies came out. When Muji rang the big bell at the end of her fire watch to signal the end of the day, I snuck back into the temple and crawled into bed.

The next morning I went looking for old Jiko and found her in her room. She was sitting on the floor with her back to the door, bent over her low table. She was reading. I stood in the doorway and didn't even bother to go in. "Yes," I told her. "I'm angry, so what?"

She didn't turn around but I could tell she was listening so I went on, giving her an executive summary of my crappy life.

"So what am I supposed to do? It's not like I can fix my dad's psychological problems, or the dot-com bubble, or the lousy Japanese economy, or my so-called best friend in America's betrayal of me, or getting bullied in school, or terrorism, or war, or global warming, or species extinctions, right?"

"*So desu ne,*" she said, nodding, but keeping her back to me. "It's true. You can't do anything about those things."

"So of course I feel angry," I said, angrily. "What do you expect? It was a stupid thing to ask."

"Yes," she agreed. "It was a stupid thing to ask. I see that you're angry. I don't need to ask such a stupid thing to understand that."

"So why did you ask?"

Slowly she turned herself around, pivoting on her knees, until finally she was facing me. "I asked for you," she said.

"For me?"

"So you could hear the answer."

Sometimes old Jiko talks in riddles, and maybe it's because I spent so many years in Sunnyvale that I still have some trouble with the Japanese language, but this time, I think I got her meaning. After that, I started telling her little things about what was going on in school and stuff, even when she didn't ask. And as I talked, she just listened and made her juzu beads go round and round the string, and I knew that every bead she moved was a prayer for me. It wasn't much, but at least it was something.

105才106

That's what she just texted me. That's how old she says you have to be before your mind really grows up, but since she's a hundred and four, I'm pretty sure she's joking.

---

106. *sai* (才)—years (of age).

# *Ruth*

## I.

The power was out for four days, which was relatively brief for a winter blackout. During these outages, they could keep their computers and some appliances running, but only if the generator was working, and only for as long as they had gas. When they ran out of gas, they could get more only if one of the two pumps on the island had its generator going, and if the roads had been cleared of the trees that had brought down the power lines in the first place.

When their generator stopped working, the well pump stopped, too, so they ran out of water. Indoor toilets, running hot water, baths, electric lights—after four days, these seemed like unimaginable luxuries from another age and planet.

"Welcome to the future," Oliver said. "We're on the cutting edge."

Ruth moved through the house in a darkened, kerosene-scented dream, listening to the pounding of the rain and the groan of the wind. Inside, without the constant ambient humming of fans and compressors, the house was quiet and still. At first she found herself straining to hear the twin engines of the seaplane, bringing in the hydro crew, but after a day or two of not hearing, she gave up and surrendered to the silence. She sat in front of the woodstove with the cat and read by the light of an oil lamp. She was trying to read Proust. She was trying not to read ahead in Nao's diary. Mostly she stared into the flames. Sometimes, at dusk, she stood in the doorway listening to the wolves as they moved through the mist-enshrouded forest. Their call started low, a singular uneasy moan that threaded through the trees and gathered, as one by one the pack joined in, their voices wild and raw, rising into a full-throated howl. She shivered. Oliver insisted on going running in spite of the rain, and she waited for him, worried. She'd seen cougar scratchings on trees behind their house, fresh scat on the path, wolf paw prints in the mud.

The wolf population was on the rise, and the packs had become bolder. They approached people's houses, snatched cats, and lured dogs into the forest to eat. Back in the 1970s, when the wolves killed cattle and sheep, the islanders responded with a wolf cull, hunting them down, shooting as many as they could, and stacking their bleeding carcasses like firewood in the backs of their pickups. People still remembered this, and so did the wolves, and for a while they stayed away. But now they were back. Provincial wildlife officers had come to the island to teach people what to do. Haze them, the officers said. Shout at them. Throw things. Easier said than done. Once she had looked out her office window to see Oliver in his running shorts, brandishing a huge stick and bellowing as he chased a wolf up their driveway. Oliver was running full tilt. The wolf was barely loping, taking his time.

How had she become a woman who worried about wolves and cougars eating her husband? She had no answer. Her mind just hung there, in a strange kind of limbo.

When the power came on, the house slammed back into the twenty-first century: lights blazed, appliances hummed, aquarium pumps gurgled, the taps sighed, and Ruth jumped over the cat and scrambled through the tangle of extension cords on her way upstairs to check her email. The world was restored to its place in time, and her mind was back online.

She logged on. Nothing from the professor. It had been almost a week. Was he ignoring her, or was he having a power outage, too? Did they have power outages in Palo Alto?

She checked the meteorological service. Another storm was brewing. There was no time to waste. With so many loose ends and unanswered questions, she chose the issue she thought could most easily be resolved. She launched her browser and typed in *Japanese Shishōsetsu and the Instability of the Female "I."* The Internet was fast for a change, as though it had come back refreshed from a much-needed vacation. Within seconds she had returned to the academic archives site, and there it was, the preview of the article she was reading just before the crash. She clicked the <read more> link, which took her to the website of a publication called *The Journal of Oriental Metaphysics*. Brilliant. The article was listed in the index. She clicked through, and the same preview came up, but this time there was an ORDER NOW button at the bottom of the page. She clicked it, quickly filled out the order form, and then turned her office upside down to find her credit card. On the island, she could go days without needing her wallet and often lost track of its whereabouts completely. When she finally found it, wedged behind a cushion in the corner of the armchair, she entered her credit card number. She clicked the CONFIRM PURCHASE button and waited for the download to begin, but instead a new message appeared.

> The article you have requested has been removed
> from the database and is no longer available. We
> apologize for this inconvenience. Your order has been
> canceled, and your credit card will not be charged.

*"NO!"* she cried, so loudly that Oliver heard her from his office, even with his noise-canceling headphones on. He paused and waited for a moment to see what would happen next.

### 2.

Outside in the cedar tree by the woodpile, the Jungle Crow cocked its head, listening, too. A few moments passed, maybe a minute. The windows of the house were bright again—glowing squares that floated in the darkness of the forest. Another cry, longer this time, emerged from the window closest to the woodpile.

*NOOOOOOOOOOOoo—!*

Silence followed, and then the window went dark. The crow lifted up its slick black shoulders and shuddered, which was the corvine equivalent of a shrug. It flapped its feathery wings once, twice, thrice, and then rose up from its perch, flying through the heavy cedar boughs. It circled the roof of the house. Down below, a ragged line of wolves ran silently, in single file, following a deer trail through the salal. The crow cawed out a warning, in case anyone was listening, and then flew higher, away from the little rooftop in the clearing, until finally it cleared the canopy of Douglas fir.

Soaring now above the treetops, it could see all the way to the Salish Sea and the pulp mill and the logging town of Campbell River. A cruise liner bound for Alaska was passing through the Strait of Georgia, all lit up like a birthday cake, covered with candles. Circling higher still, up and up, and the mountains of the Vancouver Island Range came into view, the Golden Hinde, the white glaciers glowing in the moonlight. On the far side stretched the open Pacific and beyond, but the crow could not fly high enough to see its way home.

# Nao

## 1.

The vibe in the Apron is definitely weird today and I don't know if I'm going to be able to write much. Babette just came over to ask me if I was interested in a date, which I'm not, but when I lied and told her I had my period, her smile froze and her face got cold and hard, and she whipped around and almost took out my eye with the lacy edge of her petticoat. I don't think she knew I was lying, but I can tell that writing in this diary is becoming a problem, and my antisocial behavior is starting to piss off Babette and the other maids. I hope they don't try to make me pay the table charge, because it's insanely expensive and I'll have to find someplace else to write. I can see their point, though. I didn't know this before, but I get it now that writers aren't exactly the life of the party, and I'm not doing my part to help create an upbeat and cheerful atmosphere around here.

Today Fifi's Lonely Apron feels even lonelier than usual.

Oh well. That's what's going on in my world. How about in yours? You doing okay?

## 2.

I don't know why I keep asking you questions. It's not like I expect you to answer, and even if you did answer, how would I know? But maybe that doesn't matter. Maybe when I ask you a question like "You doing okay?" you should just tell me, even if I can't hear you, and then I'll just sit here and imagine what you might say.

You might say, "Sure thing, Nao. I'm okay. I'm doin' just fine."

"Okay, awesome," I would say to you, and then we would smile at each other across time like we were friends, because we are friends by now, aren't we?

And because we're friends, here's something else I will share with you. It's kind of personal, but it's really helped me out a lot. It's Jiko's instructions on how to develop your superpower. I thought she was kidding when she said it. Sometimes it's hard to tell when a really, really old person is kidding or not, especially if she's a nun. We were in the temple kitchen, helping Muji with the pickle-making at the time. Jiko was washing these big white daikons, and I was cutting them up and salting them and putting them into plastic freezer bags. It was after old Jiko had found my scars, and I was telling her about my funeral and how my classmates had chanted the Heart Sutra for me, and how I became a living ghost and launched a tatari attack on Reiko and stabbed her in the eye. Jiko stood at the sink, scrubbing this big old daikon that was longer and fatter than her arm, and when I finished talking, she plunked the radish on top of a stack of other radishes that were piled next to her like firewood and said,

"Well, Nattchan, you don't have to worry. You're not really dead. Your funeral wasn't real."

I was like, Huh? I kinda already knew that.

"They chanted the wrong sutra," she explained. "You do not chant Shingyo at a funeral. You must chant Dai Hi Shin."[107]

Then, before I could say how relieved I was, she said, "Nattchan. I think it would be best for you to have some true power. I think it would be best for you to have a superpower."

She was talking in Japanese, but she used the English word, *superpower*, only when she said it, it sounded like supah-pawah. Really fast. *Supapawa*. Or more like *SUPAPAWA—!*

"Like a superhero?" I asked, using the English word, too.

"Yes," she said. "Like a *SUPAHIRO—!* With a *SUPAPAWA—!*"

---

107. *Dai Hi Shin Dharani*—Great Compassionate Mind Dharani. An esoteric mantra or invocation said to have magical powers to protect against evil spirits.

She squinted at me from behind her thick glasses. "Would you like that?"

It's weird to hear a really, really old person talk about superheroes and superpowers. Superheroes and superpowers are for young people. Did they even have them back then when Jiko was a kid? I was under the impression that in the olden days, they only had ghosts and samurai and demons and oni. Not *SUPAHIRO*—! With *SUPAPAWA*—! But I just nodded.

"Good." She slowly dried her hands and took off her apron and gave Muji some instructions about the pickles, and then she took me by the hand.

First we went to the foot-washing place, and we said a little foot-washing prayer, which goes like this:

*When I wash my feet*
*May all sentient beings*
*Attain the power of supernatural feet*
*With no hindrance to their practice.*

Of course I immediately started to think about the power of super-natural feet, and how I wanted some, but I wasn't sure if I wanted all beings to have them, too, because then what's the point? But that's the difference between me and Jiko. I'm sure she wants all beings to have supernatural feet. Anyway, we washed our feet, and then she led me into the hondo.[108]

The hondo is a special room, very dark and still. There's a big gold statue of Shaka-sama and a smaller one of Lord Monju, the Wisdom Lord,[109] at the other end, and in front of each is a place with candles, where you can offer incense. Jiko and Muji spend a lot of time doing services, but not many danka come anymore, since most of the people in this village are either old or dead, and the young ones aren't interested

108. *hondo* (本堂)—shrine room.
109. Manjushri (Sanskrit)—bodhisattva associated with wisdom and meditation.

in religion and have moved away to the cities to get jobs and lead interesting lives. It's like throwing a party that nobody shows up for, but Jiko doesn't seem to mind.

There are lots of services you have to perform, even at a tiny temple like Jiko's. Muji explained it to me once. There used to be more nuns living there, but now it's just the two of them. From time to time, a couple of younger nuns come from the main temple headquarters to check up on things and help with the bigger ceremonies. They're really nice. When old Jiko dies, one of them will probably move in to help Muji, unless the main temple decides to sell Jigenji to a real estate developer, who will probably tear down the old buildings to build a hot spring resort or a driving range. Old Jiko looks sad when they talk about this kind of thing. The little temple is falling apart and there's no money to repair it, and Muji says she wonders what's even holding it to the mountain. She worries about earthquakes and is afraid the buildings will just collapse and slide down into the gulch and wash out to sea.

Zazen usually happened insanely early, like five o'clock in the morning when I was still asleep, and also later in the evening, after dinner, when I was tired. Actually, the whole meditation thing made me a little nervous because I don't really like sitting still, but I liked the feeling in the hondo, so when Jiko showed me how to offer incense to Lord Monju, touching the stick to my head before I stuck it into the bowl of ashes, I felt excited. She did three raihai[110] bows and I did, too, just like she taught me, kneeling and touching my forehead and elbows to the floor and lifting my hands, palms up, toward the ceiling. Then when we were finished she led me to a zafu[111] and told me to sit down, and that's when she gave me the instructions.

Hmm. Wait a sec. I didn't actually ask her if I could tell you this, and now that I think about it, maybe I should ask her first.

Okay, I texted her and asked her if I could tell my friend how to do

---

110. *raihai* (礼拝)—a full prostration. Raising the palms symbolizes lifting the entire world above one's own head.

111. *zafu* (座蒲)—round black cushion for zazen.

zazen. It will probably take her a while to answer, but since the Apron's totally dead and nobody's bothering me right now, I might as well tell you about how old Jiko became a nun. She told me this story once and it's pretty sad. It was right after the war. In Japan if you say "the war," people know you mean World War II, because that was the last one that Japan fought in. In America it's different. America is constantly fighting wars all over the place, so you have to be more specific. When I lived in Sunnyvale, if you said "the war" it meant the Gulf War, and a lot of my friends at school didn't even know about World War II because it happened so long ago and there were so many other wars in between.

And here's a funny thing. Americans always call it World War II, but a lot of Japanese call it the Greater East Asian War, and actually the two countries have totally different versions of who started it and what happened. Most Americans think it was all Japan's fault, because Japan invaded China in order to steal their oil and natural resources, and America had to jump in and stop them. But a lot of Japanese believe that America started it by making all these unreasonable sanctions against Japan and cutting off oil and food, and like, ooooh, we're just a poor little island country that needs to import stuff in order to survive, etc. This theory says that America forced Japan to go to war in self-defense, and all that stuff they did in China was none of America's business to begin with. So Japan went and attacked Pearl Harbor, which a lot of Americans say was a 9/11 scenario, and then America got pissed off and declared war back. The fighting went on until America got fed up and dropped atom bombs on Japan and totally obliterated Hiroshima and Nagasaki, which most people agree was pretty harsh because they were winning by then anyway.

Around that time, old Jiko's only son, Haruki #1, was studying philosophy and French literature at Tokyo University, when he got drafted into the army. He was nineteen, just three years older than I am now. I'm sorry, but I would totally freak out if someone told me I had to go to war in three years. I'm just a kid!

Jiko said it freaked Haruki out, too, because he was a peaceful boy.

Think about it. One day you're sitting in your little boardinghouse room, warming your feet over a charcoal stove, sipping green tea and maybe reading a little *À la recherche du temps perdu*, and then a couple months later, you're in the cockpit of a suicide bomber, trying to keep the nose of your plane pointed at the side of an American battleship, knowing that in a few moments you're going to explode in a great big ball of fire and be totally annihilated. How awful is that? I can't even imagine. I mean, talk about temps perdu! I know I keep saying that I'm going to exit time and end my life, but it's a totally different thing, because it's my own choice. Being annihilated in a great big ball of fire was not Haruki #1's choice, and from what old Jiko said, besides being peaceful, he was also a cheerful, optimistic boy who actually liked being alive, which is not at all the situation with me or my dad.

And even though I said I can't imagine how awful it was, maybe I can, just a little. If you take all the feelings I felt when we were packing up to leave Sunnyvale, and when Mom found my scars in the sento, and Dad fell onto the train tracks, and my classmates tortured me to death, and then you multiply those feelings by a hundred thousand million, maybe that's a little of how my great-uncle Haruki #1 felt when he was drafted into the Special Forces and forced to become a kamikaze fighter pilot. It's the cold fish dying in your stomach feeling. You try to forget about it, but as soon as you do, the fish starts flopping around under your heart and reminds you that something truly horrible is happening.

Jiko felt like that when she learned that her only son was going to be killed in the war. I know, because I told her about the fish in my stomach, and she said she knew exactly what I was talking about, and that she had a fish, too, for many years. In fact, she said she had lots of fishes, some that were small like sardines, some that were medium-sized like carp, and other ones that were as big as a bluefin tuna, but the biggest fish of all belonged to Haruki #1, and it was more like the size of a whale. She also said that after she became a nun and renounced the world, she learned how to open up her heart so that the whale could swim away. I'm trying to learn how to do that, too.

When Jiko found out that her only son was going to die as a suicide bomber, she wanted to commit suicide, too, but she couldn't because her youngest daughter, Ema, was only fifteen years old and still needed her. So instead of committing suicide, Jiko decided to wait until Ema was a little older and could be independent, and then she would shave her head and become a nun and devote the rest of her life to teaching people how to live in peace, and that's pretty much exactly what she did.

Old Jiko says that nowadays we young Japanese people are heiwaboke.[112] I don't know how to translate it, but basically it means that we're spaced out and careless because we don't understand about war. She says we think Japan is a peaceful nation, because we were born after the war ended and peace is all we can remember, and we like it that way, but actually our whole lives are shaped by the war and the past and we should understand that.

If you ask me, Japan is not so peaceful, and most people don't really like peace anyway. I believe that in the deepest places in their hearts, people are violent and take pleasure in hurting each other. Old Jiko and I disagree on this point. She says that according to Buddhist philosophy, my point of view is a delusion and that our original nature is to be kind and good, but honestly I think she's way too optimistic. I happen to know some people, like Reiko, are truly evil, and many of the Great Minds of Western Philosophy back me up on this. But still I'm glad old Jiko believes we're basically good, because it gives me hope, even if I can't believe it myself. Maybe someday I will.

Oh, hang on. Cool. Jiko just texted me back and she said it's okay if I teach you how to do zazen as long as we're both serious and not just horsing around. I'm not horsing around, are you? I don't think you are horsing. At least, I'm going to imagine you're not, and then maybe you won't. I'll just give you the instructions, and if you don't want to do them, you can skip ahead.

112. *heiwaboke* (平和 ぼけ)—stupefied with peace; lit. "peace" + "addled."

# INSTRUCTIONS FOR ZAZEN

First of all, you have to sit down, which you're probably already doing. The traditional way is to sit on a zafu cushion on the floor with your legs crossed, but you can sit on a chair if you want to. The important thing is just to have good posture and not to slouch or lean on anything.

Now you can put your hands in your lap and kind of stack them up, so that the back of your left hand is on the palm of your right hand, and your thumb tips come around and meet on top, making a little round circle. The place where your thumbs touch should line up with your bellybutton. Jiko says this way of holding your hands is called hokkai jōin,[113] and it symbolizes the whole cosmic universe, which you are holding on your lap like a great big beautiful egg.

Next you just relax and hold really still and concentrate on your breathing. You don't have to make a big deal about it. It's not like you're thinking about breathing, but you're not <u>not</u> thinking about it either. It's kind of like when you're sitting on the beach and watching the waves lapping up on the sand or some little kids you don't know playing in the distance. You're just noticing everything that's going on, both inside you and outside you, including your breathing and the kids and the waves and the sand. And that's basically it.

It sounds pretty simple, but when I first tried to do it, I got totally distracted by all my crazy thoughts and obsessions, and then my body started to itch and it felt like there were millipedes crawling all over me. When I explained this to Jiko, she told me to count my breaths like this:

Breathe in, breathe out . . . one.

Breathe in, breathe out . . . two.

---

113. *hokkai jō-in* (法界定印)—cosmic mudra.

She said I should count like that up to ten, and when I got to ten, I could start over again at one. I'm like, no problem, Jiko! And I'm counting away, when some crazy revenge fantasy against my classmates or a nostalgic memory of Sunnyvale pops into my mind and totally hijacks my attention. As you've probably figured out by now, on account of the ADD, my mind is always chattering away like a monkey, and sometimes I can't even count to three. Can you believe it? No wonder I couldn't get into a decent high school. But the good news is that it doesn't matter if you screw up zazen. Jiko says don't even think of it as screwing up. She says it's totally natural for a person's mind to think because that's what minds are supposed to do, so when your mind wanders and gets tangled up in crazy thoughts, you don't have to freak out. It's no big deal. You just notice it's happened and drop it, like whatever, and start again from the beginning.

One, two, three, etc. That's all you have to do. It doesn't seem like such a great thing, but Jiko is sure that if you do it every day, your mind will wake up and you will develop your *SUPAPAWA—!* I've been pretty diligent so far, and once you get the hang of it, it's not so hard. What I like is that when you sit on your zafu (or even if you don't happen to have a zafu handy, for example, if you're on the train, or on your knees in the middle of a circle of kids who are punching you or getting ready to tear off your clothes . . . in other words no matter where you are) and you return your mind to zazen, it feels like coming home. Maybe this isn't a big deal for you, because you've always had a home, but for me, who never had a home except for Sunnyvale, which I lost, it's a very big deal. Zazen is better than a home. Zazen is a home that you can't ever lose, and I keep doing it because I like that feeling, and I trust old Jiko, and it wouldn't hurt for me to try to see the world a little more optimistically, like she does.

Jiko also says that to do zazen is to enter time completely.

I really like that.

Here's what old Zen Master Dōgen has to say about it:

> Think not-thinking.
> How do you think not-thinking?
> Nonthinking. This is the essential art of zazen.

I guess it doesn't make a whole lot of sense unless you just sit down and do it. I'm not saying you have to. I'm just telling you what I think.

# Ruth

### 1.

One. Two. Three. Whenever Ruth tried to sit still and count her breaths, her mind constricted like a slow, dull fist around her cosmic egg and she nodded off.

Over and over again.

How could this be her mind awakening? It felt like boredom. It felt like what happened when the power went out. But Nao was right. It also felt like home, and she wasn't sure she liked it.

### 2.

Over and over she tried. When her head fell forward, she jerked awake and started counting, but over and over she nodded off again. In the interstices between sleeping and waking, she floated in a darkened liminal state that was not quite a dream, but was perpetually on the edge of becoming one. There she hung, submerged and tumbling slowly, like a particle of flotsam just below the crest of a wave that was always just about to break.

### 3.

*What if I travel so far away in my dream that I can't get back in time to wake up?*

Ruth had asked her father this once, when she was little. He used to tuck her into bed, and kiss her on the forehead and bid her sweet dreams, but the exhortation always made her anxious. *What if my dream isn't sweet? What if it's horrible?*

"Remind yourself it's just a dream," he said. "And then wake up."

*But what if I can't get back in time?*

"Then I'll come and get you," he said, turning out the light.

## 4.

"Maybe you're trying too hard," Oliver suggested. "Maybe you should take a break."

He was standing in the doorway to her office, watching her adjust the cushion on the floor.

"I can't take a break," she said, sitting back down and crossing her legs. "My whole life is a break. I really need to do this."

She shifted her weight forward and arched her spine. Maybe she was too comfortable. Maybe she should be more uncomfortable. She reached around and gave the cushion a punch and then tried it again.

"Maybe you're just tired," Oliver said. "Maybe you should stop trying to meditate and take a nap."

"My whole life is a nap. I need to wake up." She closed her eyes and exhaled. Immediately she felt the dull shimmer of fatigue, pressing from somewhere deep inside her, dragging her down. She shook herself and opened her eyes again.

"Listen," she said. "You're the one who said the universe provides. Well, the universe provided Nao, and she says this is the way to wake up. Maybe she's right. Anyway, I want to try. I need something. I need a supapawa." She closed her eyes again. Her mind was her power. She wanted her mind back.

"Okay," he said. "Do you want to go get some clams and oysters after you finish? The rain's stopped and it's a nice low tide."

"Sure," she said, keeping her eyes closed.

The cat, who had been sharpening his claws on the doorjamb, now squeezed between Oliver's legs and went straight for her, thrusting his head into her mudra.

"Pest," she said, breaking the circle of her cosmic egg to scratch his ear. "Oliver, will you please come get your cat and close the door on your way out."

"That's his superpower," Oliver said, as he scooped him up. "He knows how to be annoying."

He paused at the doorway again, still holding the cat. "We should go get clams soon, though, while the tide's still low. How long are you going to sit there for? Do you want me to come wake you up?"

## 5.

The clam garden they liked best was a secret one that Muriel had shown them. Islanders kept a lot of secrets: secret clam gardens and oyster beds, secret pine mushroom and chanterelle patches, secret underwater rocks where sea urchins grew, secret marijuana grow-ops, secret telephone lists for salmon and halibut, meat and cheese and unpasteurized dairy. In recent years, the three small grocery stores had upgraded their stock and you could now buy most foods, but in the old days, if you were a newcomer, you could starve if an old-timer didn't take pity on you and let you in on some of the secrets.

The clam garden was on the western edge of the island, facing the deep cold waters of the passage. The oysters there were small and sweet, and the clams were bountiful. Muriel said that the garden was ancient and had been cultivated by the Salish for generations, but now few people harvested there, which was a pity because the gardens benefited by frequent harvesting. Still, every forkful of sand turned up a dozen or more fat clams, and in about twenty minutes they had their combined daily limit of a hundred and fifty littlenecks and thirty oysters.

They sat on a smooth rock just above the sandy flat, looking west across the ocean toward the jagged silhouette of the mountains. The dark indigo sky was streaked with pale clouds, reflecting the dying glow of the day. Overhead, the first stars dotted the sky. Small waves licked the rock at their feet.

Oliver took a can of beer out of his coat pocket, popped it open, and handed it to Ruth. He took out an oyster knife and a lime. His knife flashed, and the top half of the oyster shell arced and sank in the dark water. He held out the bottom half to her. The flayed mollusk glistened on the pearly shell; plump grey meat, dark frill. She thought she saw it flinch when he sprayed it with lime.

She accepted the offering, tipping the shell to her lips and letting the oyster slip into her mouth. It was cold and fresh-tasting. He pulled another from the bucket, shucked it, and sucked it back.

"Ahhh," he sighed. "*Crassostrea gigas*. The essence of the sea." He washed it down with a swig of beer.

He looked so happy. And healthy, too. He'd lost weight when he was sick. It was good to see him looking well again. She thought about what the oysterman, Blake, had said about radiation, what Muriel had said about drift.

"Some of the oyster guys are worried about nuclear contamination," she said. "From Fukushima. What do you think?"

"The Pacific is a pretty big place," he said. "You want another?"

She shook her head.

"It's kind of ironic," Oliver said, shucking one for himself. "This Pacific oyster isn't native."

She knew this. Everybody knew this. It was impossible to live on the island and not know this. Oyster farming was the closest thing they had to an industry, now that the salmon run was depleted and the big trees had been cut.

"They were introduced in 1912 or '13," he said, "but didn't really acclimate until the thirties. But once they did, they took over. Crowded out the smaller native species."

"Yes," she said. "I know."

"You used to be able to walk barefoot on the beaches. That's what the old-timers say."

She'd heard this, too. Now the local beaches were covered with razor-sharp oyster shells, so it was hard to imagine walking barefoot. "And why is this ironic?"

"Well, maybe *ironic* is the wrong word. It's just that *Crassostrea gigas* originally came from Japan. From Miyagi, actually. In fact, the other name for them is the Miyagi oyster. Isn't that where your nun is from?"

"Yes," she said, feeling the wide Pacific Ocean suddenly shrink just a little. "I didn't know that."

The cold from the rock had seeped through the seat of her jeans. She stood and jumped up and down to get warm. It was still too cold to be sitting on rocks, drinking beer, but she didn't mind. The sea air was fresh and felt good in her lungs, dissolving the sleepiness and the murky claustrophobic feeling that overwhelmed her after a day in front of the computer. Here, she felt awake again.

"Do you know how lucky we are?" Oliver was saying. "To live in a place where the water is still clean? Where we can still eat the shellfish?"

She thought about the Salish who used to tend these gardens. She wondered when the last oyster was harvested in the beds around Manhattan. She thought about the leak in Fukushima. She thought about old Jiko's temple, clinging to the side of the mountain in Miyagi. Or was it?

"I wonder how much longer we have . . ." she said.

"Who knows?" he said. "Better enjoy it while you can." He held out an oyster. His fingers were wet and raw. "You want another?"

"Okay." The sharp-edged shell was rough against her lips, the cold flesh soft on her tongue. She swallowed and savored the brine. The tide was rising around their rock, lapping at her toes. "I'm cold," she said. "Let's go home."

# *Nao*

## 1.

Have you ever tried to bully a wave? Punch it? Kick it? Pinch it? Hit it? Beat it to death with a stick?

Stupid.

After old Jiko found my scars, she took me on an errand into town. On the way back, she wanted to stop and buy some rice balls and soft drinks and some chocolate treats. She had this idea that we could take the bus to the seaside and have a picnic there. I didn't particularly care, but she seemed to think it would be a big treat for me to eat store-bought food and play by the ocean, so I was like, whatever, you know, willing to go along because it's hard to disappoint someone who's a hundred and four years old.

Because of her cataracts, Jiko can't really walk very well, and she always carries a stick, but what she really likes is when you hold hands with her. I think holding hands makes her feel more confident, and so I got into the habit of holding her hand when I was next to her, and to tell you the truth, I liked it, too. I liked the feeling of her thin little fingers in mine. I liked being the strong one, and keeping her tiny body close to me. It made me feel useful. When I wasn't there, she used her stick. I liked feeling more useful than a stick.

Before getting on the bus to the seaside, Jiko wanted to stop at the Family Mart in town to buy our picnic, but there happened to be a gang of yanki[114] girls hanging out in the parking lot in front, so I lied and said

---

114. *yanki*—a delinquent, from the English *Yankee*. The popular image of yanki is a tough juvenile delinquent with shaved eyebrows, wearing a long, brightly colored, garishly embroidered workcoat called a tokkō-fuku. The word *tokkō-fuku* means "Special Attack uniform"; these uniforms were issued to the Tokkōtai, the Special Attack Force of kamikaze pilots during World War II.

I wasn't hungry. They were speed-tribe biker chicks, with bleached orange and yellow shaggy hair and baggy construction-worker pants and big flapping lab coats that looked like the kind that doctors and scientists wear, only they weren't white. They were neon bright and graffitied all over with giant black kanji.

The girls were squatting on the pavement by the door, chewing gum and smoking. A couple of them were leaning on wooden swords, the kind you use for kendo, and I was like, No way, Grandma, I'm really not hungry, but old Jiko had her heart set on making a picnic for me, so what could I do? I held her little hand real tight, and when we got near the girls, one of them spat and it landed at our feet, and then they started to say stuff. It was nothing I hadn't heard at school before, but it shocked me because of Jiko being so old, and how can you say rude stuff about manko[115] and chinchin[116] to an old lady who is a nun? It took us forever to get past them because Jiko walks so slow and they were kind of blocking our way. They kept on shouting out and spitting, and I could feel my heart racing and my face growing hot, even if old Jiko didn't bat an eyelid.

Finally we made it into the Family Mart. The whole time we were looking for rice balls and drinks and deciding whether to buy chocolate or sweet bean cakes or both for dessert, I kept looking through the window at the girls squatting outside the store. I knew that when we left they would say more stuff to us. Maybe they would throw things at us or trip us. Maybe they would follow us to the beach and get their boyfriends to rape us and beat us and throw our dead bodies into the ocean, or maybe they would just do the business themselves with their wooden swords. I'd gotten plenty of practice at school imagining this kind of thing happening to my own body so it didn't bother me that much, but the idea of someone hurting my old Jiko was brand new to my mind, and it made me feel like throwing up.

But old Jiko wasn't paying any attention. She was concentrating on selecting the flavors of our rice balls, and eventually she decided on sour

---

115. *manko*—cunt, pussy.
116. *chinchin*—penis.

plums, flavored seaweed, and spicy cod roe. She wanted me to choose a chocolate treat, either Pocky or Melty Kisses or both, but how could I focus on something so unimportant? I had to protect us from our enemies outside the door, even if she was too old and blind to comprehend the danger we were in, and I was trying to calculate my chances of fighting off a dozen yanki bitches with serious sticks, when all I had was my pathetic little *supapawa!*

It took forever for Jiko to pay the cashier—you know how it is with old people and their coin purses—but I didn't mind, or offer to help. I was kind of hoping that maybe she would take all day, and by the time we'd finished, the gang would have gone, but no such luck. They were still there, squatting on the pavement, and the minute we walked out of the store, they kind of locked on to us, spitting and sizing us up. I tried to hurry Jiko past them, but you know old Jiko. She always takes her time.

The girls started calling out, and as we got closer their cries grew louder and more screechy, and a couple of the squatting ones got to their feet. I moved in front, but when we were even with them, suddenly old Jiko stopped. She turned to face them, peering as if she was noticing them for the first time, and then she tugged on my hand and started shuffling in their direction.

I held back, whispering, "Damē da yo, Obaachama! Ikō yo!"[117] but she didn't listen. She went up and stood right in front of them and gave them a long look, which is how she looks at everything. Long and steady, probably on account of the time it takes for an image to form through the milky lenses of her cataracts. The girls, in their neon-colored pants and blue and orange and red mechanical coats with the big black kanji, must just have been a confusion of lines and bright colors to her eyes.

No one said anything. The girls were jutting out their chins and hips and shifting restlessly from side to side. Finally, I guess old Jiko understood what she was looking at. She dropped my hand and I held my breath. And then she bowed.

---

117. *Damé da yo, Obaachama! Ikō yo!*—No, that's no good, Grandma. Let's go!

I couldn't believe it. It wasn't a little bow, either. It was a deep bow. The girls were, like, what the fuck? One of them, a fat girl squatting in front, kind of nodded back—not quite a bow, not completely respectful, but not a punch in the face either. But then the tall one in the middle, who was clearly the girl boss, reached over and gave the fat one a swift punch in the head.

"Nameten no ka!" she snarled. "Chutohampa nan da yo. Chanto ojigi mo dekinei no ka?!"[118]

She smacked the fat girl once more, and then she stood up straight, put her palms together, and bowed deeply from the waist. The rest of her crew jumped up and did the same. Jiko bowed to them again, and nudged me, so I bowed, too, but I did it half-assed, so she made me do it again, which made things even because now it was like old Jiko was the girl boss of our gang, and I was the fat screwup who couldn't bow properly. I didn't think this was so funny, but the gangbangers thought it was hilarious, and Jiko smiled, too, and then she took my hand and we walked on. When the bus came, Jiko sat by the window and looked back out at the parking lot.

"I wonder what omatsuri[119] it is today?" she said.

"Omatsuri?"

"Yes," she said. "Those pretty young people, dressed up in their matsuri clothes. They look so gay. I wonder what the occasion is. Muji remembers these things for me . . ."

"It's not a matsuri! Those were gangbangers, Granny. Biker chicks. Yanki girls."

"They were girls?"

"Bad girls. Juvenile delinquents. They were saying stuff. I thought they were going to beat us up."

"Oh no," Jiko said, shaking her head. "They were all dressed so nicely. Such cheerful colors."

---

118. *Nameten no ka! Chutohampa nan da yo! Chanto ojigi mo dekinei no ka?!*— Are you messing with me? That's half-assed. Can't you even bow properly?!

119. *omatsuri* (お祭り)—festival.

## 2.

"Have you ever bullied a wave?" Jiko asked me at the beach.

We had eaten rice balls and chocolate and were hanging out. Jiko was sitting on a small wooden bench, and I was lying on the sand at her feet. The sun was beating down. Jiko had tied a damp white hand towel around her bald head and seemed as cool as a cucumber in her grey pajamas. I was hot and sweaty and feeling restless, but I hadn't brought a bathing suit and didn't really want to go for a swim. But that's not what she was asking.

"Bullied a wave?" I repeated. "No. Of course not."

"Try it. Go to the water and wait for the biggest wave and give it a punch. Give it a good kick. Hit it with a stick. Go on. I will watch." She handed me her walking stick.

There was no one around, except for a couple of surfers way down the beach. I took old Jiko's stick in my hand and walked and then ran to the edge of the ocean, waving it above my head like a kendo sword. The waves were big, breaking on the beach, and I ran into the first one that came at me, yelling *kiayeeeee!* like a samurai going into battle. I smacked the wave with the stick, cutting through it, but the water kept coming. I ran back up the beach and escaped, but the next one knocked me over. I got to my feet and attacked again and again, and each time the water crashed down on top of me, grinding me against the rocks and covering me with foam and sand. I didn't mind. The sharp cold felt good, and the violence of the waves felt powerful and real, and the bitterness of salt in my nose tasted harshly delicious.

Over and over, I ran at the sea, beating it until I was so tired I could barely stand. And then the next time I fell down, I just lay there and let the waves wash over me, and I wondered what would happen if I stopped trying to get back up. Just let my body go. Would I be washed out to sea? The sharks would eat my limbs and organs. Little fish would feed on my fingertips. My beautiful white bones would fall to the bottom of the ocean, where anemones would grow upon them like flowers. Pearls would rest in my eye sockets. I stood up and walked back to where old

Jiko was sitting. She took the small towel from her head and handed it to me.

"Maketa," I said, throwing myself down in the sand. "I lost. The ocean won."

She smiled. "Was it a good feeling?"

"Mm," I said.

"That's good," she said. "Have another rice ball?"

### 3.

We sat there for a while longer, waiting for my shorts and T-shirt to dry. Down the beach, in the distance, the surfers kept falling into the water and disappearing.

"The waves keep beating them up, too," I said, pointing.

Jiko squinted, but she couldn't see them through her flowers of emptiness.

"There," I said. "See that one? He's just standing up . . . he's up . . . he's up . . . oh, he's down." I laughed. It was funny to watch.

Jiko nodded, like she was agreeing with me. "Up, down, same thing," she said.

It's a typical Jiko comment, all about pointing to what she calls the not-two[120] nature of existence when I'm just trying to watch some cute guys surfing. I know better than to argue with her, because she always wins, but it's like a knock-knock joke, where you have to say "Who's there?" so the other person can tell you the punch line. So I said, "No, it's not the same thing. Not for a surfer."

"Yes," she said. "You are right. Not same." She adjusted her glasses. "Not different, either."

See what I mean?

"It *is* different, Granny. The whole point of surfing is to stand on top of the wave, not underneath it."

"Surfer, wave, same thing."

---

120. nondualistic—*funi* (不二), lit. "not" + "two."

208

I don't know why I bother. "That's just stupid," I said. "A surfer's a person. A wave is a wave. How can they be the same?"

Jiko looked out across the ocean to where the water met the sky. "A wave is born from deep conditions of the ocean," she said. "A person is born from deep conditions of the world. A person pokes up from the world and rolls along like a wave, until it is time to sink down again. Up, down. Person, wave."

She pointed to the steep cliffs along the shoreline. "Jiko, mountain, same thing. The mountain is tall and will live a long time. Jiko is small and will not live much longer. That's all."

Like I said, this is pretty typical of the kind of conversation you have with my old Jiko. I never completely understand what she's saying, but I like that she tries to explain it to me anyway. It's nice of her.

It was time to go back to the temple. My shorts and T-shirt had dried out and my skin was superitchy from the salt. I helped Jiko to her feet and we walked back to the bus stop together, holding hands again. I was still thinking about what she said about waves, and it made me sad because I knew that her little wave was not going to last and soon she would join the sea again, and even though I know you can't hold on to water, still I gripped her fingers a little more tightly to keep her from leaking away.

# Ruth

## I.

You can't hold on to water or keep it from leaking away. This was a lesson that Tepco learned in the weeks following the tsunami, when they pumped thousands of tons of seawater into the reactor vessels at the Fukushima nuclear plant in an attempt to cool the fuel rods and prevent the reactor meltdowns that in fact had already happened. They called it the "feed and bleed" strategy, and it created about 500 tons of highly radioactive water each day—water that needed to be contained and kept from leaking.

On the opposite side of the Pacific, Ruth pored over reports of the disaster. The International Atomic Energy Agency, which was monitoring the situation, published the daily 2011 Fukushima Nuclear Accident Update Log, describing the details of the desperate efforts to stabilize the reactors. Here's a very short excerpt from the April 3 log:

> On 2 April, transferring of water from the Unit 1 condenser storage tank to the surge tank of the suppression pool was completed in preparation for transferring water in the basement of the Unit 1 turbine building to the condenser.
>
> Also on 2 April, transferring of water from the Unit 2 condenser to the condenser storage tank was started in preparation for transferring water in the basement of the Unit 1 turbine building to the condenser.

Paragraph after paragraph, page after page, the log detailed the intricate system of pumps and drains, surge tanks and feed-water lines, intakes and injection lines, suppression pools and pits, flow rates and leakage paths, trenches and tunnels and flooded basements, that were being used to hold on to the water.

This Update Log of April 3 was the first to mention a crack, discovered in the side wall of a containment pit below Reactor #2, next to the seawater inlet point. High concentrations of radioactive iodine-131 and cesium-137 were found in samples of seawater as far away as thirty kilometers from the reactors, with levels measuring tens of thousands of times higher than before the accident. The containment pit was leaking what *The New York Times* later reported to be rivers of highly radioactive water, which flowed directly into the sea.

On April 4, the Update Log reported that Tepco received permission from the Japanese government to release 11,500 tons of contaminated water into the Pacific Ocean. That much water is roughly equivalent to the contents of five Olympic swimming pools.

On April 5, the Update Log noted that the dumping had begun. It lasted for five days.

The radioactive levels of the contaminated water were about a hundred times over the legal limits, but the Pacific Ocean is vast and wide, and Tepco didn't foresee a problem. According to the Update Log, the company estimated that a member of the public, eating seaweed and seafood harvested from nearby the nuclear plant every day for a year, would receive an additional annual radiation dose of 0.6 millisieverts, well below the level that would be dangerous to human health. The company didn't estimate the consequences to the fish.

Information is a lot like water; it's hard to hold on to, and hard to keep from leaking away. Tepco and the Japanese government tried to contain the news of the reactor meltdown, and for a while they were successful in covering up crucial data about dangerous radiation levels in the region surrounding the crippled plant, but eventually the information began to leak. Japanese people pride themselves on being stoic and slow to anger, but the ongoing disclosures of mismanagement, lies, and cover-ups touched a deep core of rage.

## 2.

In medieval Japan, people used to believe that earthquakes were caused by an angry catfish who lived under the islands.

In the earliest legends, the *mono-iu sakana,* or "Saying-things Fish," ruled the lakes and rivers. This supernatural fish could shapeshift into human form and speak in human tongues, and if any humans trespassed against his watery realm, he would appear to them and deliver a warning. If the offenders failed to heed this warning, the enraged *mono-iu sakana* would punish them by sending a flood or some other natural disaster.

By the middle of the nineteenth century, the *mono-iu sakana* had morphed into the *jishin namazu*, or Earthquake Catfish, an enormous whalelike creature who caused the earth to shake and tremble by his furious thrashing. The only thing holding him in check was a large stone wielded by the Kashima Deity, who lives at the Kashima Shrine.

This stone is called the *kaname-ishi,* an untranslatable Japanese term that means something like "keystone" or "rivet stone" or "lodestone." The Kashima Deity uses the *kaname-ishi* to immobilize the catfish by pinning its head to the ground. If the Kashima Deity dozes off or gets distracted, or is called away on business, the pressure on the catfish's head is released, allowing it to wiggle and thrash. The result is an earthquake.

If you go to the Kashima Shrine, you won't see much, since most of the stone is buried underground. A small roofed enclosure shelters a bare patch of earth, from which a small, round stone, about twelve inches in diameter, emerges from the earth like the crowning skull of an infant trying to be born. It's impossible to know how big the stone might be underneath the earth. How amazing to think that the fate of the Japanese islands rests on the assumption that the buried and largely invisible crowning keystone is large and hefty enough to subdue an angry earthquake catfish!

## 3.

The Earthquake Catfish is not solely a malevolent fish, despite the havoc and calamity it can wreak. It has benevolent aspects as well. A subspecies of the Earthquake Catfish is the *yonaoshi namazu* or World-Rectifying Catfish, which is able to heal the political and economic corruption in society by shaking things up.

Belief in the World-Rectifying Catfish was especially prevalent during the early nineteenth century, a period characterized by a weak, ineffective government and a powerful business class, as well as extreme and anomalous weather patterns, crop failures, famine, hoarding, urban riots, and mass religious pilgrimages, which often ended in mob violence.

The World-Rectifying Catfish targeted the business class, the 1 percent, whose rampant practices of price-fixing, hoarding, and graft had led to economic stagnation and political corruption. The angry catfish would cause an earthquake, wreaking havoc and destruction, and in order to rebuild, the wealthy would have to let go of their assets, which would create jobs in salvage, rubble-clearing, and construction for the working classes. The redistribution of wealth is illustrated in satirical drawings of the time, which depict the World-Rectifying Catfish forcing wealthy merchants and CEOs to vomit and shit out gold coins, which are being pocketed by laborers.

But sadly, earthquakes result in collateral damage, and often the catfish is filled with remorse. In one poignant drawing, *seppuku namazu*, the Suicide Catfish, slices open his stomach to atone for all the deaths he's caused. Gold coins pour from the wide slit in his belly. In one hand, he's gripping the ritual disemboweling knife that he has thrust into his stomach. In the other, he's holding a gold bar and offering it up to a group of humans, while overhead, the Kashima Deity and the spirits of the dead look on.

### 4.

The association between catfish and earthquakes has persisted into modern times. The Yure Kuru mobile phone app warns users of a coming earthquake, providing information about the location of its epicenter, the arrival time, and the seismic intensity. Yure Kuru means "Shaking Coming," and the app's logo is a cartoon catfish with a goofy smile and two lightning bolts coming out of his head.

"That's cute," Oliver said, reaching for his iPhone. "We should have that. We're due for a big one here. I wonder if it'll work in Whaletown."

They were sitting in front of the fire in the living room after a dinner of clam-and-oyster chowder, fresh-baked rosemary bread, and a salad of tender young kale and spicy mustard greens from the greenhouse. It was still only February, but Oliver was managing to keep them supplied with fresh greens even during the winter months.

"In Stuttgart, where my parents grew up, they had gigantic catfish that lived at the bottom of the river Neckar. Nobody ever saw them except right before an earthquake, when the catfish would rise to the surface. Huge, whiskery things, weighing up to two hundred pounds."

"Were they really that big?"

"That's what my dad said, but they're pretty much all fished out now. You don't see catfish that big anymore, except in Chernobyl. There's a bunch of them that live in the channel that used to bring cooling water to the condensers in the reactor. They hang out under the railway bridge. Nobody fishes there anymore, so the catfish thrive. They've gotten really enormous, some even twelve or thirteen feet long. They're bottom-feeders, and apparently the mud still contains a lot of radioactive particles, but the catfish don't seem to mind."

Ruth thought once again about the clams. She had been purging them on the porch for twenty-four hours to get them to expel the mud and sand. She had a technique, which entailed soaking them in buckets of seawater, to which she'd add a handful of cornmeal and a rusty nail. She'd agitate the water several times a day, and change the water after twelve hours.

She'd read about this method in a novel, but she'd forgotten which one. She seemed to recall it was a story about a family with a summer house in Maine or Massachusetts or possibly Rhode Island. An East Coast enclave of beautiful summer people, with lanky golden children and a comfortable lifestyle, and a mother who knew how to make bivalves spit. The clams that this beautiful New England family ate would have no unpleasant grit to grind between their strong, white teeth. Maybe it was the Hamptons. Memory is a funny thing. The mother's technique to achieve this grit-free end had stayed with Ruth, even though she had forgotten the plot of the novel, or why the technique was effective.

When she had related this to Oliver, he supplied a theory. "I think two things are happening. The cornmeal is simply food, which the clams ingest and which cleanses the green stuff from their digestive tracts and intestinal organs."

Ruth had been dicing potatoes for the chowder at the time he was explaining this. As she wielded the knife and listened, she could clearly see the image of the mother in the novel. She was wearing a long dress made of fine white linen. Her clams would not have green stuff in their intestines.

"That's the first process," Oliver was saying. "It's biological. The second process is electrochemical. Saltwater is an ionic solution and functions as an electrolyte. The rusty nail, which is made of iron, acts as a conductor, and I imagine the bodies of the clams do, too."

Actually, it probably was the Hamptons, Ruth was thinking. There were sand dunes and Atlantic breezes, green-and-white-striped awnings and canvas-covered deck chairs. The mother wore a white dress that billowed in the afternoon breeze, or perhaps she was in shorts, and the gauzy curtains in the tall open windows of the house were what billowed.

"When you introduce the nail into the saltwater," Oliver said, "it generates a small electrical charge, which is just enough to irritate the clams and cause them to purge the sand."

But then again, maybe she'd conflated the scene from the novel with something else. Maybe the beautiful blond mother in the billowing white dress didn't put the rusty nail in the bucket with the clams. It didn't sound like something she'd do. Maybe the nail in the bucket was a Japanese trick that Ruth had picked up from her own mother or from one of her Japanese friends.

"So basically," Oliver had concluded, "you're simultaneously feeding them and electrocuting them to make them shit and spit."

Ruth, who was by this time chopping onions, wiped the tears from her eyes with the back of her hand. "Actually," she said, "the novel was more about the family—tall cool drinks and tennis whites and human relationships, that sort of thing. It didn't go into a lot of detail about the electrochemistry."

They ate in the living room in front of the fire and listened to the wind howl. It was too cold to wear billowing white dresses here, and besides, people in the Pacific Northwest wore practical clothes, polypropylene and synthetic fleece, but Ruth couldn't complain. The fire was nice and the chowder was delicious, rich and creamy. Whatever its origin or explanation, the technique for purging the bivalves worked, and the clams were both plump and free of grit and sand. The cat liked the chowder, too. He'd been circling around all during their meal, trying to lick their soup bowls. When Oliver shooed him away, the cat took a swipe at his hand, so Oliver grabbed him and pinned his head to the ground. Subdued but offended, Pesto had turned his back to them, shunning them, and now he stared moodily into the fire.

"This sucks," Oliver said. "I can download Yure Kuru, but it only works off data from the Japan Meteorological Agency. It won't tell us anything about earthquakes in Canada."

Ruth stared into the flames. "I thought Canada was safe."

"No place is safe," Oliver said. "Okay, I've got it. Now we'll know all about seismic activity in Japan."

"Maybe we should go to Japan so you can use the app."

"Maybe we don't have to, since Japan is coming here."

## 5.

"What?"

"Japan is coming here."

"What are you talking about?"

"The earthquake," Oliver said. "It moved the coast of Japan closer to us."

"Really?"

Oliver looked puzzled. "Don't you remember? The release of subduction caused the landmass near the epicenter to jump about thirteen feet in our direction."

"I didn't know that."

"Yes, you did. We talked about it. It also caused the planet's mass to shift closer to the core, which made the earth spin faster. The increase in the speed of rotation shortened the length of the day. Our days are shorter now."

"They are? That's terrible!"

He smiled. "You sound just like your mother . . ."

She ignored his comment. "How much time did we lose?"

"Not much. One point eight millionth of a second a day, I think it was. Do you want me to look it up?"

"I'll take your word for it."

"I'm sure we talked about this," Oliver said. "It was all over the Internet. Don't you remember?"

"Of course I remember," she lied. "I thought the days seemed awfully short. I figured it was my imagination."

# Nao

## I.

By the end of the summer, with Jiko's help, I was getting stronger. Not just strong in my body, but strong in my mind. In my mind, I was becoming a superhero, like Jubei-chan, the Samurai Girl, only I was Nattchan, the Super Nun, with abilities bestowed upon me by Lord Buddha that included battling the waves, even if I always lost, and being able to withstand astonishing amounts of pain and hardship. Jiko was helping me cultivate my *supapawa!* by encouraging me to sit zazen for many hours without moving, and showing me how not to kill anything, not even the mosquitoes that buzzed around my face when I was sitting in the hondo at dusk or lying in bed at night. I learned not to swat them even when they bit me and also not to scratch the itch that followed. At first, when I woke up, my face and arms were swollen from the bites, but little by little, my blood and skin grew tough and immune to their poison and I didn't break out in bumps no matter how much I'd been bitten. And soon there was no difference between me and the mosquitoes. My skin was no longer a wall that separated us, and my blood was their blood. I was pretty proud of myself, so I went and found Jiko and I told her. She smiled.

"Yes," she said, patting me on the arm. "Plenty of good food for mosquitoes."

She explained to me that young people need lots of exercise and that we should exhaust ourselves on a daily basis or else we would have troublesome thoughts and dreams, which would result in troublesome actions. I knew enough about young people's troublesome actions to agree with her, so I didn't mind that every day she made me work in the kitchen with Muji. I know Muji was happy to have me there, because she told me so. Before I came, there was too much work for a single nun to do. I've probably said this before, but the thing you have to realize about temple life is that it's like living in a whole different era, and everything takes about a hundred times longer than it does in the twenty-first century. Muji and Jiko never waste anything. Every rubber band or twist-tie, every piece of string or paper or scrap of fabric, they carefully collect and reuse. Muji has a thing for plastic bags and she would make me wash them carefully with soap and water and hang them outside, where they would catch the sunlight and spin in the wind like jellyfish balloons as they dried. I didn't mind, because I didn't have much else to do, but in my opinion, it took way too long. I tried to explain that it would be quicker and easier just to throw the old bags away and buy new ones, and then they would have more time for zazen, but Jiko disagreed. Sitting zazen, washing freezer bags, same thing, she said.

The only time they ever throw anything away is when it's really and truly broken, and then they make a big deal about it. They save up all their bent pins and broken sewing needles and once a year they do a whole memorial service for them, chanting and then sticking them into a block of tofu so they will have a nice soft place to rest. Jiko says that everything has a spirit, even if it is old and useless, and we must console and honor the things that have served us well.

So you can see how, with all this extra work, having an extra young person around really helps, and we were able to pickle more plums and cabbages, and dry more gourds and daikons, and take better care of the temple garden. We were able to visit many parishioners who were old or sick, and sometimes when we visited them, I weeded their gardens, too.

I started getting up at five in the morning to sit zazen with them, and after the offerings and service and sōji,[121] while Muji was cooking breakfast, Jiko would make me run all the way down the mountain to the road and then all the way up to the temple again. She would be there to meet me as I came panting up the last few steps, my legs like noodles. She'd

---

121. *sōji* (掃除)—cleaning.

be standing there with Chibi, the little black-and-white temple cat, and she would hand me a towel and a big jar full of cold water, and she'd watch me as I drank it down.

"You have good straight legs," she said once. "Nice and long. Strong."

I was pleased and would have blushed if my face wasn't already red from running.

"They are your father's legs," she continued. "He was a strong runner, too. Just a little faster than you."

"You made him run up and down, too?"

"Of course. He was a young boy with many troublesome thoughts. He needed lots of exercise."

I poured the remaining water from the jar over my head and then shook it. Water drops flew from the tips of my hair, showering Chibi, who jumped and moved away.

"I'm sorry, Chibi!" I cried, but of course he ignored me. He sat at a distance with his back turned and started licking himself. He seemed really offended, but he's a cat so I didn't take it personally.

"Dad still has troublesome thoughts," I said, watching the cat ignore me. "Maybe he should come back and live here with us. Maybe you could train him and teach him to be strong again. He could run up and down, and do zazen, and work in the garden . . ."

The more I thought about it, the better my idea seemed, and before I knew it, the words were just falling out of my mouth. Please, Granny! I said. I'm serious. He needs help! And then I told her all about the night he fell in front of the train, and how he and Mom were pretending it was an accident but it wasn't, and about how he never left the apartment during the day, but went out late at night and stayed out for hours and hours, and I knew because I stayed up and listened for him because I was afraid he wouldn't come back. And how one night, when I couldn't stand it anymore, I snuck out after him, because I needed to know if he was stalking someone or going to meet a lover, which would kind of suck for Mom, but at least would give him a raison d'être, and I followed him through the streets, staying in the shadows and keeping close to the walls. The route he walked made no sense, but he didn't care, like he was a robot and his feet had been programmed to execute the kind of random algorithm we learned about in computing class, but his mind had been turned off so he didn't notice where he was going. Maybe he was sleep-walking. Sometimes he entered different neighborhoods, and sometimes the streets got so old and narrow and twisting I was sure we were lost. He never stopped or spoke to anyone or bought anything, not even cigarettes or beer from a vending machine, and now that I think of it, we never passed anyone on the streets either, so maybe he had an avoid-ance algorithm built into his program, the way some robots do so they don't bump into things.

We walked for hours. I was scared because I knew I'd never find my way back home alone, and I didn't want him to know I'd been following, but I was too tired to keep up. And just then he made one last turn, and we came out into the same small park on the bank of the Sumida River that I'd seen in my bed in my metal-bound dream. It was exactly like I pictured it. Off to one side, next to the riverbank, there was a playground area with a swing set and a slide and a teeter totter, and I knew that's where he was headed. And sure enough, he walked straight over to the swing set and sat down. He had his back to me, so I went around and hid behind a cement panda where I could see his face. He lit a Short Hope and began to swing. He was facing the water, and he started pumping his legs and swinging higher and higher, with his cigarette clenched between his teeth, grinning like he really meant business. It looked like he was trying to get that swing going as high as he could so that when it reached the top of its arc and he let go, the momentum of his swinging would send him sailing over the low safety wall and into the Sumida River, where he would drown and his body would sink to the bottom and get eaten by a kappa or a giant river catfish. I swear, I could see it, the moment when his hands slipped from the chain and his body shot out of the seat, flying forward, his arms and legs spread wide to hug the oncoming air and the dark, deep water. *No . . . no . . . no!* I heard myself whispering, and my heart was beating in time to the swinging. *Now . . . now . . . now!*

But it never happened. He never let go, and then slowly his pumping lost its power and the arc of the swing grew smaller and more uneven, until he was barely moving at all, and the toes of his plastic sandals were just dragging backward and forward, tracing small aimless circles in the dust under the swing. He stood up and walked to the safety wall and looked over, and then he took one last drag from his cigarette and flicked it into the river. He stood there for a long time, staring into the oily water. I was afraid he was going to climb over then and jump. I wanted to run out from my hiding place and stop him.

"But you didn't," Jiko said.

"No. I was going to, but then he turned away from the water and started walking again."

"Did you follow?"

"Yes. He walked home. I waited outside the door of our apartment until I thought it was safe and then let myself back in with my key. I don't think he heard me. He was snoring by then."

Old Jiko nodded. "He was a good sleeper as a boy."

"So don't you think he should come back and stay here with us?" I asked. "I think it would do him a lot of good, don't you? You should have seen his face when we were walking up the steps to the temple. He looked really happy."

"He always liked it here," Jiko said.

"So he should come back, right?"

"Maa, soo kashira,"[122] she said, which is one of those Japanese answers that mean absolutely nothing.

## 2.

By August, it was hotter than you can imagine, and in the afternoon, when Jiko and Muji were teaching flower arrangement or sutra singing to the neighborhood ladies and I was supposed to be doing my summer homework, I would drag myself out onto the engawa[123] that overlooked

---

122. *Maa, sō kashira*—Well, I wonder . . .
123. *engawa* (縁側)—a narrow wooden veranda that wraps around a traditional Japanese building.

the pond and sit there and zone out. I liked to lean up against the thick wooden beam with my headphones on, and my legs sprawled out in front of me, watching the dragonflies flit around the lotus pads in the tiny pond, and listening to Japanese pop covers of French chansons that I was into even back then before I knew about *À la recherche du temps perdu*. Jiko didn't like it when I sprawled, and when she caught me doing it she told me so. She said it wasn't good manners to sit with my legs spread wide open for all the world to see, especially when I wasn't wearing any panties, and generally I agreed with her, but it was so hot! I just couldn't stand the feeling of the skin on the insides of my legs touching, and the old wood of the engawa was smooth and cool, and nobody was watching. Even Chibi the cat, who normally loved hot laps, stayed away. He was passed out on a cool mossy rock underneath some ferns. Mostly the air was dead still, but sometimes the tiniest breezes blew up the side of the mountain and entered the temple gates and found their way into the garden, where they ruffled the surface of the water and tickled up between my legs, making me shiver. Sometimes I think that the spirits of the ancestors live in the breezes, and you can feel them swishing around.

It was coming up to Obon, and spirits were cruising about like travelers arriving at the airport with their suitcases, looking for a place to check in. Obon was their summer vacation, too, when they could come back from the land of the dead to visit us here, in the land of the so-called living. The hot air felt pregnant with ghosts, which is a funny thing for me to say, since I've never been pregnant, but I've seen women on the train who are about to pop, and I imagine it must feel like this. They heave themselves around, belly first, and if someone is nice enough to give them a seat, they plop down, and then they just sit there with their legs open, rubbing their bellies and fanning their sweaty red faces, which is just how August feels, as Obon approaches, like the whole round world is pregnant with ghosts, and at any moment the dead will burst through the invisible membrane that separates them from us.

When I wasn't sitting on the veranda, zoning out, I was following

Jiko around the temple, carrying stuff for her and bugging her with questions about our ancestors.

"How about Grandma Ema? Is she coming? Did I ever meet her? I'd like to meet her. How about Great-Aunt Sugako and Great-Uncle Haruki? I'd like to meet them, too. Do you think they might want to meet me?"

I was excited because even though none of my dead relatives had ever bothered to show up for Obon before, at least to my knowledge, I had a feeling that this year would be different. First of all, I was an ikisudama now, and as a living ghost, I figured the dead ghosts would feel more comfortable with me. And I figured, too, that they would be more likely to come here to Jiko's temple, where everyone was expecting them and knew how to treat them properly, than to Sunnyvale, say, where the neighbors would simply freak and treat them like tacky Halloween spooks. It's like a birthday party. If you have parents like Kayla's who are really awesome event planners and take everybody bowling or rock climbing, then it's great to be the birthday girl, but if you have parents like mine who are pretty clueless, then birthdays suck, and really you'd rather be a thousand miles away than stuck there at your boring little party with your American friends who keep sighing and rolling their eyes at each other and then going all gushy and fake whenever your mom walks into the room with another plate of sushi. And you pretend you're having a good time, too, smiling like a crazy person, but you know it's a sales job, and you're only doing it to make your parents happy, and because it's good for their self-esteem. Anyway, all I'm trying to say is that if you were a ghost, which party would you rather go to?

Jiko and Muji are awesome party planners, and we spent every Buddhist nanosecond preparing the altars and arranging the flowers and dusting and deep cleaning even the tiniest corners and cracks of the temple so it would be spotless for the spirits and ancestors. We also made different kinds of special food to offer them, because they get hungry after their long journey back, and if you don't feed them, they might get angry. Food is a big part of Obon. In Japan, there are thousands of different spirits and ghosts and goblins and monsters who can do tatari and attack you, so just to be on the safe side we were going to kick things off with a big osegaki[124] ceremony, with lots of guests, as well as priests and nuns from a nearby temple who were coming to help us feed the hungry ghosts.

Muji told me the story behind this, about how back in the old days, Lord Buddha had this one disciple named Mokuren, who got really upset when he happened to see his mother hanging upside down like a side of beef in the Hell Realm of the hungry ghosts. He asked Lord Buddha how to rescue her, and Lord Buddha told him to make special offerings of food, which seemed to do the trick, and which just goes to show that kids have to look after their parents' well-being, even when their parents are dead and hanging upside down from meat hooks in hell. Old Mokuren was a pretty amazing dude, with lots of *supapawa!* like being able to walk through walls, and read people's minds, and talk to the dead. I would like to walk through walls and read people's minds and talk to the dead. That would be cool. I'm just a beginner, but as you know, I think it's important to have concrete goals in life, and walking through a wall seems doable, don't you think?

Anyway, finally we had everything ready, and the night before the first guests arrived, Jiko and Muji and I took a bath together so we would be clean and extra spiffy, and I got to shave both their heads with the razor. Jiko and Muji are superstrict about personal hygiene, and they never let their hair grow for more than five days, which is about an eighth of an inch, and sometimes they let me help. I liked doing it. I liked the way the stiff little stubbles came off in front of the blade, leaving the skin all nice and smooth and shiny. Muji's stubbles were tiny and black, like dead ants falling off a clean white page, but old Jiko's stubbles were bright and sparkling silver, like glitter or fairy dust.

There's a prayer for shaving heads, too, that goes like this:

*As I shave the stubble off my head*
*I pray with all beings*

---

124. *segaki* (施餓鬼)—hungry ghosts; also a derogatory name for homeless people.

*that we can cut off our selfish desires*
*and enter the heaven of true liberation.*

That night I was so excited, thinking about the arrival of the ghosts, I stayed up until Muji finally made me go to bed, but as soon as she and Jiko were asleep, I sneaked out again. I don't know what I expected. I walked through the garden and went to sit on the top step of the temple, under the gate, to wait. The stone step felt cold and damp through my pajamas, and all I could hear was the sound of the frogs and the night insects, singing.

Some people think that the night is sad because it is dark and reminds them of death, but I don't agree with that point of view at all. Personally I like the night, especially at the temple, when Muji turns off all the lights and only the moon and the stars and the fireflies are left, or when it's cloudy and the world is so black you can't even see your hand in front of you.

Everything seemed to grow blacker as I sat there, except for the fireflies whose tiny pulsing lights drew arcs through the dark summer air. On off . . . on off . . . on off . . . on off. The longer I stared, the dizzier I got, until I felt as if the world was tipping and pitching me forward down the mountainside into the long throat of the night. I put my hand down to touch the step to steady myself, but instead of the cold stone, I felt something prickly that moved like electricity under my hand. I screeched and pulled away, but of course it was only Chibi, who had come out to greet the ghosts with me. He froze like a cartoon cat with his green eyes as round as glowing coins, but when I laughed and petted his electric fur, he pressed up against my knee and pushed his head into my hand.

"Baka ne, Chibi-chan!"[125] I said, my heart still pounding. Even though I could barely make out his shape, it felt good to have him there.

A gust of wind rattled the bamboo, and it felt like spirits moving. What would a ghost look like, anyway? Would it even look human? Would it be big and fat like a daikon monster? Would it have a tremendously

---

125. *Baka ne, Chibi-chan!*—Idiots, aren't we, dear Chibi!

long nose like a red-faced tengu?[126] Would it be green like a goblin or disguised like a fox, or would it be more like a headless man-sized lump of decaying human flesh, with massive slabs of fat for arms and legs and a hideous smell? These ones are called nuppeppo. Muji told me about them. They hang around old abandoned temples and graveyards and they enjoy long, aimless walks after dark. Maybe my dad was turning into a nuppeppo. And there are other ghosts who look like dead human men with bad haircuts, whose bloodshot eyeballs pop from their sockets, and whose skin peels off their bones like lichen. They are dressed in cheap polyester business suits, and they hang from trees in the Suicide Forest, slowly turning. These are the ghosts that scare me the most because they look a little like my dad, and just when I was starting to freak myself out, I felt something settle beside me. I turned, and there he was. Dad was sitting there next to me on the stone step, and even though his eyes weren't popping and he wasn't dressed in his business suit, still I knew that he was dead, that he had killed himself at last, and this was his ghost, coming to let me know.

"Dad?" I tried to whisper, but my mouth was so dry that no sound came out.

He stared off into the darkness.

"Dad, is that you?" My voice still wouldn't make any sound, so my words were only thoughts in my head. No wonder he couldn't hear me. He stared off into the darkness. I took a deep breath, cleared my throat, tried again.

"Otosan," I said, speaking in Japanese this time. The word escaped through my lips like a tiny bubble. My dad's ghost turned his head slightly, and I noticed now that he seemed really young, and he was wearing a uniform of some kind, with a cap on his head. It looked like a school uniform, only a different color. He still didn't say anything. It occurred to me that maybe with ghosts you have to be superpolite, even if they

---

126. *tengu* (天狗)—supernatural red-faced demons with long, phallic noses, often dressed like Buddhist monks. Tengu can be evil or benevolent and are protectors of mountains and forests.

are your parents, otherwise you'll offend them, so I tried again in my most formal and polite schoolgirl voice.

"Yasutani Haruki-sama de gozaimasu ka?"[127]

He heard this time, and slowly turned to look at me, and when he spoke, his voice was so soft I could barely hear him over the wind.

"Who are you?" he asked.

He didn't recognize me. I couldn't believe it! My dad was dead and he had already forgotten all about me. My throat clenched and my nose started to itch, the way it does when I am trying not to cry. I took another deep breath.

"I am Yasutani Naoko," I announced, trying to sound bold and self-confident. "I am very pleased to see you."

"Ah," he said. "The pleasure is mine." His words were thin and blue, curling like the smoke from the burning tip of an incense stick.

Something was wrong. I didn't want to be rude and stare, but I couldn't help it. He looked like a young version of my dad, only a couple of years older than me, but he sounded different, and the clothes were all wrong, too. And that's when I figured it out: if this ghost who had answered to my father's name wasn't my father, then he must be my father's uncle, the suicide bomber, Yasutani Haruki #1.

"Have we met before?" he seemed to be asking.

"I don't believe so," I replied. "I believe I am your great-niece. I believe I am the daughter of your nephew, Yasutani Haruki Number Two, who was named for you."

The ghost nodded. "Is that so?" he said. "I wasn't aware that I had a nephew, never mind a great-niece. How quickly time flies . . ."

We both got silent then. Actually, I didn't have a choice, because I'd run out of polite phrases. I'm not very good at the real formal Japanese because I grew up in Sunnyvale, and the ghost of Haruki #1 didn't seem all that chatty, either. He seemed kind of moody and withdrawn, which made sense given what Jiko had told me about him liking French

<hr/>

127. *Yasutani Haruki-sama de gozaimasu ka?*—Are you the honorable Mr. Haruki Yasutani?

philosophy and poetry. I wished I'd paid more attention when my dad was reading to me about the Existentialists, because then maybe I could have said something intelligent to him, but the only French poetry I knew was the refrain to a song by Monique Serf called "Jinsei no Itami,"[128] which maybe wasn't the best choice to sing to a dead person.

> Le mal de vivre
> Le mal de vivre
> Qu'il faut bien vivre
> Vaille que vivre[129]

I hummed into the darkness, singing the words under my breath even though I wasn't quite sure what they all meant. I thought I heard him chuckle next to me, or maybe it was the wind, but when I looked over to where he had been sitting, Haruki #1 was gone.

### 3.

Stupid Nao! What a foolish girl! There I was, sitting with the ghost of my dead great-uncle, who just happened to be a kamikaze fighter pilot in World War II, and who was probably the most fascinating person I will ever get to meet, and what did I do? Sing some stupid French chanson to him! How idiotic is that??? He must have thought I was just another typical dumb teenager, and his time on earth was precious, so why waste even a moment of it with me? Better to just shimmer off and hang with someone who can think of more interesting conversational topics.

What is wrong with me? I could have asked him about all sorts of things. I could have asked him about his interests and his hobbies. I could have asked him if only depressed people cared about philosophy, and if reading philosophy books ever helped. I could have asked him about what it felt like to be ripped from his happy life and forced to become

---

128. *Jinsei no Itami* —The Pain of Life.
129. It's brave to live . . . ?

a suicide bomber, and if the other guys in his unit picked on him because he wrote French poetry. I could have asked him how he felt when he woke up on the morning of his mission, which was also his last morning on earth. Did he have a big cold fish dying in the hollow of his stomach? Or was he filled with a luminous calm that emanated from him so that everyone around him stood back in awe, knowing that he was ready to take to the sky?

I could have asked him what it felt like to die.

Stupid, baka Nao Yasutani.

## 4.

In the morning after breakfast, when Muji and Jiko were busy greeting the first carload of priests from the main temple who had come to help with the osegaki ceremony the next day, I sneaked off to Jiko's study. She doesn't mind me being there, so I don't know why it felt like sneaking. It's my favorite room in the temple, overlooking the garden, with a low desk where she likes to write, and a small bookshelf with a lot of fat old religious and philosophy books with faded cloth bindings. Jiko told me that the philosophical ones belonged to Haruki #1, from when he was in university. I tried to read some of them, but the kanji in the Japanese books was crazy difficult, and the other books were in languages like French and German. Even the ones in English didn't sound like any English I ever heard. Honestly, I don't know if there are still people who can read books like these anymore, but if you took out all the pages, they'd make great diaries.

Opposite the bookshelf, at the back of the room, was the family altar. A scroll with the image of Shaka-sama hung at the top, surrounded by the ihai[130] for all our ancestors and a book with all their names. Below that were different shelves for flowers and candles and incense burners and offering trays with fruit and tea and candy.

On one of the shelves, just off to one side, was a box wrapped in a

---

130. *ihai* (位牌)—spirit tablet, a memorial tablet.

white cloth and three small black-and-white photographs of Jiko's dead children, Haruki, Sugako, and Ema. I'd seen these pictures before but I never paid any attention. They were just stiff, old-fashioned strangers, time beings from another world who meant nothing to me. But now everything was different.

I stood on my tiptoes and reached across the altar for the picture of Haruki. In the photo, he looked younger than his ghost, a pale student with a school cap and a poetic expression, frozen under glass. He also looked a little like my dad, before my dad got flabby and stopped getting haircuts. The glass was dusty, so I rubbed it with the hem of my skirt, and just as I was wiping, something in his face seemed to move a little. Maybe his jaw tightened. A tiny spot of light seemed to shine from his eye. If he had turned his head and looked at me and spoken I wouldn't have been surprised, and so I waited, but nothing else happened. He just kept on staring off toward a faraway place beyond the camera, and then the moment was gone, and he was just an old picture in a frame again.

I turned the frame over and saw there was a date on the back, Showa 16. I counted back on my fingers. Nineteen forty-one.

He was still in high school. Just a couple of years older than me. He could have been my senpai.[131] I wondered if we would have been friends and if he would have protected me from the bullies. I wondered if he would have even liked me. Probably not. I'm too stupid. I wondered if I would have liked him.

One of the fasteners on the back of the frame was loose, but when I tried to push it into place, the whole thing came apart in my hands. I was like, oh, shit, because I really didn't want Jiko to know I'd broken it, so I tried to line the pieces up again, but something was jamming it and getting in the way. I was really sweating now. I thought maybe I could hide it, or just leave it on the floor and blame Chibi, but instead I sat down on the tatami and took it apart again, and that's when I discovered the letter. It was only one page, folded and tucked in between the photo and the cardboard backing. I unfolded it. The handwriting was strong

---

131. *senpai* (先輩)—one's senior at work or school, one's superior.

and beautiful, like Jiko's, in that old-fashioned way that's hard to read, so I folded it back up and stuck it in my pocket. I didn't mean to steal it. I just needed a dictionary and some time to figure out what it said. The frame was still broken, but I stuck the photograph back and bent one of the fasteners, which sort of held it together. Before I put it back up on the altar I held it close to my face.

"Haruki Ojisama!" I whispered, in my most sincere and polite Japanese. "I'm very sorry I broke your picture frame, and I'm very sorry I was such a fool. Please don't be mad at me for taking your letter. Please come back."

## 5.

Dearest Mother,

This is my last night on earth. Tomorrow I will tie a cloth around my forehead, branded with the Rising Sun, and take to the sky. Tomorrow I will die for my country. Do not be sad, Mother. I picture you crying, but I'm not worthy of your tears. How often have I wondered what I would feel in this moment, and now I know. I am not sad. I am relieved and happy. So dry your tears. Take good care of yourself and my dear sisters. Tell them to be good girls, to be cheerful and to live happy lives.

This is my last letter to you, and my formal letter of farewell. The Naval Authority will send it to you along with the notice of my death and my auxiliary pension to which you will now be entitled. I'm afraid it won't be very much, and my only regret is that I can do so little for you and my sisters with my worthless life.

I am also sending you the juzu you gave me, my watch, and K's copy of the Shōbōgenzō, which has been my constant companion these last few months.

How can I express my gratitude to you, dear Mother, for struggling to raise such an unworthy son? I cannot.

There are so many things I cannot express or send to you. It is too late. By the time you read this, I will be dead, but I will die believing that you know my heart and will not judge me harshly. I am not a warlike man, and everything I do will be in accordance with the love of peace that you have taught me.

> *Soon the waves will quench this fire*
> *— my life—burning in the moonlight.*
> *Listen! Can you hear the voices*
> *calling from the bottom of the sea?*

Empty words, you know, but my heart is full of love.

Your son,
Navy Second Sub-Lieutenant Yasutani Haruki

# Ruth

## I.

"Le mal de vivre," Benoit repeated. He was a short man, wide-faced and barrel-chested, wearing a pair of filthy Carhartts held up by red suspenders over a torn flannel shirt, and a toque jammed down over his curly black hair. His wiry beard was streaked with grey. He held a cluster of wine bottles in one large hand and gripped a Tanqueray bottle in the other. He stared past Ruth's head into some middle distance where French verse seemed to reside. The din and clatter of the recycling center seemed to quiet down just long enough to let him speak.

"Yes, of course it means the pain of life," he said. "Or the sickness, or perhaps the evil of living, as in 'les fleurs du mal.' Or, simply, the sorrow of life, contrary to la joie de vivre."

He paused for a moment to savor the sound of the words before tossing the bottles into the square hole of the crusher. The clatter of shattering glass was deafening. "Why?" he shouted.

"Oh, nothing," Ruth said. She felt suddenly unsure about how much she should tell Benoit, how much she would be able to convey over the racket. "They're just the words of a song I heard." How to explain the circumstances: that they were lyrics from a song being sung to a ghost; that she'd read them in a diary she'd found in a barnacle-encrusted freezer bag on the beach? She wanted to ask him for help translating the French composition book, and she had brought it along with her, but it all seemed too difficult. The dump wasn't a great place for nuanced conversations on a Saturday morning.

In the parking lot behind her, pickup trucks sloshed through the mud to the Dumpsters or backed up into the bays. Even though the transport center had recently introduced a garbage pickup program, islanders still liked to do things the old way. They liked to come to the dump to dispose of their waste personally. They liked to haul their sodden boxes of cans and plastic bottles to the recycling table, sort their paper from their cardboard, and hurl glass into the crusher. They liked to browse through the racks and shelves at the Free Store, which was the closest thing the island had to a department store. A trip to the dump was like a trip to the mall. It was what passed for entertainment on a Saturday morning. Children ran around outside, pretending to play World of Warcraft amid the dripping wreckage of rusting cars and doorless refrigerators. Dreadlocked punks scavenged for chains and derailleurs in the tangle of bicycles. Crows and ravens and bald eagles circled overhead, fighting for territory and meat scraps.

"Yes," Benoit said. "It is a very famous song. By Barbara." He pronounced the name in French, wrapping his lips around the three syllables, giving each equal weight and caressing the guttural *r*'s deep in his throat.

"No, actually. It was a singer named Monique—"

He flapped his hand impatiently. "Serf, yes, yes, it is the same. Barbara is her stage name, for her many fans. Are you a fan, too?"

"Well, I've actually never heard her," Ruth said. "I just ran across the lyrics in a book and wondered what they meant . . ."

Benoit closed his eyes and began to speak. She had to lean in to catch what he was saying over the steady din of the crusher's motor.

"*Le mal de vivre*, 'the pain of life.' *Qu'il faut bien vivre* . . . 'that we must live with, or endure.' *Vaille que vivre*, this is difficult, but it is something like 'we must live the life we have. We must soldier on.'"

He opened his eyes. "Does that help?"

"Oh, yes," she said. "Yes, I think it does. Thank you."

Benoit studied her. "Is this all you want? You do not need help with the rest of the translations? There is still the booklet in French, *non*?"

She eyed the crusher's gaping maw. "Muriel?"

"Dora," Benoit answered. He grinned, exposing the hole where a front tooth should have been.

"Of course."

"Mais, j'adore Barbara," he said, "and now I'm interested to help you. Here is too noisy. Perhaps we should adjourn to the library?"

He hollered for one of his dreadlocked dump punks to replace him, whistled for his dog, and then led her through the parking lot, up a dirt embankment that had been elaborately terraced with geranium-filled truck tires, to a small room at the back of the garage where the forklift was parked. His little dog ran ahead, barking.

The room was surprisingly neat, with windows overlooking the Dumpsters below. The furnishings were sparse and what you might expect: a banged-up metal desk in the corner; two office chairs on wobbly casters; a dented metal filing cabinet. But above the desk and covering the two adjacent sides of the room were floor-to-ceiling bookshelves, lined with books. The fourth wall was decorated with discarded paintings, mostly stoner art, faux native iconography, and paint-by-numbers northern landscapes of moose and grizzlies that were so bad they were good. Tacked to the wall, as well, was a sheet of ruled binder paper with a copy of the Serenity Prayer, neatly written by hand. *God give me the serenity to accept the things I cannot change* . . .

"Voilà," Benoit said, spreading his arms. "Ma bibliothèque et galerie. Welcome."

He sat down on the chair at the desk. The little dog, a wiry-haired mutt with a lot of terrier in him, jumped up onto one of the chairs, but Benoit called him off, and then used a rag to wipe the seat and offered it to Ruth. The dog gave Ruth a rueful look, then curled up at Benoit's feet.

She walked slowly past the shelves, scanning the spines. Some titles were in French, but many were in English, a good collection of the classics, interspersed with some science fiction, history, and political theory. It was better than what she could find at the library.

"All from the dump," he said, proudly. "Help yourself." He watched her, intently, as she pulled a collection of Kafka's stories from the shelf. "You look very much like your mother," he said, as she sat down across from him.

She looked up from the book, surprised.

"Ah, you didn't know?" he asked. "Your mother and I were great friends. She was one of our most loyal customers."

She remembered then. Oliver used to bring her mother to the dump every Saturday morning. They had a standing date, and her mother never forgot, even when the rest of her world was fading.

"Masako," Oliver would say, loudly, into her ear so she could hear him even without her hearing aids, which she'd stopped wearing by then. "I don't suppose you'd like to accompany me to the Free Store this Saturday?"

Her face would light up with a great toothless smile. She'd stopped wearing her dentures by then, too. "Well!" she'd exclaim. "I thought you'd never ask . . ."

She loved a bargain. She had grown up during the Depression and used to shop at thrift stores near her home before they moved her west. Soon after she arrived on the island, they brought her to the Free Store and left her to rummage through the racks. She was standing in the sweater aisle, examining a cardigan, when she called Ruth over.

"Where's the price tag?" she whispered. "The price tag is missing. How do I know how much it is?" Her voice sounded agitated. Missing things upset her. Missing price tags. Missing memories. Missing parts of her life.

"There's no price tag, Mom," Ruth said. "It's free. Everything here is free."

She stood there, stunned. "Free?" she repeated, looking around at the aisles of clothes and shelves of toys and books and housewares.

"Yes, Mom. Free. That's why it's called the Free Store."

She held up the sweater. "You mean, I can have this. Without paying? Just like that?"

"Yes, Mom. Just like that."

"My goodness," she said, looking at the sweater and shaking her head. "It's like I've died and gone to heaven."

Every Saturday after that, Oliver would drive Masako to the dump in the pickup. He'd park and help her down from the truck, and then escort her carefully up the hill, over the rocky terrain, and past the mounds of rusting junk to the door of the Free Store, where he'd hand her over to one of the volunteer ladies. They soon got to know her and saved her all the best things in her size. When he was done with the recycling, Oliver would collect her and escort her back downhill, where Benoit would be waiting to ask her how her shopping had gone and if she'd found any good bargains. This joke always made her laugh.

When her closets got full and her dresser drawers no longer closed, Ruth slipped things out from the bottom of her piles and returned them to the Free Store, where her mother could discover them all over again.

"Isn't this pretty?" Masako said, showing Ruth a blouse she'd just brought home. "I'm so glad I found this. I used to have one just like it, you know . . ."

Benoit laughed when she told him this story. "Your mother was very funny," he said. "She probably knew exactly what you were doing. Was there ever a memorial for her? No? I didn't think so. It's too bad."

He leaned forward in the chair. His dark eyes gleamed. "So, now, what can I do for you?"

He had already heard about the freezer bag and knew all about the contents. He asked to see the sky soldier watch, and so she took it off and showed him. What was it about men and that watch? He whistled through the gap in his teeth, waking the dog, who lifted his head, expectantly. When he was done admiring it, she took the letters and the composition booklet from her backpack and carefully unwrapped them. The little dog yawned and went back to sleep.

"The letters are in Japanese," she said, setting them aside and holding up the booklet. "But this is in French."

She hesitated, looking at his stained, work-hardened hands. Black grime caked the cracks in his calloused skin and under his nails. She wished she'd thought to make a photocopy. The slim booklet looked antique and flimsy between his thick fingers, but he handled it gently, turning the tissue-thin pages with a careful reverence that surprised her. He started to read aloud:

*"10 décembre 1943— Dans notre grand dortoir, les soldats de l'escadron et moi, on dirait des poissons qui sèchent sur un étendoir. Seule les nuits de pleine lune, quand le ciel est dégagé, me procurent assez de lumière pour écrire . . . Mes dernières pensées, mesurées en gouttes d'encre."*

He looked up. "Do you understand any of that?"

"Only a little," she admitted. "December. Something about fishes and the full moon. And maybe someone's last thoughts . . . ?"

His smile was tinged with pity. "Perhaps you would allow me to keep this and make a translation for you?"

The condescension in his tone irritated her, but she could get over that. Her real concern was for the safety of the old notebook. She didn't want to let him take it away, but she didn't want to offend him, either. The dog woke up, and sensing that the meeting was almost over, stood and nudged his nose into Benoit's hand.

"All right," she said, watching as he leaned over to scratch the dog's head. "Do you think it will take you a long time?"

He shrugged. Questions about time were meaningless on the island, but then his black eyes lit up. "Ah," he said. "Is this for your new book?"

"Oh, no," she said. "I'm just curious."

He looked disappointed. He folded the booklet back up and reached across the small table for the wax wrapping and the envelope. At least he was careful. The stack of folded letters caught his eye.

"Are these all written by the same man?" he asked.

"I don't actually know," she said. "I haven't read them yet. The Japanese handwriting is hard . . ."

He seemed uninterested in her excuses. He picked up the stack of letters and flipped through it. He unfolded one and spread it flat on the table. The dog, tired of waiting, lay back down.

"Don't tell me you read Japanese, too," she asked.

"Of course not. To me, this is the scratching of a chicken. But look. The pen is the same, and the ink." He opened the composition book again and laid it next to the letter. "And see? The handwriting is similar, even though your man is writing in different languages."

He was right. The writing had a similar feeling, precise and delicate, but full of energy and life. Ruth wondered how she could have missed that. "What makes you think the writer is a man?"

"Absolutely he is a man," Benoit said, tapping on the paragraph he'd read out loud in French, and then he read it again, only this time he translated into English.

"*December 10, 1943—We sleep together in one large room, my squadron members and I, laid out in rows like small fish hung to dry.*"

He reached across the table and tapped the face of her watch. "It is only my guess, but I believe these were all written by your sky soldier."

## 2.

On her way home from the dump, she noticed that the wind was picking up again, so she stopped at the Squirrel Cove store to buy groceries and top off the gas. She didn't have the spare gas can with her, but if the tank in the truck was full, Oliver could siphon out gas if the generator ran out. Provided the generator was working again. The clouds hung low on the mountains, and the waves in the mouth of the inlet were choppy and crested with white. A small fishing boat was crossing to the government dock. A bald eagle wheeled in great arcs overhead. It was only early afternoon, but the sky was already growing dark, and the lights from the Klahoose reservation twinkled on the far side of the cove.

The lights at home were still on, too. She parked the truck and unloaded the box of groceries. As she passed the woodpile she heard a crow cawing. She stopped and looked around, wondering if it was the Jungle Crow, but she couldn't see it. Did they have a different call? This one sounded alarmed. She heard it again, from farther away this time, followed by the low, drawn-out baying of a wolf, coming from over by the inlet. She continued into the house.

Oliver, anticipating the storm, already had the generator hooked up and ready to go. She put the groceries away and then followed the trail of extension cords upstairs. His office door, which was across the hall from hers, was open, and so she looked in. He was sitting at his desk, wearing his noise-canceling headphones and whistling a tuneless tune as he surfed the Internet. Next to him, the cat was asleep in the old swiveling office chair they'd gotten for him from the dump. They called it his co-pilot chair, and it was where he most liked to be. They'd gotten the cat from the dump, too.

The noise-canceling headphones had belonged to her, but she'd given them to Oliver when she saw how much he liked them. He liked the way they squeezed his head. The pressure helped him to think, he said, and now she had to shout to make herself heard.

"Hey!" she yelled from the doorway, waving her arm.

The cat blinked and opened one eye. Oliver looked up and waved back. "You're home," he said, too loudly. "I didn't hear you come in. Any luck?" The cat, annoyed at all the noise, opened the other eye.

She motioned for him to take off the headphones. "Sorry," he said, in a normal voice. "Any luck?"

"He's going to translate it. He thinks it was written by the sky soldier."

"Haruki Number One," Oliver said. "Interesting." He nudged the arm of the co-pilot chair and watched Pesto slowly rotate. "I wonder why he wrote it in French . . ."

"So nobody could read it? Benoit said he was hiding it from the other soldiers in his squadron."

Oliver pensively spun the cat. "'An excellent security feature,'" he said.

The minute she heard it, she recalled the reference. How could he remember things he'd heard with such clarity?

"'Who would pick up an old book called *À la recherche du temps perdu*?'" he continued. "That's what Nao wrote. So she's hiding her diary inside Proust, and he's hiding his diary by writing in French. Secret French diaries seem to run in the family." He gave the co-pilot chair one last happy spin and withdrew his hand quickly as Pesto, fully awake and disgruntled, swatted at him, catching his hand with a claw.

"Ow!" he said, putting his finger in his mouth.

"Serves you right," Ruth replied. The cat jumped off the co-pilot chair and stalked down the stairs and out the cat door. "I heard the wolves as

I was coming in," she said. "They're really close. It'll be your fault if he gets eaten."

Oliver shrugged. "It would serve him right if he got picked off by a wolf. Karmic retribution for all the baby squirrels he's killed." He put his headphones back on, but she could tell he was worried. Good. She crossed the hallway to her office.

Secret French diaries run in the family. Of course. Why hadn't she made that connection?

She entered her office and saw the meditation cushion on the floor, and it occurred to her that in her present state of mind, maybe she should try sitting zazen again—maybe it would help her memory—but she didn't. She sat down at her computer and logged on to Gmail, instead.

Still no reply from Professor Leistiko.

### 3.

It had been more than a week since she'd sent the email, and now she had a sudden thought: Had she actually sent it? Perhaps she had written it and forgotten to hit SEND. Or perhaps the connection had failed and the email hadn't gone out. These things happened more frequently than she liked to admit. She checked her sent-mail folder. No, there it was, stamped with the date and time. Good. She counted back. Nine days! Where had the time gone?

The cursor pulsed with steady impatience. She made a copy of the email, adding a polite little note of apology for her persistence, and sent it off again. She didn't want him to think she was a stalker, but nine days?

Her face was flushed and she put her hands on her cheeks to cool them, feeling vaguely guilty, but for what? For bothering the professor? For neglecting her own work? For all the time she was wasting online trying to track down clues about Nao? The sudden disappearance of "The Instability of the Female 'I'" had upset her. It was the corroboration from the real world that she'd been waiting for, and it had slipped away. Was she cheating to want to know more than what the girl had written? The world of the diary was growing increasingly strange and unreal. She didn't know what to make of the girl's ghost story. Did Nao really believe what she was writing?

The professor was her only hope. As she stared at the restless pixels on her screen, her impatience grew. This agitation was familiar, a paradoxical feeling that built up inside her when she was spending too much time online, as though some force was at once goading her and holding her back. How to describe it? A temporal stuttering, an urgent lassitude, a feeling of simultaneous rushing and lagging behind. It reminded her of the peculiar arrhythmic gait of Parkinson's patients in the hospice where her mother spent the last months of her life, the way they lurched and stalled as they made their way down the hallways to the dining room and eventually to their deaths. It was a horrible, stilted, panicky sensation, hard to put into words, but which, if she were to try to represent it typographically, would look something like:

*this is* **what** te**M** por *al* stut **ter** *ing* ***FEELS*** LIKE like a *stutstut* STUTTERY ***RUSHING*** FORWARD *in* TIMEWITHOUT*a*MOMENT*OR an* INSTANT *to* DI STINGUISH*One* ***INSTANCE*** *from* THE *next* GRO WING *ever* ***LOUDER*** AND ***LOUDER*** WITH *OUT* PUNCTUATION *until* ***SUDD*** ***ENLYWITHOUTWARNI*** ***NG*** IT...

243

## 4.

"I think I'm going crazy," she said. "Do you think I'm going crazy?"

They were lying in bed. Oliver was checking his email on his iPhone. He didn't reply, but Ruth didn't notice.

"I've been having premonitions," she said. "Do you remember that dream I had about old Jiko? I told you about it, right? The first one that felt so real? She was typing something into her computer, and even though I couldn't see it, I knew what she'd written."

She waited. When he didn't respond, she went on.

"She'd written, 'Up, down, same thing.' And then later when they were at the beach, Jiko said those exact same words . . . 'up, down, same thing.' I had that dream over a week before I read about the beach, so how did I know that?"

"How did you know that?" he repeated.

"Well, it was like old Jiko was texting me the message, too, only tele-pathically. Is that crazy?"

"Hm," Oliver said.

"It felt like a premonition. What do you think?"

"Premonitions are coincidences waiting to happen," he said, without looking up.

"I suppose, but it's weird, right? Stuff appearing out of nowhere, like the freezer bag and then the Jungle Crow. Stuff disappearing, like that article. I tried to find it again, but I couldn't. And the publication? *The Journal of Oriental Metaphysics*? Gone, too. I can't find it anywhere."

"Stuff doesn't usually just vanish," he said, typing a message with his forefinger. "It's got to be somewhere. Can't you do a search for the author and find out where—"

"I tried! That's the problem. I can't even find the author's name. I could have sworn it was listed in the academic archives site, but when I went back to find it, it was gone. Vanished! And Professor Leistiko won't answer my email. It's like the harder I look, the more stuff slips away. It's so frustrating!"

"Maybe you're looking too hard . . . ," he suggested.

"What's that supposed to mean?"

"Nothing." He tapped his screen and she heard the whoosh of an email being sent.

"Are you listening to me or checking your email?"

"Listening, checking email, same thing . . ."

"No it's not!"

"You're right," he said, looking up from the small screen. "Okay, I was checking my email, and at the same time I was listening to you, and at the same time something came up in my newsfeed that might be pertinent. And I now have two thoughts and one nice piece of news. Which would you like to hear first?"

"The nice news, please."

"I just got an email from an artists' collective in Brooklyn. They want to publish my monograph on the NeoEocene."

"That's fantastic!" she said, her annoyance vanishing. "Who are they?"

He smiled, modestly, trying not to show how pleased he was. "They call themselves the Friends of the Pleistocene."

"Amazing."

"It is. I mean, it's not perfect. I'm more of an Eocene guy myself, and they've got some pretty newfangled ideas. But hey, you know, one million years, fifty million years . . ."

"They're interested. That's what matters."

"Yeah," he said, sounding doubtful. "I just hope they don't disappear, too."

"They won't. Not if they've been around for that long."

"You're right," he said. "The Friends of the Pleistocene make *The Journal of Oriental Metaphysics* sound like lightweights."

"Was that your thought?"

"No." He held up his iPhone so she could see. "First of all, this came up in my newsfeed."

On the tiny screen was an article from *New Science* about a recent development in the construction of qubits for quantum computing.

She squinted to read the tiny text. "So?"

Oliver enlarged the font and pointed. She saw it then. The name of the researcher filled the tiny screen: H. Yasudani.

"Oh my god," she cried, sitting up. "Do you think that's him? It could be, right? Or it could be a typo. That's so crazy. Email me the link. I'll see if I can get in touch—"

"Already done," Oliver said.

She was half out of bed, one foot in its slipper, heading upstairs to her computer to go online and start the search.

"Don't you want to hear my other thought?" he asked.

"Of course," she said, fumbling for her glasses.

"It's just that I'm wondering if maybe there's a quantum element to what's happening."

She sat back down and let the slipper dangle. "What do you mean?"

"Well, maybe that's the wrong way to put it, but I'm just thinking that if everything you're looking for disappears, maybe you should stop looking. Maybe you should focus on what's tangible in the here and now."

"What do you mean?"

"Well, you've got the diary and you're reading it. That's good. Benoit is translating the composition book. That's good. But there's still the letters. You could get someone to help you with them."

Ruth frowned. It made sense, and it didn't. "I showed them to Ayako, but she said she couldn't—"

"Not Ayako," Oliver said. "Arigato. Hang on, let me check the weather . . ."

"What does the weather have to do with this?"

"Great," he said. "The storm is just missing us. Should be a calm crossing tomorrow." He looked up. "I need to bring that damn generator into the shop before it craps out again. You feel like going for sushi in the Liver . . . ?"

## 5.

Campbell River, or Scrambled Liver as it was called by islanders, was the closest city of any size to Whaletown, although "close" and "city" are relative terms. A trip to the Liver required two ferry rides and a drive across an intermediary island and took close to two hours, not counting ferry lineups, which in the summer season could be interminable. Once in the Liver, there was not much in the way of entertainment, just some big-box stores and half-vacant strip malls, a court, a jail, a hospital, a scattering of thrift stores and pawnshops, a couple of peeler bars, and a derelict pulp mill that left many people jobless when it closed.

Still, the ferry trip to town was beautiful, a slow chug across the steely sea, past tiny green islets that glowed under the brooding skies. Sometimes a pod of dolphins or porpoises would race the ship or play in its wake. In the distance, the snowcapped mountains rose high up above swathes of low-hanging mist.

They didn't go to town for the scenery, though. There were practical real-life reasons for the trip, like hospital visits or car repair, buying insurance, and stocking up on staples and supplies. It was customary for islanders to wince and exhibit a kind of exquisite pain at the thought of leaving their paradise for the bleak but necessary reality of the Liver.

Ruth, however, enjoyed her trips to town. For her, Campbell River felt refreshing. She liked shopping, and if they stayed overnight they could eat dinner at an ethnic restaurant, although compared with Manhattan, the choice was not huge: two Chinese buffets, a Thai restaurant, and her favorite, a Japanese sushi bar called Arigato Sushi.

The chef was a former auto mechanic named Akira Inoue, who had emigrated with his wife, Kimi, from Okuma City in Fukushima prefecture. Akira was an avid sports fisherman, and had brought his family to coastal B.C. for the world-class salmon fishing, before the runs went dry. They opened their restaurant, choosing the name Arigato as an expression of their gratitude to Canada for giving them a nice lifestyle, and in exchange, they worked hard to refine the palettes of their Campbell River neighbors. They had raised their son here and sent him to university in Montreal, but now that they were getting older and the salmon runs were in decline, Kimi had finally managed to convince Akira to sell Arigato

Sushi and retire to their hometown in Japan. The meltdown at the Fukushima Daiichi Nuclear Plant changed all that. Overnight, Okuma City had turned into a radioactive wasteland, and now Akira and Kimi were trapped in the Liver.

"Okuma City wasn't very special," Kimi said. "But it was our hometown. Now nobody can live there. Our friends, family, everybody had to evacuate. Walk out of their homes. Leave everything behind. Not even time to wash the dishes. We invited our relatives to come here. We told them Canada is safe. No guns. But they don't want to come. For them, this is not home."

Restaurants closed early in the Liver, and Kimi had taken a break from washing up in the kitchen to sit with Ruth and Oliver at the sushi bar, while Akira cleaned his knives and put away his fish. Their son, Tosh, had graduated from McGill University, and now worked in Victoria, but on the weekends he often drove up to help his father behind the sushi counter.

"Is this home for you?" Ruth asked Tosh.

"Do you mean Canada or Campbell River?" Tosh asked, looking amused. He was a tall, quiet kid, well-spoken, who had majored in political science. "Canada, yes. Montreal, absolutely. Montreal felt like home. Victoria, less so. Campbell River, uh, not so much."

"How about you?" Ruth asked Kimi.

Kimi hesitated and Akira answered for her. "She never care about fishing." He nodded to Ruth. "How about you?"

Ruth shook her head. "I don't know," she said. "I don't know what home would feel like."

Akira tore off a length of plastic wrap and laid it over a gleaming slab of bright red tuna. "I think you are more big-city girl. But you . . ." He leaned over the counter to refill Oliver's saké and then raised his glass in a toast. "You are country boy. Like me. Campbell River is plenty good for us, eh?"

Beside her, Ruth could feel Oliver hesitate, but he raised his glass. "To the Liver," he said.

It was getting late. Ruth pulled her backpack onto her lap and took out the letters. She had explained her problem earlier, and Kimi had agreed to try and help. Now Ruth watched as Kimi wiped down the countertop before accepting the letters with both hands and a formal little bow.

"Yes," Kimi said, inspecting the envelope on top. "It is a man's handwriting. The address is in Tokyo. The postal mark says Showa 18." She counted on her fingers. "That is 1943. This canceling mark is not so clear, but I think it is from Tsuchiura. There was a naval base, so maybe you are right, he was a soldier." She opened the letter and spread it on the counter in front of her, gently smoothing the creases. Tosh came around the counter and leaned over her shoulder.

"It is very nice handwriting," she said. "Old-fashioned, but I can read this. I will write down the translation, but please forgive my poor English. I have lived here for twenty years but still . . ."

Tosh put his hands on her shoulders and squeezed. "No excuses, Mom," he said. "I can't read the Japanese, but I'll help you with the English."

Akira gave a short laugh. "Yes," he said. "No excuses. Now we have lots of time to practice."

They spent the night at the Above Tide Motel and the next morning got coffee and muffins and made it to the terminal in time to catch the first ferry home. At that hour there wasn't a lot of traffic—only three vehicles in the lane bound for their island. One of the ferry crew, a beefy young Campbell River kid in shorts, came over and stood in front of their car, waiting to give them the signal to load. He eyed the vehicles in their lane and radioed the count to the bridge.

"Three for Fantasy," he muttered into his walkie-talkie.

Ruth had her window down and was feeding muffin crumbs to the sparrows.

"Did you hear that?" she asked Oliver, who was reading an old *New Yorker* in the passenger seat beside her.

"Hear what?"

"What the ferry guy just said."

"No. What did he say?"

"Three for Fantasy."

Oliver looked out the window at the kid. "That's a good one."

"How would he even know? He's too young to remember the show."

Oliver smiled. "Maybe. But he knows the island."

# *Nao*

### I.

I wasn't sure whether to tell Jiko about meeting the ghost of Haruki #1. First of all, I was afraid it might make her sad, because what if he hadn't visited her? Maybe he'd only visited me because I'm an ikisudama? And then if she knew, I would have to confess how I'd blown it by not asking him good questions or making him feel welcome. Probably there's a proper way you're supposed to treat ghosts, stuff you're supposed to say and special presents you're supposed to give them. Maybe Jiko would be upset with me for not doing it right, but how was I supposed to know?

Or maybe she would think I was lying. Maybe she would think I'd made the whole thing up to cover for the fact that I was snooping around the altar and broke the picture frame and stole the letter. By the next day, I was beginning to think I'd made the whole thing up, too, and it wasn't like I had a whole lot of opportunities to talk to her, so I decided just to wait to see if Haruki #1 would come back.

On the morning of the osegaki ceremony, I got up early and sneaked out to the temple gate. It was still dark out, but the lamps were lit in the kitchen, and I could hear Muji and some of the nuns who'd come to help. I knew if they saw me, they would make me help, too, so I was really quiet. I went and sat on the cold stone step by the gate, half hidden behind one of the huge pillars. It felt creepy and kind of damp, exactly the way you might think a ghost would like it, and I started to feel hopeful.

"Haruki Ojisama wa irasshaimasu ka?"[132] I whispered.

---

132. *Haruki Ojisama wa irasshaimasu ka?*—Uncle Haruki, are you there?

But the only person who answered was Chibi, the cat, who isn't a person at all.

I tried again. "Haruki Ichibansama . . . ?"[133]

I heard a noise then, a kind of low murmuring and humphing sound, and when I looked down to the very bottom of the steps, I could see there was a ghostly monster climbing toward me. It looked like a gigantic brown and grey caterpillar. *Tatari!* I thought. Spirit attack! I jumped up and ran behind the pillar before it could see me, holding Chibi tight to keep him from darting out.

The monster had white spots and bristly bumps and lots and lots of legs jutting out to the sides, and it moved in a kind of winding, galumphing way, slowly rising and falling up the steep stone steps. I watched it, trying to figure out what it was. It was too slow to be scary, and at first I thought maybe it was an ancient and very pathetic dragon. Sometimes temples have dragons, and maybe because Jiko was so ancient, her dragon was, too. But when it got closer, I could see that it wasn't a dragon or even a caterpillar monster. It was just a long line of very old people from the danka, and from above, their round humped backs and wobbling white heads looked like the caterpillar's body, and their arms and their walking sticks looked like the jutting legs, climbing up through the darkness.

I ran back into the temple and announced that the guests were coming, and things went into overdrive, with Muji running around and bowing and showing people into the shrine room. Across from the main altar for Shaka-sama, we'd set up a special osegaki altar for the hungry ghosts, and old Jiko sat in a fancy golden chair. There was a whole bunch of chanting and praying and incense offering, and then Jiko unrolled this scroll and started reading all the names of the dead. They were all names of family and friends that people from the danka had put on the list, and the scroll was really long, and Jiko's old voice droned on and on. The room was still and hot and quiet, and nothing was moving except for the names, and it was kind of boring, but just as I was starting to drift

---

133. *Haruki Ichibansama?*—Mr. Haruki Number One?

off, something strange happened. Maybe I was half-asleep and dreaming, but it seemed like the names were alive, like they were alive and floating through the shrine room, and nobody needed to feel sad or lonely or afraid of dying, because the names were here. It was a nice feeling, especially for the old people who knew they were going to be names on the list very soon, and when Jiko was finally done reading, everybody got a turn to stand up and make an offering of incense, which took forever but was nice, too.

So it was a long ceremony, but I didn't mind, because the visiting nuns and priests helped Jiko and Muji with the chanting and bells and the ceremonial stuff, and I got to play the drum. Muji had trained me to play it and I'd been practicing for weeks. I don't know whether you've ever played a drum before, but if you haven't you should really try it, because first of all, it feels good to beat something with a stick as hard as you can, and second of all, it makes an amazing sound.

The temple drum is as big as a barrel, and it sits on a tall wooden platform. When you play it, you stand in front, facing the stretched hide, trying to control your breathing, which is jumping all over the place because you are so nervous. The priests and nuns are chanting by the big altar, and you listen for your cue, which is getting closer and closer. Then, at just the right moment, you take a big breath, raise your sticks, draw back your arms, and

*boom*BOOM*BOOM*BOOMBOOM . . .
. . . *BOOM!*

You have to get the timing just right, and even though I was scared to make a mistake in front of all those people, I think I did a pretty good job. I really like drumming. While I'm doing it, I am aware of the sixty-five moments that Jiko says are in the snap of a finger. I'm serious. When you're beating a drum, you can hear when the *BOOM* comes the teeniest bit too late or the teeniest bit too early, because your whole attention is focused on the razor edge between silence and noise. Finally I achieved my goal and resolved my childhood obsession with *now* because that's what a drum does. When you beat a drum, you create *NOW,* when silence becomes a sound so enormous and alive it feels like you're breathing in the clouds and the sky, and your heart is the rain and the thunder.

Jiko says that this is an example of the time being. Sound and no-sound. Thunder and silence.

2.

After the osegaki ceremonies were over, we had a party for the guests, and I helped serve the food, which was hideous because I'm such a clumsy girl, so I'm not even going to bother to describe it. Finally Muji, who was a total wreck by then anyway, got fed up and sent me out on some errand, I don't remember what, and I happened to walk by Jiko's study and noticed that the sliding door was open. It looked like someone was inside. I was still worried about the picture frame and the letter, so I went over to see.

The room was dark, but the candles on the family altar were lit, and an old man was kneeling in front. His back was bent, and his hands were pressed together in front of his face. He bowed, touching his head to the floor, and then he stood up and shuffled to the altar. His body was as thin as a skeleton, and his suit was hanging off his bones. He had some kind of sash decorated with rows of medals that he wore around his shoulder, which gave the impression that maybe he was a soldier. When he reached the altar, he lit an incense stick and touched it to his forehead in offering, and as he reached forward toward the bowl, the trembling ember at the tip of the long thin stick of incense looked like a tiny firefly, wobbling around in the darkness.

He shuffled back and knelt at his place in front of the altar and stayed there for a long time. Sometimes he pressed his hands together with his juzu, and his lips would move. Sometimes he stopped and listened and then started muttering again. I watched for a while, and then I noticed that Jiko was in the room, too, kneeling in a shadowy corner by the bookshelf, with her eyes closed, like she was waiting for the old guy to finish whatever it was that he was doing. Of course, I was totally freaked out and afraid they were going to notice that the picture frame was broken and the letter was missing, but just as I was about to escape, I heard a noise behind me, like an old door sliding open or someone clearing his throat.

*The first thing they taught us was how to kill ourselves.*

The words were quiet but clear. I looked around but there was no one there, just the late-afternoon sunlight casting shadows across the garden, and the bamboo rustling in the breeze. I recognized the voice, though.

*Maybe you think that's strange? We were soldiers, but even before they showed us how to kill our enemies, they taught us how to kill ourselves.*

A small wind blew through the garden, causing the water in the pond to shiver. A dragonfly, resting there, flew away.

"Is that you?" I whispered as softly as I could. "Haruki Ojisama . . . ?"

*They gave us rifles. They showed us how to use our big toe to pull the trigger. How to lodge the tip of the barrel in the V of our jawbone so it wouldn't slip . . .*

My hand rose to my face, and my fingers brushed the underside of my chin.

*Here.*

My fingers folded themselves into the shape of a gun, thumb up, index and middle fingers pressing into the spot right beneath my jaw. I couldn't move.

*That's right. We were supposed to kill ourselves rather than allow ourselves to be taken prisoner by the Meriken.[134] They made us practice this over and over again, and if we hesitated or didn't get it right, the officers would kick us and beat us with batons until we fell down. Well, they would beat us anyway, no matter if we did it right or wrong. It was to build our fighting spirit.*

He laughed, a ghostly chuckle.

My hand dropped to my side.

---

134. Meriken (メリケン)—Americans.

The wind died then and the air was still and silent. Inside the room, the old guy was still kneeling, and I could tell by the way his body shook and his head hung down like a broken tulip that he was crying. Jiko just sat there in the corner with her eyes closed, patiently waiting, and for the first time I heard the faint rhythmic sound of her juzu beads, tapping out their tiny blessings.

When the voice spoke again, I could barely hear it. *That box on the altar. Next to the photographs. Do you see it?*

On the altar was a box wrapped in a white cloth. I'd seen it there every day. It looked like a present.

"Yes."

*Do you know what's inside?*

One day when I was helping Muji clean the altar, I'd asked her the same question. She said the box contained the remains of Haruki #1, but when I thought it over, it didn't make any sense. The word she used was *ikotsu*,[135] but if Haruki #1 died by crashing his kamikaze plane into a battleship, how could there be any leftover bones? I mean, even if there were any, who would have picked up them up? And where would they have picked them up from? The ocean floor? But Muji wouldn't answer my questions, and I couldn't ask Jiko because it wouldn't be polite to upset her. Was this a good question to ask a ghost?

"I think . . . they're your ikotsu, right? That's what Muji told me, but it doesn't make sense . . ."

I heard the sound again, like an old wooden door makes when it rattles in the wind.

*No sense. No sense at all . . .*

And then he was gone. Don't ask me how I knew. I could just tell by the absence. It was hot, but I was shivering and the little hairs were standing up on my arms, and I was afraid I'd pissed him off again with my stupid question. Inside the room, the old soldier took a large handkerchief from his pocket and wiped his eyes, and then he slowly pivoted on his knees so that he was facing Jiko, and the two of them bowed to

---

135. *ikotsu* (遺骨)—cremated remains; lit. "left-behind" + "bones."

each other. It took them forever to stand up again after all that bowing, which gave me plenty of time to run away.

## 3.

Obon lasted for a total of four days, and it's a crazy time for a couple of nuns. After osegaki was over and all the visitors had left, old Jiko and Muji and I got busy making the rounds of danka houses to do Buddhist services in front of all the family altars. Back in the old days, they used to walk to all the houses, but when Jiko finally turned one hundred, she said it would be okay if they drove in a car instead. Muji had to get her driver's license, which is really tough in Japan and costs a lot of money and takes a long time, even if you're good at driving, which Muji isn't. In fact, she is really bad at driving. The temple has an old car that one of the danka donated, and I sat next to Muji in front, and Jiko sat in back. Muji gripped the wheel with both hands so tightly her knuckles turned white, and leaned forward so far her nose almost pressed against the windshield. She stalled the car twice trying to start it, and even when she got it going, she was so nervous she kept hitting the brake. I could see why. The mountain roads were twisty and narrow, and every time we saw another car coming, she had to pull off onto the nonexistent shoulder to pass. And whenever that happened, old Muji would start bowing politely to the oncoming driver, bobbing her head up and down and almost plunging the car off the side of the mountain. I've never been so scared in my life. One time I looked behind at Jiko, figuring she must be having a heart attack or something, but she was fast asleep. I don't know how she does it. Once we got to the parishioner's house, there wasn't a whole lot I could do to help them, so mostly I just stayed outside and talked with people's cats.

I still had Haruki #1's letter in my pocket. By then I'd borrowed old Jiko's kanji dictionary from off her desk and had pretty much read the whole thing, except for a couple of words I didn't understand. At night I sneaked out to the temple gates and waited in a cloud of fireflies, hoping he would come once more, but he never did.

## 4·

After Obon, it was just the three of us again, but before we could settle back into our routine, summer vacation was over, and I only had a few days left before my dad came to pick me up and take me home. I was really bummed, so Jiko and Muji decided to make a little going-away party for me. Not that I'm a big fan of parties, but we decided to make pizza, which came out pretty badly because none of us knew how to make crusts, but we didn't mind. We had chocolates for dessert, because old Jiko really loved chocolates, and we also decided to sing some kara-oke.[136] It was Muji's idea. By then one of the danka had given us an old computer and helped us get online, and I found a pretty good karaoke website where you can download songs, and even though we didn't have a microphone, we were still able to sing and dance and make a lot of noise. We took turns, and then we voted on which song each person sang best.

My best hit was the old Madonna classic "Material Girl," and I did my dance number on the engawa, framed by the sliding doors, which looked like a stage. I translated the words for Jiko and she thought the whole thing was hilarious. Muji sang an R. Kelly number called "I Believe I Can Fly," but when she sang it it sounded like "I Bereave I Can Fry," which totally cracked me up. But Jiko won the all-around best hit of the evening with "Impossible Dream," which is a song from an old Broadway musical. I'm not a big fan of old Broadway musicals, but Jiko really liked this song, and even though her voice isn't so strong anymore, she sang it with real feeling. It's a sentimental song about how it's okay to have impossible goals, because if you follow your unreachable star no matter how hopeless or far, your heart will be peaceful when you're dead, even though you might be scorned and covered with scars like I am while you're still alive. I could really identify with the lyrics, and Jiko's quivery old voice was beautiful to hear. She really put her heart into it, and I think maybe she sang it for me.

---

136. *karaoke* (空オケ)—lit. "empty" + "orchestra" (*oke*—abbr. for *okesutora*).

That night, she came to my room to say good night, slipping along the engawa and in through the sliding doors like a breeze from the garden, so quietly I didn't hear her coming. She knelt next to my futon and put her hand on my forehead. Her old hand was dry and cool and light, and I closed my eyes, and before I knew it, I was telling her all about Haruki #1's ghost, how he'd visited me on the temple steps on the first night of Obon but he left because I couldn't think of any interesting conversational topics and I sang him a dumb French chanson instead. And how I felt so stupid and disrespectful, I had to visit his photograph on the altar so I could apologize, and while I was holding the picture his face seemed to come alive, but then I broke the frame and his letter fell out, so I took it. And how I begged him to come back, and he did, and he told me about how when he was a soldier the officers used to beat him up to build his fighting spirit, and he showed me how to shoot myself in the throat using my toe rather than be taken prisoner by the Merikens, but then he went away and I never saw him again.

I had my eyes closed, and it was like I was talking to myself in the darkness, or maybe not even talking, maybe just thinking. I could feel Jiko's hand on my forehead, drawing my thoughts out of my mind and holding me down to earth at the same time, so I wouldn't fly away. This is another one of old Jiko's superpowers. She can pull a story out of anybody, and sometimes you don't even need to open your mouth, because she can hear the thoughts that are going through your crazy mind before your voice can even find them. When I finished my story, I opened my eyes and she took her hand away. She seemed to be looking off into the distance, out into the garden, where the frogs were singing in the pond. Over and over their croaking voices swelled like a wave and then fell silent.

"Yes," she said. "That's how they were trained. They were student soldiers and very bright. The military men despised them. They bullied them and beat them every day. They broke their bones and crushed their spirits."

The word she used was *ijime*, and hearing it, suddenly I felt very small. Me and my stupid classmates. My little pricks and pokes and stabbings.

I thought I knew all about *ijime*, but it turned out I didn't know anything about it at all. I felt ashamed, but I wanted to know more.

"But it didn't work, right?" I asked. "They didn't crush Haruki Ojisama's fighting spirit, did they?"

Jiko shook her head. "No," she said. "I don't believe they did."

I thought about it some more. "Americans were the enemies," I said. "That's so weird. I grew up in Sunnyvale. Does that mean I'm an enemy?"

"No, it doesn't."

"Do you hate Americans?"

"No."

"Why not?

"I don't hate anybody."

"Did you, before?"

"No."

"Did Haruki hate them? Is that why he wanted to be a suicide bomber?"

"No. Haruki never hated Americans. He hated war. He hated fascism. He hated the government and its bullying politics of imperialism and capitalism and exploitation. He hated the idea of killing people he could not hate."

It didn't make sense. "But in his letter, he said that he was giving his life for his country. And you can't be a suicide bomber and not kill people, can you?"

"No, but that letter was just for show. It was not his true feeling."

"So why did he join the army then?"

"He had no choice."

"They made him go?"

She nodded. "Japan was losing the war. They had drafted all the men. Only the students and little boys were left. Haruki was nineteen when his notice came, calling on him, as a Japanese patriot and warrior, to report for battle. When he showed it to me, I cried, but he only smiled. 'Me,' he said. 'A *warrior*. Imagine that!'"

A single frog croaked, and then another. Jiko's words dropped like stones into the silence in between.

"He was poking fun at himself, you see. He was a kind boy, so gentle and wry. He was not the warrior type."

The frog voices began to gather and rise. Jiko kept on talking, and now her words were steady, a low drumbeat under the shrill croaking.

"It was late October. There was a pageant. Twenty-five thousand student draftees marched into the compound outside Meiji Shrine. They were given rifles to carry on their shoulders like children playing soldiers. A cold, dull rain was falling, and the red and gold colors of the shrine looked gaudy and much too bright. For three hours the boys stood at attention, and we stood there, too, listening to the fine words and phrases in praise of the fatherland.

"One of the boys, Haruki's classmate, gave a speech. 'We, of course, do not expect to return alive,' he said. They knew they would die. We had all heard about the mass suicides of soldiers at a place called Attu. Gyokusai,[137] they called it. Insanity, but by then there was no stopping. The prime minister was there. Tojo Hideki. It is not true, what I said before, because I hated him. He was a war criminal, and after the war, they hanged him. I was so happy. I wept for joy when I heard he was dead. Then I shaved my head and took a vow to stop hating."

The frog chorus fell silent.

"That boy who gave the speech survived," she said. "Every year at Obon he comes here to apologize."

It took me a moment to understand. "You mean that old man?"

She nodded. "Not a boy anymore. My son would be an old man, too, if he had survived. It is hard for me to imagine."

I lay on my back and pictured the old soldier's face. I tried to imagine him as a young man, as young as Haruki's ghost. Impossible.

"They were our finest students," she said. "They were the *crème de la crème*." She used the French words, pronouncing them in Japanese, but I knew what she meant. Her eyes, cloudy with emptiness, stared

---

137. *gyokusai* (玉砕)—suicide attack, human wave attack. Literally "shattering like a jewel," from a seventh-century Chinese saying, "A great man should die as a shattered jewel rather than live as an intact tile."

into the past. I was afraid to say anything to disturb her, but I had to know.

"I'm sorry I took the letter," I said. "I'll put it back."

She nodded, but I don't know if she really heard me.

"What's in the box?" I asked.

The question seemed to bring her back for a moment. "What box?"

"The one on the family altar."

A shadow crossed her face. Maybe it was a cloud passing in front of the moon, or maybe it was my imagination.

"Nothing."

"What do you mean, nothing?" I asked, and when she didn't answer, I prompted her. "You mean it's empty?"

"Empty," she repeated. "So desu ne."

She looked at me as though I was a fading memory. "Forgive me, Nao dear. I go on and on. You must sleep."

"No," I protested. "I like your stories! Tell me more!"

She smiled. "Life is full of stories. Or maybe life is only stories. Good night, my dear Nao."

"Good night, my dear Jiko," I answered.

In the moonlight, she looked tired and old.

## 5.

The next day, my dad came to pick me up, but before he arrived, I went back to Jiko's study one last time. I had promised to put back the letter, and the box was still sitting on the little shelf, tied in its white cloth, next to the photograph. I didn't want to disturb him again, but I really needed to see what was in that box. Jiko said there was nothing, but the way Haruki had laughed his ghostly laugh made me think there was something inside. Maybe his baby teeth, or his glasses, or his high school diploma. You can call it superstition, but I wanted to see some piece of him that really existed in order for him to be real.

I stood up on my tiptoes and reached for the box, pulling it off the shelf and into my arms. I sat down on the floor and untied the white cloth. It was like unwrapping a Christmas present. Inside the cloth there was a wooden box with some writing on it that said, "The Heroic Soul of the Late Second Sub-Lieutenant Yasutani Haruki." I felt my heart start to pound. The box was about 40 centimeters tall. I gave it a little shake and thought I heard something rattle inside. What would a soul sound like? I really wanted to look, but suddenly I was afraid if I opened the box, his heroic soul would fly out. Would it be angry at me? Would it fly in my face? I almost wrapped the box up again and put it back on the shelf, but at the last minute I changed my mind. I lifted up the lid.

It was empty.

Jiko was right. I couldn't believe it. Just to be sure, I turned it upside down and shook it. A small slip of paper fell to the floor.

"The Naval Authority sent me that," Jiko said.

She was standing in the doorway, dressed in the faded brown robe that she wore for morning service and leaning on her cane. I swear, she can appear out of nowhere. It's another one of her superpowers.

"They sent us a box with the remains of our beloved children. If the bodies weren't found, they put in a piece of paper. They couldn't just send an empty box, you see."

I looked at the paper in my hand. There was one word written on it: 遺骨[138]

"I opened it just like you did," she said. "And just like that, the paper fell out. I was so surprised! I read it and then I laughed and laughed. Ema and Suga were in the room with me. They thought I had gone crazy with grief, but they didn't understand. My daughters were not writers. To a writer, this is so funny. To send a word, instead of a body! Haruki was a writer. He would have understood. If he had been there, he would have laughed, too, and for a moment that's what it felt like, like he was there with me and we were laughing together."

She chuckled to herself and wiped her eyes with her crooked old finger. Sometimes when she told stories about the past her eyes would

---

138. *ikotsu*—remains.

get teary from all the memories she had, but they weren't tears. She wasn't crying. They were just the memories, leaking out.

"It was the nicest consolation," she said. "Given the circumstances. But I could never bring myself to put it into the family grave. That last word was not his, after all. It was the government's."

She was still leaning on her cane, but now she started looking for something in the deep sleeve of her robe, and she swayed a little like she might lose her balance, so I jumped up to help her. When I reached her, she held out her hand.

"Here," she said. She was holding one of Muji's freezer bags with some papers inside. "These were the letters that Haruki wrote to me before he died. Perhaps you'd better have them, too. You can keep them together with the one you found."

I took the bag from her, unzipped it, and looked in. I recognized Haruki's handwriting from the letter I'd taken from the picture frame.

"You may read them," Jiko said. "But please remember these aren't his last words, either."

I nodded, but I was barely listening. I was so excited! I couldn't wait to read the letters. Haruki #1 was my new hero. I wanted to know everything I could about him. She fumbled around in her robe sleeve again.

"And this," she said. "Take this, too."

She was holding an old wristwatch. It had a round black face and steel hands and a steel case and a big knob on the side for winding. I took it and held it to my ear. It made a nice ticking sound. I turned it over. Engraved in the metal back were a line of numbers and two kanji characters. The first was the kanji 空 for sky. The second was the kanji 兵 for soldier. Sky soldier. That made sense. But the character for sky can also mean "empty." Empty soldier. That made sense, too. I turned it back over and strapped it on my wrist. Not big. Not small. Just right.

"It was Haruki's," Jiko said. "You have to wind it." She tapped the little knob on the side with her bent finger. "Every day."

"Okay."

"Never let it stop," Jiko said. "Please don't forget."

"I won't," I promised. I held out my wrist to show her the watch. I made a fist. It made me feel strong. Like a warrior.

She nodded and seemed satisfied. "I'm glad you met him while you were here," she said. "He was a good boy. Smart like you. He took his life seriously. He would have liked you."

She gave another nod, taking her time, and then turned and shuffled away. I stood there listening to the sound of her cane tapping down the old wooden corridor. I couldn't believe she said that. Nobody ever called me smart. Nobody liked me.

I put Haruki's remains-that-were-not-remains back into the box and tied the whole package up and put it back on the altar. Then I lit a candle and a stick of incense and offered it to him, placing my palms together.

"It has been a great pleasure to meet you," I said, in my most polite Japanese. "I hope I may look forward to your company again next summer. Please continue to take good care of dear Jiko Obaachama until I get back, okay? Oh, and thanks for the watch."

I bowed a deep, formal raihai bow, dropping to my knees and touching my forehead to the floor and then lifting my palms toward the ceiling. When I got up again, I had another thought.

"I don't know whether this is cool or not, but if you wouldn't mind checking up on my dad from time to time, too, I would really appreciate it. He's named for you, and he could really use some help."

I bowed again quickly and left. I didn't really believe Haruki's ghost could do anything for my dad, but I figured it couldn't hurt to ask.

Dad arrived that afternoon. I didn't want to leave, but I was happy he'd shown up. I guess part of me was worried that he wouldn't. He looked older than I remembered, but I didn't say anything. I kept waiting for him to notice how strong I'd become, but he didn't say anything, either. He was going to spend the night, and we were going to leave for Tokyo the next morning.

I felt kind of bad about what happened next. At dinner he announced that he was going to take me to Disneyland on the way home. Now that I think about it, I can see how it was a big deal for him because he really suffers in places like that with all the noise and the crowds, so he must have been psyching himself up for weeks. But at the time, I couldn't see this. All I could see was how old and tired and pathetic he looked behind his big goofy smile, and in my mind I kept comparing him to Haruki #1. Jiko and Muji were sitting at the dinner table, waiting for me to jump up and down and be really happy and grateful about going to Disneyland, but instead I just kind of mumbled, "No thank you."

Dad's big smile disappeared then, and if I were a nicer person, I would have said, Hey, just kidding!, and then pretended to be superexcited, and we would have gone to Disneyland, and that would have been that. But I'm not a nice person. The truth was that I didn't want to go. After meeting Haruki #1, who was a real hero, and hearing about what he went through in the war, I couldn't get excited about seeing Mickey-chan and shaking his hand. It all just seemed kind of juvenile and dumb. I just wanted to get back home so I could start reading the letters.

# Haruki #1's Letters

December 10, 1943

Dear Mother,

Three months have passed since the Measures to Strengthen the Internal Situation were announced, terminating our student deferments and shutting down the Department of Philosophy. I'm afraid Jurisprudence has suffered, too, along with Belles Lettres, Economics, and others, of course. So there you have it. Philosophy, Law, Literature, and the Economy, all sacrificed to the glorious cause of War. How splendid is that?

Two months have passed since our great send-off at Meiji Shrine, that ceremony of sad puppets in the cold and bitter rain. Dear Mother, I fear Monsieur Ruskin was wrong. The sky does weep, and there is nothing false about pathetic fallacy.

One week has passed since I bid goodbye to you and Suga-chan and Ema-chan, and entered the barracks at T— Navy Airbase. I will try to write more of my life here, but for now, suffice it to say that you would not recognize me if you were to pass me on the street, I have changed that much.

January 2, 1944

Dear Mother,

When I learned our student exemptions were terminated, I knew I would die, and I was overcome with an emotion akin to relief upon hearing the news. Finally, after these long months of waiting and not knowing, to be certain, even if it was the certainty of death, felt exhilarating! The way ahead was clear, and I could stop worrying about all the silly metaphysical business of life—identity, society, individualism, totalitarianism, human will—that in university had so preoccupied and clouded my mind. In the face of certain death, all those notions seemed trivial, indeed.

It was only when I saw your tears, dear Mother, that I realized the selfishness of my response, but sadly, I was too immature to correct myself. Instead, I grew impatient with you. Your tears made me feel ashamed. If I'd been more of a man, I would have thrown myself onto the floor at your feet and thanked you for your tears and for the strength of your love for me. Instead, your unworthy son asked you (somewhat coldly, I fear) to stop crying and to pull yourself together.

During the physical examination in October, the recruiting officer ordered us to "switch off our hearts and minds completely." He instructed us to cut off our love and sever our attachment with our family and blood relations because from now on we were soldiers and our loyalty must lie solely with our Emperor and our homeland of Japan. I remember listening to this and thinking that I could never comply, but I was wrong. In trying to stop your tears, I was already obeying the officer's command to the letter, not out of patriotic allegiance, but out of cowardice, in order not to feel the pain of my own heart, breaking.

Since that time, on many occasions, I have realized that my exhilaration was preemptive and naïve, as well as selfish. It was a feeling born of ignorance, the kind of heady existential euphoria that gives birth to mere heroics or to the unthinking patriotism of the kind that we see so often during war. These are dangerous consequences indeed, and I am filled with chagrin at having been so misled. I am determined not to let this happen again.

As I have not much time left in life, I am determined not to be a coward. I will live as earnestly as I can and feel my feelings deeply. I will rigorously reflect upon my thoughts and emotions, and try to improve myself as much as I can. I will continue to write and to study, so that when the time of my death comes, I will die beautifully, as a man in the midst of a supreme and noble effort.

February 23, 1944

Dear Mother,

Our training is severe and our squadron received more special attention today. It is both personal and, at the same time, not. Our squadron leader is a noncommissioned officer named F, and he and the other senior officers seem to favor us student recruits and single us out for special exercises. They see us as privileged and effete, and of course they are right. They are doing us a favor, they say, turning us into military men, and I have to laugh at the brilliance of this! Oh, we are turning into fine soldiers, all right.

With my lack of physical stature and my clumsy ways, you can imagine I am quite a favorite, but the one I truly feel sorry for is K, who was senior to me in the Department of Philosophy. K is a true philosopher. He is . . . how to express it? Not "of this world." He has the unfortunate habit of losing himself in a train of thought, and when this happens, he stares off into the distance and pays no attention to the commands of the officers, which does little to endear him to those in charge. F has nicknamed K "The Professor" (as you can imagine, we all have our pet names, and mine do not bear repeating). K and I have decided that there is a kind of beauty in the ingenuity of F's training methods, which are akin to those of the brilliant French soldier the Marquis de Sade. Like the

Marquis, he has an ingenious mind and an artist's introspection that inspires him, driving him toward some kind of unspeakable perfection. We have decided this shall be his nickname from now on.

February 26, 1944

Dearest Mother,

Our days pass, and I am pleased to tell you that I am making progress in my training and seem to be advancing in both rank and status, as well as in the estimation of my superiors and peers.

Recently during one of our exercises, I became concerned about K's health, so I stepped forward and volunteered to take his place. The Marquis was only too happy to oblige, and since that time he has decided that I am a far more satisfying pupil than K, from whom he failed to elicit any significant reaction. Now, when he calls me out, it's almost as if he is seeking my collaboration in making each exercise more exquisite than the last. He refers to his training as an act of kindness, and I wouldn't be surprised if he goes over our sessions in his mind afterward, in order to hone his artistry. If his medium had been words instead of war, he would have been a poet.

April 14, 1944

Dear Mother,

I shall continue my tales of adventure where I last left off. After the evening meal and roll call, the Marquis often suggests silly games to improve the morale of the squad. Since I have now advanced and become his favorite, he invites me to be the oni, while the others circle around and sing "Kagome Kagome." Do you remember that song, Mother? It is a pretty song about a trapped bird in a bamboo cage.

Another game he likes is "bush warbler crossing the valley," which entails hopping over every bed and stopping now and then to chirp the bush warbler's song, *ho-ho-ke-kyo!* Sometimes, too, we play the train game, or the heavy bomber game. His games don't finish until the final bugle sounds, signaling lights out.

The other members of my squadron sometimes laugh and enjoy themselves, but K never laughs. He stands there, watching, committed to bearing witness to the smallest details, but there is nothing he can do. When he tries to step forward and take my place, the Marquis just brushes him away like a mosquito. In my eagerness to protect K, I fear I have caused him an even greater suffering.

June 16, 1944

Dearest Mother,

I will not write at length, because you will be coming soon for your visit, and this thought fills me with a joy I can hardly contain or express. But I felt I needed to write, briefly, to prepare you.

K disappeared three days ago. At first we didn't know what happened. The Marquis questioned us, but none of us knew anything, although I feared the worst. And indeed, the following day we received news that he had died. I don't know how, although I have my suspicions. All I know for certain is that I feel such grief for the suffering of my friend, and I fervently hope that he will be reborn in a far better world than this one.

August 3, 1944

Dear Mother,

The memories of your visit linger, and I can call to mind every detail of your strong, beautiful face, of Suga's charming shyness and Ema's sweet smiles. These images comfort me every night as I lie down to sleep, and I try not to think of my dear sisters weeping and waving as the train pulled away. Thank you for the juzu. It is such a comfort, and I will carry it under my uniform, next to my heart.

I will also not forget the shocked expression on your face when you first laid eyes upon me. Has your dear son changed so much? I can still feel the touch of your gentle fingertip caressing the bruise on my cheek and the cut on my jaw. You would not believe me when I said that the injuries were minor, and in that moment I felt such shame for failing to prepare you for what are, in truth, merely the routine banalities of military life. I was not thinking how extremely you would suffer on my behalf. How selfish and indulgent I've been! My only excuse is that sometimes I forget you cannot read my mind. We are so close, you and I, the same flesh and blood, and you have always known my heart.

Your reports of the situation in Tokyo frighten me, and I beg you to be careful. I fear for your safety and the safety of my sisters. I wish you would consider evacuating to the countryside. Meanwhile, here, it seems this phase of our training is complete, so you may now cease your worrying. The Marquis has been assigned a squadron of new recruits, and we have graduated and are now learning to fly.

December 1944

Dear Mother,

Yesterday we were called together to hear a rousing speech and fiery appeal to our patriotic spirit, culminating in a call for volunteers to receive accelerated training as Special Attack Force pilots. Dear Mother, please forgive me. Death is inevitable, no matter what choice I make. I see that and understand it in ways that I could never have before. Please dry your eyes, and let me explain.

Choosing this death has various benefits associated with it. First, and most important, it guarantees a posthumous promotion of two ranks, which of course is meaningless, but it comes with a substantial increase in the pension paid to you upon my death. I can hear you protesting, wringing your hands and insisting that you don't need the money, and the thought makes me smile. You would rather starve to death than benefit from my dying. I understand this. But for my sake and my sisters' sake, I beg you to accept my decision. Choosing this death gives me tremendous consolation. It gives meaning to my life and profound satisfaction to my filial heart. If the extra compensation helps feed you and my sisters, and helps them find good husbands, that will be enough for me.

So that is one benefit, and it is practical. The other benefit is perhaps more philosophical. By volunteering to sortie, I have now regained a modicum of agency over the time remaining in my life. Death in a ground offensive or bombing attack seems random and imprecise. This death is not. It is pure, clean, and purposeful. I will be able to control and therefore appreciate, intimately and exactly, the moments leading up to my death. I will be able to choose where and how, precisely, my dying will occur, and therefore what the consequences might be. If you dry your tears and think about this, Mother, I am sure you will understand what I am saying.

Spinoza writes, "A free man, that is to say, a man who lives according to the dictates of reason alone, is not led by fear of death, but directly desires the good, that is to say, desires to act, and to preserve his being in accordance with the principle of seeking his own profit. He thinks, therefore, of nothing less than death, and his wisdom is a meditation upon life."

The point being that my death in this war is inevitable, and so how I die is academic. Since there is no possibility of preserving my being or seeking my own profit in this life, I have chosen the death that will bring most benefit to the ones I love, and that will cause me the least grief in the next life to come. I will die a free man. Please console yourself with thoughts like these.

March 27, 1945

Dear Mother,

You will be happy to know that as I wait to die, I have been reading poetry and novels again. Old favorites by Sōseki and Kawabata, as well as the books you sent me by your dear women writer friends, Enchi Fumiko-san's *Words Like the Wind* and the poems by Yosano-san in *Tangled Hair*.

Reading these women writers makes me feel closer to you. Did you share their racy past, my dear Mother? If so, I applaud you, and will ask nothing further, knowing it's unbecoming of a son to tease a mother so.

I find myself drawn to literature more now than in the past; not the individual works as much as the <u>idea</u> of literature—the heroic effort and nobility of our human desire to make beauty of our minds—which moves me to tears, and I have to brush them away, quickly, before anyone notices. Such tears are not becoming in a Yamato danshi.[139]

Are you still writing? Nothing would make me happier than to know that you are writing poems or working on a novel, but I imagine you have little time for that.

Today during a test flight, I remembered Miyazawa Kenji's wonderful tale about the Crow Wars. People think of it as a children's tale, but it is so much more than that, and as I was soaring in formation at an altitude of two thousand meters, I recalled the Crow Captain lifting off from his honey locust tree, and taking to wing to do battle. *I am Crow!* I thought, ecstatically. The visibility was good, and since this was the very last of the special training flights, I flew in all directions to my heart's content.

I love to fly. Have I mentioned that? There is truly no feeling more splendid or more transcendental. Sometimes zazen comes

---

139. *Yamato danshi* (大和男子)—lit. "man of Yamato." The masculine archetype of a true Japanese man.

close. I am sitting zazen every day. Thank you for suggesting it. I am comforted to know that you are sitting, too.

I'm afraid my day is approaching and my next "official" letter to you may be the last one you receive from me. But no matter what nonsense I write in it, please know that those are not my last words. There are other words and other worlds, dear Mother. You have taught me that.

# Part III

*Do not think that time simply flies away. Do not understand "flying" as the only function of time. If time simply flew away, a separation would exist between you and time. So if you understand time as only passing, then you do not understand the time being.*

*To grasp this truly, every being that exists in the entire world is linked together as moments in time, and at the same time they exist as individual moments of time. Because all moments are the time being, they are your time being.*

—Dōgen Zenji, Uji

# *Nao*

## 1.

It took me a week to read all of his letters. His handwriting was difficult because the characters all ran together, and I didn't understand a lot of the terms he used, but I was determined. Every evening as I wound my great-uncle Haruki's watch, I thought about his whispered stories, and they haunted me and filled me with shame. Every morning, when I woke up early to do zazen, these were the words that crowded through my head as I sat on my cushion:

"What a fool you are, Yasutani Naoko! A coward, who cannot even withstand a little bit of ijime by children who are equally as pathetic as you! What they did to you is just a peanut compared to what your great-uncle endured. Haruki #1 was only a couple of years older than you, but he was a superhero, and brave and mature and intelligent. He cared about his education and he studied diligently. He knew about philosophy and politics and literature, and he could read books in English and French and German as well as Japanese. He knew how to shoot himself in the throat with a gun, even though he didn't want to. You, Yasutani Naoko, are pitiful compared to him. What do you know about? Manga. Anime. Sunnyvale, California. Jubei-chan and her Lovely Eyepatch. How can you be so stupid and trivial! Your great-uncle Yasutani Haruki #1 was a War Hero who loved life and peace, and still he was willing to fly his plane into a battleship and die to protect his country. You are a sad little bug, Yasutani Naoko, and if you don't get your shit together immediately, you do not deserve to live another instant."

Now that I think about it, I can understand that I was probably very hard to be around after I got back from the temple. I was mad at myself but I was even madder at my dad. I mean, I was a girl and still pretty young, so I had an excuse for being lame, but my dad was a grown-up man and had no excuse. He was supposed to go to the doctor over the summer and get better, but as far as I could see, he was exactly the same or worse, and I could tell my mom thought so, too.

One day, right after I started reading the letters, there was a kanji that I couldn't find in the dictionary. I copied it out as best I could, and that night I showed it to my mom and asked her what it meant. She said it was an old-fashioned word, and she rewrote it the modern way and we looked it up together. The next time I had trouble, I asked her again, and soon I was making a list every day and asking her for help every night, which made my reading go a lot faster. One night when we were sitting at the kitchen table, she asked me what I was working on and if it was a project for school. Dad was out on the balcony, smoking, and I knew he couldn't hear us, so I decided to tell her about H #1's letters.

She looked surprised. "Your great-grandmother really gave them to you?"

Her question made it sound like I'd stolen them or something. "Yes, she really gave them to me. And they're really interesting. I'm learning a lot about history and stuff." I hated that I sounded so defensive.

"Have you shown them to your dad?"

"No." Now I was really regretting that I'd told her.

"Why not? They were written by his uncle, and I think he would want to read them, too. Your dad knows a lot more about his side of the family than I do. You could read them together."

Okay, this pissed me off. I didn't want to show them to my dad. He didn't deserve to see them, and besides, I figured she was just trying to unload me on him as part of his so-called rehabilitation, or mine.

"If you don't want to help me, fine. I'll figure it out on my own."

This was a pretty snotty thing to say, but instead of getting mad, she reached her hand across the kitchen table and laid it on my wrist, kind of holding me in place. "Naoko-chan," she said. "I love helping you. It's not that. I know how difficult all this has been for you, but don't be too hard on your father. He's a good man and I know deep down you love him. He's trying really hard, and you should, too."

If she hadn't been holding my arm down at that moment I would have jumped up and thrown something at her. She didn't know anything about how difficult stuff was for me or how hard I was trying! And I totally didn't believe her about my dad, either. She was lying. He was sitting on the balcony on his bucket with a cigarette, reading a manga, and I could tell by her tired face and the nervous way she looked at him that she didn't think he was trying hard at all.

But she was right about one thing. I still loved him. I thought about her suggestion in bed that night and realized that maybe I did want to tell him about the War and Haruki #1. Dad was named after him, and if he knew how brave and cool Number One was, he might get inspired to turn things around.

So the next day when I got home from school, I decided to show him the letters. He was sitting at the kotatsu, folding a Japanese rhinoceros beetle from a page of The Great Minds of Western Philosophy. On account of what I'd learned about Number One, I was a little bit more interested in philosophy now.

"What are you folding?" I asked.

"A *Trypoxylus dichotomus tsunobosonis*," he said, holding it up and showing me its great pronged horn.

"No, I mean, what philosopher?"

He turned the insect over, squinted, and started to read, rotating the body to follow the line of words around the folds and edges. " '. . . existent Dasein . . . comes to pass in time . . . historizing which is 'past' in our Being-with-one-another . . . handed down . . . regarded as 'history' in the sense that it gets emphasized,' " he read, and then he smiled. "Mr. Martin Heidegger-san."

For some reason, this really pissed me off. I didn't know anything about Mr. Martin Heidegger-san or understand what he was talking about, but I recognized his name from one of H #1's old philosophy books, so I knew he must be important, and here was my dad, turning Mr. Heidegger's great mind into a bug. That did it. It was time my dad learned what a contemptible being he was.

"You know your uncle Haruki studied philosophy for real," I blurted out. "He was in the Department of Philosophy at Tokyo University. He didn't sit around at home all day playing with origami like a child."

My dad's face went pale and still. He put his beetle on the table and stared at it.

I knew my words were harsh. Probably I should have stopped there, but I didn't. I wanted to inspire him. I wanted to snap him out of it. I slapped the letters on the table in front of him.

"Jiko Obaachama gave me his letters. You should read them, too, and maybe you'll stop feeling so sorry for yourself. Your uncle Haruki Number One was brave. He didn't want to fight in a war but when the time came, he faced his fate. He was a navy second sublieutenant and a true Japanese warrior. He was a kamikaze pilot, only his suicide was totally different. He wasn't a coward. He flew his plane into the enemy's battleship to protect his homeland. You should really be more like him!"

My dad didn't look at me or the letters. He just kept staring at his beetle. Finally he nodded. "*Soo daro na . . .*"[140]

His voice sounded really sad.

Maybe I shouldn't have said anything.

## 2.

School started again. In Japan, September is only halfway through the school year, and so I was still in the same class with those stupid, hypocritical kids who had ignored me to death in the first semester and then pretended to be sad at my funeral. But this semester I decided things were going to be different. I was not going to let them bully me anymore or break my spirit. I knew I could always stab old Reiko in the eye again, but I didn't want to resort to physical violence if I didn't have to. Instead, I was going to use my *supapawa* that Jiko taught me. I was going to be brave and calm and peaceful, like her and Number One.

When I walked into school that first day back, my heart was pounding,

---

140. *Sō darō na*—Mm, you're probably right.

but the fish in my stomach felt strong and powerful like a dolphin or a killer whale. The kids must have noticed the difference, or maybe they sensed Number One's ghost hovering next to me, and even though nobody seemed overjoyed to see me, at least they didn't punch me in the face.

With nobody torturing me, my focus started to improve, and I was able to concentrate on my studies. Classes were still boring, but after reading Number One's letters, and seeing how smart he was and how much he liked studying, I felt ashamed of my ignorance. Of course, you could ask what's the point of having an education if you're just going to fly your plane into the side of an enemy aircraft carrier? That's true, but I felt it wouldn't kill me to learn something before I died, and so I started to apply myself, and you know what? School got more interesting, especially science class. We were studying evolutionary biology, and that's where I got fixated on extinctions.

I don't know why I found the subject so fascinating, except that the Latin names of the dead life-forms sounded beautiful and exotic, and memorizing them helped keep my stress levels down. I started with prehistoric sea cucumbers, and then moved on to the brittle stars. After that, I did jawless fishes, and then cartilaginous fishes, and finally bony fishes, too, before starting on the mammals. Acanthotheelia, Binoculites, Calcancorella, Dictyothurites, Exlinella, Frizzellus . . .

Jiko had given me a bracelet of pretty pink juzu beads, kind of a starter set, and for every dead species I would move a bead around, whispering their beautiful names to myself during recess, or walking home from school, or lying in my bed at night. I felt a sense of calm, knowing that all these creatures had lived and died before me, leaving almost no trace.

I wasn't so interested in the dinosaurs and ichthyosaurs and stuff because they're kind of a cliché. Every elementary school kid goes through a phase of dinosaur love, and I wanted my knowledge base to be more subtle than that. So I skipped over the great lizards and in November, just around the time I'd started on the extinct Hominidae, my dad committed suicide again.

## 3.

I need to back up a little, to September 11, in order to really explain this properly.

September 11 is one of those crazy moments in time that everybody who happened to be alive in the world remembers. You remember it exactly. September 11 is like a sharp knife slicing through time. It changed everything.

Something had already started to change in my dad. He was complaining about insomnia, and even his sleeping pills weren't working, or maybe he wasn't taking them. I don't know. He still went out walking at night, and my eyes still popped open in the dark just in time to hear the metal bolt clank shut and his footsteps scuff down the outside corridor. Plastic on cement. I didn't have to go out after him anymore. I just followed him in my mind.

But the big change happened on September 11. It was about a week after I gave him Haruki #1's letters, and I woke to the sound of the television in the living room. The volume was low, but the sirens and the fire engines were loud enough to wake me. I looked over to where Mom and Dad slept. I could see Mom's shape, but Dad's futon was empty. The digital clock said 10:48 p.m. I got up and went into the living room.

He was sitting on the floor in front of the TV, wearing boxer shorts and an undershirt, with an unlit cigarette in his mouth. On the screen was the image of two tall, skinny skyscrapers against a bright blue city sky. The buildings looked familiar, and I sort of recognized the skyline. I knew it wasn't Tokyo. Smoke was coming out from the sides of the buildings. I stood in the doorway and watched for a while. At first I thought it was movie, but the picture stayed the same for too long and didn't do anything. It was just these two skyscrapers leaking smoke into the air without any music or soundtrack except for the low voices of newscasters in the background.

"What's that?" I asked.

Dad turned around. In the light of the TV, he looked sick. His face was pale and his eyes were glazed. "It's the Boeki Center," he said.

I grew up in America so I recognized the name, but I couldn't remember exactly where it was. "Is it New York?" I asked.

He nodded.

"What happened?"

He shook his head. "They don't know. A plane flew into one of the buildings. They thought it was an accident, but then it happened again. There, look!"

On the screen was the shaky image of a plane disappearing into the face of the silver building. It slipped in like a knife going into a stick of butter. A cloud of flame and smoke burst out from the side. Where did the plane go?

"That was the second plane," my dad said. "Now they're saying it's a terrorist attack. They're saying it's suicide bombers."

The light from a spurt of flame reflected on his skin.

"There's people trapped inside," he said.

I sat down next to him. Flames and black smoke leaked from the wounds in the building. Bright scraps of paper blew out of the holes and sparkled and twinkled like confetti in the air. Tiny people waved things from the windows. Small dark shapes dropped down the sides of the shining building. I reached for my dad's hand. The shapes were alive, they were people, too. Some of them had suits on. Like my dad's. I saw one man's necktie.

Above the sirens and the honking car horns, I could hear the voices of the people standing on the street near the camera. They were speaking English. A man's voice was calling, *Clear the road, clear the road.* Some other guys were talking about a helicopter that was hovering over the towers. Was it going to try to land?

And then a woman screamed, and then everybody screamed, and a man started crying out, *Oh my god! Oh my god!* over and over, as the first tower fell. It went straight down, disappearing into itself, into a white cloud of smoke and dust that rose up and swallowed the world.

People were running down the street. They were hurt. They were trying to escape. *Oh my god! Oh my god!* Time passed, and then the second tower fell.

I held on to my dad's arm. We sat there, side by side, and watched until dawn. One after the other, the towers fell. Over and over, we watched them. When I left for school, he was still watching. When I came home, he was still watching.

## 4.

He became obsessed with the people who jumped. That first night we saw them, small dark human shapes, dropping down the sides of the buildings, and we kept expecting to see them again on television or in the newspapers, but instead they disappeared. Did we just imagine them? Was it a dream?

For the next couple of weeks, he hunted for them on the Internet. He stopped walking. Late at night, I'd wake up and see him sitting at my desk in our bedroom, staring at the computer screen, running searches. He said the government and the networks were censoring the images, but finally the picture of the Falling Man showed up. You've probably seen him. The photograph shows a tiny man in a white shirt and dark pants, diving headfirst down the slick steel side of the building. Next to that gigantic building, he's just a small, dark squiggle, and at first you think he's a piece of lint or dust on the camera lens that got onto the picture by mistake. It's only when you look closely that you understand. The squiggle is human. A time being. A life. His arms are next to his body, and his one knee is bent, like he's doing an Irish jig, only upside down. It's all wrong. He shouldn't be dancing. He shouldn't be there at all.

From my futon on the floor, I watched my dad watching the photograph. He would sit with his nose inches from the screen, and it looked like he and the Falling Man were having a conversation, like the man had stopped falling in midair for a moment to consider my dad's questions. *What made you decide to do it? Was it the smoke or the heat? Did you have to decide or did your body just know? Did you jump or dive or just step into the air? Did the air feel refreshing after the heat and smoke? How does it feel to be falling? Are you okay? What are you thinking? Do you feel alive or dead? Do you feel free now?*

I wonder if the Falling Man answered.

I know what me and Dad would have done if we'd been trapped inside those buildings. We wouldn't have even needed to discuss it. We would have found our way to an open window. He would have given me a quick hug and a kiss on the head before he held out his hand. We would have counted to three just like we used to do in Sunnyvale, standing on the edge of the swimming pool when he was teaching me how to not be afraid of the deep water. One, two, three, and then at exactly the same moment we would have jumped. He would have held on to my hand really tight as we fell, for as long as he could, before letting go.

## 5.

What would you do?

Does falling scare you? I've never been afraid of heights. When I stand on the edge of a tall place I feel like I'm on the edge of time, peering into forever. The question *What if . . . ?* rises up in my mind, and it's exciting because I know that in the next instant, in less time than it takes to snap my fingers, I could fly into eternity.

Back when I was a little kid in Sunnyvale, I never thought about suicide, but when we moved to Tokyo and my dad fell down in front of the train, I started thinking about it a lot. It seemed to make sense. If you're just going to die anyway, why not just get it over with?

At first, it was all pretty much a mind game. How would I do it? Hmm. Let me think. I know kids who cut themselves, but razor blades are messy and bleeding takes too long. Trains are messy, too, and some poor slob would have to clean up all the guts and stuff, not to mention there's that fine that your family has to pay. It wouldn't be fair to Mom, who works really hard to support us.

Pills are hard to get and how would you know if you'd taken enough? The best would be to find a nice place outside in nature, maybe a steep cliff that goes straight down into a deep ravine where nobody would find you, and your body could just decompose naturally or the crows could eat you. Or, better yet, a steep cliff into the sea. Yes, that's a good one.

Near to the little beach where me and Jiko had our picnic. I could probably even see the small bench where we sat and ate our rice balls and chocolate together. From the top of that cliff, the beach would look as small as a pocket. I would think fondly about Jiko and how she taught me the uselessness of fighting a wave, and that would be a nice last thought to have as I jumped off the edge of the world and went flying toward the ocean. It's the same big Pacific Ocean where Number One crashed his plane into the aircraft carrier. That's nice. The jellyfish would eat my flesh, and my bones would sink to the bottom, and I would be with Haruki forever. He's so smart, we would have lots to talk about. Maybe he could even teach me French.

# *Ruth*

## I.

On September 11, they were in the Driftless. A few days earlier, Ruth had given the keynote address for a conference on food politics at the University of Wisconsin in Madison, after which she and Oliver had gone to visit their friends John and Laura, who had a house in the country. The Driftless is a rural area in southwestern Wisconsin, one that Oliver had long wanted to see on account of the unique geology of the Paleozoic Plateau, which had somehow escaped glaciation and was named for the absence of drift: the silt, sand, clay, gravel, and boulders usually left behind by the retreating sheets of ice. He was particularly interested in the cave systems, the disappearing streams, blind valleys, and sinkholes that characterized the topography, but Ruth was feeling anxious. Her mother was still alive then and living with them on the island, and although Ruth had arranged for a neighbor to drop in and bring food and check up on her, she didn't like leaving her alone for so long. But the fall weather in Wisconsin was beautiful, and it felt good to be with their friends. They spent a long, lazy afternoon in canoes on the Mississippi, watching turtles basking on logs in the golden sunlight.

The next morning the four of them were sitting around the kitchen table after a leisurely breakfast, enjoying a second cup of coffee, when they heard the neighbor's pickup truck approaching. John went out to see what he wanted. He came back a few minutes later looking serious.

"Something's happened in New York," he said. The farmhouse had no television. He turned on the radio to NPR just as the second plane hit the North Tower.

Ruth spent the next hour standing on a picnic table at the top of a small rise on the property, trying to get a mobile phone signal so she could call her friends in New York. Finally she managed to get through to her editor, who was watching the disaster unfold from her kitchen window in Brooklyn.

Her editor's voice cut through the static. "It's falling!" she cried. "Oh my god, the tower's falling down!" And then the connection went dead.

They drove back to Madison, turned on the television, and spent the rest of the afternoon watching the planes slice into the towers and the towers collapse. She thought about her mom, all alone in the little house in Canada. Her mom always watched the news, even if she couldn't remember what was going on from day to day. Ruth tried calling, but nobody picked up. Her mom was almost deaf and couldn't hear the phone ringing.

"Mom's watching this on TV," she told Oliver. "She'll think we're in New York. She'll be crazy with worry."

"Call the neighbors," he said. "Tell them to unplug the set."

By the time she got through to anyone, it was already the next morning. "I need you to go to Mom's house and find out if she's seen anything," she said. "If she has, just reassure her. Tell her we're okay and that we're nowhere near New York. Then unplug the television and tell her it's broken."

There was a long silence on the end of the line. "Sure thing," the woman said. "Is there a problem?"

"I'm afraid she's going to see the news and panic."

Again, a long silence. "What news . . . ?"

Ruth explained briefly and then hung up the phone. "We have to get back," she told Oliver.

## 2.

The airports were closed, so they rented a car, a white Ford Taurus, and drove west, skirting the Canadian border. Their plan was to drop the Taurus off in Seattle and take the hydrofoil back to Canada. Canada was safe.

As they made their way across the country, American flags began popping up like flowers after a rain, fluttering from poles and car antennae, and taped to the windows of stores and homes. The country was awash in red, white, and blue. At night, in Super 8s and Motel 6s, they watched the president vow to hunt down the terrorists. "Dead or alive," he promised. "Smoke 'em out of their caves. Git 'em running so we can git 'em."

One evening they stopped for dinner at the Great Wall of China restaurant in Harlem, Montana. The restaurant was empty and closing early. It was an extra security precaution, their waitress explained, when she brought their bill.

"You never know who they're gonna target next," she said.

"You think Arab terrorists will attack us here in Harlem, Montana?" Oliver asked. Harlem, Montana, had a population of just under 850. It was two thousand miles from New York City, and surrounded by desert.

The waitress, who looked like she might be Mexican, shook her head. "We're not taking any chances," she said.

Later, at the Super 8 motel, they watched a news report about the spate of hate crimes against Muslim Americans being committed across the country.

"You know, I think I was wrong," Oliver said.

"About what?"

"Our waitress. I don't think it was Arab terrorists she was afraid of."

### 3.

They made it across the border, and Canada had never felt safer. Back on the island, their neighbors expressed concern for their well-being, but news of the world had little relevance to their daily lives, and they were only vaguely aware of what was going on down south, which didn't keep them from having opinions.

"I'm pretty sure it's all a hoax," one neighbor said, when he dropped in to deliver Masako's Alzheimer's medication, which he'd picked up for her at the clinic.

"A hoax?" Ruth repeated. "You mean, you don't think it happened?"

"Oh, no," he said. "It happened all right. It's just not what they're saying it is." He looked around and then took a step closer, standing so that his face was inches from hers. "If you ask me, it's a government conspiracy."

He was American, a Vietnam vet. He had been awarded a Purple Heart, which he handed back to the U.S. immigration authority at the border when he crossed into Canada. His spinal injuries had never healed and he required a steady dose of morphine in order to control the pain. Ruth didn't have the energy to argue. She offered tea and then sat with him, listening to his theories and thinking about the box in the basement. How nice it would be to crawl inside and fall asleep.

From their fog-enshrouded outpost on the mossy margin of the world, she watched the United States invade Afghanistan and then turn its sights on Iraq. While troops were quietly being deployed to the Middle East, she sat on the couch with her mother, in the little house in the middle of the dark and dripping rain forest, staring at the small, glowing television screen.

"What program is this?" her mother asked.

"It's the news, Mom," she answered.

"I don't understand," her mother said. "It looks like a war. Are we at war?"

"Yes, Mom," she said. "We're at war."

"Oh, that's terrible!" her mother exclaimed. "Who are we at war with?"

"Afghanistan, Mom."

They watched together in silence, until the commercial break. Her mother got up and shuffled to the bathroom. When she came back, she stopped and looked at the screen. "What program is this?"

"It's the news, Mom."

"It looks like a war. Are we at war?"

"Yes, Mom. We're at war."

"Oh, that's terrible! Who are we at war with?"

"Iraq, Mom."

"Really? But I thought that war was over."

"No, Mom. It's never over. America has always been at war with Iraq."

"Oh, that's terrible!" Her mom leaned forward and peered at the screen.

Days pass, and weeks. Months pass, and then years.

"Now, who did you say we are at war with?"

# *Nao*

## I.

After 9/11 we thought the world was going to end more or less immediately, but it didn't. School just kept plodding along. My classmates were nice to me for a while because of my connection to America. We folded a thousand origami paper cranes to send to Ground Zero for the twenty-four Japanese victims and all the other people who had died in the towers. But by the end of September, everybody was tired of feeling kind and compassionate, and there was a noticeable increase in hostilities. It wasn't organized like before, at least not at first, just minor random sniper attacks coming out of nowhere when someone felt impatient or restless. A shove in the hallway, a punch in the breast. War and treachery were in the air. The whole world was waiting for America to attack Afghanistan, but nothing was happening, which seemed to cause a lot of tension, even in our classroom. We took our preliminary exams, which weren't the real ones but still made it clear who was going to get into a good high school and have a fabulous life, and who was a loser. Me. I should have been prepared, but I wasn't. Still, what's the point in beating yourself up when other people will do it for you?

Finally, on October 7, the United States started bombing Afghanistan, and I got my period again, and in a way both of these felt like a huge relief.

I know a lot of people think it's gross to talk about this kind of thing, so I hope you don't mind. I'm not the kind of girl who gets an erotic kick out of telling everyone about her menstrual cycles, and I wouldn't even bring it up if it wasn't important to what happened next.

I started having periods in Sunnyvale, when I was twelve, which is pretty normal in America but early for Japan. I was fourteen when we moved back to Tokyo, but then suddenly my period just stopped for almost the whole year, probably on account of all the stress and ijime. I think my body was trying to go backward in time to my younger, happier days. Anyway, it didn't start again until the last class that day, when Sensei was announcing that the U.S. had started bombing Afghanistan, and suddenly I felt myself starting to bleed. Stupidly, I'd gotten out of the habit of carrying around pads and supplies. I knew it wasn't safe to hang around after school for even a minute, but I wasn't going to make it home without a big bloody disaster, so as soon as the bell rang, I grabbed my stuff and ran to the washroom.

The junior high school I was going to was old, and the old-style Japanese toilets are different from American ones. The bowls are in the ground and you have to squat over them instead of sitting. I was squatting there with my skirt up and my stained panties down at my ankles when I heard the washroom door open and close. Someone had come in.

As quietly as I could, I wrapped some toilet paper around my hand and made a wad. A noise, kind of a scrabbling sound like rats climbing the wall, came from the stall next to me. I froze. The stalls are built all the way to the floor so you can't see under, thank god, but still it's a terrible feeling to be squatting with your panties down and your bare butt hanging out, listening to rats. Nothing makes you feel more vulnerable. I held my breath. Everything was still. I hiked up my skirt and leaned over to stick the wad into my panties, when I heard the sound again, only this time it was coming from the top of the partition. I heard someone snicker and looked up to see two raggedy lines of little keitai phones thrust over the partition walls on both sides, aiming down at me. I stood up real quick and pulled up my panties.

"Oooh!" a voice cried. "Nice shot!"

One by one, the phones disappeared. I pulled my skirt down and backed into the corner of the stall.

"Gross!" someone said. "There's blood! She didn't even flush!"

I leaned against the tiled wall, hugging myself. Should I flush? Should I try to escape? If I'd had a rifle I would have shot myself in the throat.

"Baka! It's blurry!"

I pushed away from the wall and reached for the latch.

"That's not blurry! That's her pubes!"

I unlocked the door and opened it. They were standing at the sinks, clustered around Reiko, comparing their keitai screens. I ducked my head and pushed past them toward the exit, but Reiko held out her hand like a traffic cop.

"Where are you going?" she asked.

"Home," I said.

"I don't think so," she said.

Someone grabbed me by the collar then and pushed me into the corner, where Daisuke was filming with a video camera. Three of the big girls forced me to my knees and then onto my stomach. The floor tiles smelled of urine and bleach and felt cold against my cheek. I could feel someone's hard knee in my back, pinning me down, and someone's hands yanking my skirt up to my armpits. Someone else kicked me in the ribs.

"Pass me the rope."

They had planned this. They held my hands together, and then they pulled my skirt up over my head and used a skipping rope to tie it like a sack so I couldn't see. They held my ankles so I couldn't kick and then they pulled off my panties.

"Ooh, score!" I heard one of them say. "There's stains! You get more for stains!"

"That's disgusting. It stinks. Put it in the bag before I have to throw up!"

"Daisuke, you baka. Are you shooting this? We need video."

It was dark inside my plaid skirt sack, and hot and wet because I was breathing hard and my breath had nowhere to go. I could see only the faintest bit of light and shadow through the weave of the skirt fabric. Someone stuck a toe under my ribs and rolled me over onto my back, and now the shadows were moving above me, and the tiles were cold against my bare bottom. They were talking about who was going to rape me first. They decided to make Daisuke do it.

"Hand over the camera," Reiko ordered. "Pull down his pants."

They held my legs apart and made him kneel and then lie down on top of me. I could feel the weight of his scrawny body and his bony hips poking into me, but he was way too scared for anything to happen, so they kicked him off and I heard him run away. They started talking about how they needed a rape scene for the video, but after Daisuke's failure, nobody wanted to try. Maybe they were all scared. I don't know.

"Somebody's gotta do it."

"She's bleeding. It's too gross."

"You guys are pathetic."

"Fine, so you do it, Reiko. It'll be a lez scene. That's even better."

"Baka. I'm no lez."

I just lay there, perfectly still. It was pointless to struggle or scream. There were too many of them, and no one would hear me or come to help, but really it didn't matter, because I was thinking about Number One, and he was giving me courage. They could break my body but they wouldn't break my spirit. They were only shadows, and as I listened to them arguing, I felt my face relax into a gentle smile. I summoned up my supapawa, and soon the shadows were just mosquitoes, buzzing in the distance and bothersome only if you let them be.

"Hey," I heard someone say. "She's stopped moving."

"She's not breathing."

"That's way too much blood."

"Shit. Let's get out of here!"

Do you remember what it feels like to be a little kid playing dead? You're out in your backyard in Sunnyvale with the other kids, and there's a war going on, and suddenly BANG! somebody points a stick at you and shoots? So you fall to the ground, clutching your chest. The earth is cold and damp. Your enemy is watching you die, so you make it good, groaning and clutching at your bleeding heart, but by the time you're done, the war has already moved on to a different part of the backyard.

You lie there, feeling the cold of the earth pressing against your cheek, your chest, your whole body. There are wet patches on your knees from where you first went down. You shiver. The earth smells like mud and rain and lawn chemicals. It makes your head ache, but you don't move. You can't move because you are dead.

Where did everyone go? you're wondering. Did they forget about me? How much longer do I have to lie here?

Will they just play around my dead body and then go home? How will I know if the game is over? What if nobody tells me?

It's boring to be dead!

Finally, you can't take it anymore, so you roll over onto your back and open your eyes, and above you is the great, big, goofy, cloud-spotted sky. You blink, half believing that it's not pretend and you might actually be dead. Slowly you move your arm, your leg, to see if you still can, and then . . . hey! You're not dead! Relieved, you scramble to your feet, pick up your gun, and declare yourself alive again, and run off to rejoin the war.

That's what I felt like, only I couldn't see the sky at all, only the hazy blur of the fluorescent light tubes through the plaid fabric. The bathroom and the hallway outside were silent. The tiles were still cold, and I could feel the sticky blood against my bottom. Slowly I sat up and pushed at the knotted fabric above my head until the rope gave way and released me from my skirt. The bathroom was bright and empty. I used my teeth to untie the rope around my wrists. They hurt, and so did the place in my rib where someone kicked me, but mostly I was okay. I wet some paper towels and went back into the toilet stall to clean myself up, and then I took the train home.

They posted the video on the Internet that night. One of my classmates emailed me the link. The image quality from the keitai phone cams was crap, grainy and shaky, and you couldn't really see my face too clearly, which I was grateful for, but the video was awfully clear. With my arms and head tied up in my skirt and my naked legs kicking, you could almost say I looked like a giant prehistoric squid, squirming and oozing ink from my ink sac in a futile attempt to confuse my predators.

Next to the video was a link to a burusera fetish[141] site where hentais could bid on my blood-stained panties. The auction was scheduled to

---

141. *burusera* (ブルセラ)—schoolgirl uniform fetish; lit. *buru* (abbr. for *bloomer*) + *sera* (abbr. for *sailor*).

last for a week, and the bidding was fast, but this time I didn't feel any satisfaction at my rising hit count. I shut down the computer, remembering to clear the cache in case my dad happened to get curious.

We still only had the one computer, so I had to share it with my dad. For a long time he never went online, but after his whole obsession with the Falling Man started, he was on all the time. And once the U.S. invaded Afghanistan, that was it. He put away his philosophers and his origami bugs and spent all day following the war, which was really inconvenient because I was dealing with this highly sensitive burusera material, and I didn't want him snooping on me when I was monitoring the price of my panties. It gave me the creeps. He would lurk around behind me, waiting for his turn, until finally I had to ask him to leave so I could have some privacy. But even then he'd poke his head into the bedroom like every five minutes.

"Just let me know when you're off, okay?" he'd say, until finally I gave up and let him have a turn, at which point he'd hog it for hours. When Mom asked him what he was doing, he lied and told her he was looking for a job. She pinched her lips together and turned away before the cutting words escaped from her mouth. She didn't believe him, and neither did I, because we'd both been checking out his browsing history and we'd seen the websites he was hanging out on. Weapons technology pages. War blogs. Military fan sites. Al Jazeera. Missile footage that looked like first-person shooter games, only grainy and dark. Bombs exploding. Buildings collapsing. Beatings. Bodies.

## 2.

It was me who found him.

I stopped going to school after the Panty Incident, while the auction was in progress. Instead, I left the house dressed in my school uniform and went to an Internet café, where I could change into street clothes, and either I'd hang out there and watch the bidding and read manga if the weather was bad, or take the train into the city and look at the shops. Then I changed back into my uniform and came home in time for supper.

The days were getting colder and the leaves on the ginkgo trees that lined the streets were turning to gold. It was raining a lot, too, and the rain knocked the leaves to the ground where they lay plastered on the wet black asphalt like little gilded fans. Ginkgo trees remind me of Jiko, and it always makes me sad to see the leaves and nuts getting crushed under people's shoes and turning into yellow smears that look and smell like dog shit or vomit.

On the day the auction was ending I don't know if I was depressed or nervous, knowing that some disgusting hentai would soon be rejoicing over my panties. It was not a nice feeling, kind of heavy and dirty and blue, so I went to the DIY craft shop in Harajuku to cheer myself up. And it was lucky I did, because that's when I found my beautiful *À la recherche du temps perdu* diary, and I remember feeling cheerful on the train home, like as long as I had a secret diary, I could survive.

But as soon as I let myself in the door with my key, my optimism vanished. I knew something was wrong on account of the smell. The apartment smelled like stinky ginkgo trees. It smelled like the alley on a Saturday morning after the hostesses brought their dates home drunk. It smelled like garbage and throw-up.

I took off my shoes and stepped up into the kitchen.

"Tadaima . . ." I called. Have I mentioned tadaima? Tadaima means "just now," and it's what you say when you come in the door to your home. Just now. Here I am.

Dad didn't answer, because, just then, he wasn't.

He wasn't in the kitchen. He wasn't in the living room. Volume I of The Great Minds of Western Philosophy was sitting on the table, and the television was off. This was a detail I especially noticed because he always had the television tuned to CNN or BBC so he could catch the latest breaking news about the war. But the screen was blank and the room was silent. He wasn't in the bedroom, either.

I found him in the toilet. He was lying on the floor, facedown in a puddle of vomit, and I wish I could tell you that I rushed to his side to help him, but I didn't. I walked in and saw him and gagged on the smell, and then this big empty space opened up in time when everything was quiet and still. I think I may have said "Oh, sorry" or something stupid like that and then backed up and closed the door behind me.

I stood there for a while, staring at the door. It was like I'd walked in on him while he was taking a dump and caught sight of his penis or something. I can't explain it. It felt so private and personal, him lying there, and I just knew he wouldn't want me to see him like that, so I backed across the hallway and sank down against the wall until I was sitting on the floor.

"Dad?" I asked, but my voice sounded like it was coming from another person who lived far away. "Dad?"

He didn't answer. I had my keitai on a chain around my neck so I called 911, and then I remembered that in Japan the emergency number is 119, so I called that instead, and then I sat there until the ambulance came. The paramedics put him on a stretcher and took him away. I asked if my dad was dead, and they said no. I asked if he was going to be okay, but they wouldn't tell me. They wouldn't let me ride with him. They wanted to call for a policewoman to keep me company until my mom came home, but I told them I was almost sixteen and used to being alone. The apartment was really quiet when they were gone. I stared at the card in my hand. The paramedic had written the name of the hospital where they were taking him on it, but I didn't know how to get there by train. I called my mom's number but just got her voicemail, so I tried leaving a message.

"It's me."

I hate talking to machines, so I hung up and texted her instead.

"Dad vomited and passed out. He's at N— Hospital in T— Ward."

What else was there to say?

I was thirsty. I went to the refrigerator to get a glass of milk, but the smell from Dad's throw-up got mixed up with the taste of the milk so I had to pour it down the sink. The milk made a thick white puddle on the stainless steel that trickled down the drain, leaving a pale film. I turned on the taps to rinse it off with water, and then washed the glass and wiped down the sink. I thought maybe I should clean up Dad's mess while I was at it, so I got a bucket and a mop from the balcony. The smell was still sick-making, so I tied a clean dish towel around my mouth and nose and went into the toilet.

The vomit was clear but kind of yellowish, with melting white lumps in it that looked like little sugar candies. One of the paramedics had noticed them, too. He'd put on rubber gloves and scooped up a whole bunch of them with a little scraper from his kit and put them into a tube with a stopper.

"Is your father taking any medications?" he asked me.

I didn't know. The other paramedics were trying to get my dad and the stretcher down the narrow hallway. The man looked quickly around the base of the toilet and then in the trash can.

"Do you know where he kept his medicines?" he asked.

I didn't want to get Dad in trouble, so I didn't say anything.

"It's important," the paramedic said.

I pointed to the medicine cabinet and he opened it, but there was nothing inside except for the usual stuff: aspirin, Band-Aids, some laxative and hemorrhoid cream, and a bunch of my mom's hair products.

The other medics were wheeling my dad out the door.

"Where's the bedroom?"

I led him down the hallway. The curtains were drawn, so the room was pretty dark. The only light was coming from the computer in the corner and my Hello Kitty screensaver that was making everything pinkish. The pinkish futon was lying on the floor, neatly laid out, like someone had just gone to bed and then gotten up again because they'd forgotten to turn off a light. Next to the pinkish pillow was a glass, and a half-empty pitcher of water, and an empty bottle of pills. The paramedic put the bottle into another plastic bag and headed toward the door. He turned back and gave me the card and then looked at me closely.

"You okay?"

"I'm okay," I said in the faraway voice that didn't sound like mine. I tried to smile at him, but he was already out the door and running down the corridor.

The vomit on the floor had dried up a little. I went back into the kitchen and got an empty guava juice carton from the trash and cut it open with a pair of scissors, and then I used the edge of the cardboard to scrape the goo off the floor and into the toilet. I've seen enough cop shows on TV to know that I was destroying evidence, but I didn't need evidence. I knew what had happened, and I knew everyone would be happier if we just pretended like it was an accident. Silly Dad. Careless Dad. Accident-prone Dad. Then I thought of something else.

I put the guava juice carton in a plastic bag and went downstairs to throw it in the garbage can on the street. When I got back to the apartment, I locked the door behind me. Volume I of The Great Minds of Western Philosophy was sitting on the table, but he had finished the Hellenists a long time ago, so I knew something was wrong. I found the note tucked inside the chapter called "The Death of Socrates," on a sheet of my Gloomy Bear stationery, folded neatly in thirds. I pulled it out. There was no name on the note, so I wondered if he meant for me to find it, or Mom, or both of us, or maybe he just wrote it for himself. I didn't want to read it just then, so I folded it back up and put it in the pocket of my school blazer.

Here is what I thought: If I read this note and he is already dead, then I will know that he was serious this time and really meant to die, and it was my fault for being harsh and mean to him. And if he isn't already dead, then reading the note might kill him, and it will still be my fault.

It made no logical sense, but that's what I thought at the time, and I knew that whatever I did, I would feel crummy. I was still wearing my school uniform. I went to the bedroom and changed into jeans and a hoodie, transferring the note to my sweatshirt pocket, and then went back to the toilet to finish mopping up. Two nasty Toilet Incidents in one week. Weird.

Mom called from her office. She'd been in a meeting. She made me describe what had happened and exactly what I'd seen, and then she made me read the name of the hospital and the address and phone number off the card. Then she asked me if I was going to be okay by myself.

"Of course," I said.

"Are you hungry?" she asked. "Did Dad leave you any food?"

"I'm not hungry." Probably I would never eat again.

"I'll call you from the hospital. Wait for me. Don't go out."

"Mom?"

"Yes?"

I wanted to tell her about the note but I didn't know if I should.

"What is it, Naoko?" Her voice was strained. She wanted to get going.

"Nothing."

We hung up. I took the note out of my hoodie pocket. Maybe I was wrong. It wasn't addressed to anyone, so maybe it wasn't a note at all. I unfolded it. There were two sentences on it in my dad's passionate manic handwriting. The first one said this:

> *I should only make myself ridiculous in my own eyes if I clung to life and hugged it when it has no more to offer.*

I recognized the sentence. It was what Socrates said to his friend Crito just before he drank the poison hemlock. Crito was stalling, trying to get Socrates to hold off a little longer. He was like, "What's the big hurry? There's still lots of time. Why not hang out and have some dinner and enjoy a couple glasses of wine with us?" But Socrates was like, "Forget it. I don't want to feel like an idiot. Let's get this over with," and so he did. Dad really liked that story and told it to me one afternoon. He had some theory about how it exemplified the Western Mind, but I didn't know what he was talking about. I just remember he pronounced Crito like Kuritto, and I liked the way it sounded. Like a cracker breaking in half, or crickets in the grass.

Underneath the first sentence was a second.

> *I should only make myself ridiculous in the eyes of others if I clung to life and hugged it when I have no more to offer.*

A horrible thought occurred to me. I went back into the bedroom. Hello Kitty glowed pinkly at me from the screensaver, but when I woke the computer up, Hello Kitty disappeared, and I was staring at the burusera hentai website, at the page with my panties for sale. I had forgotten to clear the cache in the web browser. He must have seen it. The auction was over. Someone named Lolicom73 had won. I looked at the bidding history. It had reached a peak and flattened out, but in the final hour, a new bidder named C.imperator had jumped in, and there was a flurry of raising and counter-raising, but with just two seconds to go, Lolicom73 beat C.imperator's last bid.

Lolicom73 was the proud owner of my panties. C.imperator had lost. I went to the bathroom and leaned over the toilet and threw up, but at least I did it neatly into the bowl.

I went back into the living room. The note was still sitting on top of the book where I'd left it. I picked it up and crumpled it in my fist and threw it across the room, but it just bounced off the sofa and landed on the rug. I wanted it to be a rock or a bomb. I wanted it to blow a huge hole in the middle of our living room or blow up the whole stupid building. But I didn't have a bomb, so I picked up Volume I of The Great Minds of Western Philosophy instead and heaved it at the glass balcony door. It was a heavy book, but the glass was strong, and the book bounced off and landed facedown on the floor. This made me even madder, so I picked it up again, only this time I opened the sliding door before I threw it. As I watched the Hellenists go sailing out over the balcony rail, pages fluttering like the underfeathers of the last archaeopteryx, I felt a tremendous sense of relief. I listened for what seemed like many moments for the tiny thud to come.

"Hey!"

I froze. The voice was coming from the street below.

"Hey! Don't try to hide yourself. I know you're up there!"

It was a young female voice and it didn't sound too angry, so I stepped onto the balcony, and peered down over the rail. A pretty round face looked up at me. It was one of the hostesses who lived in the neighborhood. I recognized her from the public baths. She always had a smile for me, and now she recognized me, too.

"Oh, it's you," she said. She was holding the book in her hands. "You drop this?"

She looked uninjured so I nodded.

"You should be more careful," she said, like it was no big deal. "You could kill somebody."

"I'm sorry," I said. My voice still wasn't working very well, so I don't know if she heard me or not.

"I'll just leave it here, okay?" She placed it on the low cinder-block wall that ran between the sidewalk and the building. "You better come down and pick it up or someone might take it." She looked at the title. "Or maybe not. Anyway, I'll just leave it here, okay?"

"Thank you!" I whispered, but she had already rounded the corner and disappeared.


They pumped Dad's stomach to make sure they got all the pills out, and he didn't die after all, and in fact, it wasn't even close. Mom got home from the hospital and told me he was going to be fine. I didn't tell her about the note in Socrates.

When Dad was discharged, we all sat down in the living room for another heart to heart, or maybe you could call it a family debriefing. Dad spoke dully, like he'd memorized his lines and didn't believe them. He apologized to me. He said it was an accident, that he was so tired, but he couldn't sleep. He lost track of how many pills he had taken. It wouldn't happen again. He didn't mention the note or the auction.

My mom watched his performance carefully, and when he got to the end, she sounded so relieved. "Of course it was an accident," she said, appealing to me. "We knew that, didn't we, Nao?"

She turned back to Dad and started scolding him. "Silly Papa! How could you be so careless? From now on, Naoko and I will keep all your medications safe for you and you must ask us if you need a pill. Isn't that right, Nao-chan?"

Don't drag me into this, I thought, but I just picked at my split ends and nodded. I couldn't bear to look at either of them. After the debriefing was over and Mom went to bed, I handed Dad a sheet of Gloomy Bear stationery, folded neatly in thirds. It looked exactly like his Socrates note, and he turned pale and opened and closed his mouth like a dying fish.

"You better read it," I said.

He unfolded it and read. It was two sentences long. When he finished, he nodded and folded it up again. "Yes," he said. "You're right."

Here's what my first sentence said:

*Your uncle Haruki #1 would not keep screwing up like this.*

And here's the second:

*If you're going to do something, please do it properly.*

Sometimes you have to say what's on your mind.

That night, when my parents were finally asleep, I sneaked into the bathroom with a pair of scissors and the electric clipper my mom bought to give Dad haircuts when he still cared about grooming and personal hygiene and employment and stuff. In the cold bathroom light, I chopped off my hair in chunks. It took me a long time to cut it all off until it was short enough to buzz. I plugged in the electric clipper and turned it on. It was so loud! I switched it off quickly and listened, but there was no sound from the bedroom, so I closed the door and wrapped the clipper in a towel to muffle the sound of the motor. When I was done with the buzzing, I cleaned up all my long hair and hid it in a paper bag in the trash, then wiped the sink with toilet paper. I covered my bare head with my hoodie and crawled back into my futon. It was such a weird feeling, and I had to keep reaching up to touch my head.

I sat zazen under my covers for the rest of the night, and as soon as the sky grew light, I got dressed and left the apartment. I was wearing my hoodie under my school blazer, which is totally against the rules, but I had to hide my naked head. Since it was so early, I bought a can of hot coffee from a vending machine and went to sit on the stone bench in the temple garden to kill some time. The monk came out to rake the gravel. He glanced up and saw me. Maybe he understood what I had going on under my hoodie because something passed between us and he nodded to me. I set my can of coffee on the bench and stood up and pulled my hood off, and then I bowed to him, a proper Buddhist bow, with my palms pressed together, nice and deep like Jiko taught me. When I straightened up, I saw he'd stopped raking and was returning my bow properly, too. That made me feel good, and it's why I like monks and nuns so much. They know how to be polite to everyone, regardless of how fucked-up she might be.

I waited until I knew the last bell had rung, and then I jogged the rest of the way to school. There was no one in the playground. I slipped through the empty corridors as silent as a ghost until I reached my classroom. Since I still couldn't walk through walls, I threw open the door instead. Sensei was in the middle of roll call, but I didn't bother to apologize for interrupting or for being late. Some of Reiko's gang started to snicker when they saw me, and I caught the words "auction" and "panties" and "bottom line." I figured that everyone in the class had heard about the Panty Incident and had been following the bidding over the last few days. It was an all-class project.

But I ignored the whispering and marched to my seat. Maybe it was the hoodie under my blazer that signaled something was different, or maybe it was my erect posture, like a soldier marching to battle, or maybe the energy of my *supapawa* cast a spell over them and struck them dumb. One by one they fell silent. I reached my desk, but instead of sitting down on my chair, I climbed up on it and then onto my desk, and I stood there, tall and straight. Then, when everybody was looking, I flipped back my hoodie.

A gasp went around the room that sent shivers up my spine. The *supapawa* of my bald and shining head radiated through the classroom and out into the world, a bright bulb, a beacon, beaming light into every crack of darkness on the earth and blinding all my enemies. I put my fists on my hips and watched them tremble, holding up their arms to shield their eyes from my unbearable brightness. I opened my mouth and a piercing cry broke from my throat like an eagle, shaking the earth and penetrating into every corner of the universe. I watched my classmates press their hands over their ears, and saw the blood run through their fingers as their eardrums shattered.

And then I stopped. Why? Because I felt sorry for them. I climbed down from my desk and walked to the front of the classroom. I turned to face my teacher and I bowed, pressing my palms together, and then I turned to my classmates and bowed to them, too, nice and deep, and then I left the room. It was fine to leave then, and I even managed to feel a little sad, knowing I was never coming back.

## 3.

My dad had gotten so good at not looking at me that after I shaved my head and defeated my classmates with my awesome *supapawa*, I went home and waited for the rest of the day for him to notice that I had no hair, but he never did. Mom noticed right away, of course. The minute she walked in the door that night and saw me in my hoodie, she freaked out and demanded that I tell her what had happened. I skipped over the whole Panty Incident and instead just announced that I was dropping out of school and leaving home to become a nun. I was half serious. Part of me really wanted to do that, to go to old Jiko's temple and sign up for a lifetime of zazen and cleaning and pickle-making.

No way, Mom said. I was too young to leave home, and I had to go to high school first. Big mistake. She should have let me, but instead we fought for three days, and in the end, I agreed to at least take the entrance exams, which were coming up. It didn't matter to me, since I knew I'd never get in anywhere good, but I promised her I'd try, and at least it got her off my back.

That same week at the public baths, I saw the bar hostess I'd almost hit with The Great Minds of Western Philosophy, and even with no hair, she recognized me immediately. But instead of looking away like most people, she narrowed her eyes and inspected me, and finally she nodded.

"It's cute," she said. "Nice shape. You have a pretty head."

We were sitting in the soaking tub, up to our necks. In the clouded mirror, I could see my smooth white skull, bobbing on the surface of the steaming water like a boiled egg.

"I don't give a shit about pretty," I informed her. "I'm a superhero. Superheroes don't need pretty."

She shrugged. "Well, I don't know about superheroes. But it couldn't hurt, could it? To be a little pretty?"

I guessed not. "My mom is freaked out," I told her. "She wants me to buy a wig."

She nodded and stretched her pretty arm and watched the water drip from the tips of her graceful fingers. "Okay," she said. "I'll take you. I know a good place."

Like I'd even asked.

She told me her name was Babette, which is not a typical Japanese name. Babette wasn't always Babette. Before that, she was Kaori when she worked as a hostess in an Asakusa club, which was before she got fired for sleeping with the mama-san's boyfriend. She was sick of the club life anyway, she said. The patrons were too sentimental and wet. She changed her name to Babette and got a job at Fifi's Lovely Apron, which was a very cheerful and upbeat place to work when it was still lovely, before it got lonely.

Babette's life passion is cosplay, and at Fifi's she can wear her pretty little petticoats and pinafores and stockings and lace. When she's all dressed up for work, she looks like a fancy cupcake decorated with marzipan flowers and sparkles and sugary hearts, so sweet and delicious you just want to gobble her right up, but don't be fooled. There is nothing wet about Babette.

Since I wasn't going to school anymore, I didn't have much to do during the days, so we made a date and took a train to Akiba together.

"I like riding with you," she said. "People look at us. We could get you some pretty fashions. You would look very shibui[142] with a nice outfit and your adorable bald head. Maybe you could dress up like a nun. Or no, wait, a baby doll! Yes. With a lacy bonnet, you'll look just like a pretty little bald baby doll. Oh, that'll be totally sweet!"

---

142. *shibui* (渋い)—cool, chic.

"You're supposed to be helping me get a wig," I reminded her, but secretly I was pleased.

Akihabara means Field of Autumn Leaves, but the fields and leaves have all been replaced by electronics stores, and these days people call it Akiba or Electricity Town. I'd never really hung out there before. I thought it was where manga otaku and loser geeks like my dad went to sell their computer hardware when they ran out of money, but I was totally wrong. Akiba is wild and weirdly awesome. You walk through these narrow alleyways and shopping streets lined with stores and stalls spilling over with circuit boards and DVDs and transformers and gaming software and fetish props and manga models and inflatable sex dolls and bins filled with electronics and wigs and little maid costumes and schoolgirl bloomers. Everywhere you look, you can see bright anime posters and gigantic banners hanging from the tops of buildings, with pictures of towering moe[143] girls with round sparkling eyes the size of kids' swimming pools and humongous luscious tits busting out of their galactic superhero reformer costumes, and all you can hear is the crazy *clang! clang! clang!* of the game arcades, and the *ping! ping! ping!* of the pachinko parlors, and loudspeakers screaming limited-time offers from the storefronts, and the little French maids in the street crying out to otaku boys as they walk by. There are no fields or autumn leaves around here anywhere.

Babette steered me through the crowds, holding me by the arm so I wouldn't get distracted or lost. I felt like a goofy tourist with my mouth hanging open like an American, which reminded me of Kayla. I hadn't thought about her in a million years, and suddenly I wished I could somehow make Kayla materialize in the middle of Akiba Electricity Town, just to blow her little Silicon Valley mind. This was a side of Tokyo I could totally get into, and I couldn't wait to find a wig—at that moment I was thinking long and superstraight and pink, like Anemone from *Eureka Seven*—and maybe some kind of cute costume so I would fit in with the scene, when we happened to pass the window of a DVD store

---

143. *moe* (萌え)—sprouting, budding. Slang for an adorable, crushworthy manga-type girl.

stacked with rows of flat-screen TVs. Tinny fight music blared from the speakers. Fireworks exploded as the title burst onto the screens. *INSECT GLADIATORS!* Then the fight announcer screamed, *Next up, Orthopteran Cricket versus Praying Mantis!*

We stopped and watched as a monster cricket wrestled a pale green praying mantis into the corner of a glass terrarium. The image was repeated on every screen, and the video picked up every microscopic detail. *Look at those powerful bolt-cutter jaws, crunching that mantis's eye! Pulverizing her gossamer wings!*

The fight ended when the cricket tore the mantis's head off.

*And the winner is . . . Orthopteran Cricket! Next up, Staghorn Beetle versus Yellow Scorpion!*

The pale scorpion used its pincers to flip the staghorn beetle into the air. The beetle reared up and fell over on his back, exposing his underside. The scorpion's segmented tail curled over to deliver its venomous sting. *Sasu! Sasu! Yellow Scorpion stings!* The staghorn beetle shuddered. In the small, bare terrarium, he had no place to hide. His spindly legs writhed and flailed in the air, until they didn't anymore. *It looks like Staghorn Beetle is the loser, yes, he's dying, he's dying, he's . . . DEAD!*

Neon-colored titles flashed across the screen. *Yellow Scorpion Wins!*

I started to cry.

I'm not kidding. Until then nothing could make me cry, not losing all our money, not moving from my wonderful life in Sunnyvale to a crappy dump in Japan, not my crazy mother, or my suicidal father, or my best friend dumping me, or even all those months and months of ijime. I never cried. But for some reason, the sight of these stupid bugs tearing each other apart was too much for me. It was horrible, but of course it wasn't the insects. It was the human beings who thought this would be fun to watch.

I crouched down next to the building and hugged myself and cried. Babette stood guard over me, fiddling with the eyelet lace on the edge of her pinafore and lightly tapping my hairless scalp with the tips of her fingers like she was testing a melon or practicing scales. From the inside of my head, her fingertips felt like raindrops bouncing off my skull. After a while, she lit up a cigarette and smoked it, and by the time she stubbed it out under the six-inch heel of her platform boot, I was okay again.

"Sorry," I said.

"No problem," she said. She inspected my face, and then started digging in her handbag. "You crazy about bugs or something?"

"Not really. My dad is. He likes to fold them out of paper. It's one of his hobbies."

"Weird," she said, pulling out a tissue and wiping something from my cheek. "What's his other hobby?"

"Committing suicide."

She handed me the tissue. "Hmm. Well, if he's still alive, it sounds like he's not very good at it."

"He's better at bugs." I blew my nose and stuffed the tissue in my pocket. "He won third prize in the Great Origami Bug War for his flying staghorn beetle."

"Awesome," she said. "You must be proud of him."

"Yeah," I said, and for a moment I actually was.

"You okay to go shopping now?"

"Sure," I said, following after her.

We bought a cute little knit cap for me, and a shoulder-length wig, and a lacy petticoat, and a pair of loose socks, then she took me to Fifi's to meet the maids. Babette was only a couple of years older than me, but she knew just how to take care of me and make me feel better.

# Ruth

## 1.

"That Babette seems pretty cool," Oliver said.

"She seems like a nice friend for Nao to have . . ." he said.

"It's good that she finally has somebody to talk to . . ." he said.

"I'd like to go to Akiba . . ." he said.

"It's sad about the bugs."

She closed the diary, took off her glasses, and placed both on the bedside table. Pushing the cat off her stomach, she switched off the light. "Good night, Oliver," she said, turning her back to him.

"Good night," he replied. The cat curled up in the gap between them and fell back to sleep. They lay there, side by side, in silence. A few thousand moments passed.

## 2.

"Did I say something wrong?" he asked into the darkness.

She could pretend she was asleep, or she could answer. "Yes," she said.

She could almost hear him thinking. "What?" he asked, finally.

She spoke to the far wall, keeping her voice even. "I'm sorry," she said. "But I just don't understand you. The girl is attacked, tied up and almost raped, her video gets put up on some fetish website, her underpants get auctioned off to some pervert, her pathetic father sees all this and instead of doing anything to help her he tries to kill himself in the bathroom, where she has to find him—after all that, the only thing you can say is Babette is cool? It's sad about the *bugs*?"

"Oh."

A few more hundred moments passed.

"I see your point," he said. "But it's good that she has a nice friend, isn't it?"

"Oliver, Babette is a pimp! She's not being nice to Nao, she's recruiting her. She's running a compensated-dating operation out of that awful maid café."

"Really?"

"Yes. Really."

### 3.

He sounded genuinely surprised. "Are all the maid cafés like that?"

"You mean are they all brothels? Probably not. But this one is."

He thought about this for a while. "Well, I guess maybe I was wrong about Babette."

"Yes. You were."

"But it's not true that Nao's father didn't try to help."

She lost it then, sat up and switched on the light. "Are you fucking kidding me?" she said, bringing her fists down hard onto the puffy folds of the comforter. "He learns about the hentai site and so he takes pills and tries to kill himself? How exactly is that helpful?"

He didn't look at her, or he would have seen she was even angrier than she sounded and he might have backed down. The cat knew. The minute Ruth started pounding on the covers, Pesto was off the bed and out of the room. They heard the sound of the cat door slam as he slipped out into the safety of the night.

Oliver stared up at the ceiling and defended his point. "He did try to help. He was bidding. He was trying to win the auction. It wasn't his fault that he lost."

"What?"

"Bidding." He looked confused. "On her underpants. You didn't realize that?"

"How do you know?"

"C.imperator? The guy who lost the auction? That was him. That was Nao's father."

She felt the heat rising to her face as she listened.

"*Cyclommatus imperator*," he continued. "Don't you remember?"

She didn't.

"It's the Latin name for the staghorn beetle," he explained. "The one he folded out of paper? It was a flying *Cyclommatus imperator*. He won third place for it in the origami bug wars."

Of course she remembered *that*. She just hadn't recalled the Latin name, and she hated that he had. She hated that now he felt he needed to speak slowly and carefully and explain everything as if she were an imbecile or had Alzheimer's. He used to use this tone of voice on her mother.

"Nao recognized the Latin name immediately," he said. "That's why she was so upset. As soon as she saw the suicide note, she knew. 'I should only make myself ridiculous in the eyes of others if I clung to life and hugged it when I have no more to offer.' Her father was referring to the bidding, and Nao figured it out, which was why she went to check her computer. That's my theory."

She hated that he had a theory and that he sounded so smug.

"He had no more to offer, you see? In the auction, which is why he lost. And he didn't want to appear ridiculous in the eyes of—"

"I get it," she said, cutting him off. "It's disgusting. He was bidding on his daughter's panties. What kind of sicko bids on his daughter's underpants?"

Oliver looked surprised. "He was just trying to rescue them so no one else would get them. He didn't want some hentai to buy them. It's not like he was getting off on them himself."

"How do you know?"

"Oh, wow. You're crazy. If that's what you think, you're the sicko."

"Thanks."

"I mean, the guy may be a loser, but—"

"Well, I guess you should know."

## 4.

As soon as the words were out of her mouth, she wanted to take them back.

"I didn't mean that," she said. "You called me crazy. You called me a sicko. I was angry."

But it was too late. She watched his blue eyes veil over as the wall went up and he pulled his tender parts in behind it. When he spoke, his voice was distant, alien.

"He's not a hentai. He just loves her is all."

She turned off the light again. It was too late to fix things. She spoke into the dark. "If he loves her, then he should stop trying to kill himself. Or he should do a better job of it."

"I'm sure he will," Oliver answered, quietly.

## 5.

They didn't fight often. Neither of them liked to argue, and there were certain places they were careful not to go. He knew better than to needle her about her memory. She knew better than to call him a loser.

He wasn't. He was the most intelligent person she knew, an autodidact, with a mind that opened up the world for her, cracking it like a cosmic egg to reveal things she would never have noticed on her own. He'd been an artist for decades, but he called himself an amateur as a matter of principle. He had passionate botanical hobbies: growing things, grafting, and interspecies hacking. He would come in from the orchard, triumphant, crying "It's a red-letter day!" after he'd succeeded in getting a rare tree to germinate or a whip graft to take. He grew cacti from seed on his windowsill, collecting specks of yellow dust from the males with a tiny sable paintbrush and transferring them gently to the female flowers. He made little mesh hats that looked like dunce caps for his *Euphorbia obesa*, which he placed on the females' round heads to catch the fertilized seeds as they sprayed into the air.

Before he got sick and they moved to the island, he used to get grants and the occasional land art commission, supplementing their income by teaching and giving talks. After they moved, he kept up his art practice, even when he was ill. He wrote papers, participated in arts events remotely, and started projects like the NeoEocene. He traveled down to Vancouver to create an urban forest called Means of Production, growing plants and trees for local artists to use: wood for instrument makers, willow for weavers, fiber for papermakers. Wherever they traveled, he collected seeds and cuttings: ghetto palms from Brooklyn; metasequoia from Massachusetts; ginkgos, a living Chinese fossil, from the sidewalks in the Bronx. In the Driftless before 9/11 he'd collected hawthorn root stock onto which he'd grafted a medlar.

"It's my greatest triumph!" he said, and while she cooked, he sat on the stairs and told her all about the history of the medlar, about the applelike fruits, which were best eaten rotten, in spite of their nasty, unmistakable smell.

"Kind of like sugar-frosted baby shit."

"Nice," she said, stirring sage into her soup.

"They're much maligned," he said. "In Elizabethan times, the English used to call them open-arse fruit. The French called them cul de chien, or dog's asshole. Shakespeare used them as a metaphor for prostitution and anal intercourse. Where's your copy of *Romeo and Juliet*?"

She sent him upstairs to her office to fetch her Riverside Shakespeare, and a moment later he was back, with the heavy book on his lap, reading the passage out loud.

*If love be blind, love cannot hit the mark.*
*Now will he sit under a medlar tree,*
*And wish his mistress were that kind of fruit*
*As maids call medlars, when they laugh alone.*

"It's Mercutio, making fun of Romeo for not getting it on with Juliet," he told her.

She turned the burner down and covered the soup. "Where do you find this stuff?"

He told her about the website he'd found for medlar enthusiasts, where he'd come across the Shakespearean references. The idea for the medlar–hawthorn graft he'd found while perusing *Certaine Experiments Concerning Fish and Fruite,* published in London in 1600, by John Taverner, Gentleman.

"It's a book of that gentleman's observations of fish ponds and fruit trees," he said, wistfully. "I would like to publish a book like that."

He was the least egotistical man she'd ever met, nor was he particularly ambitious. His land art projects, like the Means of Production, he deemed successful only when he himself had disappeared from them.

"I want viewers to forget about me."

"Why?" she asked. "Don't you want credit for your work?"

"That's not the point. It's not about any system of credit. It's not about the art market. The work succeeds when all the cleverness and artifice have disappeared, after years of harvest and regrowth, when people begin to experience it as ambience. Any residual aura of me as artist or horticultural dramaturge will have faded. It will no longer matter. That's when the work gets interesting . . ."

"Interesting, how?"

"It becomes more than 'art.' It becomes part of the optical subconscious. Change has occurred. It's the new normal, just the way things are."

By his own measure, then, his work was successful, but the more successful he became, the more difficult he found it to make a living.

"I'll never be a captain of industry," he said, ruefully, one night when they were looking over their finances and trying to figure out how they would pay their bills. "I feel like such a loser."

"Don't be ridiculous," she said. "If I'd wanted a captain of industry, I would have married one."

He shook his head, sadly. "You picked a lemon in the garden of love."

# *Nao*

Sometimes when I sit here at Fifi's writing to you, I find myself wondering about you, what you look like, how tall you are, how old you are, and whether you're a female or a male. I wonder if I would recognize you if I passed you on the street. For all I know, you could be sitting a couple of tables over from me right now, even though I doubt it. Sometimes I hope you're a man, so you'll like me because I'm cute, but sometimes I hope you're a woman because then there's a better chance you'll understand me, even if you don't like me as much. Mostly I've decided it doesn't matter. It's not such a big deal, anyway, male, female. As far as I'm concerned, sometimes I feel more like one, and sometimes I feel more like the other, and mostly I feel somewhere in-between, especially when my hair was first growing back after I'd shaved it.

Here's a good story about in-between. The first date that Babette set me up on was with this guy who worked for a famous advertising agency that you'd probably recognize only I can't mention the name of it because I don't want to get sued. He had loads of cash and suits and watches that were to die for, all the best Armani and Hermes and stuff, and Babette said she thought we would really hit it off. We would be a perfect couple. It was my first time and Babette chose him, I'll call him Ryu, for me because he was rich but also very polite and gentle. He asked me if I wanted to go out to dinner first, but I was so nervous I thought I might throw up, so I told him I just wanted to get it over with. He took me to a nice place on Love Hotel Hill in Shibuya, and he opened a bottle of champagne and took off all my clothes. We had a bath together and he got me pretty drunk. He kissed me a lot, until I started to get annoyed, and I told him, so he stopped. He washed me all over, and he was polite enough not to say anything about my little scars or to ask for a refund on account of them.

Afterward, he dried me off and took me to bed, and that's when I kind of freaked out. I mean, it was my first time, and I was scared because I didn't know what to do. Probably if he'd just been an asshole and held me down and gotten on with it, I would have just gone to my silent place inside the iceberg where I can freeze out the world, and probably I wouldn't have even noticed what he was doing to me or felt anything at all.

But Ryu wasn't an asshole. He was being really nice and gentle, but I was too tense, and it was like trying to push a breakfast sausage through a glass window—it just wouldn't go. Every time he tried to put it in, I started trembling and couldn't stop, and suddenly I was overcome with sadness that was like a wave washing over me. Maybe it was the champagne making me weepy, but it hit me that here was this really nice guy who I thought would be a total jerk but it turned out he wasn't, and he'd paid all this money for a date with me, and now just when he was hoping to have some nice virgin sex, instead he had a hopelessly weeping schoolgirl with an impenetrable vagina on his hands. I felt like such a loser. It seemed like all I could do was cry these days, first over some stupid bug wars, and now this.

He was way too polite to force me when I was crying. He sat up in bed and watched me for a while, and then he went over to the chair where his suit was laid out and he got a beautiful pressed linen handkerchief from his pocket and gave it to me to blow my nose on. Then, because I was shivering, he brought his shirt over and draped it around my shoulders. It was so soft and silky feeling, and before I knew it, I had slipped my arms through the sleeves, so he buttoned it up. The next thing was his pink silk necktie, which he tied in a lovely Windsor knot for me. Then his pants, and then the suit jacket, and by the time I was dressed in his clothes, I had stopped crying, and he took my hand and led me over to the mirror and turned me around and around to admire my reflection.

I was beautiful in his suit. He was a little bit bigger and taller than me, but really we weren't so different. I'd taken off my wig, and under it, my head still looked pretty buzzed, which he said he liked. He said I looked just like a bishōnen,[144] but actually I was cuter than any boy. Honest. I swear I could have fallen in love with myself. He was standing behind me, naked, and he reached around into my breast pocket and took out a pack of cigarettes. He shook out two, put them in his mouth, and then lit them with a classy platinum lighter that was hardly bigger than a match. He put one of the cigarettes between my lips and then went back to the bed to smoke the other one and watch me. Luckily I'd had puffs from my dad's cigarettes before, so I knew how. I cocked my head to one side and studied my reflection. I let the smoke trail from my pouting lips, which were red and puffy from all that kissing we'd done. Out of the corner of my eye, I could see him in the mirror. He lay on the bed, smoking his cigarette, and I could see he was really turned on. I turned and poured myself another glass of champagne and drank it down, and then I stubbed out my cigarette and went over to the bed and climbed on top of him.

"Close your eyes," I said. "Pretend you're me."

He closed his eyes and let me kiss him for a while, and then he reached up and undid the Windsor on his pink silk tie and unbuttoned his shirt. He unzipped the zipper on his fly. He pulled down his pants and I kicked them off, but I kept his shirt on while I straddled his hips, and he guided me down, and it hurt, but only for a while.

Afterward, we lay side by side, and he lit another cigarette, and he asked me if I wanted one. I told him no thank you. Then he asked if the sex had been okay for me, and I said sure, and thanks for asking. I mean, that's nice, right? I bet a lot of guys wouldn't even bother.

"Did it hurt?" he asked, and I told him a little, but I didn't mind because I have a really high pain threshold. He smiled and told me I was funny.

"How old are you anyway?" he asked, and I was just about to say fifteen, when suddenly I remembered.

---

144. *bishōnen* (美少年)—beautiful youth, beautiful boy.

"Sixteen," I said. "I'm sixteen."

He laughed. "You sound surprised."

"Yes," I said. "It's my birthday. I almost forgot."

He said he was sorry he didn't have a gift for me and then gave me his slick little lighter. We had a couple more dates after that, and we always did it the same way, with me wearing his suit. Once, I made him put on my school uniform, but he looked so ridiculous with his knobbly knees sticking out from under the pleats that I got angry and wanted to hit him, so I did. I was wearing his beautiful Armani, which is a cruel suit, and he stood passively in front of me, wearing my skirt and my sailor blouse, and kept his eyes fixed on the floor. His passive attitude made me even angrier, and the madder I got, the harder I wanted to hit him. I slapped him until I was almost hysterical, and when he raised his eyes, they were so full of sadness and pity for me, I thought maybe I would have to kill him. But the next time my hand came toward him, he caught my wrist.

"Enough," he said. "You're only hurting yourself."

I was wearing Haruki #1's sky soldier watch. The old metal buckle on the watchband cut into my wrist, where he was gripping it. The skin on his face looked red and angry. I put my other hand on his swollen cheek.

"I'm sorry," I said, starting to cry.

He brought my stinging palm to his lips and kissed it.

"I forgive you," he said.

He really liked Number One's sky soldier watch, and once he asked me if I would trade it for his Rolex. The Rolex had real diamonds in it. I was tempted, but of course I said no.

**2.**

Sometimes, after we made love, Ryu just wanted to lie in bed and drink Rémy and watch porno on the television, so I would get dressed in his suit and leave him there and walk around. Sometimes I even left the hotel, making sure I walked by the side where our room was, so he could see me from the window if he happened to be looking. He liked that.

I kept to the shadows mostly, just slouching around, enjoying being a male. Sometimes I took a cigarette from his pocket and lit it with the platinum lighter. The lighter had a little diamond in it, too. Ryu was a really classy guy, with his slim diamond lighters and beautiful suits, but he smoked Mild Seven, which is not a classy brand of cigarettes. Honestly, they taste like shit. Next time I have to remember to find a boyfriend who smokes Dunhills, or at least Larks.

If it wasn't too late at night, sometimes I texted old Jiko at the temple, but I felt a little weird about telling her what was going on. I'd pretty much stopped sitting zazen so we weren't really on the same wavelength anymore, and we weren't really on the same time schedule anymore, either, since she went to bed early, and I was dating, so I stayed up late. It's funny how time can make all the difference in whether or not you feel close to somebody, like when I moved away to a different time zone, and Kayla and I couldn't be friends anymore. I wondered what Kayla would say if she could see me now. Maybe she would think I was cute and come on to me. That's what happened on the street sometimes, if I kept to the shadows. Girls would think I was a host from a host club[145] and try to flirt with me, and I'd have to escape before they figured out that I was a girl and got mad and beat me up for making fools of them.

You couldn't really call Ryu my boyfriend. It wasn't like that. We dated for almost a month, but when my hair started getting longer, he vanished. I was really starting to love him, and I didn't know any better, so when he stopped calling I thought my heart would break. I kept asking Babette if she'd heard from him, but she said no, which may or may not have been true. Babette did matchmaking for a lot of girls, and she just shrugged and said I must have done something wrong, but other than the time I hit him, which he forgave me for, I really don't think I did.

After that I hung around Fifi's, sulking and listening to Edith Pilaf

---

145. A club or bar with bishōnen hosts who serve drinks and entertain female customers.

and Barbara, refusing to go out on any more dates until Babette finally got fed up. She said I should stop being so selfish, and I should feel grateful to her for fixing me up with such a nice, kind guy for my first time. Then she told me to cheer up or get out, and threatened to give my table to a happier girl.

## 3.

It wasn't that I wasn't grateful to her. I really was. She was my only friend, and if I couldn't hang out at Fifi's Lonely Apron, where could I go? My home life was a disaster. Mom had gotten a promotion at the publishing company and was now an editor, which meant she was killing herself working overtime. Dad was entering a new phase as he prepared for his third and final suicide challenge. Before, when he went through his Pretending to Have a Job Phase, and then his Hikikomori Phase, and the Great Minds Phase, and the Insect Origami Phase, you could say that at least he was interested and engaged with his insanity. Even during the Night Walking Phase and Falling Man Phase, his craziness had a focus and he was holding it together. But this time it was different. He was depressed like I've never seen him before, like he'd finally and truly lost all interest in being alive. He avoided any contact with me and Mom, which is a trick in a small two-room apartment. He pretended we were invisible and stayed glued to the computer screen, but sometimes, if I happened to pass him in the narrow hallway and catch his eye, his face would twitch and start to crumple with the weight of his shame, and I had to turn my head away because I couldn't bear to see it.

Dad and I were still sharing the computer, and one day when I was searching his browser cache, I happened to find his links to an online suicide club. He had made some friends, it seemed, and they were chatting and making plans.

How pathetic is that? You can't do it alone, so you have to find a stranger to hold your hand? And what's worse, one of his club mates was a high school student, and he had the nerve to be trying to talk her out of suicide. I found his chat stream and read it. I mean, is that hypocritical or what? He wants to kill himself but he's telling her that she shouldn't? That she has her whole life in front of her? That she has so much to live for?

The idea came to me then. Maybe I wouldn't go to Jiko's temple and become a nun after all. Maybe I would just kill myself, too, and be done with it.

# *Ruth*

## I.

Dear Ruth (if I may call you that),

I was delighted to find your email in my inbox, and I must apologize for taking so long to reply. I do, of course, remember you from your visit to Stanford. Prof. P-L in Comparative Literature is a good friend of mine, so you need no further introduction. Unfortunately I was just leaving for sabbatical at the time of your residency and was unable to attend your talk, but I trust that I will have the pleasure of hearing you read from your next book soon.

Now, in regard to your urgent query, while I feel I must still exercise some discretion regarding information told to me in confidence, I think that I can be of some help.

First, I agree that it seems likely that the "Harry" who authored the testimonial on my website is the father of the Nao Yasutani whose diary has somehow come into your possession. Mr. Yasutani was a computer scientist, working at a large information technology company here in Silicon Valley back in the '90s. I suppose you could say we were friends, and he did indeed have a young daughter named Naoko, who could not have been more than four or five years old at the time when I first met him.

I hasten to say that I am using the past tense not from any knowledge of their outcome or fate, but only because I am no longer in touch with Mr. Yasutani and so our relationship has, regrettably, receded into the past. As you may be aware, he moved back to Japan with his family shortly after the dot-com bubble burst. After that, we corresponded sporadically by email and by phone, but little by little we fell out of touch, and it has been several years since our last exchange.

Now, let me tell you something of our acquaintance. I met Mr. Yasutani at Stanford in 1991, about a year or so after he moved to Sunnyvale. He came to my office late one afternoon. There was a knock at the door. Office hours were over, and I remember being slightly annoyed at the interruption, but I called out "Come in" and then waited. The door remained shut. I called again, and still there was no response, so I got up and went to the door and opened it. A slight Asian man carrying a messenger bag was standing there. He was dressed somewhat casually in khaki pants, a sports jacket, and sandals with socks. I thought at first that he might be a bike courier, but instead of handing me a package, he bowed deeply. This startled me. It was such a formal gesture, at odds with his casual dress, and we are not accustomed to bowing to each other at Stanford University.

"Professor," he said, in slow, careful English. "I am very sorry to disturb you." He held out his business card and bowed again. The card identified him as Haruki Yasutani, a computer scientist at one of the rapidly growing IT companies in the Valley. I invited him in and offered him a seat.

In stilted English, he explained that he was originally from Tokyo and had been headhunted to work on human–computer interface design. He loved his work and had no problem with the computer end of things. His problem, he said, was the human factor. He didn't understand human beings very well, so he'd come to the Psychology Department at Stanford to ask for help.

I was astonished, but curious, too. Silicon Valley is not Tokyo, and it would be natural for him to be suffering from culture shock or having problems relating to his co-workers. "What kind of help do you want?" I asked.

He sat with his head bowed, gathering his words. When he looked up, I could see the strain in his face.

"I want to know, what is human conscience?"

"Human consciousness?" I asked, not hearing him correctly.

"No," he said. "Con-sci-ence. When I search for this word in the English dictionary, I find that it is from Latin. *Con* means 'with,' and *science* means 'knowing.' So *conscience* means 'with knowing.' With science."

"I've never quite thought about it that way," I told him. "But I'm sure you're right."

He continued. "But this does not make sense." He pulled out a piece of paper. "The dictionary says 'A knowledge or sense of right and wrong, with a compulsion to do right.'"

He held out the piece of paper for me to see, so I took it. "That seems like a reasonable definition."

"But I do not understand. Knowledge and sense are not the same thing. Knowledge I understand, but how about sense? Is sense the same as feeling? Is conscience a fact that I can learn and know, or is it more like an emotion? Is it related to empathy? Is it different than shame? And why is it a compulsion?"

I must have looked as baffled as I felt, because he went on to explain.

"I'm afraid that even though I am trained in computer science, I have never felt such a sense or feeling. This is a big disadvantage for my work. I would like to ask you, can I learn to feel such a feeling? At my age, is it too late?"

It was an extraordinary question, or rather barrage of questions. We continued to talk, and eventually I managed to piece together his story. While his company was primarily involved in interface development for the gaming market, the U.S. military had an interest in the enormous potential his research might have for applications in semiautonomous weapons technology. Harry was concerned that the interface he was helping to design was too seamless. What made a computer game addictive and entertaining would make it easy and fun to carry out a massively destructive bombing mission. He was trying to figure out if there was a way to build a conscience into the interface design that would assist the user by triggering his ethical sense of right and wrong and engaging his compulsion to do right.

His story was moving and tragic, too. Although he claimed not to understand matters of human conscience, it was precisely his own conscience that led him to question the status quo, and which would cost him his job later on. Needless to say, technology design is not value-neutral, and military contractors and weapons developers do not want these kinds of questions raised, never mind built into their controllers.

I did what I could to reassure him. The very fact he was asking these questions in the first place demonstrated that his conscience was in fine working order.

He shook his head. "No," he said. "That is not conscience. That is only shame from my history, and history can easily be changed."

I didn't understand and asked him to explain.

"History is something we Japanese learn about in school," he said. "We study about terrible things, like how the atom bombs destroyed Hiroshima and Nagasaki. We learn this is wrong, but that is an easy case because we Japanese people were the victims of it.

"A harder case is when we study about a terrible Japanese atrocity like Manchu. In this case, we Japanese people committed genocide and torture of the Chinese people, and so we learn we must feel great shame to the world. But shame is not a pleasant feeling, and some Japanese politicians are always trying to change our children's history textbooks so that these genocides and tortures are not taught to the next generation. By changing our history and our memory, they try to erase all our shame.

"This is why I think shame must be different from conscience. They say we Japanese are a culture of shame, so maybe we are not so good at conscience? Shame comes from outside, but conscience must be a natural feeling that comes from a deep place inside an individual person. They say we Japanese people have lived so long under the feudal system that maybe we do not have an individual self in the same way Westerners do. Maybe we cannot have a conscience without an individual self. I do not know. This is what I am worrying about."

Of course, I'm paraphrasing here, remembering what I can of that stilted conversation many years ago. I don't recall how I answered, but the exchange was mutually satisfying and resulted in further conversations and eventually in friendship. You can see how this inquiry into notions of individual self would lead to, among other things, the topic of shame, honor, and self-killing, which was the subject of the letter that caught your attention. My own interest in cultural influences on suicide, while initially prompted by the activity of suicide bombers in the Middle East, was informed over the years by my exchange with Mr. Yasutani. He always asserted that in Japan, suicide was primarily an aesthetic, not a moral, act, triggered by a sense of honor or shame. As you may or may not know, his uncle was a WWII war hero, a pilot in the Tokkotai, who died while carrying out a kamikaze mission over the Pacific.

"My grandmother felt so much pain," Harry said. "If my uncle's plane had a conscience, maybe he would not have done such a bombing. For the pilot of the *Enola Gay*, it is the same thing, and maybe there would not have been a Hiroshima and Nagasaki, too. Of course, technology was not so advanced then, so such a thing was not possible. Now it is possible."

He sat perfectly still, studying his hands in his lap. "I know it is a stupid idea to design a weapon that will refuse to kill," he said. "But maybe I could make the killing not so much fun."

Toward the end of his stay in the Valley, Mr. Yasutani was having trouble with his employer, which was unwilling to jeopardize its relations with the military and investors on account of one Japanese employee's tortured conscience. They asked him to refrain from pursuing this line of research, but he refused. He was dropped from his project team. He grew anxious and depressed, and while I do not have a clinical practice,

I counseled him as a friend. The company fired him shortly after.

That must have been March of 2000, because less than a month later, in April, the dot-com bubble burst and the NASDAQ crashed. He came in to see me and told me that he'd had most of his family's savings tied up in the company's stock options, and that he'd lost everything. He was not a practical man. In August of that year, they moved back to Japan, and I didn't hear from him for a while.

The following year, I decided to make some of my research available online and I launched my website. A few months later, I received an email from Harry, an excerpt of which you read online. It was a beautiful and moving cry for help, and I corresponded with him for several months after that by email and also by phone. It was during that time that I asked if I could post his comments on my website, and he said if I thought it would help others, I could have his permission. I felt strongly that he needed professional counseling, and I suggested the names of a few clinicians in Tokyo. I don't know whether he followed through on that or not. I suspect not.

I lost track of him after the September 11 bombings. It was a busy time for me, as world events prompted much media interest in my research. I recall we may have had one exchange a few years later, but around the same time, a virus obliterated my computer files and much of my archived email, including those from him, was lost. I wanted to contact him after the

earthquake and tsunami, but I discovered I no longer
had his email address. I consoled myself with the
thought that he and his family lived far from Sendai;
however now, after hearing from you, I feel motivated
to try to track him down.

You mentioned some letters in addition to the diary
belonging to the daughter. If these contain any
information that might help me locate Mr. Yasutani
and his family, I would appreciate it if you would
share it with me. I would like to ask, too, what it was
that led you to be concerned for the daughter's well-
being. You said you felt it was a matter of some
urgency. Why is that?

Finally, I would also be interested to know how the
diary and letters found their way into your
possession, but that is perhaps a story for another
time.

And speaking of stories, I trust you are working on a
new book? I look forward to reading it, as I enjoyed
your last one very much.

Sincerely yours,

etc.

## 2.

She skimmed the email quickly, and immediately wrote back, describing
her discovery of the diary in the tangle of kelp, her theory as to its origins
in the tsunami, and her failure thus far either to corroborate this theory

or to explain how else the freezer bag might have wound up on the beach. She summarized, briefly, the passages in Nao's diary that were causing concern: the descriptions of her father's precarious mental health, his suicide attempts, and Nao's decision to commit suicide herself. She explained that she couldn't help but feel a strong sense of almost karmic connection with the girl and her father. The diary had washed up on Ruth's shoreline, after all. If Nao and her father were in trouble, she wanted to help.

She concluded her email with a mention of the article about qubits in *New Science* that Oliver had found, citing H. Yasudani, whom she had tried, and failed, to track down. She sent the email off and sat back in her chair, savoring the rush of relief and excitement. This was it, then. The corroboration she'd been waiting for. Nao and her family were real!

She stood up and stretched and wandered across the hallway to Oliver's office. He was sitting with the noise-canceling headphones clamped to his ears. The co-pilot chair was empty.

"Where's Pesto?" she asked, waving her hand to catch his eye.

Oliver took off the headphones and looked at the catless chair. "He hasn't been here all day," he said, glumly.

They had made up at breakfast. Ruth apologized again for calling him a loser, and he apologized for calling her a sicko, but there was still tension lingering between them. Sometimes the cat, feeling a chill in the air, would stay away. Ruth felt it, too, which was why she'd crossed the hall to share the good news about the professor's email, but now, seeing Oliver slumped in his chair, she hesitated.

"What's wrong?" she asked.

"Oh," he said. "It's nothing. Just that I've got a whole flat of baby ginkgos, ready to be planted, but the covenant holder won't let me. They're saying the ginkgos are potentially invasive." He took off his glasses and rubbed his hands across his face. He had a particular fondness for *G. biloba*. "It's insane. That tree is a living fossil. It survived major extinction events over hundreds of millions of years. The entire population disappeared except for a tiny area in central China where some of them managed to hang on. And now they're going to die on our porch if I can't get them in the ground soon."

It was unlike him to sound so discouraged or to cast a relatively small problem like this in such dire terms. He must be upset about the cat.

"Can't you make a nursery bed here on our property?"

He sighed, heavily, staring at his empty hands in his lap. "Yeah, I'll do that. I just don't see why I bother, though. What's the point? Nobody understands what I'm trying to do . . ."

He must be really upset about the cat. She decided to save the news about the professor's email for later, but just as she turned to leave, he looked up. "Did you want something?" he asked.

And so she told him. She recounted what Leistiko had written, his surprising revelation of Nao's father as a man of conscience who had been fired for his beliefs, and she summarized her reply, but then she broke off, realizing Oliver was looking at her strangely.

"What?" she said. "You're giving me a look. What's wrong?"

"You told him it was a matter of some urgency?"

"Of course. The girl is suicidal. So is her father. The whole diary is a cry for help. So, yes. Urgency. I'd say that about describes it." She heard the defensive edge in her voice but she couldn't help it. "You're still looking at me."

"Well . . ."

"Well, what?"

"Well, you're not making a lot of sense. I mean, it's not like this is happening now, right?"

"I don't understand. What's your point?"

"Do the math. The dot-com bubble burst back in March of 2000. Her dad got fired, they moved back to Japan, a couple of years passed. Nao was sixteen when she started writing the diary. But that was more than a decade ago, and we know the diary's been floating around for a least a few years longer. My point is that if she was going to kill herself, she's probably already done it, don't you think? And if she didn't kill herself, then she'd be in her late twenties by now. So I just wonder if *urgency* is really the right word to describe it, that's all."

338

Ruth felt the floor tip. She put her hand on the doorjamb to steady herself.

"What's wrong?"

"Nothing," she said, swallowing hard. "I . . . of course, you're right. Stupid. I just . . . forgot." She could feel her cheeks burning, and a tingling sensation inside her nose, like she was going to sneeze, or cry.

"You forgot?" he repeated. "Seriously?"

She nodded, already backing away. She wanted to run somewhere and hide.

"Wow," he said. "That's crazy."

She turned, crossed the hall, and headed downstairs.

"I didn't mean *you're* crazy," he called down after her.

### 3.

She didn't get far. Just to the bedroom. She crawled into bed, pulled the covers up to her nose, and lay there, breathing rapidly. Outside, the bamboo tapped against the windowpane. Tall sword ferns had grown up from below. The blades of the bamboo, ensnared by the thorns of roses, cut off much of the light. She stared at the entangled foliage and thought about the email she'd just sent the professor. She felt the blood rush to her face. How could she have been so stupid?

It wasn't that she'd forgotten, exactly. The problem was more a kind of slippage. When she was writing a novel, living deep inside a fictional world, the days got jumbled together, and entire weeks or months or even years would yield to the ebb and flow of the dream. Bills went unpaid, emails unanswered, calls unreturned. Fiction had its own time and logic. That was its power. But the email she'd just written to the professor was not fiction. It was real, as real as the diary.

Oliver knocked on the door and then opened it a crack. "Can I come in?" She nodded. He walked over and stood by the bed. "You okay?" he asked, studying her face.

"I got confused," she said. "In my mind, she's still sixteen. She'll always be sixteen."

Oliver sat down on the edge of the mattress and put his hand on her forehead. "The eternal now," he said. "She wanted to catch it, remember? To pin it down. That was the point."

"Of writing?"

"Or suicide."

"I've always thought of writing as the opposite of suicide," she said. "That writing was about immortality. Defeating death, or at least fore-stalling it."

"Like Scheherazade?"

"Yes," she said. "Spinning tales to forestall her execution . . ."

"Only Nao's death sentence was self-imposed."

"I wonder if she ever carried it out."

"Keep reading," Oliver said. "You won't know until the end."

"Or not . . ." She thought about how not knowing would make her feel. Not great. Then something else occurred to her.

"Oh!" she said, sitting up in bed. "She doesn't know!"

"Know what?"

"About why her dad got fired! She doesn't know that he's a man of conscience. We have to—"

There. She was doing it again. She slumped back down against the pillow. At least this time she caught herself.

"It's too late," she said, glumly.

"Too late for what?"

"To help her," she said. "So what's the point? The diary's just a distrac-tion. What difference does it make if I read it or not?"

Oliver shrugged. "None, probably, but you still have to finish. She wrote to the end, so you owe her that much. That's the deal, and anyway, I want to know what happens."

He stood and turned to go. She reached for his hand.

"Am I crazy?" she asked. "I feel like I am sometimes."

"Maybe," he said, rubbing her forehead. "But don't worry about it. You need to be a little bit crazy. Crazy is the price you pay for having an imagination. It's your superpower. Tapping into the dream. It's a good thing, not a bad thing."

The phone started to ring, and he headed out to answer it, but then paused at the door. "I'm really worried about Pesto," he said.

## 4.

Benoit sat in a battered armchair in front of the woodstove, smoking and staring into the flames. He looked up when he heard Ruth enter. His eyes were red, as though he'd been crying, and he'd been drinking, too. The cloying scent of Canadian whiskey mingled with the smell of cigarettes and wood smoke and wet socks.

His wife stood in the doorway of the living room. She did not look pleased. She had been the one who'd called, and Oliver had spoken to her. Her husband had finished the translation of the French diary, she said. Would Ruth please come to their house to collect it, tonight. Oliver hung up the phone, put the chainsaw in the truck, and offered to drive. The wind was picking up, and the tall trees were beginning to sway. Another storm was coming, this one heading right toward them.

Benoit held out a sheaf of about twenty sheets of ruled notebook paper, which shook in his outstretched hand.

"Le mal de vivre," he said. "You ask me what it means. *This* is what it means. Evil, sorrow, suffering. How can there be so much pain in the world?"

Ruth took the pages from him.

"Thank you," she said, glancing down at the translation.

"Take this, too," he said. He held out the thin composition booklet that contained the diary, wrapped in its waxy paper.

"I really appreciate . . ." she started, but he shook his head and stared back into the flames.

His wife stepped forward then and touched her on the arm. She led Ruth from the room and showed her to the door. "He's been drinking."

Ruth didn't know what to say. "I'm so sorry . . ."

His wife softened. "It's not just your fault," she said, lowering her voice. "His little dog got snatched by the wolves last night. They sent a young bitch out and he followed. Stupid dog. The pack was waiting on the far side of a ravine. Set on him and killed him, just like that. Tore him to shreds and ate him." She looked back toward the living room, where her husband was still sitting. "He watched it happen. Called him and chased after, but couldn't get across the ravine. He's too big. Too slow. There were just pieces of fur left by the time he got there. He loved that little dog." She opened the door and cocked her head, listening. "You better go. Wind's picking up. It's going to be a bad one."

# *Haruki #1's Secret French Diary*

## 1.

December 10, 1943—We sleep together in one large room, my squadron members and I, laid out in rows like small fish hung to dry. It is only when the moon is nearly full and the sky is clear that I have enough light to write. I slip these pages out from inside the lining of my uniform, where I keep them hidden, careful not to rustle. I unscrew the cap on my fountain pen, worried that the ink might run dry and be insufficient for my thoughts. My last thoughts, measured out in drops of ink.

We have been instructed to keep a diary of our training and our feelings as we face certain death, but I have been warned by one of the other student soldiers that the senior officers will inspect these diaries, as they will read our letters, without warning, so I should be careful not to write truthfully from my heart. Duplicity is a hardship I am unwilling to suffer, so I have decided I will keep two records: one for show, and this hidden one for truth, for you, even though I hardly expect you will ever read this. I will write in French, ma chère Maman, following the good example of your idol, Kanno-san, who faithfully persisted in her English lessons right up until the moment they led her to the gallows. Like her, we must keep up our studies even as civilization collapses around us.

## 2.

*Clench your teeth. Bite down hard!* our commanding officer, le Marquis de F—, orders. He punches K in the face with his fist until K's knees buckle, and then he kicks him when he's down. Last week, he crushed two of K's back teeth, but K acted as though he didn't feel a thing, blinking and smiling his sweet, otherworldly smile as the blood ran from his mouth.

K is my senior in the Philosophy Department and I have a duty to him. Yesterday, when the beating got particularly bad, I stepped in front of K to take his blows. The Marquis de F— was delighted. He punched me on both sides of my face and beat me with the heel of his boot. Afterward, the inside of my mouth was like minced meat and even the smallest sip of miso soup brought tears to my eyes, the salt in the wounds was so painful.

Chère Maman, I am wrapping this composition book in oilskin and hiding it under the rice in the bottom of my lunchbox. I will try to find a way to get it to you before I die. I cannot write candidly in my letters to you, but the hope that someday you will know the truth about this imbecilic lynching comforts me. No matter how much bullying they inflict on my body, as long as I have this hope, I can endure any pain.

### 3.

Last night, during the pleasure quarters game, I sensed a change come over K as he watched my humiliation. As I crouched behind the rifle rack, following the orders of le Marquis, reaching out my arms through the slats and waving my hands seductively like a lady of the night, I saw K turn away for the first time, as though the sight of me was too much to bear.

Le Marquis, noticing K's withdrawal, perhaps, ordered me do it again and again. He feeds me my lines. *Hey there, soldier*, I call. Like a director, an auteur, he studies my performance with his head cocked to one side. He tells me to make my voice higher and sweeter. There is a seriousness, almost an innocence, to his attention. *Won't you come inside and play with me?* I cry, and it is only a matter of time before he obliges. The games don't finish until long after the final bugle call, signaling lights-out. At night, sometimes I can hear K, weeping.

Tu marches sur des morts, Beauté, dont tu te moques;

De tes bijoux l'Horreur n'est pas le moins charmant . . .[146]

Did Baudelaire know of such things, Maman? Are these the dark petals of les fleurs du mal?

### 4.

The bush warbler's song is a beautiful song. I will never be able to hear it again without thinking of F— and wanting to kill him. We hear whispered stories about hated officers who have been shot from behind or beaten to death by their own troops in the confusion of a skirmish. I am counting the blows I receive from the Marquis. I will return each one to him someday. The number as of tonight is 267.

I don't mind dying. We all understand that death is the only outcome for us. I only hope that I will not die before I taste the sweetness of revenge.

### 5.

No sense. No sense. K escaped at dawn, and later we were told that he committed suicide in front of a supply train, but one of the men who'd seen his body told me that he'd been shot in the back. That night, I discovered his worn copy of Master Dōgen's *Shōbōgenzō* tucked inside my duffel. I lie here and long for the hot tears I used to cry, but my heart is frozen. I am frozen, inside and out. I have ceased to feel. Even the Marquis's blows have no effect and fail to move me to anger. They are like torpedoes, missing their mark. At one point in my life, I learned how to think. I used to know how to feel. In war, these are lessons best forgotten.

### 6.

During your visit, Maman, I was planning to find a way to slip these pages to you, but your shocked expression when you laid eyes upon my

146. Beauty, you walk on corpses of dead men you mock. / Among your stores of gems, Horror is not the least . . .

face caused me to change my mind. I lied to you and told you that the bruises were due to a routine training accident. I do not think you believed me, but in that moment, my lie made it impossible to follow through with my plan to slip you this diary, containing as it does such lengthy and self-indulgent accounts of what are the routine and quite banal cruelties of military life. So as a result of my lack of self-restraint and mental training, here I am once again, writing alone by the light of the moon. I do not regret my lie, however. I would do anything to spare you more grief.

And in fact, my feelings toward the Marquis have begun to transform. At first, when he beat me, I was afraid. I do not mind admitting this. How could I not be? I had never been beaten before! Few boys have been as fortunate as I, raised into manhood with only the gentlest of words and blandishments in my ears and the kindest of caresses upon my person, by a mother who sheltered us from everything that is harsh and ugly in the world. I was spoiled, utterly unprepared for cruelty, and perhaps this sounds like I'm complaining, but I'm not! You mustn't think I blame you. I'm afraid I must sound like the most ungrateful son in the world, when in fact the opposite is true. I am more grateful now than ever for the way you raised us, teaching us the value of kindness, of education, of independent thinking and liberal ideals, in the face of the fascism that is sweeping our country. The cruelest punishments now fail to bring even a tear to my eye, but the thought of the hardship you've suffered on behalf of your ideals makes me weep like a baby.

There, now I have spoiled this page with my tears so I can barely make out the words. Paper is precious, although these words are hardly worth the paper or the ink required to write them.

Where was I? Oh, yes. I was telling you about the transformation of my feelings toward F—. After the first few weeks of punishment and training, I began to notice that my initial fear and self-pity were transforming into resentment, and then from resentment into rage. When he called my name, instead of anxiety, a boiling excitement shot through my body like a drug, and I worked to keep my gaze lowered, certain that if I looked at his despicable face, he would see the white-hot fire of rage in mine. My anger frightened me more than my fear once had.

But recently, my feelings have changed once again. Last week, he called me out to correct me for some small infraction—perhaps I dropped a grain of rice when I served him, or left a speck of dust on his shoe, or maybe he'd just suffered indigestion or a poor night's sleep. I don't remember, but he ordered me to kneel on the floor with my hands tucked beneath my thighs, and he began to beat me with his belt across my face and body.

Normally, I would keep my eyes downturned, staring fixedly at a point on the floor until my eyes would swell or fill with blood and I could no longer see, but that day, for some reason, I raised my gaze. I looked F—straight in the eye, which is against the rules, for we are never to make eye contact with a superior, and when I did, oddly, I felt my heart soften. I know it sounds strange, but that's what it felt like. For the first time, I noticed the fever in his narrow-set eyes and the greasy sweat upon his brow, and I was filled with pity, and even after a dozen blows, I could forgive him sincerely. Of course, this was not a good strategy, since my steady gaze and disobedience made him even angrier, and twelve blows turned to twenty and then thirty. When I lost consciousness, I also lost count. Eventually the beating must have come to an end. Someone must have carried me back to the barracks and covered me with a blanket. When I woke, my body must have hurt, but I couldn't feel the pain. Instead, I was enveloped in a warm sensation of peace, which comes from the knowledge of inner power.

This, I think, was the source of the smile I remember seeing on K's face when he was being beaten, before I stepped in to take his punishment for him. He could tolerate his own pain, but mine, taken on his behalf, was more than he could bear. It still torments me to imagine that I was the one responsible for his death, but in this tangled world of cause and effect, it is impossible to know.

Since then, although there have been one or two punitive sessions, it seems that F— has grown bored with me, too, or perhaps he is scared. It might be my imagination, but his heart just doesn't seem to be in it anymore.

Should I be grateful to him? Having lost count of the blows I have received, I no longer care to return them. Perhaps this means I have outgrown this childishness. Perhaps I have graduated and am finally a man.

### 7.

August 3, 1944—Here is what I could not say in my letter. Rumors abound, Maman. The war is not going well. Our troops have withdrawn from northern Burma, and American forces have landed on Guam. If this continues, a U.S. invasion of Japan may follow, and our deployment will be the last attempt to stem the tide. I was deeply disturbed to read your account of the visit from the military police, and I fear you may be targeted because of your political activities. I beg you to be careful. I wish you would reconsider taking my sisters and evacuating to the countryside.

### 8.

I have written to you of my decision to die. Here is what I did not tell you. On either side of me, my comrades sigh and groan, restless in their sleep, and outside the insects cry, but the ticking of the clock is the only sound I am able to hear now. Second by second, minute by minute . . . tick, tick, tick . . . the small, dry sounds fill every crevice of silence. I write this in the shadows. I write this in the moonlight, straining my ears to hear beyond the cold mechanical clock to the warm biological noises of the night, but my being is attuned only to one thing, the relentless rhythm of time, marching toward my death.

If I could only smash the clock and stop time from advancing! Crush the infernal machine! Shatter its bland face and rip those cursed hands from their torturous axis of circumscription! I can almost feel the sturdy metal body crumpling beneath my hands, the glass fracturing, the case cracking open, my fingers digging into the guts, spilling springs and delicate gearing. But no, there is no use, no way of stopping time, and so I lie here, paralyzed, listening to the last moments of my life tick by.

I don't want to die, Maman! I don't want to die!

I don't want to die.

❖

I'm sorry. I was just talking to the moon.

❖

Silly. The amount of ink I waste on foolish outpourings, smashing clocks in my mind, crying out in my imagination. Forget the clock. It has no power over time, but words do, and now I am tempted to rip up these pages. Is this how I want to be remembered? By these words? By you?

But no, I will leave them for now, since you will never see them. I write them for my own benefit, to conjure you in my mind. They are meant only for me.

"To study the Way is to study the self," Dōgen said. I have vowed to sit zazen and study my thoughts and feelings meticulously, the way a scientist would dissect a cadaver, in order to improve myself as much as I can in the few short weeks I have left. I have vowed to reveal myself to you, even if you never read this. Ripping up the pages will not excise the cowardice from my heart any more than ripping the hands from a clock face will stop time.

Really, I am one of the lucky ones. I have been educated and my mind has been trained. I have the capacity to think things through.

"To philosophize is to learn to die."

So wrote Montaigne, paraphrasing Cicero, although the thought, of course, was not a new one, going back at least as far as Socrates in the

West, and the Buddha in the East . . . although certainly the notion of what it meant "to philosophize" differed.

"To study the Way is to study the self. To study the self is to forget the self. To forget the self is to be enlightened by all the myriad things."

❖

I mentioned to you in a letter my fanciful thoughts about Miyazawa's tale of the Crow Wars, and now I feel very silly indeed. I am no Crow Captain, taking to wing to do battle! But the truth is, I cannot deny my love of flying. And foolish as it might seem, the tale remained in my mind, and later on, I found myself recalling the scene where the Crow Captain is burying his dead enemy and he prays to the stars. Do you remember the passage? It goes something like this:

*Blessed Stars, please make this world into a place where we will never again be forced to kill an enemy whom we cannot hate. Were such a thing to come about, I would not complain even if my body were torn to pieces again and again.*

These beautiful words I believe are true and, now that I know I will sortie, they have such poignant meaning for me. Recalling this passage during dinner brought tears to my eyes. Unfortunately, as I was brushing them away, I dropped a bowl of pickles onto the floor. My new rank, however, seems to protect me from scolding, and the Marquis just looks the other way.

## 9.

Time is so interesting to me now that I have so little of it. I sit zazen, or run the juzu through my fingers, counting with beads and breath the moments until my death. Somewhere Dōgen wrote about the number of moments in the snap of a finger. I don't remember the exact figure, only that it was large and seemed quite arbitrary and absurd, but I imagine that when I am in the cockpit of my plane, aiming the nose at the hull of an American battleship, every single one will be clear and pure and discernible. At the moment of my death, I look forward at last to being fully aware and alive.

Dōgen also wrote that a single moment is all we need to establish our human will and attain truth. I never understood this before, because my understanding of time was murky and imprecise, but now that my death is imminent, I can appreciate his meaning. Both life and death manifest in every moment of existence. Our human body appears and disappears moment by moment, without cease, and this ceaseless arising and passing away is what we experience as time and being. They are not separate. They are one thing, and in even a fraction of a second, we have the opportunity to choose, and to turn the course of our action either toward the attainment of truth or away from it. Each instant is utterly critical to the whole world.

When I think of this, I am both cheered and saddened. Cheered at the thought of the many instants that arise and are available to do good in the world. Saddened by all the misspent moments that have piled on top of each other and led us to this war.

In the end, then, what volition will arise in me? Will I bravely hold my plane's course steady, knowing that at the moment of contact my body will explode in a ball of flames and kill so many of my so-called enemy, whom I have never met and whom I cannot hate? Or will cowardice (or my better human nature) rally one last time, just long enough to nudge my hand on the control stick and turn my plane off course, so that by choosing to end my life in watery disgrace rather than inflamed heroics, I will at the very same instant forever alter the fate of those enemy troops on the battleship, as well as their mothers and sisters and brothers and wives and children?

And in that same fraction of time, that minuscule movement of my hand through space will determine the fates of all the Japanese soldiers and citizens that these same Americans (enemies, whose lives I save) may live to kill. And so on and so on, until you could even say that the very outcome of this war will be decided by a moment and a millimeter, representing the outward manifestation of my will. But how am I to know?

My, how grandiose one can become in the face of death! But I have no interest in being a Hero. In *Sein und Zeit*, Martin Heidegger raises this notion of the Hero within the context of a discussion of authentic temporality, historicality, and Being-in-the-World, and while I once would have applied myself diligently to an analysis of my current predicament in Heideggerian terms, now I am finding greater satisfaction in Dōgen's Zen and my own Japanese traditions, which perhaps only proves MH right. "Language is the house of being," he once wrote, and Dōgen (a wordy man himself!) would no doubt have agreed. But MH's labyrinthine Teutonic chambers I find exhausting in my present fevered state of mind, and what draws me instead are the quiet, empty rooms of Dōgen. In between the words, Dōgen knew the silences.

❖

The cherry blossoms on the base have bloomed and fallen, and still I am waiting to share their fate.

❖

"Tomorrow I will die in battle," said Captain Crow.

Montaigne wrote that death itself is nothing. It is only the fear of death that makes death seem important. Am I afraid? Certainly, and yet . . .

"Que sais-je?" Montaigne asked. The answer is nothing. In reality, I know nothing.

And yet, at night I lie on my bed, counting my beads, one for every thing on earth I love, on and on, in a circle without end.

## 10.

We arrived yesterday in Kyushu. Two veteran soldiers from the China Offensive, who'd been discharged and then called up for a second tour of duty, have been assigned to our squadron. They are hard men, coarse and lean, with glittering eyes that know evil, and even F— seems nervous in their presence. The mood in the barracks changed the moment they entered. Last night after dinner they sat in our midst, surrounded by the fresh young faces of our newest student soldiers, picking their teeth and boasting about the time they'd served in Shandong province.

It sickens me to recall their stories now, how they laughed when they spoke of the old Chinese grandmothers they'd found cowering in a hut with their grandchildren. One by one they pulled the old women into the center of the room and raped them, and then they used their bayonets to mutilate their genitals when they were done. Still laughing, they imitated the comical way the old women begged for mercy for their grandchildren. One by one, they tossed the babies into the air and skewered them on the ends of their bayonets.

How their eyes glittered when they described the Chinese men they hung upside down like meat over open fires, and then watched as their burning flesh peeled from their living bodies and their arms danced like grilled squid legs. When the men died, they cut their charred corpses down and fed them to the dogs.

How they leered at us as they regaled us with stories of young Japanese recruits, callow boys like me and K, ordered to do bayonet practice on living Chinese prisoners to build their fighting spirit. They tied the prisoners to posts and drew targets over their hearts. "Stab anywhere but here," their officers commanded, pointing to the circles. The point was to keep the prisoners alive for as long as possible, and the boy soldiers trembled so hard their bayonets shook and they defecated in their pants. Our two fine soldiers laughed, recounting their terror. By end of the exercise, they assured us, when the prisoners had died and their bodies were shredded and running with blood, those Japanese boys had become men.

These deeds they described as they'd performed them, with no shame. They were carrying out orders, they said, to teach the Chinese a lesson, performing these massacres in front of entire villages, while the victims' children and parents, neighbors and friends, looked on. And in their retelling, they were teaching us a lesson, too, to toughen us up and inure us for what was to come.

"Chacun appelle barbarie ce qui n'est pas de son usage," Montaigne wrote. "Everyone calls barbarity that to which he is not accustomed."

Thankfully, I will not live long enough to grow accustomed, and in one way I am grateful to these two devils: their monstrous barbarity shines a new light on my own small suffering. I am deeply ashamed to have wasted so much ink complaining. The time has come for me to close the book on my life. Maman, I am scheduled to sortie tomorrow, so this is goodbye. Tetsu no Ame[147] has commenced, and tonight, my fellow student officers and I will have a party. We will drink saké and write our wills and our official letters of farewell. These empty words the naval authorities will send to you, along with my personal effects—the juzu you gave me, my watch, and K's copy of the *Shōbōgenzō*. This diary, however, will not be among my possessions. I must confess, I've had a change of heart, and now I wish there were some way of getting it to you, but I do not dare. Its contents undermine this fine pageant of patriotism we are so grimly playing out, and I'm afraid it would jeopardize the compensation you are due to receive in return for the sacrifice of your only son's life. I do not know what I will do with it. Perhaps I will burn it tonight when I'm drunk, or take it with me to the bottom of the sea. It has been my consolation, and without being overly fanciful, I truly believe that although you have not laid eyes on these pages, still you have read every word I have written. You, dear Mother, know my true heart.

What I have to tell you now, I cannot write in any official document that may be read or intercepted. I have made my decision. Tomorrow morning I will wrap my head tightly in a band that bears the insignia of the Rising Sun and fly south to Okinawa, where I will give my life for my country. I have always believed that this war is wrong. I have always

---

147. *Tetsu no Ame* (鉄の雨)—Typhoon of Steel (also Battle of Okinawa), which resulted in the highest number of casualties in the Pacific Theater during World War II. More than 100,000 Japanese troops were killed or captured, or committed suicide. Allied casualties numbered over 65,000. Somewhere between 42,000 and 150,000 Okinawan civilians were also killed or wounded, or committed suicide (between one-tenth and one-third of the indigenous Okinawan population).

# *Ruth*

## I.

She read the last of Benoit's translated pages and placed it on top of the pile on the sofa next to her. She stared out the window at the horizon. Storm clouds darkened the sky with such heavy striation that, were it not for the tiny flecks of whitecaps kicked up by the wind and adding texture to the water, she would have been unable to trace the line between dark sky and dark sea. The waves looked so small from where she sat on the couch. Hard to imagine. From up close, they would look much bigger. Hard to miss.

*He flew into a wave*, she thought.

The gusty wind battered the house, making the old wood beams creak. Outside, the trees groaned and swayed. Living wood.

*Nao doesn't know this yet. She still thinks her great-uncle flew his plane into the enemy's battleship. She thinks he died a war hero, carrying out his mission. She doesn't know he scuttled it. How can this be?*

The electricity was on, but already the lights had flickered several times. Somewhere a tree had come down across a power line. The generator was still at the shop in Campbell River. They were hanging by a thread.

*She's read his Japanese letters—the official one she found in the picture frame and the others that Jiko gave her—but she hasn't mentioned anything about a secret French diary. Does she even know about it? Where is it? If Haruki #1 had gotten drunk and burned the diary, or taken it with him on his mission, then it would long ago have turned to ashes scattered in the wind, or cellulose dissolving in the sea.*

She picked up the waxy packet containing the composition booklet that Benoit had returned with the translated pages. She turned it over and studied it carefully.

*It's real, but how did it get here? How did it end up in the freezer bag and here in my hands?*

She wanted to discuss this with Oliver, to ask these questions out loud, but he was out in the rain looking for Pesto. She unwrapped the waxy paper and unfolded the booklet. She ran her fingers across the page. The paper was cheap. The ink was faded, but she could tell it had once been a dark shade of indigo blue. He'd hidden it in his lunchbox, under his rice. He'd hidden it inside his coat, next to his chest. She closed her eyes and held the booklet to her face, inhaling deeply, but the only smell was from the wax and the sea.

*Nao must read this, and her father, too. They have to know the truth.*

She opened her eyes and folded up the diary again, packing it away. It was growing dark outside. She looked at the sky soldier watch to check the time. The watch was still ticking. Where was Oliver?

*Haruki #1 was struggling with the most profound moral and existential issues of genocide and war and the consequences of his imminent death, and we're upset about a missing cat? How is this even possible?*

But it was possible and true. They'd been distracted ever since the cat had run away, and even more so after they'd learned about Benoit's dog being eaten by wolves. Every time Oliver heard a noise outside he would stop what he was doing and go to the door, open it, and listen. He listened to the screech of the owls, the howling of the wolves, and even the cawing of the ravens with equal trepidation.

"I'm sure he's fine," he said, trying to make himself feel better. "He's such a little guy. Just a scrawny morsel. Who would bother to eat him?" But they both knew that the forest was full of predators who would love to eat a little cat for dinner. Finally, he couldn't stand it any longer, and when the wind picked up he went out to search for him.

Ruth felt bad. It was her fault for getting angry and scaring Pesto out of bed and into the night. She wished she'd been able to contain her anger. She wished Oliver hadn't made her mad in the first place.

## 2.

The rain was starting to fall in earnest, so she went downstairs to throw some wood on the fire and found that the stack was getting low. She put on her raincoat and gum boots, grabbed a headlamp and the firewood sling, and headed out to the woodpile. The wind had really picked up and the cedar limbs were thrashing. Where was he? It wasn't safe to be out in the woods in high winds like this. The trees were groaning and creaking under the gale's assault. For such tall trees, their roots were surprisingly shallow, and the forest floor was soggy from rain. She thought for a moment she should go out and look for him, but then realized that was foolish. She started pulling the split logs from the pile and stacking them up in the leather sling. Just then she heard a harsh cry from overhead. She looked up. It was the Jungle Crow, perched on its usual spot on the branch of the cedar. The crow looked down at her, fixed her with a beady eye. "*Caw!*" it cried, with an urgency that sounded like a warning. She looked behind her at the house. The windows had gone black. The power was out. Suddenly, she felt afraid.

"What should I do?" The rain beat against her face as she turned back to the crow. "Go," she said. "Please, go and find him."

The crow just continued to watch her.

Stupid, she thought. Talking to a bird, but there was no one else nearby, and somehow just hearing her own voice helped to calm her.

The crow stretched its neck and shook its feathers. She heaved the heavy sling filled with firewood onto her shoulder and headed toward the darkened house. "*Caw!*" cried the crow again, and when she turned back, she saw Oliver emerging from the wind-lashed trees, dripping with rain. Seeing her standing there with the wood, he spread out his arms. His wet hands were empty. No cat.

# *Nao*

### 1.

Making the decision to end my life really helped me lighten up, and suddenly all the stuff my old Jiko had told me about the time being really kicked into focus. There's nothing like realizing that you don't have much time left to stimulate your appreciation for the moments of your life. I mean it sounds corny, but I started to really experience stuff for the first time, like the beauty of the plum and cherry blossoms along the avenues in Ueno Park, when the trees are in bloom. I spent whole days there, wandering up and down these long, soft tunnels of pink clouds and gazing overhead at the fluffy blossoms, all puffy and pink with little sparkles of sunlight and blue sky glinting between the bright green leaves. Time disappeared and it was like being born into the world all over again. Everything was perfect. When a breeze blew, petals rained down on my upturned face, and I stopped and gasped, stunned by the beauty and sadness.

For the first time in my life, I had a project and a goal to focus on. I had to figure out everything I wanted to accomplish in my remaining time on earth, and that's how I came to realize that I wanted to write down old Jiko's life story. Jiko was so wise and interesting, and now, when I think about how I've failed in my goal to tell her story, I want to cry.

### 2.

The reason I was spending my days in Ueno Park, getting lost in the blossoms, was because Babette was still pissed off at me, and of course I still wasn't going to school. I hadn't been back since I shaved my head and found my superpower, and mostly I just felt a huge sense of relief, but now that the school year was almost over, I also felt some regret. I'd taken my high school entrance exams like I'd promised my mom, and I really blew it. The minute I sat down at my seat, I knew I was in trouble. The examination room was incredibly hot and crammed with rows of jittery kids in uniforms, stinking of teenage sweat and polyester. You could almost see the smog of pheromones in the air, turning my juicy, interesting brain into lead. Dense, heavy, inert. All I wanted to do was to put my head down on the desktop and sleep.

It turned out I knew a lot of the material, after all, especially in the English section, but I didn't even bother to answer most of the questions. My scores were so low it was a joke, like I was mentally handicapped or something, but I was like, whatever. It didn't bother me a lot, but it bothered me a little, knowing that I would never go to high school and learn all the things that my great-uncle Haruki #1 had learned before he died. I mean, you could say what's the point in learning stuff if you're only going to kill yourself, and that's true, but there is something noble about the effort some people put into trying. Like old Jiko's superhero, Kanno Sugako, who continued to study English and write in her diary, right up until the day they hanged her. I think she is a good role model, even if she did try to assassinate the emperor with a bomb.

Anyway, now that I knew my time on earth was limited, I didn't want to waste my precious moments with any more stupid dates, and this really pissed Babette off. She said that I was taking up valuable table space at Fifi's, and that my scribbling was bringing the mood down. I tried to convince her that having a writer there made the place feel more authentic, like a real French café, but she disagreed, and then finally she gave me an ultimatum. Either go on a date or get out.

Fine. Whatever.

That was yesterday.

She flounced away and I kept on writing, watching her out of the corner of my eye. She started talking to a customer at one of the nearby tables, and the guy turned around to look at me, and I couldn't believe it, but it was that creepy hentai I mentioned at the beginning. The one with the greasy hair and the bad complexion who liked to watch me pull up my socks? He's a regular, but he seemed like just a peeper, and not like the type who would actually have enough cash to pay for a date. Babette was doing a real sales job on him now, which actually I found kind of insulting if you want to know the truth. I mean, I'm a fairly adorable sixteen-year-old girl in a school uniform. You'd think he would be happy to be given the chance to date me, right? Finally he took out his wallet and handed Babette some money. Babette folded up the bills and tucked the roll between her tits and then glanced over at me.

"Date," she mouthed.

Sighing, I closed my diary and followed her out into the coatroom, where she fished out the thin wad of cash, peeled off a few bills, and handed them to me.

I looked at her, surprised.

She shrugged. "Ryu spoiled you," she said. "It's time you got realistic."

"I'm not doing it for this!" I said, handing back the bills. "I have some self-respect, you know."

Her smile spread, slow and dangerous, across her cute doll face. She backed me up against the wall of coats and grabbed me by the chin, digging her knuckle deep into the soft part where the jawbone makes a vee, just above the throat. I gagged on the pain, which was sick-making.

"That's amusing," she said. "People like you don't deserve to have self-respect. So you better get over it."

She took my cheeks in both hands and pinched so hard that my eyes filled with tears. She pulled me toward her until my forehead was almost touching hers, and her two eyes became one, a single hideous eye, dark and glittering, surrounded by ruffles and lace.

"You're lucky I'm generous and sharing with you at all," she said. "The trouble with you is that you're too American. You're lazy and selfish. You should learn to be loyal and work hard." She gave my face one last hard shake and released me.

I fell back against the coats and slumped down the wall. She cocked her head and looked me over, and then she reached down and stroked my burning cheek.

"So pink," she said. "So pretty." And then she slapped me. She located my date's coat and threw it at me. "Have fun," she said, pivoting so neatly that her petticoats lifted, and from where I was sitting on the floor I could see the frill of her panties as she flounced out the door.

I don't remember the hentai's name. Maybe I never knew it. He was waiting for me in the reception area by the nude lady in the fountain. I handed him his coat. He took it and didn't even look me in the eye. He mumbled something that I didn't quite catch and walked out, expecting me to follow. The tiny elevator was empty, and we stood there awkwardly, watching the doors close, not knowing what to say or how to make conversation. A few floors down, the doors opened again and a big, happy party pushed in, laughing and drunk, and suddenly I was jammed up against him. I could feel his sour breath on the back of my neck as he groped underneath my skirt, pushing against me from behind. I wanted to scream, CHIKAN![148] like you're supposed to do on the subway when some perv starts fondling you, but I stopped myself. He'd paid, after all, and if he wanted to get a head start, what could I say? When the elevator doors opened and everyone got out, he held his overcoat in front of his pants and stumbled down the street, glancing back every couple of steps to make sure I was still following. I could have slipped away, but I didn't. I just followed because he'd paid, and that was the honorable thing to do. I couldn't believe how pathetic he was, but I had no self-respect, so it didn't matter. He had no social skills to speak of. He didn't offer to buy me a cute sweater or a keitai. He didn't offer me a drink, and the kind of hotel he took me to didn't even have a minibar. There was no champagne, no brandy, just a vending machine in the hall with cans of beer and One Cup Saké. One Cup Saké reminded me of my dad because that's what he'd been drinking the night he fell onto the tracks in front of the Chuo Rapid Express. It was totally depressing, but my so-called date was too cheap to buy me one, anyway.

If you don't mind, I'd rather not go into a lot of detail about what

---

148. *chikan* (痴漢)—masher, molester. A man who sexually gropes a woman in public.

happened next because just thinking about it makes me feel sad and sick, and I haven't even had time to take a bath yet. Let's just say that the bed wasn't round and it didn't have a zebra-skin cover, but the rest of my imagining was pretty accurate. When we got to the room, he didn't waste any time, and while he did things to my body, I just went to the silent frozen place in my mind that was clean and cold and very far away.

And really I don't remember very much, only that partway through, I was lying on my stomach when my keitai started to ring, and I drifted back to this world just enough to wonder who was phoning me. I thought maybe it was Jiko, and the tears started leaking out of my eyes because I knew how sad she would feel if she could see me now, and I missed her and wanted to talk to her so badly. Then the thought occurred to me that maybe she knew I was in trouble, and that's why she was calling, and maybe right now she was clicking her juzu beads and saying prayers for my well-being. And maybe the sound of the phone ringing actually did save me, because thinking of Jiko made me realize that I didn't want to end up being one of those girls who the police have to find on the floor days later, because that would break her heart, and if you live to be a hundred and four, you don't deserve to have your heart broken by your careless great-granddaughter. And just at that moment, my date did something that hurt so much, the pain shocked me back into my body, and I heard myself cry out, and then I reacted. I pushed him off me long enough to twist out from under. Ryu had taught me how sometimes men enjoy a little ijime, so I summoned up my superpower and pushed the hentai down onto his back, and then I straddled him and started smacking him hard across the face. And wouldn't you know it, he was delighted. I used his belt to tie his wrists together, and I didn't even have to hurt him too much to get him off. It's amazing how quickly a man can turn from a sado into a maso. I know what old Jiko would say. Sado, maso, same thing.

As soon as he fell asleep, I got up and checked my phone, and sure enough, the call was from her. She knew and she had saved me! But when I read the text message, I saw that it wasn't from Jiko, after all. It was from Muji. Just one line. I read it, but I couldn't take in the meaning. I read it again.

先生の最期よ．早くお帰り．[149]

I stood there in the middle of the tacky mirrored room, staring at the little screen. My so-called date was snoring on the bed. I looked up and caught sight of a naked girl in the mirrors, endlessly reflecting. Her body was raw-looking, gawky and awkward. I hugged myself and the girl did, too. I started to cry and we couldn't stop. I turned away from her and quietly gathered up my school uniform and put it on. I tiptoed over to the pile of clothes belonging to my date and quickly went through his pockets. I emptied his wallet and took the last remaining bills. I bundled his clothes up into a ball and forced myself to stop crying long enough to turn the doorknob. As I slipped out of the room and the door clicked behind me, I heard him call. I started to run. I pictured him frantically searching for his clothes, so I dumped them in the stairwell at the end of the hallway. I could have taken them with me and thrown them on the street, but I didn't need to. I guess I'm a nice person at heart.

When I got outside, I kept running, cutting through the crowded narrow alleys of Electricity Town. Akiba at dusk is really something, a huge, strobing hallucination of neon lights and giant manga action heroes that loom down at you like they're going to crush your head. And then there's the noise, the crazy jangle of the pachinko parlors and game arcades, and the screaming hawkers and kyakuhiki[150] calling out to the drunken salarymen and tourists and otaku who merge and swell like plankton in the sea.

Usually I love it. Usually I feed off all that energy, but you have to be in the right mood, and I wasn't. I pushed through the crowds, keeping my face down to hide the tears. All I wanted was to get home to my dad. I needed my dad. I needed to tell him that Jiko was dying, so he would drop everything and take me to the station, and together we would catch the next express train bound for Sendai, and since it was night and the buses wouldn't be running, we could take a taxi all the way from the station up to the temple. We could be there in no time at all. Maybe five

---

149. *Sensei no saigo yo. Hayaku okaeri.*—Sensei's last moments. Come quickly.
150. *kyakuhiki* (客引き)—a tout; lit. "customer" + "pulling."

or six hours. And when we arrived, everything would be peaceful and quiet, and Muji would come running out to greet us and tell us that Jiko was fine, and it was all just a false alarm, and she was so sorry for calling us and disturbing us for no reason, but now that we were here, would we like to have a bath?

This was what I wanted. To find my dad, to know Jiko was fine, and to take a bath. I concentrated on these thoughts on the train, all the way to my stop, keeping my head down and wiping my nose with the cuff of my uniform sleeve.

The apartment was quiet when I got home.

"Tadaima," I said softly. My voice sounded hoarse from all the crying.

There was no answer, which was not unusual if my dad was on the Internet and couldn't hear me. I wondered if my mom was still at work. Had Muji phoned them? Maybe they'd already left for Sendai without me.

"Dad?"

I heard the toilet flush, and then a shaft of light cut across the darkened hallway as the washroom door opened. I took off my shoes and stepped up into the entryway. There was a shopping bag from the local supermarket on the floor, in the place where we put things we don't want to forget. I opened the bag and looked inside, and then I closed it and walked toward the light.

I found him in the bedroom, dressed in his dark blue suit, neatly shaved and putting on his socks.

"Dad?"

His bony feet looked sickly white. He looked up. "Oh," he said. "Naoko. I didn't hear you come in."

He was looking right through me, and his voice was flat and lifeless. He bent down to adjust the sock. "You're home early," he said. "You're not going out with your school friends tonight?"

Wow. He still believed I had school friends. That shows you how clueless he was. I watched him from the doorway. There was something strange about him, even stranger than usual, like he had turned into a zombie.

"Where's Mom?" I asked.

"Zangyō,"[151] he said. He stood and straightened out his trousers.

"Are you going out or something?"

"Yes," he said, sounding a little surprised. He was even wearing a tie. It was the tie I bought for him that first Christmas, when he was still pretending to have a job. It wasn't silk, but it had a nice butterfly pattern on it.

"Where are you going?"

"To meet a friend," he said. "Someone from my university days. We're going to have a drink for old times' sake. I won't be long." He spoke the words like he'd written them down and memorized them. Did he really think I'd believe that?

Zombie Dad was putting on his suit jacket.

"Did anybody call?" I asked.

He shook his head. "No." He put his wallet in his suit pocket, and then he paused and frowned. "Why? Were you expecting someone?"

It figured. Muji was such a space case, and besides, she knew he never answered the phone.

"No, I just wondered." I studied him as he stood there. He looked okay in his suit. It was a cheap, ugly suit, but it was better than the dirty old trainer he wore in the house.

I followed him out into the hallway and watched as he used the shoehorn to slide his heel into his loafer.

"Don't forget your bag," I said.

He reached for it automatically, and then he froze. "What bag?" Pretending like he was confused. Like he didn't know.

"That one," I said, pointing to the bag next to the door.

"Oh. Right. Yes. Of course." He picked up the bag and glanced at me, and I could tell he was wondering if I'd looked inside. I turned away and went into the kitchen.

"Ittekimasu . . ." he called, but there was a catch in his voice, like he wasn't sure.

---

151.  *zangyō* (残業)—overtime.

*Ittekimasu* is what you say when you know you're coming back. That's literally what it means: I'm going and I'm coming back. When somebody says "Ittekimasu" to you, you're supposed to answer "Itterashai," which means: Yes, please go and come back.

But I couldn't say it. I stood next to the sink with my back to the door, picturing him standing there with his shopping bag full of charcoal briquettes and his Nick Drake songs. Time Has Told Me. *Day Is Done.*

He must have thought I hadn't heard him the first time, because he said it again, "Ittekimasu!"

Why didn't he just leave! A moment later, the door clanged shut.

*Liar*, I whispered, under my breath.


That was last night.

I didn't need my dad after all. I caught the last train to Sendai and then transferred to the local and managed to get to the town closest to the temple. The buses had stopped running for the night, but even with the hentai's money, I didn't have enough for a taxi up the coastline to Jiko's village, so I sat on a bench in the dinky little station and waited. I thought about calling the temple. I could imagine how the ringing of the phone would break the deep, dark silence of the night, and it seemed wrong, so I texted instead. I knew nobody would answer, and I really felt like talking to someone, so I wrote all these pages to you. I knew you wouldn't answer, either. I guess I fell asleep then.

The sky was just turning grey when the stationmaster woke me up and showed me where to catch the bus. I got a hot can of coffee from the vending machine, and now I'm waiting here for the first bus to come. I tried calling the temple, but nobody's answering, so I don't know what's going on there. I hope Jiko's okay. I hope she isn't dead already. I hope she waits for me. I'm praying. Can't you hear me praying?


I know this is stupid. I know you don't exist and no one is ever going to read this. I'm just sitting here on this stupid bus stop bench, drinking a can of too sweet coffee, pretending that I have a friend to write to.

But the fact is, you're a lie. You're just another stupid story I made up out of thin air because I was lonely and needed someone to spill my guts to. I wasn't ready to die yet and needed a raison d'être. I shouldn't be mad at you, but I am! Because now you're letting me down, too.

The fact is, I'm all alone.

I should have known better. I knew when I started this diary that I couldn't keep it up, because in my heart of hearts, I never believed in your existence. How could I? Everyone I believed in is dying. My old Jiko is dying, my dad is probably already dead by now, and I don't even believe in myself anymore. I don't believe I exist, and soon I won't. I am a time being about to expire.

Babette was right. I am selfish, and I only cared about my own stupid life, just like my dad only cared about his own stupid life, and now I've gone and wasted all these beautiful pages and failed to achieve my goal, which was to write about Jiko and her fascinating life while I still had time, before she died. And now it's too late. Talk about temps perdu. I'm sorry, my dear old Jiko. I love you, but I screwed up.

It's cold. The blossoms in front of the station have mostly fallen, and the ones still clinging to the branches of the trees are an ugly shade of brown. There's an old man in a blue-and-white jogging suit sweeping the petals from the sidewalk in front of his pickle shop. He doesn't see me. The stationmaster is opening the station doors. He knows I'm here but he doesn't look at me. A dirty white dog is licking its balls across the street. An old farmer woman with a blue-and-white tenugui on her head is bicycling by. Nobody sees me. Maybe I'm invisible.

I guess this is it. This is what now feels like.

# Ruth

## I.

The storm blew in from the northeast at dusk, rounding the Aleutians, sliding down the Alaska coast, and funneling into the Strait of Georgia with gale-force winds that knocked out the power and extinguished the entire island in the blink of an eye. One minute the island was there, its presence marked by clusters of tiny glinting lights, and the next instant it was gone, plunged into the darkness of maelstrom and sea. At least that's how it must have looked from above.

Over the next couple of hours, the wind continued its assault on the clearing in the tall trees. The little house that usually blazed far into the night was now discernible only by the insipid glow that emanated from the small square bedroom window.

## 2.

". . . this is it," Ruth read, straining to make out the letters in the dim light of the kerosene lamp. "This is what now feels like."

Her voice sounded so small in the howling vastness of the storm-whipped night, but for a single long moment, the words brought everything to a standstill. The lamp flickered. The world held its breath.

"She caught up with herself," Oliver said into the silence.

They sat there, side by side in bed, thinking about what Nao had written, conscious that they were waiting for the wind to pick up, but when the quiet persisted, Oliver finally spoke. "Go on," he said. "Don't stop."

Ruth turned the page, felt her heart miss a beat.

The page was blank.

She turned another. Blank.

And the page after that. Blank.

She skipped ahead further. There were perhaps twenty pages still remaining in the book, and all of them were blank. The wind started up again, lashing the trees and pummeling the tin roof with sheets of rain.

It made no sense. She knew the pages had once been filled because on at least two occasions she had checked, riffling through to see if the girl's handwriting had persisted to the end of the book, and indeed it had. The words had once been there, she was sure of it, and now they weren't. What had happened to them?

She groped for her headlamp, which was hanging on the bedpost, switched it on, and slipped the band around her head. The bright LED beam was like a searchlight. Carefully, she raised the book and glanced down at the bedspread, scanning the small hillocks and vales, half expecting to catch sight of the letters scurrying away into the shadows.

"What are you doing?" Oliver asked.

"Nothing," she muttered, searching the blank pages once again, in case a stray word or two had gotten left behind, trapped in the gutter or stuck in the spine.

"What do you mean, nothing?" he asked. "Keep reading. I want to know what happens."

"Nothing happens. That's what I mean. The words are all gone."

He exhaled, softly. "What do you mean, all gone?"

"I mean they were here, and now they're not. They're missing."

"Are you sure?"

She held the book up to show him. "Of course I'm sure. I checked. Several times. The writing used to continue all the way to the very last page."

"Words can't just disappear."

"Well, they did. I can't explain it. Maybe she changed her mind or something."

"That's a bit of a stretch, don't you think? She can't just reach in and take them back."

"But I think she did," Ruth said. She switched off the headlamp. "It's like her life just got shorter. Time is slipping away from her, page by page . . ."

He didn't answer. Maybe he was thinking. Maybe he'd fallen asleep. She lay there for a long time, listening to the storm. The rain was blowing sideways now, beating against the window like a creature trying to come in. The kerosene lamp on the bedside table was still lit, but the wick wanted trimming and was sputtering badly. She would need to reach over and blow it out soon, but she disliked the stench of kerosene and smoke, and so she waited. Oil lamps and LEDs. The old technologies and the new, collapsing time into a paradoxical present. Did whale oil smell any better? In the jittery light, she was aware of Oliver lying next to her, a dim, unstable silhouette, moving in and out of darkness. When at last he spoke, as though no time at all had passed, the proximity of his voice startled her.

"If that's the case," he said, "then it's not just *her* life that's at risk."

"What do you mean?"

"It calls our existence into question, too, don't you think?"

"Us?" she said. Was he kidding?

"Sure," he said. "I mean, if she stops writing to us, then maybe we stop being, too."

His voice seemed farther away now. Was it her ears or the storm? A thought occurred to her.

"We?" she said. "She was writing to me. I'm her *you*. I'm the one she was waiting for. Since when did I become us?"

"I care about her, too, you know," he said. His voice sounded close again, right next to her ear. "I've listened to you read the diary, so I think I qualify as part of you by now. And besides, 'you' can be either singular or plural, so how do you know she wasn't referring to both of us from the beginning?"

It was hard to tell with all the racket of the wind, but she thought she caught an undertone, a simmering amusement, in his voice. She switched on her headlamp again and turned the beam on his face.

"Do you think this is *funny*?"

He held up his hand to deflect the harsh light. "Not at all," he said, squinting. "Please . . ."

She obliged, turning her head away.

"I'm serious," he said, as he receded into the dimness. "Maybe we don't exist anymore. Maybe that's what happened to Pesto, too. He just fell off our page."

### 3.

Outside in the tall cedar tree by the woodshed, the Jungle Crow raised its shoulders against the heavy rain. The wind whipped through the boughs, ruffling the shiny black feathers. *Ke ke ke*, said the crow, scolding the wind, but the wind couldn't hear over the din, and so it didn't answer. The branch swayed and the crow tightened its talons, preparing to launch forward and fly.

### 4.

"You sound even crazier than I do," she said.

"Not at all," he said. "On the contrary. We just have to approach this problem logically. Take it step by step." There was something careful and deliberate in his speech that made her uneasy.

"You're baiting me," she said. "Stop it."

"If you're so sure the words were there," he continued, "then you have to go find them."

"That's ridiculous—"

"The words were there," he said. "And now they're gone. Now, where do missing words go?"

"How would I know?"

"Because it's your job to know?" He had been directing his remarks to the ceiling, and now he turned to face her. "You're a *writer*."

It was perhaps the cruelest thing he could have said.

"But I'm *not*!" she cried, her anguished voice rising to compete with the wind. "I used to be, but I'm not anymore! The words just aren't there . . ."

"Hm," he said. "Maybe you've been trying too hard. Or looking in the wrong place."

"What do you mean?"

"Maybe they're here."

"Here?"

"Why not?" He gazed back up at the ceiling. "Think about it. Where do words come from? They come from the dead. We inherit them. Borrow them. Use them for a time to bring the dead to life." He rolled onto his side and raised himself up on one arm. "The ancient Greeks believed that when you read aloud, it was actually the dead, borrowing your tongue, in order to speak again." He moved his long body over hers, reaching toward the oil lamp on the bedside table. He cupped his hand over the tall glass chimney to blow out the flame, and for just a moment, the light shining from below, up onto his face, cast the deep sockets of his eyes into skeletal shadows. "The Island of the Dead. What better place to look for missing words?"

"You're freaking me out . . ."

He laughed and then blew across the funnel of the chimney. The room went dark and the acrid scents of kerosene and smoke rose like ghostly leavings.

"Sweet dreams," he whispered.

## 5.

*What if I travel so far away in my dreams that I can't get back in time to wake up?*

*"Then I'll come and get you."*

What does separation look like? A wall? A wave? A body of water? A ripple of light or a shimmer of subatomic particles, parting? What does it feel like to push through? Her fingers press against the rag surface of her dream, recognize the tenacity of filaments and know that it is paper about to tear, but for the fibrous memory that still lingers there, supple, vascular, and standing tall. The tree was past and the paper is present, and yet paper still remembers holding itself upright and altogether. Like a dream, it remembers its sap.

But she holds her edge, pushing until the fibers give way, like cambium to an ax blade, like skin to a knife—

The boughs part then, revealing a path that winds and twists, growing narrower and narrower, leading her into an ever-thickening forest. The rain has stopped now. Crickets chirp. The fragrance of temple incense, cedar and sandalwood, lingers in the air.

In the distance, something catches her eye amid the leaves—a pixelation, a form, a figure? Hard to say. It darts from limb to limb. A bird? The pixels cohere, darken, and the image dissolves. She strains after it and then remembers. *Maybe you've been trying too hard.* She stops trying.

*Sometimes the mind arrives but the words don't.*

*Sometimes words arrive but the mind doesn't.*

Where are these words coming from? She stops walking, too. She sits down on the thick forest floor in the roots of a giant cedar. The mossy humus forms a cushion underneath her, cool and damp, but not unpleasant. She crosses her legs.

*Sometimes mind and words both arrive.*

*Sometimes neither mind nor words arrive.*

A spider drops on a silvery thread from the branch overhead. A faint breeze stirs the treetops. Dew and rain cling to the leaves and ferns of the understory. Each drop holds within itself a small, bright moon.

*Mind and words are time being. Arriving and not-arriving are time being.*

Something moves in the periphery of her vision. She turns her head and sees a heel. The heel is clothed in a dark sock, and next to it is a second, matching heel, dangling a meter or so above a pair of cheap slip-on loafers, which have been left neatly aligned upon an emerald green tussock of moss. She looks up at the silent bodies hanging in the shadows from the limbs of trees and knows this is wrong, but she can no longer stand up and run. Her body is as heavy and helpless as the hanged men, rotating slowly in the slush-thick currents of air.

Or is it water? Yes, she is swimming now. She is cold and swimming, and the sea is black and thick and filled with debris. She starts to sink and the ceiling of sludge closes over her.

Sounds merge and separate, coalesce and differentiate. Words shimmer, a darting cloud of tiny minnows ripples beneath the surface of the water. Ungraspable. *We sleeptogether in onelargeroom laid outin rowslike smallfish-hungtodry . . .*

But something's gone wrong with the words in time—syllables linger, refusing to dissipate or fall into silence—so that now there's a pileup of sounds, like cars colliding on a highway, turning meaning into cacophony, and before she knows it, she is adding to the din, wordlessly, soundlessly, with a cry that rises from her throat and goes on and on forever. Time swells, overwhelming her. She tries not to panic. Tries to relax and hold herself loosely, resisting the instinct to tense and flee. But where would she go? She remembers Jiko's elevator. *When up looks up, up is down . . .* But there is no up. No down. No in. No out. No forward or backward. Just this cold, crushing wave, this unnameable continuum of merging and dissolving. Groundless, she struggles to the surface.

Feelings lap at her edges like waves on the sand. Jiko holds out her glasses, and Ruth takes them and puts them on because she knows that she must. The murky lenses smear the world, as fragments of the old nun's past flood through her: spectral images, smells and sounds; the gasp of a woman hanged for treason as the noose snaps her neck; the cry of a young girl in mourning; the taste of a son's blood and broken teeth; the stench of a city drowned in flames; a mushroom cloud; a parade of puppets in the rain. For a moment she vacillates. The words are there at her fingertips. She can feel their shape, could grab them and bring them through, but she also knows she can't stay much longer. In a split second, she makes a decision, and opens the fist of her mind and lets go. She can't hang on to the old nun's past and still find Nao, too.

*Nao*, she thinks. *Nao, now, nooooo . . .*

With a flip of its tail, the fish slips away, but she follows, doggedly, her arms and legs moving through the water in time to some distant music, like a synchronized swimmer in an old film reel, until exhaustion overwhelms her, cracking the world into a kaleidoscope of fractal patterns—recursive limbs and glinting wavelets—that spin and then re-organize themselves into a mirrored room with a round bed and a zebra-skin coverlet. Good, she thinks. I must be getting close. She looks for Nao in the mirror, a logical place, but sees only a reflection of herself that she does not recognize.

"Who are you?" she asks.

Her reflection peers out at her and shrugs, causing the surface of the mirror to ripple like a pond when a stone drops into the water. The ripples settle, and her reflection is replaced by another, slightly different, which isn't her, either.

"Do I know you?" she asks.

*Do I know you?* Wordlessly, her reflection apes her.

"What are you doing here?" she asks.

*What are you doing here?* the reflection echoes, mutely.

"Why are you mocking me?" she asks.

Her reflection replies by unhinging its jaw. Its mouth gapes, bloodred, dripping with saliva—a terrible orifice. When it cracks a smile, the earth shudders, and from inside its tunnel-like throat, a long, forked tongue shoots out, rears up, and writhes like a snake about to strike.

"Stop it!" she cries, and just then she notices the young girl, standing behind her in the mirror. The girl is naked except for a man's shirt, which she wears unbuttoned. A necktie hangs loosely around the collar. Their eyes meet, and the girl starts to button up the shirt, but when Ruth turns, the girl is already gone and the zebra-skin bed is empty.

*Don't be fooled!* her reflection howls as the room explodes into a vortex of mirrors and light.

"Wait!" she cries, but just as her edges begin to dissolve into the blinding brightness, she sees out of the corner of her eye something quick and black, a gap, more like an absence. She holds her breath and waits, not daring to turn and look at it directly. The small black gap starts to preen as its pixels cohere, and then she hears a faint, familiar cawing.

Crow?

The word appears on the horizon, black against the unbearable light, and as it comes closer, it starts to turn and spiral, elongating its *C* to create a spine, rounding its *O* into a sleek belly, rotating its *R* to form a forehead and a wide-open beak. It stretches wide its *W*ings, flaps them once, twice, thrice, and then, fully feathered, it starts to fly.

It's her Jungle Crow come to save her! She pulls herself back together and follows as it flies from limb to limb, but she's on the ground and the terrain is rocky. When she slows or stumbles, Jungle Crow stops to wait, cocking its head and watching her with a beady black eye. It seems to be leading her somewhere. She hears traffic in the distance, clambers up a rocky incline, and finds herself in a sprawling city park, overlooking a wide pond. The edges are overgrown with lotuses and rushes but the middle is clear. It's dusk, but a few pastel-colored paddleboats, shaped like long-necked swans, still crisscross the glassy water, leaving smears of pink and blue and yellow in their wavering V-shaped wakes. A broad asphalt path rings the pond, punctuated with stone benches at regular intervals like the hours on a clock.

A man is sitting on one of the benches, underneath a weeping willow, feeding a mangy flock of crows who flap and strut and vie for bread. Crow lands at the man's feet, scattering the others and raising a small cloud of dust. She follows and sits down on the bench next to him.

He straightens and then bows his head in a tentative greeting. "Are you the one I'm waiting for?" he asks.

"I don't know," she answers. She takes a better look at him. He's a middle-aged guy in a shiny blue suit, but the evening is warm and he's taken off the jacket and folded it neatly, draping it over the back of the bench. He's wearing a short-sleeved white dress shirt and a butterfly tie.

"Are you a member?" he asks.

"A member?"

"Of the club . . . ?"

"I don't think so."

"Oh." He looks crestfallen. He checks his watch.

She notices a shopping bag at his feet.

"Briquettes?" she asks, and sees him shrink back in alarm. "Funny time of year for a barbecue." She stares out at the pastel-colored paddle-boats floating on the lake. They have long, graceful necks, in the shape of question marks, and soulful swan eyes.

The man clears his throat, as though something has gotten stuck in it. "Are you sure you're not the one I'm waiting for?"

"Pretty sure."

"Perhaps you're here to meet someone, too?"

"Yes," she says. "I'm here to meet you."

"Me?"

"Yes. You are Haruki #2, aren't you?"

He stares at her. "How did you know?"

"Your daughter told me." She's working on a hunch, on a wing and a prayer.

"Naoko?"

"Yes. She, uh, said you might be here."

"She did?"

"Yes. She wanted me to give you a message."

He's suspicious now. "How do you know my daughter?"

"I don't," she says, thinking quickly. "I mean, we're . . . pen pals."

He looks her over. "You're a little old to be her pen pal," he says, bluntly.

"Thanks a lot."

"I didn't mean . . . ," he starts to say, and then another thought occurs to him. "Did you meet her online? Are you one of those online stalkers?"

"Of course not."

"Oh, good," he says, relaxing. "The Internet's a toilet bowl. Excuse my language." He throws a small chunk of bread to the crows, as his attention turns inward. "We never thought it would turn out like this . . ."

They watch the birds fight over bread.

"It's okay," she says. "Actually, I met her walking on the beach. It was after a storm."

"Oh," he says, nodding. "That's good. She should spend more time outdoors. We used to go to the beach quite often when we lived in California. I worry about her. She dropped out, you know."

"Of school?"

He nods, and tosses another scrap of bread to the crows. "I don't really blame her. She was getting bullied. They were posting horrible things about her on the Internet."

He sighs and hangs his head. "I'm a programmer, but there was nothing I could do. Once stuff is up there, it sticks around, you know? Follows you and it won't go away."

"Actually, I've been having the opposite experience," she says. "Sometimes I'll search for something, and the information I'm looking for is there one minute, and then the next minute, *poof!*"

"Poof?"

"Obliterated. Wiped out. Just like that." She snaps her fingers.

"Obliterated," he says. "Hmm. Where are you getting these results?"

"Well, mostly on the island where I live. We're a bit behind the times, and our connection with the world is a little iffy."

He raises his eyebrows. "That's an interesting idea," he says. "I've always thought time was a little iffy, myself."

It's nice sitting on the park bench and chatting with him, but a sudden constriction in her brain tells her that her time is almost up. She shakes herself and tries to focus. "Do you want to hear your daughter's message or not?"

She sees him wince, but then he nods. "Of course."

"Okay." She turns on the bench to face him, so he will know she is serious. "She says to tell you please don't do it."

"Don't do what?" he asks.

She points to the shopping bag at his feet.

His gaze follows her finger, and his shoulders slump. "Oh. That."

"Yes, that," she says, sternly. "She worries about you, you know."

"Does she?" A tiny glimmer of some emotion shows in his face, but dies just as quickly. "Well, that's why it's best just to get it over with, so she can get on with her life."

His answer makes her angry. "Please forgive me for saying so, but you really shouldn't be so selfish."

He looks surprised. "Selfish?"

"Of course. She is your daughter. She loves you. How do you suppose she's going to feel if you abandon her? It's not something she'll ever get over. She knows what you're up to, and if you go through with this, she intends to kill herself, too."

He slumps forward, resting his elbows on his knees and covering his face with his hands. The collar of his white shirt is damp with sweat and she can see the outline of his sleeveless undershirt through the fabric. His shoulder blades move like the wings of a newly hatched bird, scrawny and spastic, not terribly useful.

"Do you really believe that is true?" he asks through his fingers.

"Yes. I'm certain. She told me. She's planning to kill herself, and you're the only one who can stop her. She needs you. And we need her."

He shakes his head slowly from side to side, and then rubs his hands over his face. He stares out over the pond. They sit for a long time, watching the cheerful boats. Finally he speaks.

"I don't understand," he says. "But if what you say is true, I can't take the chance. I'll go home and talk to her . . ."

"She's not at home. She's at the bus stop in Sendai. She's trying to get to the temple. Your grandmother is—"

"Yes?" He looks up at her, expectantly, but his expression quickly turns to concern. "Are you all right?" he asks. "You look very pale."

There's so much more she wants to tell him but the words won't come. Her brain is tightening, and her time is almost up, but there's something else she must do, if only she can remember. She stands, and a wave of vertigo overwhelms her. The mangy crows at her feet caw and squabble, demanding more food. She looks around for Jungle Crow, who seems to have vanished.

"Crow!" she cries, as gravity fails, and the world releases her from its embrace, tilting out from underneath her, while she is blown back.

A storm of moonlit petals. A temple graveyard at night. Wind whips the ancient cherry tree, stripping petal from limb and filling the darkness with a pale confusion of blossoms that swirl around her shoulders and settle on the old stone tombs. The wooden memorial plaques chatter and tap like the rotting teeth of ghosts, and in the wind she hears a voice, which is not quite a voice, but more an impression. "*It is only when the moon is nearly full . . .*" it seems to say, this voice that is not quite a voice but more like a haunted breeze across the neck of an empty bottle. Why here? she asks. She looks down and realizes she is holding the old composition book in her hands, carefully wrapped in creased wax paper, and suddenly she remembers. She knows her way through the temple grounds to the altar in the study. She knows where the box rests, high on the shelf, and it takes her no time at all to unwrap the white cloth, lift the lid, and slip the packet with the booklet inside. She hears a noise and looks up to see the old nun standing in the doorway, watching. Behind her is the garden. She's wearing black robes, and when she stretches out her arms to enfold the world, her long sleeves billow. Longer and wider they grow until they are as vast as the sky at night, and when they are big enough to hold everything, Ruth can finally relax and fall into her arms, into silence, into darkness.

## 6.

The storm passed in the night, and in the cold light of day, she stood at the kitchen counter, waiting for the tea water to boil. It was late, still technically morning but in fact closer to noon. Oliver had woken earlier and had gone out to see how many trees had blown down, and whether Pesto had returned, but now he was back in the kitchen, on his stool at the counter, where he normally sat with the cat on his lap. He was drinking tea and checking his email on his iPhone, while Ruth tried to tell him about her dream. The cat still seemed to be somewhat there with him, but only as an absence, a cat-shaped hole.

"I couldn't find her words," she said. "I looked and looked, but I couldn't find them. I came back empty-handed." She spread her fingers and studied her ineffectual palms.

"Well," he said. "At least you tried."

The water boiled and she filled the teapot. "Actually, at one point I felt I had something, right there at my fingertips, but then I realized it was old Jiko's story, not Nao's, and so I let it go. I didn't want to get distracted, you know?"

Oliver nodded. He knew all about distraction. She heard the whoosh of an outgoing email, as he put down the phone and took a sip of cold tea.

"The Friends of the Pleistocene are asking me when my monograph will be ready for submission," he said, glumly. "I should have had it done by now. Why can't I focus? Why are they in such a hurry?"

The questions were rhetorical, so she didn't bother to answer. She topped off his tea and poured a cup for herself. "The only other words I found were Haruki's," she said. "The ones in his secret French diary, but we'd already read those, so I left them behind."

"That's the trouble with the Pleistocene," he said. "It's always rush rush rush. They want everything yesterday."

"I put it in the box of his remains right before I woke up. It seemed like the right thing to do."

"But it's not their fault," he said. "I know that. It's mine. I just can't concentrate without Pesto."

"Did you hear a word I was saying?"

He looked up at her. "Of course I did. It sounds like quite a dream. Have you checked the diary?"

She put down her tea. "Oh," she said. "Do you think I should?"

# Part IV

*A book is like a large cemetery upon whose tombs one can no longer read the effaced names. On the other hand, sometimes one remembers well the name, without knowing if anything of the being, whose name it was, survives in these pages.*

—Marcel Proust, *Le temps retrouvé*

# Nao

### 1.

Are you still there?

I wouldn't blame you if you'd totally given up on me this time. I mean, I gave up on myself, right? So why should I expect you to stick around? But if you did, and if you are still there (and I really hope you are) then I want to thank you for not losing faith in me.

So now where were we? Oh, right. I was sitting on the bench at the bus stop, waiting for the bus to take me to the temple so I could watch my old Jiko die, and there was an old guy in a jogging suit sweeping up the petals from the sidewalk, and a dirty white dog licking its balls, and the stationmaster was opening the doors to the station. The first commuters started to arrive, and then a train pulled in, and some passengers got off, just like you'd see at any small train station early in the morning. Nothing special, right? But after a few minutes, the stationmaster came back out again with some guy in a suit, and he looked around and caught sight of me and pointed. The guy who was with him bowed in thanks, and when he straightened up, I saw that it was my dad.

I couldn't believe it. I thought he was dead. Actually, I'd been trying not to think, because every time I did, I would picture him in a car in the woods somewhere with his suicide friends, suffocating and listening to Nick Drake.

But he wasn't. He was walking toward me, and so I quickly looked away and pretended I hadn't seen him. When he got to my bench, he stood there while I watched the dog scratch its fleas. He knew I knew he was there, but we didn't have much to say to each other, and the conversation, when it finally started, was pretty lame and went something like this:

"Hi," he said.

"Hi," I said.

"Have you been here long?"

"Uh, yeah? Like all night?"

"Oh."

"Do you mind if I sit down?"

"Whatever."

I scooched over to make room because I didn't want to touch him. He sat down, and we watched the dog together until it finished scratching and walked away.

"Did you come to see Obaachama?" he asked.

I nodded.

"Is she sick?"

I nodded.

"Is she dying?"

I nodded.

"Why didn't you tell me?"

I laughed, but not like *ha-ha*. More like *yeah, right, and what the fuck good would that have done?*

He understood my meaning and didn't say anything.

The bus came around the corner just then, and we both stood up. We were the only passengers, but we lined up politely anyway, me in front and my dad behind, like we were strangers. When the bus pulled to a stop, I said,

"I thought you were dead."

It was like I was talking to the side of the bus, and I wasn't sure if he'd even heard me. The words were in my head and they leaked out of my mouth before I could stop them. I really didn't want to get into it with him, so when he didn't answer, I felt relieved. The bus doors opened and we got on. Dad paid for our tickets, and I went to the very back of the bus and sat down, and he followed. He hesitated for a moment, but then he sat down next to me. He gave a big sigh, like we'd just accomplished something major, and then reached over and patted my hand.

"No," he said. "I'm not dead yet."

When we arrived at the temple, old Jiko was still alive but there were a lot of people waiting around for her to die. Some of the danka and a few nuns and priests and even some newspaper reporters had come on account of her being just a little bit famous for being so old.

We were her family, so we got special VIP treatment and got to go right in to see her. Muji took us. Old Jiko was lying in her futon. She looked so tiny, like an ancient child. Her skin was almost transparent, and under it you could see the beautiful round bones of her cheeks. She was staring up at the ceiling, but when I knelt beside her and took her hand, she turned her head and looked at me through her milky blue flowers of emptiness.

"*Yokkata*," she whispered. "*Ma ni atta ne.*"[152]

Her fingers were like thin, dry sticks, but hot. I thought I felt her squeeze my hand with her hot fingers. I couldn't make any words come out of my mouth, because I was trying not to cry. What was there to say? She knew I loved her. Sometimes you don't need words to say what's in your heart.

But she had something she wanted to tell us. I think she'd been waiting. She raised her arms and struggled to sit up. I tried to help her, but her body was just bones in a skin bag, and I was afraid to hurt her.

"Muji," she whispered.

Muji was right there, and my dad was, too.

"Sensei," Muji pleaded. "Please lie down. You don't have to . . ."

But old Jiko insisted. She wanted to sit in seiza,[153] so they had to lift her by the armpits onto her knees, and I honestly thought her arms would fall off or the effort would kill her. You could see how hard it was, but finally they got her balanced and upright. Muji straightened her collar.

---

152. *Yokkata. Ma ni atta ne.*—I'm glad . . . You made it in time.
153. *seiza* (正座)—formal kneeling posture.

Old Jiko sat there for a while with her eyes closed, recovering, and then she raised her hand. Muji knew. She had a brush and ink standing ready on a small table, and she moved them over to Jiko's futon and placed them carefully in front of her.

In case you don't know, it's an old tradition among Zen masters to write a final poem on their deathbeds, so this whole business wasn't as strange as it sounds, but it kind of freaked me out because one minute I swear she was about to take her last breath, and the next minute she's sitting up in bed with a brush in her hand.

She kept her eyes closed while Muji got everything ready, placing a clean white sheet of rice paper on the desk in front of her and then carefully grinding the ink against the inkstone. When she was done, she replaced the ink stick in its holder and bowed.

"*Hai, Sensei. Dōzo . . .*" [154]

And then Jiko opened her eyes. She dipped her brush in the thick black ink, pressing and tapping it lightly against the inkstone like she had all the time in the world, which she did, because time slowed down to give her the moments she needed. In honor of her great effort and her supernatural ability to slow time, we all sat up straighter—me and my dad, kneeling in front of her, and Muji off to one side—and the room grew very still, except for the pressing and tapping. Then, when the point of her brush was just right, Jiko took a deep breath and held it over the white paper. Her hand was motionless. A drop of black ink began to swell at the brush's tip, but before it fell, the brush swooped like a black bird cutting across a pale grey sky, and a moment later, five dark, bold slashes lay wetly across the page.

It wasn't a poem. It was a single character.

生

Five strokes. Sei. Ikiru. To live.

---

154. *Hai, Sensei. Dōzo*—Here, Sensei. Please . . .

Still holding the brush, she looked at me and my dad.

"For now," she said to both of us. "For the time being."

A lot of Zen masters like to die sitting up in zazen, but old Jiko lay down. It's no big deal. It doesn't mean that she wasn't a true Zen master. You can be a true Zen master and still lie down. The Buddha himself died lying down, and all that sitting-up business is just a big macho add-on. The way old Jiko died was perfectly fine. She put the brush carefully back onto the holder and then she keeled very slowly over onto her right side, just like old Shaka-sama. Her knees were still all folded up from seiza and she didn't even bother to stretch them out. When her head touched the ground, she just put her hand under her cheek to cradle it and closed her eyes like she was getting ready to take a nap. She looked really comfortable. She took a long, rattling breath, and then another, and then the whole world exhaled with her. And then she stopped. Just like that. We waited, but nothing else happened. She was all gone.

Muji knelt down next to her and wet her lips with matsugo-no-mizu,[155] and then she made raihai bows in front of her, and me and my dad made some, too. Then they rolled her tiny body over onto her back and straightened out her knees, and Muji lit incense and put a white cloth over her face. She had already prepared the altar with fresh candles and incense and flowers, and now she went off to tell all the people who were waiting outside.

I just sat there, trying to understand what had happened. I couldn't believe old Jiko was really dead, and I kept wanting to peek underneath the white cloth. I was worried that she might be suffocating under there, but the cloth wasn't moving or anything, so I knew she wasn't breathing. The thin trickle of incense rose from the burning tip into the rafters, but nothing else moved.

Time was still acting slow and strange, and I couldn't tell if minutes or hours or days were passing. I could hear different things going on in other parts of the temple. The tatami mats were disappearing from the

---

155. *matsugo-no-mizu* (末期の水)—last-minute water.

room. Eventually some men brought in a big wooden tub. Muji filled it with sakasamizu, starting with the cold water,[156] because when a person dies, you have to do everything upside down and backward. When the tub was filled, she carefully undressed old Jiko's body and then asked me if I wanted to help wash her. I could see my dad was worried about me, and he said I didn't need to, but I told him of course I would. I mean, after all the baths Jiko and I had taken together and all the times I'd scrubbed her back, I knew how to do it, right? It was like I'd been practicing for this. I knew exactly how hard to rub, and it didn't feel strange just because now she was dead. It felt pretty normal.

Afterward, Muji and I dressed her in a special pure white kimono that Muji had sewn for her without making any knots in the sewing thread so old Jiko would not be tied to this world. We crossed her kimono right over left, which is backward from the way a living person wears it, and we laid her out so that her head faced north instead of south. Muji put a little knife on her chest to help cut her remaining ties to the world. Old Jiko lay like this for the whole next day, while the danka and other priests came to bow to her and pay their last respects. Then they put her in the coffin.

I thought I knew something about Japanese funerals because of the one my classmates had for me, but Jiko's funeral wasn't anything like mine. It was very grand, and held in the main shrine room, and there were tons of people there from all over, and priests and nuns from the main temple headquarters. My mom finally showed up, all proper and dressed in black. She brought a black suit for my dad to wear, and a clean school uniform for me. The priests and nuns chanted lots of sutras, and everybody took turns going up and offering incense at the altar. I got to go up second, right after my dad, which made me feel nervous and important. After all the guests got a chance to offer incense and bow, we had to say goodbye to old Jiko before they nailed the coffin shut. We put flowers in with her and stuff that she might find useful in the afterlife,

---

156. *sakasamizu* (逆さ水)—upside-down water. Normally a bath is filled with hot water first, and then the cold is added.

like her sutra books and slippers and reading glasses and the six coins she will need to get across the River of Three Crossings on Mount Fear. When no one was looking, I slipped some Melty Kisses into her hand, too. Zen masters don't usually take chocolates with them to the Pure Land, since they're supposed to be so unattached to things of this world, but I knew how much old Jiko loved her chocolates, and I figured it wouldn't matter. When I touched her fingers, they were stiff and icy cold. She'd already changed so much since she died. The day before, when we were washing her, it felt like she was still there in her body, but now this body was empty. A sack. A skin bag. A cold thing. No Jiko at all.

They closed the coffin and nailed it shut with a stone, and the whole time, the priests and nuns were chanting. Memories, like little waves, licked the edges of my mind. I remembered back to my own funeral, and Ugawa Sensei's sad voice and the words he was chanting. *Form is emptiness and emptiness is form.* It made sense to me now, because one moment old Jiko was form and the next moment she wasn't. Then I remembered the karaoke party we had, when Jiko sang the "Impossible Dream" song. Somehow, I connected that song to her vow to save all beings, and as I watched her lying there, I felt sad for her because she had failed, and the world was still filled with creeps and hentai. But then something else occurred to me, that maybe her failure didn't matter, because at least she'd been true to her impossible dream until the very end. I wondered if her heart was feeling peaceful and calm as she was laid to her rest, or if she was still worrying about stuff. I wondered if she was worrying about me. It's selfish, but I kind of hoped she was. I mean, it's one thing to fail to save all beings, but at least she could have waited for me. Her own great-granddaughter. But she hadn't. She'd just gone ahead and gotten on the elevator anyway.

*Gone, gone,*
*Gone beyond . . .*

We took her body off the mountain in a fancy hearse and down to the crematorium near the bigger temple in town. The nuns and priests did some more chanting as they put old Jiko's coffin on the metal tray and then they slid her into the oven like a pizza. The oven doors shut, and suddenly I worried about the Melty Kisses melting all over her pure white kimono, but it was too late to do anything about it. We went outside to wait, and I could see the smoke rising into a cloudless blue sky. My dad came out and stood with me and held my hand, and I didn't mind. We didn't talk or anything. When it was done, we went back and they slid out the tray. There was no sign of the chocolate. All that was left of her was a tiny broken skeleton of warm white bones. She was so tiny I couldn't believe it.

The crematorium man took a little hammer and broke up the bigger bones, and then we all stood around the tray with wooden chopsticks, which we used to pick up the pieces. You do this with a partner, and each pair picks up a bone together and puts it in the funeral urn. You start with the feet bones and move up to the head, because you don't want her to be upside down for the rest of eternity. Me and my dad were one team, and we were both really careful, and as we did it, Muji explained what each bone was. Oh, that is her ankle. That is her thigh. That is her elbow. Oh, look, there's her nodobotoke!

Everyone was superhappy because finding the nodobotoke is a good sign. Muji said it's the most important bone, the one we call an Adam's apple in English, but in Japanese it's called the Throat Buddha, because it's triangular and looks a little bit like the shape of a person sitting zazen. If you can find the Throat Buddha, then the dead person will enter nirvana and return to the ocean of eternal tranquillity. The Throat Buddha is the last bone that goes in, and you put it on the very top, and then they close the urn.

We didn't need the big hearse for the ride back because now Jiko was so small she could sit on my lap, which is where I held her all the way back up the mountain. When we got home, we went into Jiko's room and put her urn and her picture on the family altar, next to Haruki #1's.

Muji went and got Jiko's 生 from the main shrine room. Somebody had already brought it to be mounted on a scroll during the wake, and now Muji hung it by the family altar, next to old Jiko's funeral portrait. The reporters had made a big deal about her final word, going around asking all the muckety-muck priests from the temple headquarters for their profound interpretations and explanations. Nobody could agree. Some of them said it was the start of a poem that she hadn't been able to finish. Others said no, that it was a complete statement which showed she was still clinging to life, so that even after a hundred and four years, her understanding was still imperfect. And others disagreed, claiming that writing *life* at the moment of death meant that she understood that life and death were one, and so she was fully enlightened and freed from duality. But the fact is, nobody understood what she really meant except me and my dad, and we weren't saying.

My mom went to help Muji and the other danka ladies clean up in the kitchen, and then suddenly it was just me and Dad, sitting there in front of the family altar, alone for the first time since he'd found me at the bus stop. It was really quiet. Until that moment, everything had been so crazy, with all the nuns and priests and danka and services and chanting, and reporters asking questions, but now it was just me and my dad and all the words that were unspoken, drifting around like ghosts between us. And the one big word that Jiko had written was the scariest ghost of all.

It was a little awkward. From the kitchen I could hear the murmur of faraway voices and the sound of food being prepared and insects buzzing around the garden. It was spring and getting warm again.

"I wonder what's in that box," Dad said.

I think he was just trying to make polite conversation, but he was pointing to the shelf on the altar, where the box containing Haruki #1's remains-that-were-not-truly-remains sat, and I was so relieved he'd asked something I actually knew the answer to that I ended up telling him the whole story. Of course he knew most of it already, but I didn't care. I was proud because it was a good story, and Jiko had told it to me, and now I could tell it to him and chase the unspoken word ghosts away. So I told him all about how Haruki #1 got drafted, and the pageant in the rain, and about all the training and punishment and bullying he had to endure, but despite all these hardships, how he bravely completed his suicide mission, flying his plane into the enemy target. And because he was a military hero, completing his mission and fulfilling his duty, the military authorities sent Jiko the not-quite-empty box of remains.

"There was nothing left of him," I explained, "so they just stuck a piece of paper inside that says ikotsu. Do you want to see?"

"Sure," Dad said.

I went to the altar and brought down the box. I took off the lid and looked inside, expecting to see the single slip of paper. But something else was there instead. A small packet. I reached in and pulled it out.

It was wrapped in an old piece of greasy waxed paper, stained with mildew and eaten by insects. When I turned it over, bits fell off. I brushed away the dust.

"What's that?" Dad asked.

"I don't know," I said. "It wasn't here before."

"Open it."

So I did. I peeled off the oily outside paper, taking care not to tear it. Inside was a thin booklet folded into quarters. I opened it to the first page. It was covered with words, written in a faded blue ink, that traveled from left to right across the page. Not up and down like Japanese. Like English, only I couldn't understand.

"I can't read it."

Dad held out his hand. "Let me see."

I passed him the booklet.

"It's in French," Dad said. "Interesting . . ."

I was surprised. I didn't expect him to know anything about French.

Dad leaned forward, turning the brittle pages with care. "I think it might be Uncle Haruki's," he said. "Jiko Obaachama said something about a diary once. She said Haruki always kept a diary. She figured it must have gotten lost."

"So how did it get here?" I asked.

Dad shook his head. "Maybe she had it all along?"

That didn't seem right to me. "No way," I said. "She would have told us."

"He wrote the dates, see?" Dad said. "1944. 1945. He must have been serving in the navy at the time. I wonder why he wrote in French."

I knew the answer to that one, too. "It was safe," I explained. "If the bullies found it, they wouldn't have been able to read it."

"Mm," Dad said. "You're probably right. It's a secret diary."

I felt pleased. "Uncle Haruki was really smart," I said. "He could speak French and German and English, too." I don't know why I was bragging, like it was me who could do all these things.

He looked up at me. "Shall we take this home with us? Aren't you curious to know what it says?"

Of course I was! I felt happy because I really wanted to know what Uncle Haruki had written in his secret French diary, but also because it had been so long since my dad and I had a project we could do together. I looked at him, kneeling by the altar, peering at the pages, trying to make out the French. He looked like my nerdy old studious dad, happily lost in another world. But then the image of him leaving the house with his shopping bag full of briquettes popped into my mind, and my heart flipped and sank. We were already in the middle of an unfinished project. Our last project. Our suicide project.

He must have sensed me watching him, because he looked up, and I turned away quickly so he wouldn't see me trying not to cry. I had this sad vision just then of me and my dad, side by side in our dusty urns on the family altar, with nobody left to take care of our remains. It wouldn't be long.

"Nao-chan?"

"What."

I knew my tone of voice was rude, but I didn't care.

He waited until he knew I was really listening, and then he spoke softly. "It's like Grandma Jiko wrote, Nao-chan. We must do our best!"

I shrugged. I mean, sure, it sounded good, but how could I trust him?

"*Ikiru shika nai!*" he said, half to himself, and then he looked up and repeated it, urgently, in English this time, as if to make absolutely sure I understood. "We must live, Naoko! We have no choice. We must soldier on!"

I nodded, barely daring to breathe as the fish in my stomach thrashed its tremendous tail and twisted up into the air. Then, with a great splash, it reentered the water and swam away. Slowly, the water settled.

*Ikiru shika nai.* My fish would live, and so would me and Dad, just like my old Jiko wrote.

My dad went back to reading. Chibi-chan was mewing from the veranda, so I got up to let him in. When I slid back the sliding door, he shot through the opening and between my ankles like he was being chased by ghost dogs from hell. The hair on his spine was standing straight up. A strong warm breeze followed him in from the garden, rattling the paper doors in their frames. It sounded just like Jiko's chuckle. Dad looked up from the pages of his uncle's diary.

"Did you say something?"

I shook my head.

Mom left the next day because she had to get back to work, but me and Dad stuck around to help Muji get old Jiko's stuff in order. Not that she had much stuff. She owned almost nothing, except for some of Haruki #1's old philosophy books, which Dad said he'd take. The only thing Jiko really cared about was the fate of Jigenji, but the little temple didn't belong to her. It belonged to the main headquarters, and they were still hoping to sell it to a developer, but luckily, the real estate market had crashed on account of the bubble economy bursting, and moving all the graves was going to be expensive, so they decided to wait. This meant Muji would get to stay, at least temporarily, and we could keep the family altar there, too. Muji promised to take care of it as though it were her own, which it more or less was, in my opinion, because she was like an auntie, and I promised her I would come back to the temple in the summers and also every year in March to help with old Jiko's memorial services. It was a good arrangement, at least for the time being.

# *Ruth*

## I.

The little cemetery in Whaletown wasn't very far from their home, but Ruth didn't get around to visiting as often as she should. She had planted a small dogwood tree next to her parents' grave, but that first summer they'd had a drought, and she'd forgotten to water it, so although the little tree had survived, it had lost some limbs and its pleasing symmetry. She felt bad about this.

"Sorry, Mom," she said, using a whisk broom to brush the winter's accumulation of dust and dead leaves from the small granite plaque that bore her mother's name. "I'm not very good at this."

Of course, her mother didn't answer, but Ruth knew she wouldn't have cared. Masako never had much use for ritual, never remembered birthdays or celebrated anniversaries, and generally thought occasions of this sort were just a bother. And Ruth generally agreed, but after reading Nao's account of old Jiko's funeral, she found herself wishing she'd done more to commemorate her mother's passing.

Her death had been a low-key affair. In the last years of her life, she had developed mandibular cancer, but by then, even without the complications posed by Alzheimer's, she was too old and frail to survive the surgery, which would have required removing half of her jawbone. Her oncologist recommended palliative radiation, which wouldn't cure the cancer, but might alleviate her suffering. And it did. The tumor receded and the lesion healed, but by then she needed more care than Ruth and Oliver could provide on the island, so they moved her to a nursing home in Victoria, where she spent the last two years of her life. When the tumor came back, they tried another round of radiation, but this time her mother had neither the strength nor the will to recover, and she fell into a coma.

Death came quickly. It was late at night and the nursing home was quiet. Ruth and Oliver were by her side, reading. Suddenly her mother's eyes popped open, blind and unseeing, and she struggled to sit up. Her breathing became shallow and jagged. Ruth held her mother's small, rigid body in her arms. Oliver touched her forehead. She relaxed. Her eyelids fluttered as the light drained from her face. For a while she hung there, subtle and liminal, and then she exhaled one last time and was gone.

They stayed with her for a while, keeping her company, in case her spirit was still lingering. They held her hands, and they talked to her until her body grew cold.

That was on a Tuesday night. The cremation took place on Friday. Several days had passed, and Ruth was nervous about how her mother might look, but when they were led into the small anteroom of the crematorium where Masako's body was laid out under a white sheet in a brown cardboard box, Ruth just felt happy to see her again. They'd brought some of her favorite things to send with her: photographs and letters and cards from friends and family; a crocheted lap robe from the Free Store that she'd especially liked; her favorite sneakers and her mittens; a couple of bars of chocolate. A calendar to help her remember dates. Emery boards. Scotch tape. A watercolor painting. Flowers. Oliver wanted to get tropical flowers, from Hawaii because she'd grown up there, so he'd bought anthuriums from Hilo and ti leaves for good luck, ginger and a big gaudy bird of paradise. They filled up her cardboard coffin and sat with her for a little while longer, and then not knowing what else to do, they kissed her goodbye. Ruth thought she looked nice in the box with all her things. Comfortable. The funeral director put the lid on the box and his assistants wheeled it into the retort chamber, lining up the gurney with the mouth of the oven. The doors opened and the box slid in. Ruth turned the dial to start it up. Her mom was so tiny, the director said, only seventy-four pounds. It wouldn't take long. A couple of hours. They could pick up her ashes after two.

They took a walk around the memorial garden, which was next to the funeral home. It was a beautiful morning. The Pacific sky was streaked with clouds, but the sun was shining through, and everything was wet and sparkling and golden. Big Douglas firs, the kind her mom used to love, surrounded the garden. All the deciduous trees had turned colors, and their yellow and orange foliage looked brilliant against the darkness of the conifers. The grass was littered with bright fallen leaves. They walked around the pond, following the path until they could see the chimney of the crematorium. They watched for a while. There was no smoke coming from it, but they could see a dense column of shimmering heat, which was all that was left of her mother's body as she became air. Oliver said that in this etheric form she could ride the trade winds back to Hilo and be there in no time. Ruth said her mom would like that.

They brought her ashes back to Whaletown, and Ruth talked to Dora, who, as secretary of the community club, was in charge of the cemetery as well.

"Anywhere's fine," Dora said. "Just choose a spot and dig a hole, but try not to dig anyone else up."

"It'll be small," Ruth said. "It's just for her ashes, and my dad's. But I'd like to plant a tree, if I could. A Japanese dogwood. They both liked Japanese dogwoods."

"Shouldn't be a problem," Dora said. "As long as you don't shade out somebody else. Just don't forget to water it."

The crooked little dogwood hadn't grown much in the years since her mother's death, but it did manage to produce a few blossoms every spring, although few people were ever around to notice. Ruth's mother hadn't wanted a funeral, and neither had her father. They'd outlived most of their friends, and the remote location of the island prevented any survivors from ever visiting their graves. Sometimes, though, Ruth found a dead rose or a small stuffed animal by her mother's stone, which meant somebody was dropping by. She guessed the roses were from Dora, but the stuffed toys baffled her, although her mother would have liked them.

"I hope you guys aren't too lonely," Ruth said, giving her father's stone a final brushing. She looked dubiously around at the other graves. Many of the oldest were just sunken depressions, marked by small decaying wooden crosses. The graves with stones were easier to locate. One or two of the older headstones had maritime themes, honoring fishermen and boat captains who'd died at sea. Some of the more recent graves were marked by rough stupas or wooden totem plaques carved by shamanistic hippies. A few of the graves showed signs of care, but most were untended. Old offerings of shells and stones, guttered candles and macramé dream catchers, lay scattered about. A torn Tibetan prayer flag hung from the bough of a cedar. It was a lonely place. Ruth's mother, a solitary person, wouldn't have minded, but her father had enjoyed company.

Ruth returned the whisk broom to her knapsack and took out a small hand scythe, which she used to cut back the dead grasses. She inspected the dogwood tree. It was still crooked, but it had put on some more growth. Little leaf buds were forming on the ends of the twigs, and she vowed to come back later in the spring to see it blooming. She had bought some incense at the local health food co-op, and now she took a stick from her backpack and lit it with a cigarette lighter. She pushed it into the soil, and then sat on the ground in front of the graves . . . to do what? She didn't know. The ground was still damp from all the rain. A thin curl of smoke rose from the tip of the incense into the air. Overhead, the sky was blue and streaked with high clouds. She thought of Nao's fake funeral and Jiko's real one and wished she knew a chant she could sing. How did the words go? Gone, gone, gone completely beyond, awakened, hurray . . .

Something like that.

## 2.

"The Japanese take funerals and memorials very seriously," Ruth said.

"Your mother didn't," Oliver replied.

They were standing out on the deck with Muriel, testing out the birding lens mount that Oliver had ordered for his iPhone. Muriel was hoping for another look at the Jungle Crow, and Ruth wanted Oliver to take a picture of it to send in, along with the GPS coordinates, to the Cornell Ornithology Lab's Citizen Science database.

"Yeah, Mom was weird. She wasn't very Japanese."

"Neither are you." He held up the long telephoto lens, onto which the iPhone was attached like an afterthought, and studied the little screen as he scanned the branches of a tall Douglas fir. The trees were dark against the blue sky, and he was having trouble with the contrast.

"I know," Ruth said. "But I try. It was nice being at the cemetery this morning. The dogwood tree is looking a little less lopsided."

He panned over to a grove of cedars. "The roots should be well established by now. It should be able to survive a few more years of drought and neglect."

He fiddled with the lens, trying to bring the image into focus. Muriel had brought her own high-powered binoculars. She'd been surveying the branches as she listened to their conversation.

"I don't think your mother was weird," she said. "I really liked her. A lot of people on the island liked her. She had friends here, even if she couldn't remember who they were. It's a shame you didn't at least have a small memorial. If not for her, for everyone else."

"I know, I know . . ."

"Did you know that Benoit visits her grave? He brings her little toys from the Free Store."

Ruth fell silent. Benoit. Of course. Muriel was right, it was a shame. She changed the subject.

"Actually, my point was really about Nao and Jiko. The Japanese take these memorials really seriously. Old Jiko died in March, right? Nao promised to go back to Jiko's temple in March every year to help with the memorial. The temple was located north of Sendai, near the coast and the epicenter of the earthquake, and more or less in the path of the tsunami. So the question is, was she there on March eleventh of 2011? I think the evidence is pretty strong. She was there, she knew the wave was coming, she grabbed some of Muji's plastic bags and stuffed her most precious things inside—her diary, Haruki's letters and the watch . . ."

"What's the point in speculating?" Oliver asked. "You haven't even finished reading."

Muriel lowered her binoculars and looked at Ruth, aghast. "You haven't finished reading?"

"No," Ruth said. "I've still got a few pages left to go."

Muriel shook her head. "I don't understand you," she said. "I would have sat down and read the damn thing from start to finish, and found out everything I could, before looking for evidence to support my conclusions. Nothing would have stopped me from getting to the end."

Ruth gazed up at the wispy clouds in the sky and thought about how best to answer this. "Well," she said. "I know what you mean, but I was trying to pace myself. I felt I owed it to Nao. I wanted to read at the same rate she'd lived. It seems silly now." She paused, wondering whether or not to continue. "And then there's the problem with the end . . ." she said, finally.

"What's wrong with the end?"

"Well, nothing. It's just that it keeps . . . changing."

"Changing?"

"Receding," Ruth said.

"Interesting," Muriel said. "Would you care to explain?"

So Ruth did. She explained how she had riffled through to the end of the book to ascertain that all the pages were filled, only to have those same pages suddenly go blank, just as she was about to read them. She looked at Oliver for confirmation. He raised his eyebrows and shrugged.

"Weird," Muriel said. "Excuse me for asking, but have you guys been smoking a lot of pot?"

"Of course not," Ruth said. "You know we don't smoke pot."

"Just checking," Muriel said. She sat down on the splintery deck chair, which groaned ominously, causing Oliver to glance up nervously. The deck furniture, like the deck, and the entire house for that matter, was in disrepair, and he was always waiting for the weather-worn planks to give way and for someone to fall through.

"What you're describing is interesting," Muriel said, twisting the end of her braid around her finger. "The reader confronting the blank page. It's like writer's block, only in reverse."

Ruth thought about this. "You mean, as her reader, I'm blocked, and so her words disappear? I don't like that. Besides, it doesn't make any sense."

"Hard to say. Agency is a tricky business. What was she writing about when the pages went blank?"

"She'd just caught up with herself. With the *now* of her story. She was sitting on a bench at the bus stop in Sendai, and her last words were 'I guess this is what now feels like.' And then, nothing. Blank. She ran out of words, that is until . . ."

She hesitated. The part about her dream was even weirder, and she felt unsure as to whether she should tell Muriel about it or not, but Muriel was looking at her intently, so she described how the Jungle Crow had led her to the park bench in Ueno where Nao's father was waiting for his suicide hookup, and how they'd talked about Nao, and he'd gone off to Sendai to find her.

"And then, the next morning, when I checked the diary, she'd written a whole new entry about old Jiko's death and funeral, and her reconciliation with her father, and her promise to Muji to return to the temple every March."

"That sounds like a happy enough ending," Muriel said.

"Well," Ruth said. "It would be, except I *still* haven't reached the end. Every time I open the diary, there are more pages. Like I said, the end keeps receding, like an outgoing wave. Just out of reach. I can't quite catch up."

"Curiouser and curiouser," Muriel said. "Okay, I have two more theories. In indigenous myth, crows are pretty powerful. So let's assume this Jungle Crow is your familiar, your totem animal, just like the cat was Oliver's." She broke off and turned to Oliver. "I was sorry to hear about Pesto," she said. "You know Benoit lost his little dog, too, don't you?"

"Yeah," he said, tersely, keeping his back turned. "It sucks." He was still hoping that Pesto would return safely—his spine was rigid with hope—but as the days passed, this outcome seemed less and less likely.

Muriel, who had lost a favorite cat to a cougar, sighed deeply, and her whole body seemed to deflate into the rickety chair.

"It does suck," she said. "I keep telling myself we're lucky to live in an ecosystem that's intact enough to support large predators, but I miss my Erwin." She stared at her lap, and then she took a deep breath and roused herself. "Anyway," she continued, "my theory is that this crow from Nao's world came here to lead you into the dream so you could change the end of her story. Her story was about to end one way, and you intervened, which set up the conditions for a different outcome. A new 'now,' as it were, which Nao hasn't quite caught up with."

Muriel sat back in her chair, looking pleased with herself.

Ruth laughed. "And you call yourself an anthropologist?"

"I'm retired," Muriel said.

"I see. So what's your second theory?"

"You might not like this one."

"Try me."

"Well, it's akin to my reader's block theory. That it's your doing. It's not about Nao's now. It's about yours. You haven't caught up with yourself yet, the now of *your* story, and you can't reach her ending until you do."

Ruth thought about this. "You're right," she said. "I don't like it. I don't like having that much agency over someone else's narrative."

Muriel laughed. "That's a fine way for a novelist to talk!"

"I'm not a—" Ruth started to say, when Oliver interrupted.

"Look!" he said, aiming the lens at the maple tree. "Over there. In that low branch. Isn't that your crow?"

Muriel leaned forward and held up her binoculars. "Looks like a Jungle Crow," she said. "Handsome bird. What do you think?" She passed the binoculars to Ruth.

It took Ruth a moment to get her bearings amid the tangle of branches and pale hanging wisps of old man's beard, but then she saw it, a glossy black wing against a bright green mat of moss. She focused the binocular lenses. The crow was far away, but the image stabilization allowed her to get a good look. "Yes, that's the one. I recognize the aquiline profile. I'm almost sure."

The crow stretched its neck and turned its head.

"She sees us," Ruth said. "She's staring right at us."

Oliver took a few more pictures. "They're not great," he said, "but maybe they're good enough for identification purposes. I wish I could get a better shot."

He aimed the lens again, but just as he did, the crow hunched its shoulders, spread its wings, and took off.

Ruth lowered the binoculars. "Where'd she go?"

"There," Muriel said, pointing up.

The crow had cleared the branches and was gaining in altitude as it flew across the meadow toward them. When it was directly overhead, it released something from its talon. The small object fell through the air and bounced on the deck at their feet, rolled a little, and came to rest in the gap between two rotten planks.

"Weird," Ruth said. "What was that?"

"A nut," Oliver said, bending to retrieve it. "It's stuck in the crack."

"A nut?" Ruth felt disappointed. What was she expecting?

Oliver got to his knees. "Looks like a hazelnut," he said. He took out his multitool and extracted a blade. "Probably from one of our trees last fall." He pried out the nut and turned it over in his hand.

Ruth looked up. The crow was circling overhead, climbing higher and higher on each orbit. She thought about Haruki's Crow Captain. "Do you think she was trying to bomb us?"

"I doubt it," Muriel said. "Crows drop nuts and clams on rocks to crack them."

The crow was still overhead, but higher now, just a speck in the sky. "Do you think she's waiting for us to crack it?"

"She doesn't seem to be waiting," Muriel said. "She seems to be leaving. Maybe it's a parting gift."

"Here," Oliver said, dropping the nut into Ruth's hand. "If it's a nut, it must be for you."

"Gee, thanks," she said, rolling the hard little object around on her palm. "I'm going to try not to take that personally."

Oliver was still on his knees, folding up his multitool, when something under the deck caught his eye. The house was built on the rise of a hill, and the deck extended out over a slight downward slope, creating a large crawl space underneath.

"Something's moving down there," he said. He leaned over and peered between the rotting planks, pressing his face to the crack where the nut had been lodged. "It's too dark. Hand me a phone, will you?"

Ruth turned on the flashlight app and passed it to him. He directed the beam down into the darkness.

"What is it?" she asked, but Oliver didn't answer.

He scrambled to his feet and ran across the porch. He leaped down the stairs, stomping and beating his way through the thick clumps of fern, and then he dropped to his hands and knees and disappeared under the deck. From up above, they could see the beam of light as he groped his way forward in the dirt, and then they heard a thin sound, something in between a squeak and a whimper, and Oliver's voice, crying out, "What are you doing *here*?"

"It's Pesto," Ruth said, clutching Muriel's arm. "He's come back from the dead."

### 3.

The cat had been attacked and was badly hurt. The incident must have taken place several days earlier, because the wounds had closed over and were infected. His tail, of which he'd been so proud and which usually stood up straight in the air, hung limply down, dragging on the ground. He was emaciated. His fur was matted with blood and thick with dust, and his eyes were dull and distant, as though he'd retreated deep inside to some inviolable animal place where he felt no pain. Oliver carried him out and held him while Ruth found a box and lined it with a towel. When they put him in the box, he tried to stand, but immediately fell over. His back legs weren't working.

"This is not good," Oliver said. "These gashes are really deep. They're abscessed."

He took a deep breath and then ran his hands over the cat's hindquarters. When he touched the injured tail, Pesto raised himself and tried to snarl, but even that was too much for him, and he sank back onto the towel.

"He's in too much pain," Oliver said. The pitch of his voice was high, and his words sounded brittle. He straightened and stood up next to the box, staring down into it. "Stupid cat. He's not going to make it."

"How do you know?" Ruth said. "He might—"

"No," he said, cutting her off. "The infection's spread through his body. We have to put him down."

"Do you want me to call Dora?" Muriel asked.

"No," Ruth said. "We have to take him to town. We have to take him to the vet."

"There's no point," Oliver said. He wheeled away and went to stand by the deck railing. "I *knew* this would happen. Stupid cat. Running out. Getting into fights. It was just a matter of time."

"We can catch the two o'clock ferry if we leave now," Ruth said.

"It's not worth it," he said. "He's dying. He's just a stupid barn cat."

"We can phone the vet from the boat."

"No. The vet's expensive. We'll get all the way over there and they'll just have to put him down . . ."

He stood there, back turned, gripping the railing. Ruth looked at his rigid spine. He was so angry. Angry at her, at the cat, at the world, for breaking his heart. She went into the house and got the car keys. She came out again, picked up the box with the cat, carried it over to the hatchback, and loaded it in. She backed the car out and rolled down the window. "Hurry," she called to him.

He turned his head and hesitated.

"Go," Muriel said, pushing him toward the car.

On the ferry, he stared straight ahead out the window at the waves, while Ruth phoned to tell the clinic they were coming. "Stupid cat," he kept saying. "Stupid cat." But when they got there, he carried the box in and held Pesto on the table while the vet shaved him and lanced his wounds to clean and drain them. The wounds were bad, the vet concurred, as bad as he'd ever seen, gashes from teeth and claws, probably a raccoon or a pack of raccoons. Pesto had been trying to escape, which was why the injuries were so severe on his hindquarters, but the real threat was the infection, which had spread throughout his body. The prognosis was not good. They would have to keep the wounds clean, and lance them back open if they started to close, so they wouldn't become abscessed. They needed to keep him on antibiotics, keep him contained, and soak his body in a warm Epsom salt bath three times a day. Oliver asked questions, made notes, and then asked the vet for a scalpel. Ruth sat in a chair and tried not to faint as the vet explained how to open up the wounds and drain the pus. Oliver looked grim, but his determination was back. He was going to save his cat.

She was still feeling queasy when they left, so he drove. Pesto, knocked out from the anesthesia, slept in his box in the back. In the ferry lineup, she wedged her head between the seat back and the car door, closed her eyes, and listened to Oliver process. He was going around in circles, trying to make sense of what had happened.

"At least we know," he kept saying. "Even if the Pest doesn't make it now, at least we know what happened. That's what was driving me crazy. Not knowing where he'd gone, or if he was alive or dead. But at least now we know. We'll do our best to save him, but even if we can't, even if he dies tomorrow, at least we'll know we tried. Stupid cat. There's nothing worse than not knowing . . ."

**4.**

Dear Ruth,

My efforts have borne some fruit, though perhaps my results are not as satisfying as we would have liked. Since we last corresponded, I was able to recover some of my missing computer files and locate an old email that Harry must have sent me, which, I must confess, I hardly recall ever receiving. I wrote to him immediately, but have yet to receive a reply. I took the liberty of sending him your email address and telling him about your urgent concerns, so it's possible you may hear from him directly, but then again, you may not. I am forwarding you his email, and when you read it, you will see what I mean.

Of course, this email predates the earthquake and the tsunami, so I doubt this will be of much use to you, or answer your questions as to the current whereabouts of my enigmatic friend and his family, but I can't help feeling that there are things in this email that you might find interesting. At the very least, I felt you should be privy to our most recent exchange, even though by now it is several years old.

### 5.

Dear Ron,

Thank you for not forgetting your old friend who is neglecting for so long to write to you. First let me answer your kind questions. My family is well. My wife continues her job in the textbook company and recently she has a new hobby of deep sea diving. I am very grateful to her for supporting me during my trouble times, and also to my daughter, Naoko. When at first we returned from Sunnyvale to Tokyo, she had many trouble times as well, and for a while she even dropped out of the school. But later on she was able to apply herself strictly for passing the equivalency exam, and she was successful to receive a good scholarship for an international high school in

Montreal, where she became very interested in studying the culture and language of French.

And for me, several years ago, I was able to launch my new Internet start-up company, which is an online encryption and security system called Mu-Mu[157] Vital Hygienics. I cannot tell you many details because of the agreements of nondisclosure, but Naoko gave me this idea. In her junior high school days, she was a victim of harsh bullying when her classmates teased her, including making videos of her shame that they posted onto the Internet. When I saw these, I cried many tears. I was very angry! As her father, it is my duty to keep my daughter safe, but I failed to keep her so. I was like a blind man, too selfish because I couldn't see, and only my concern was for myself.

But when I finally woke up, I began to research and was able to develop a neat little spider that could crawl up search engine databases and sanitize all instances of my daughter's name and personal information, as well as all the pictures and nasty videos, until there was not even one trace of her shame left. It was all clean again. "Super squeaky clean!" Naoko said, and she was very happy to make fresh start in her new life in Montreal, Canada.

So all that was a very good outcome, but then I got an idea that maybe my cute little spider, who I am calling Mu-Mu the Obliterator, can be useful for other people, too. For example, there are many

---

157. mu-mu (無 無?)—not, naught, nothing, nil, non-, un-.

people who make a mistake and would like to correct it, and my little Mu-Mu can help. Or, many people would like to disappear, and Mu-Mu can make it so no one can find you. For example, if you are a famous person and you are tired and want to be like an ordinary man.

For this purpose, we have developed two Mu methods. Method #1 is a quantum one that we call Q-Mu, which causes Mu to search for all the instances of you from the Internets of many worlds, and then exchange all of the instances for naughts. I don't know how to explain it, except that this one is like playing origami with time. It is most difficult and costly method because Q-Mu must collaborate between worlds and switch possible pasts, so it is only practical if you are very wealthy, and even then, some people are too famous to ever attain perfect Super Squeaky Clean, because they are too famous in too many worlds.

Method #2 is simpler and mechanical, because this Mu can alter only present and future. This one is called MechaMu, and it is more gradual, but just as successful over time. In this method, MechaMu targets only the search engines and eats your name to keep them from finding you. So when nobody can find you, you will stop being famous pretty quick, and before long you will disappear. It's like a slowly becoming invisibility cloak, and is the most cost-effective way.

I have many famous clients, who you have already never heard of! (That is joke, but it is very true.)

You see, Ron, now I understand that suicide is old-thinking, from old-fashioned materialist days. It is also messy and unnecessary. Now, with my Mu-Mu, one does not need to bother with such messy things, because my little spiders can neatly undo you if you stop wanting to be. Naoko made up a funny theory of unbeing that she calls Muyū.[158] She says Muyū is the New Yu.[159] It is new-thinking. She says anonymity is the new celebrity. She says the mark of new cool is no hits for your name. No hits is the mark of how deeply unfamous you are, because true freedom comes from being unknown. I don't know if this is true or not, but maybe it is somewhat true because my Mu-Mu is doing very well, and for the first time since the dot-com bubble burst, I can provide a comfortable lifestyle for my family again.

I hope you are doing well, too. I have been following your work on your website, and it seems you have no need of my services, but if you ever do in the future, I hope you know you can ask me.

Your friend,
"Harry"

---

158. *muyū* (無有?) —nonbeing.
159. *yū* (有?) —being, existence, antonym of mu.

# Nao

### 1.

Wow. I'm really going to miss you. It's crazy, I know, since you don't even exist yet. And unless you find this book and start to read, maybe you never will. You're just my imaginary friend, at least for now.

Still, I feel like I would recognize you if I passed you on the street or caught your eye at Starbucks. How weird is that? Even if I wimp out and decide not to leave this book someplace for you to find, even if I decide maybe it's better if you only exist in my mind, still I feel I would recognize you in a heartbeat. You may be only make-believe, but you are my true friend and you've helped me. I really mean that.

So anyway, as you can see, I'm running out of pages here, so we'd better wrap things up. I just wanted to tell you what happened after old Jiko's funeral, and let you know what's going on with me and my family so you don't have to worry too much. On the way home from Sendai, my dad actually took me to Disneyland, even though it's kind of a weird thing to do after a funeral, and I'm already too old to get superexcited about shaking hands with Mickey-chan. But it was really fun anyway, especially watching my dad in Futureland, riding through the ice cavern asteroid fields at the speed of light in pursuit of the Death Star.

And speaking of stars, one night about a month after we got home, my dad and I went out for a walk to that little park by the Sumida River, and we sat on the swings and watched the stars above and the dark water of the river flowing by. Feral cats were slinking through the shadows, eating garbage. In the darkness, swinging back and forth, it was easy to talk about difficult things. We talked about the stars and the size of the cosmos, and about war. We'd just finished reading Haruki #1's secret

French diary earlier that day. My dad got this graduate student who was studying French poetry at the university to translate it for us, and we were reading it together, and for the first time I was learning how evil people can be. I thought I understood everything about cruelty, but it turns out, I didn't understand anything at all. My old Jiko understood. That's why she always carried Haruki's juzu beads with her, so she could pray to help people be less cruel to each other. After the funeral, Muji gave the juzu to me, and now I carry them all the time, too. They're pretty intense beads, dark and smooth and heavy with all the prayers from H #1's and Jiko's fingers that have gone into them. I don't know any prayers, so I just make them go round and round and say blessings in my head for all the things and people I love, and when I run out of things I love, I move on to the things I don't hate too much, and sometimes I even discover that I can love the things I think I hate.

At the end of the secret French diary, on the night before he died, my great-uncle actually wrote about his suicide mission, and me and my dad were surprised to learn that he had made up his mind not to crash his plane into the enemy aircraft carrier after all. He couldn't get out of going on the mission, so he decided to fly his plane into the waves instead. Of course, this was totally top secret. He knew his commanding officers would execute him for treason if they found out his plan to purposefully miss his target, and he wanted to make sure that his mother and his sisters got the compensation money that the government was supposed to give to the families of dead pilots who gave their lives for their country. It made a lot of sense to me. He was like the Crow Captain. He didn't want to support a war that he hated, and he didn't want to cause any more suffering, even for his so-called enemy. When I read this, I felt a little bit ashamed, actually. I remembered how I used to ambush Daisuke-kun and beat him up, and also how I went forth as a living ghost to stab my enemy Reiko in the eye. I started to feel so bad about this, I decided I would apologize if I ever saw them again, which I probably won't. Daisuke and his mom moved away, and since I stopped going to school, I don't see Reiko anymore.

Anyway, when we read about Haruki's decision to fly into the waves, my dad totally lost it. We were at home, sitting at the kotatsu, and he was reading the translation out loud to me, and when he got to that part, he put down the page and made this loud snorting noise that sounded a bit like a gigantic sneeze, only it wasn't. It was an explosion of sadness. He stood up and went into the bathroom and shut the door, but I could still hear him crying in a deep, gulping way. This is weird, right? To hear your dad totally fall apart? I didn't know what to say, and of course it freaked me out because when your dad's already tried to commit suicide a bunch of times, this kind of thing makes you nervous. But eventually he came out again and started to cook dinner like everything was back to normal, so I dropped it, but later that night, when we were in the park and swinging in the darkness, I asked him why he'd gotten so bent out of shape, and he told me.

It was all connected to his job in Sunnyvale and how come he got downsized. I was still pretty young when that whole thing happened, so I didn't understand it at the time. All I knew was that he was designing interfaces for a computer gaming company, which seemed pretty cool to me.

"My interfaces were really good," he said. "They were so much fun. Everybody enjoyed playing them." He had this wistful, faraway look in his eyes. "We were prototyping first-person operator perspectives. They called me the Pioneer of POV. Then my company signed an agreement with a U.S. military contractor. They were going to apply my interfaces in designing weapons controllers for soldiers to use.

"Wow," I said. That sounded pretty cool, too. I didn't say so, but he heard it in my voice. He dug the plastic toe of his slipper in the bare patch of sand below the swing and brought it to a stop.

"It was wrong," he said, leaning his body forward into the chains that held up the swing. "Those boys were going to kill people. Killing people should not be so much fun."

I stopped swinging, too, and hung there next to him. My heart was pounding, pushing the blood into my cheeks. I felt so stupid and young, and at the same time something was cracking open inside me, or maybe it was the world was cracking open to show me something really important underneath. I knew I was only seeing a tiny bit of it, but it was bigger than anything I'd ever seen or felt before.

He got off the swing and started walking. I followed him. He told me how he fell into a deep depression and stopped sleeping at night. He tried to find someone to talk to about his feelings. He even went to see a California psychologist. He kept bringing up the issue at work, too, trying to convince the members of his development team to let him program some kind of reality check into the interface design, so that the poor pilots would wake up and understand the madness of what they were doing, but the military contractor didn't like this idea, and his company and team members got tired of hearing about his feelings, so they fired him.

He sat down on a cement panda and held his face in his hands. "I was so ashamed," he said.

I couldn't believe it. I stared at him, sitting all hunched over on the panda's head, and I felt like my heart would burst with pride. My dad was a total superhero, and I was the one who should be so ashamed, because the whole time he was being persecuted for his beliefs, I was just pissed off at him for getting himself fired and losing our money and ruining my life. Shows you how much I knew.

He was still talking. ". . . so that's why I cried today, when I read Uncle Haruki's diary. I understood how he felt, you see? Haruki Number One made his decision. He steered his airplane into a wave. He knew it was a stupid, useless gesture, but what else could he do? I made a similar decision, also stupid and useless, only my plane was carrying our whole family. I felt so sorry for you, and for Mom, and for everyone, on account of my actions.

"When 9/11 happened, it was clear that war was inevitable. They'd been preparing for it all along. A generation of young American pilots would use my interfaces to hunt and kill Afghani people and Iraqi people, too. This would be my fault. I felt so sorry for those Arab people and their families, and I knew the American pilots would suffer, too. Maybe not right away. At the time those young boys were carrying out their missions, it would all feel unreal and exciting and fun, because that's how we designed it to feel. But later on, maybe days or months or even years later, the reality of what they'd done would start to rise up to the surface, and they would be twisted up with pain and anger and take it out on themselves and their families. That also would be my fault."

Restless, he stood up from the panda and shuffled over to the chain-link fence that surrounded the playground. I followed. A little gate led out onto the high angled concrete embankment of the river. We sat side by side on the slope and watched the swift dark current of the river sweep by. I knew he'd thought about drowning himself in these waters. I knew he was thinking about the times he'd come here to die. He reached over and took my hand.

"I let you down," he said. "I was twisted up with my guilt. I wasn't there for you when you really needed me."

I held my breath. He was going to bring up the Panties Incident. He was going to confess that he'd been bidding on them. I tried to pull my hand away. I really didn't want to talk about it, but how could I escape? After all, I'd asked him a tough question and he'd given me a true and honest answer. I owed him. So when he asked me how my panties had gotten up on that burusera hentai website and what had happened in the video, I took a deep breath and told him everything. I know he and Mom had talked about my ijime, but I don't think he ever realized how bad it was. I could see it made him sad, but it also really pissed him off.

"Thank you for telling me," he said when I'd finished. There was a hard edge in his voice but I knew he wasn't mad at me. It sounded more like he'd made up his mind about something. He stood up and pulled me to my feet, and we walked home in silence, stopping once at a vending machine so he could buy me a Pulpy. He seemed really preoccupied. I don't know what he's planning to do, but ever since that night, he's been back working at the computer like a fiend with a raison d'être.

He's stopped reading The Great Minds of Western Philosophy completely, and spends all his time programming, which really is his superpower. I mean, there are lots of superheroes with different super-powers, and some of them are big and flashy, like superstrength, and superspeed, and molecular restructuring, and force fields. But these abilities are really not so different from the superpower stuff that old Jiko could do, like moving superslow, or reading people's minds, or appearing in doorways, or making people feel okay about themselves just by being there.

Anyway, I don't know why I'm telling you all this, except that I thought you would like to know. My dad seems to have found his superpower, and maybe I've started to find mine, too, which is writing to you. And before I run out of space, I just want you to know that me and my dad are really okay, now that I finally know what kind of man he is, and even though we haven't actually discussed the topic of suicide, I'm pretty sure that neither of us is thinking along those lines anymore. I know I'm not, anyway. As soon as I've finished these last pages, I'm going to buy a new blank book and keep my promise, which is to write the whole entire story of old Jiko's life. It's true she's already dead, but her stories are still alive in my head at least for now, so I have to hurry up and write them down before I forget. I have a pretty good memory, but memories are time beings, too, like cherry blossoms or ginkgo leaves; for a while they are beautiful, and then they fade and die.

And maybe you'll be glad to know that for the first time in my life, I really don't want to die. When I wake up in the middle of the night, I check to see if H #1's sky soldier watch is still ticking, and then I check to see if I'm still alive, and believe it or not, sometimes I actually feel scared, like *Oh my god, what if I'm dead! That would be terrible! I haven't written the story of old Jiko's life yet!* And sometimes when I'm walking down the street, I find myself thinking, *Oh, please don't let that stupid Lexus careen out of control and run me over, or that crazy hentai burusera salaryman with the comb-over stab me with a penknife, or that guy all dressed in white who looks like a cult terrorist drop a bag of sarin gas in my subway car . . . at least not until I've finished writing old Jiko's life! I can't die until I do that. I have to live! I don't want to die! I don't want to die!*

That's what I find myself thinking. At least until I finish writing her story, I absolutely don't want to die. The thought of letting Jiko down brings tears to my eyes, and I guess you could say this is a big improvement in my state of mind, to actually be worried about dying like a normal person.

And here's one last thing. I just learned something very encouraging. I learned that old Marcel Proust didn't write just one book called *À la recherche du temps perdu*. He actually wrote seven! Amazing, right? *À la recherche du temps perdu* was an incredibly long story with thousands of pages, so he had to publish it in a bunch of different volumes. And the very last volume is called *Le temps retrouvé*, which means *Time Regained*. How perfect is that? So now I just have to keep my eyes open and try to find an old copy of *Le temps retrouvé*. I'll take it to the crafty shop in Harajuku and see if I can get the lady who works there to send it to the hacker to do another book-mod for me, and then I'll write old Jiko's story in that.

Hm. You know what? On second thought, maybe I won't. Maybe I'll actually try to learn some French so I can read Marcel's book, instead of throwing out all the pages. That would be cool. And as for my old Jiko's life story, I think I'll just buy some plain old paper and get started.

# *Ruth*

## 1.

She closed the book.

She'd reached the end. The final page. She was done.

Now what?

She looked at the clock. The red numbers glowed, 3:47 a.m. Almost four o'clock. The woodstove in the living room had long gone out and it was cold in the house. If she were at Jiko's temple, she would be getting up to go sit zazen in an hour. She shivered. Outside the bedroom window, the cold, black night pressed against the pane, and only the single bright spot of her headlamp, reflected in the glass, kept it at bay. She could hear the wind in the bamboo, and the sound of a tall tree creaking. Next to her, Oliver slept soundly, his lips making a little pu-pu-pu sound. The injured cat, in the box on the floor next to his side of the bed, was silent. He must be sleeping, too.

She'd woken inexplicably an hour earlier, and after lying awake for a while, unable to get back to sleep, she'd picked up the diary. Before she knew it, she was reading the penultimate page. Only one more to go. She'd hesitated then, wondering if the pages would suddenly multiply again, but they didn't. She turned the final page. The words continued, she read them to the end, and then at the bottom of the page, they stopped. There was no doubt about it. There were no more words and no more pages.

Books end. Why was she surprised?

She thought back to the mystery of the missing words. Had she somehow found them and brought them back? It wasn't as crazy as it sounded. Sometimes, when she was writing, she would lose herself in a story so completely that the next morning, when she opened her document file and looked at the manuscript, she would find herself staring at paragraphs that she could swear she'd never seen before, and sometimes even entire scenes that she had no recollection of writing. How did they get there? It was an uncanny feeling, usually followed by a quick upsurge of panic—*someone has broken into my story!*—which often turned into excitement as she read on, leaning into the monitor as though it were a source of light or heat, trying to follow the strange new sentences as they unscrolled in front of her. Vaguely, vaguely she'd begin to recollect, the way you might recall a mothlike image from a dream, her mind groping peripherally, askance, shy to face the words full on, for fear they would flutter off into the netherworld, just beyond the pixels, and vanish there. Out of sight, out of mind.

But what had happened this time was different. She hadn't been writing; she'd been *reading*. Surely a reader wasn't capable of this bizarre kind of conjuration, pulling words from the void? But apparently she had done just that, or else she was crazy. Or else . . .

*Together we'll make magic . . .*

Who had conjured whom?

She seemed to remember Oliver suggesting this once before, but she hadn't really appreciated the importance of his question. Was she the dream? Was Nao the one writing her into being? Agency is a tricky business, Muriel had said. Ruth had always felt substantial enough, but maybe she wasn't. Maybe she was as absent as her name indicated, a homeless and ghostly composite of words that the girl had assembled. She'd never had any cause to doubt her senses. Her empirical experience of herself, as a fully embodied being who persisted in a real world of her remembering, seemed trustworthy enough, but now in the dark, at four in the morning, she wasn't so sure. She shuddered, and the sudden movement made her aware of all the places where her body touched the bed. Better. She made an effort to feel the warmth and weight of the comforter against her skin, the cold air on her face and arms, the beating of her heart.

The diary, too, still felt warm in her hands. She stared down at the red cloth cover. Was it her imagination or did the fabric look more worn than it had when she first found it? She turned it over. There was a dark spot on the back where the cat had drooled on it. She held it up to her nose. The bitter scent of coffee beans and sweetly fruity shampoo had faded. Now it smelled of wood smoke and cedar, and faintly, too, of mildew and dust. She traced the gilt lettering on the spine, and then opened it up, quickly, to the last page, as though to catch it off guard.

The page hadn't changed. Of course it hadn't. What was she thinking? That a few extra words might have slipped in between the covers when they were closed, when she wasn't looking? Ridiculous.

Still, a few extra words would have made all the difference. She closed the book again and worried the broken corner like a loose tooth. The cover seemed cooler now. Was she imagining that, too?

Enough.

She placed the diary on her bedside table and turned out the light. By morning, when she reached for it again, the book was cold to her touch.

### 2.

"Now that you're finished," she said, "I need to know if I'm crazy or not."

They were sitting at the kitchen counter having their morning tea. Pesto, shaved, covered with open wounds, and wearing the Cone of Shame, was lying on a towel on Oliver's lap, looking drugged and exceedingly cross. Oliver had just read the last pages of the diary, and when he heard her question, he held up his hand to deflect her. "I can tell that this conversation is not going to turn out well, so please let's not go there."

She ignored his protestations. "That night when the words went missing and you told me it was my job to find them, you didn't really believe that the pages were blank. You didn't believe that the end was receding, either. Did you." It wasn't a question.

He looked her straight in the eye and didn't miss a beat. "Sweetheart," he said. "I didn't ever *not* believe you."

"Oh," he said, sounding relieved. "If *that's* what you're worried about, don't bother. Everyone on this island is crazy. I'm sure Muriel didn't give it a second thought."

This answer did little to reassure her, but given that there were so many other unresolved questions, she was willing to leave it. "Okay," she said. "Supposing, somehow, that Muriel's theory was right, and in my dream I was able to follow the Jungle Crow into Ueno Park and find Nao's father and send him to Sendai . . ."

He had put the diary to one side, and now he was flipping through the most recent *New Yorker*.

"Oliver!"

"What?" He looked up. "I'm listening. You followed the crow to the park and found the father and sent him to Sendai."

"Okay, so, what does that even mean?"

"What do you mean what does that mean?"

"I mean, are you saying that the Jungle Crow led me back in time? That if I hadn't had the dream, Nao's father might have gone ahead and hooked up with his suicide date and killed himself? That Nao would never have discovered that her father was a man of conscience, or learned the truth about her kamikaze great-uncle?"

"I'm not saying anything," Oliver said. "Believe me."

"If I didn't put Haruki Number One's secret French diary into his box of remains on the altar, then how did it get there?"

He looked up then, surprised. "You put it there?"

"Yes. I told you. At the very end of my dream. I discovered it in my hand, and I was just on the verge of waking up, so I stuck it in the box."

"Smart move," he said.

She shrugged, feeling pleased. "Yeah, I thought so. I felt a little bit like a superhero just then."

"I'll bet you did," he said, admiringly.

But she wasn't convinced. "I don't know," she said, as her confidence ebbed. "If I were listening to myself, I'd think I was crazy, too. There's probably a simple, rational explanation, like old Jiko put it there. Maybe she had it all along. Maybe Haruki Number One somehow managed to send it to her before he flew, but for some reason she didn't want to let anyone know about it. Maybe she secretly supported the war and was ashamed of her son's final decision not to carry out his suicide mission. Maybe she thought he was a coward . . ."

"Stop," Oliver said. "Now you really are sounding crazy. There's not a single scrap of evidence to support that hypothesis. From everything Nao's said, her old Jiko was a pacifist and a radical, too, even if she was a hundred and four years old. So don't go cooking up far-fetched explanations and practicing revisionist history in order to make yourself feel sane. If you have to be crazy in order for Jiko to be who she is, so be it. That goes for everyone."

Ruth fell silent. He was right, of course. He picked up *The New Yorker* again, but she wasn't ready to let the subject drop.

"Okay," she said. "But what about Haruki Number Two's email? What about Q-Mu and MechaMu and all that quantum computing stuff? Do you really believe all that? He sounds even crazier than I do."

Oliver looked up from the magazine. " 'Quantum information is like the information of a dream,' " he said. " 'We can't show it to others, and when we try to describe it we change the memory of it.' "

"Wow," she said. "That's beautiful. Did you make that up?"

"No. It's a quote from some famous physicist. Can't remember his name."[160]

"That's what it feels like when I write, like I have this beautiful world in my head, but when I try to remember it in order to write it down, I change it, and I can't ever get it back." She stared disconsolately out the window and thought about her abandoned memoir. Another ruined world. It was sad. "But I still don't understand. What does quantum information have to do with any of this?"

---

160. Charles Bennett. Oliver looked up the quote later and found it's from an article about quantum computing by Rivka Galchen, which appeared in *The New Yorker*, May 2, 2011.

Oliver shifted the cat on his lap. "Okay," he said. "You were speculating about multiple outcomes, right? Multiple outcomes imply multiple worlds. You're not the first to wonder about this. The quantum theory of many worlds has been around for the last half century. It's at least as old as we are."

"Well, that's certainly ancient."

"My point is that it's not new. Nothing is new, and if you buy the many-worlds interpretation of quantum mechanics, then everything that's possible will happen, or perhaps already has. And if so, maybe it's possible that in one of those worlds, Haruki Number Two figured out how to build his Q-Mu and get objects in that world to interact with this one. Maybe he's figured out how to use quantum entanglement to make parallel worlds talk to one another and exchange information."

Ruth stared glumly at the cat. "I'm not following," she said. "I should be wearing the Cone of Shame. I'm not smart enough to understand."

"Well, neither am I. You have to be able to do the math to really get it, and that's way beyond most of us. But you know about Schrödinger's cat, don't you?"

### 3.

Of course she knew about Schrödinger's cat. Their cat was named Schrödinger, after all, even though the name hadn't stuck. But, if pressed, she would have to confess that the name Schrödinger always made her feel vaguely anxious, in much the same way that the name Proust did. She firmly believed she ought to have learned about the former's cat and read the latter's opus, but she hadn't quite gotten around to either.

She knew that Schrödinger's cat was a thought experiment, devised by the eponymous physicist, which had something to do with life and death and quantum physics.

She knew that quantum physics described the behavior of matter and energy on a microscopic level, where atoms and subatomic particles behave differently than macroscopic everyday objects, like cats.

She knew that Schrödinger had proposed putting his theoretical cat into a theoretical box with a lethal toxin, which was triggered to release if a certain set of conditions were met.

"That's right," said Oliver. "I don't remember the details either,[161] but his basic proposition was that if cats behaved like subatomic particles, the cat would be both alive and dead, simultaneously, so long as the box remains closed and we don't know if the conditions have been met. But at the very moment an observer opens the box to look inside and measure the conditions, he would find the cat either dead or alive."

"You mean he could kill the cat by looking at it?"

"No, not quite. What Schrödinger was trying to illustrate is sometimes called the observer paradox. It's a problem that crops up when you're trying to measure the behavior of very small things, like subatomic particles. Quantum physics is weird. On a subatomic level, a single particle can exist as an array of possibilities, in many places at once. This ability to be in many places at once is called superposition."

"Talk about a superpower," Ruth said. "Nao would have liked that." She liked it, too. If she were a subatomic particle, she could be here and in New York.

"This quantum behavior of superposed particles is described mathematically as a wave function. The paradox is that the particles exist in superposition only as long as no one is looking. The minute you observe the array of superposed particles to measure it, the wave function appears to collapse, and the particle exists in only one of its many possible locations, and only as a single particle."

"The many collapses into one?"

"Yes, or rather, that was one theory, anyway. That there's no single outcome until the outcome is measured or observed. Until that moment of observation, there's only an array of possibilities, ergo, the cat exists in this so-called smeared state of being. It's both alive and dead."

"But that's absurd."

"Exactly. That was Schrödinger's point. There are a couple of problems with this theory of wave function collapse. What it's saying, by extension,

---

161. For more on the Schrödinger's cat thought experiment, see Appendix E.

is that at any moment, a particle is whatever it's measured to be. It has no objective reality. That's the first problem. The second problem is that nobody's been able to come up with the math to support this theory of wave function collapse. So Schrödinger wasn't really buying it. The whole cat business was meant to point out the absurdity of the situation."

"Did he have a better idea?"

"No, but later on somebody else did. This guy, Hugh Everett, came up with the math to support an alternative theory, that the so-called collapse doesn't happen at all.[162] Ever. Instead, the superposed quantum system persists, only, when it is observed, it branches. The cat isn't either dead or alive. It's both dead *and* alive, only now it exists as two cats in two different worlds."

"You mean, real worlds?"

"Yes. Wild, isn't it? His theory, which is based on what he called the universal wave function, is that quantum mechanics doesn't just apply to the subatomic world. It applies to everything, to atoms and cats. The whole, entire universe is quantum mechanical. And here's where it gets really freaky. If there's a dead-cat world and an alive-cat world, this has implications for the observer, too, because the observer exists *within* the quantum system. You can't stand apart, so you split, like an amoeba. So now there's a you who is observing the dead cat, and another you who is observing the alive cat. The cat was singular, and now they are plural. The observer was singular, and now you are plural. You can't interact and talk to your other yous, or even know about your other existences in other worlds, because you can't remember . . ."

## 4.

Could this explain her lousy memory?

She stared at the cat, shifting uncomfortably in Oliver's lap. The cat stared back at her, a long, baleful look, before closing his eyes. Who was observing whom? It was hard for Pesto to observe anything at the moment

162. For more on Hugh Everett, see Appendix F.

with the Cone of Shame around his neck, but before the Racoon Incident, he used to like to observe himself. Could Pesto be his own observer? Interesting question. He used to like to raise his leg and study his asshole. It didn't seem like this observation caused him to split into multiple cats with multiple assholes.

Nao's words came back to her just then, or were they Jiko's? *To study the Way is to study the self.* No, it was Haruki who'd written that. He'd been quoting Dōgen and talking about zazen. It made some kind of sense. From what Ruth could tell, zazen seemed like a kind of moment-by-moment observation of the self that apparently led to enlightenment. But what did that even mean?

*To study the self is to forget the self.* Maybe if you sat enough zazen, your sense of being a solid, singular self would dissolve and you could forget about it. What a relief. You could just hang out happily as part of of an open-ended quantum array.

*To forget the self is to be enlightened by all myriad things.* Mountains and rivers, grasses and trees, crows and cats and wolves and jellyfishes. That would be nice.

Had Dōgen figured all this out? He'd written these words many centuries before quantum mechanics, before Schrödinger put his enigmatic cat into his metaphorical box. By the time Hugh Everett came up with the math to support a theory of multiple worlds, Dōgen was dead, and had been for almost eight hundred years.

Or was he?

"So you see," Oliver was saying, "we're now in a world where Pesto is alive, but there's another world where he was killed and eaten by those dastardly coons, who, by the way, I'm going to trap and drown, thereby splitting the world yet again into one with dead coons and another with live ones."

"My head hurts," Ruth said.

"Mine, too," Oliver said. "Don't worry about it too much."

"I don't think you should kill the raccoons," she said. "Not in this world, at least."

"I probably won't, but that won't stop the world from splitting. Every time the possibility arises, it happens."

"Ouch." She thought about this. Maybe it wasn't so bad. In other worlds, she had finished her memoir. The memoir, and perhaps even a novel or two. The thought cheered her. If she'd been able to be so productive in other worlds, maybe she could just try a little harder in this one. Maybe it was time to get back to work. But instead she continued to sit there.

"Do you really believe this?" she asked. "That there are other worlds where Haruki Number One didn't die in a wave, because World War Two didn't happen? Where no one died in the earthquake and tsunami? Where Nao is alive and well, and maybe finishing her book of Jiko's life, and you and I are living in New York, and I'm finishing my next novel? Where there are no leaking nuclear reactors or garbage patches in the sea . . ."

"There's no way of knowing," Oliver said. "But if World War Two hadn't happened, then you and I would never have met."

"Hm. That would be sad."

## 5.

Not knowing is hard. In the earthquake and the tsunami, 15,854 people died, but thousands more simply vanished, buried alive or sucked back out to sea by the outflow of the wave. Their bodies were never found. Nobody would ever know what happened to them. This was the harsh reality of this world, at least.

"Do you think Nao is alive?" Ruth asked.

"Hard to say. Is death even possible in a universe of many worlds? Is suicide? For every world in which you kill yourself, there'll be another in which you don't, in which you go on living. Many worlds seems to guarantee a kind of immortality . . ."

She grew impatient then. "I don't care about other worlds. I care about this one. I care whether she's dead or alive in this world. And I want to know how her diary and the rest of the stuff washed up here, on this island." She held out her arm and pointed to the sky soldier watch. "This watch is real. Listen. It's ticking. It's telling me the time. So how did it get here?"

He shrugged. "I don't know."

"I really thought I would know by now," she said, getting to her feet. "I thought if I finished the diary, the answers would be there or I could figure it out, but they weren't, and I can't. It's really frustrating."

But there was nothing she could do about it, and it was time to go upstairs and get back to work. As she reached into the cone to scratch Pesto's head, a thought occurred to her. "That cat of Schrödinger's," she said. "It reminds me of you. What quantum state were you in when you were hiding in the box in the basement?"

"Oh," he said. "That. Definitely smeared. Half-dead and half-alive. But if you'd found me, I would have died, for sure."

"Well, it's a good thing I didn't go looking for you."

He laughed. "Really? You mean that?"

"Of course. What do you think? That I want you dead?"

He shrugged. "Sometimes I think you'd have been better off without me. You could have married a captain of industry and had a nice life in New York City. Instead you're stuck with me on this godforsaken island with a bad cat. A bald bad cat."

"Now you're the one practicing revisionist history," she said. "Is there any evidence to support this?"

"Yes. There's plenty of evidence to prove the cat is very bad. And very bald."

"I'm talking about me being better off without you."

"I don't know. I guess not."

"Well, then, you should wear the Cone of Shame for even suggesting it. Because now you've gone and sentenced me to another life in another world in New York, with some boorish corporate oligarch of a husband. Thanks a lot." She gave the cat a final pat on the nose.

"Well, don't worry," he said. "You've already forgotten all about me."

He was joking, of course, but his words hurt her feelings. She withdrew her hand. "I have not."

He reached across the counter and took her wrist. "I was just kidding," he said, and then he held on a little longer so she couldn't pull away. "Are you happy?" he asked. "Here? In this world?"

Surprised, she stood there and thought about his question. "Yes, I suppose I am. At least for now."

The answer seemed to satisfy him. He gave her wrist a squeeze and then let go. "Okay," he said, returning to his *New Yorker*. "That's good enough."

# Epilogue

You wonder about me.

I wonder about you.

Who are you and what are you doing?

I picture you now, a young woman of . . . wait, let me do the math . . . twenty-six? Twenty-seven? Something like that. Maybe in Tokyo. Maybe in Paris in a real French café, looking up from your page while you search for a word, watching the people go by. I don't think you are dead.

Wherever you are, I know you are writing. You couldn't give that up. I can see you clutching your pen. Are you still using purple ink or have you outgrown that? Do you still bite your nails?

I don't see you doing a company job, but I don't think you're a freeter, either. I suspect you might be in graduate school, studying history, writing your dissertation on women anarchists in the Taishō Democracy, or the Instability of the Female "I." (For one crazy moment, I thought that monograph I found online might even be yours, but it vanished before I could discover who wrote it.) At any rate, I hope you've finished your book about your old Jiko's life. I'd like to read that sometime. I'd like to read old Jiko's I-novel, too.

I don't really know why I'm writing this. I know I can't find you if you don't want to be found. And I know you'll be found if you want to be.

In your diary, you quoted old Jiko saying something about not-knowing, how not-knowing is the most intimate way, or did I just dream that? Anyway, I've been thinking about this a lot, and I think maybe it's true, even though I don't really like uncertainty. I'd much rather *know*, but then again, not-knowing keeps all the possibilities open. It keeps all the worlds alive.

But having said this, I also just want to say that if you ever change your mind and decide you would like to be found, I'll be waiting. Because I really would like to meet you sometime. You're my kind of time being, too.

Yours,
Ruth

P.S. I do have a cat, and he's sitting on my lap, and his forehead smells like cedar trees and fresh sweet air. How did you know?

# Appendices

# Appendix A: Zen Moments

The Zen nun Jiko Yasutani once told me in a dream that you can't understand what it means to be alive on this earth until you understand the time being, and in order to understand the time being, she said, you have to understand what a moment is.

In my dream, I asked her, *What on earth is a moment?*

*A moment is a very small particle of time. It is so small that one day is made of 6,400,099,980 moments.*

When I looked it up afterward, I discovered that this was the exact number cited by Zen Master Dōgen in his masterwork, the *Shōbōgenzō* (*The Treasury of the True Dharma Eye*).

Numerals resist the eye, so let me spell it out in words: six billion, four hundred million, ninety-nine thousand, nine hundred and eighty. That's how many moments Zen Master Dōgen posited are in one day, and after she rattled off the number, old Jiko snapped her fingers. Her fingers were crazily bent and twisted with arthritis, so she wasn't very good at snapping, but somehow she got her point across.

*Please try it*, she said. *Did you snap? Because if you did, that snap equals sixty-five moments.*

The granularity of the Zen view of time becomes clear if you do the math,[163] or you can just take Jiko's word for it. She leaned forward, adjusting her black-framed glasses on her nose and peering through the thick, murky lenses, and then she spoke once more.

---

163. 1 fingersnap = 65 moments, and 6,400,099,980 moments = one day, so 6,400,099,980 ÷ 65 = 98,463,077 fingersnaps per day.

*If you start snapping your fingers now and continue snapping 98,463,077 times without stopping, the sun will rise and the sun will set, and the sky will grow dark and the night will deepen, and everyone will sleep while you are still snapping, until finally, sometime after daybreak, when you finish up your 98,463,077th snap, you will experience the truly intimate awareness of knowing exactly how you spent every single moment of a single day of your life.*

She sat back on her heels and nodded. The thought experiment she proposed was certainly odd, but her point was simple. Everything in the universe is constantly changing, and nothing stays the same, and we must understand how quickly time flows by if we are to wake up and truly live our lives.

*That's what it means to be a time being,* old Jiko told me, and then she snapped her crooked fingers again.

*And just like that, you die.*

# *Appendix B: Quantum Mechanics*

Quantum mechanics is time being, but so is classical physics. Both describe the interactions of matter and energy as they move through time and space. The difference is one of scale. At the smallest scales and atomic increments, energy and matter start to play by different rules, which classical physics can't account for. So quantum mechanics attempts to explain these quirks by positing a new set of principles that apply to atomic and subatomic particles, among which are:

- superposition: by which a particle can be in two or more places or states at once (i.e., Zen Master Dōgen is both alive and dead?)
- entanglement: by which two particles can coordinate their properties across space and time and behave like a single system (i.e., a Zen master and his disciple; a character and her narrator; old Jiko and Nao and Oliver and me?)
- the measurement problem: by which the act of measuring or observation alters what is being observed (i.e., the collapse of a wave function; the telling of a dream?)

If Zen Master Dōgen had been a physicist, I think he might have liked quantum mechanics. He would have naturally grasped the all-inclusive nature of superposition and intuited the interconnectedness of entanglement. As a contemplative who was also a man of action, he would have been intrigued by the notion that attention might have the power to alter reality, while at the same time understanding that human

440

consciousness is neither more nor less than the clouds and water, or the hundreds of grasses. He would have appreciated the unbounded nature of not knowing.

# *Appendix D: Temple Names*

After doing some research on Japanese temple nomenclature, I realized that *Jigenji* was the name of the temple, and *Hiyuzan* was the so-called mountain name, or *sangō* (山号). According to early Chinese tradition, Zen masters would retreat to a distant mountaintop, far away from the distractions of towns and urban centers, where they would build a solitary meditation hut and devote themselves to practice. As word of their spiritual accomplishments spread, disciples would climb the mountain to seek them out, and before long communities sprang up, roads were built, and vast temple complexes were constructed, bearing the name of the formerly remote mountain. (How did word spread? How did these viral networks and reputation economies develop before the Internet?)

When Zen came to Japan, the custom of giving a mountain name to a temple persisted, regardless of whether there was a mountain beneath it or not. As a result, even temples built on the coastal plains of metropolitan Tokyo bear mountain names, and no one seems to mind.

There are several possible kanji for the temple name *Jigenji*, but the most likely combination is 慈眼時, consisting of the characters for *merciful*, *eyeball*, and *temple*. The character for *gen*, or eyeball, is the same as the one in Master Dōgen's *Shōbōgenzō, The Treasury of the True Dharma Eye*.

The most probable kanji for *Hiyuzan* seems to be 秘湯山 (Hidden Hot Spring Mountain); however, when I first read the name, the combination of characters that popped to my mind was 比喩山, which can be translated as Mount Metaphor. I couldn't help but think of René Daumal's brilliant work *Mount Analogue: A Novel of Symbolically Authentic*

*Non-Euclidean Adventures in Mountain Climbing.* The object of Daumal's quest is a unique and geographically real mountain, whose summit is inaccessible but whose base is accessible. "The door," he writes, "to the invisible must be visible." Mount Analogue is where *peradam* can be found, an extraordinary and unknown crystalline object that can be seen only by those who seek it.

All of this might seem like a digression and quite beside the point, but when old Jiko's temple proved so elusive, thinking of Mount Analogue gave me an enormous sense of hope.

# Appendix E: Schrödinger's Cat

The experiment goes like this:

A cat is put into a sealed steel box. With him in the box is a diabolical mechanism: a glass flask of hydrocyanic acid, a small hammer aimed at the flask, and a trigger that will either cause the hammer to release, or not. The factor that controls the release is the behavior of a small bit of radioactive material being monitored by a Geiger counter. If within, say, an hour, one of the atoms in the radioactive substance decays, the Geiger counter will detect it and trigger the hammer to shatter the flask, releasing the acid, and the cat will die. However, there is an equal probability that no atom will decay within that hour, in which case the trigger will hold and the cat will live.

It seems simple enough; however, the point of this thought experiment is not to torture the cat. The point is not to kill it, or save it, or even to calculate the probability of its succumbing to either fate. The point is to illustrate the perplexing paradox of the so-called measurement problem in quantum mechanics: what happens to entangled particles in a quantum system when they are observed and measured.

The cat and the atom represent two entangled particles.[164] Entangled means that they share certain characteristics or behaviors, in this case their fate within the box: *decayed atom = dead cat*; and *undecayed atom = live cat*. The two behave as one. Together in their box, the entangled

---

164. Erwin Schrödinger came up with the term *entanglement* in the course of devising his thought experiment. Einstein later called entanglement "spooky action at a distance."

atom/cat are part of a quantum system that is being measured by an observer, who, let's say, is you.

Now, hold that thought for a moment, because in order to proceed, we need to understand two other fundamental quantum phenomena: *superposition* and *the measurement problem*.

Imagine that instead of an entangled atom/cat in the box, you were measuring a single electron. Before you open the box to observe it, that electron exists as a *wave function,* which is an array of itself in all of the places it might possibly be in the box. This quantum phenomenon is called *superposition*: that a particle can be in all of its possible states at once. (Think of a superimposed photograph of a pacing tiger in a pen, taken with a shutter that exposed the film every couple of seconds. In the superimposed photograph, the tiger would appear to be a blur or smear. In a microscopic quantum universe, governed by the principle of superposition, the tiger *is* the smear.)

The measurement problem arises the moment you open the box to observe the particle. When you do, the wave function appears to collapse into a single state, fixed in time and space. (To use the tiger analogy, the smeared tiger becomes a singular beast again.)

Okay, now, let's go back to the entangled cat and radioactive atom. The state we're measuring here is not the location of a tiger, but rather the entanglement of atom/cat. Instead of the possible positions of the tiger in the cage, we're measuring degrees of the cat's aliveness, its existential status, as it were.

We know that on account of the measurement problem, the moment you open the box to measure the cat's state, you will find the cat either dead or alive. Fifty percent of the time the cat will be alive. The other 50 percent of the time, the cat will be dead. Whichever it is, the cat's state is singular and fixed in time and space.

However, *before* you open the box to measure it, the cat's state must be smeared and multiple, like the blurred tiger. Due to the quantum principles of entanglement and superposition, until you observe it, the cat must be both dead and alive, *at the same time*.

Of course, this conclusion is absurd, which was exactly Schrödinger's point. But the questions his thought experiment poses are interesting: At what point in time does a quantum system stop being a superposition of all possible states and become a singular, either/or state instead?

And, by extension, does the existence of a singular cat, either dead or alive, require an external observer, i.e., you? And if not you, then who? Can the cat be an observer of itself? And without an external observer, do we all just exist in an array of all possible states at once?

There have been many attempts to interpret this paradox. The Copenhagen interpretation, formulated by Niels Bohr and Werner Heisenberg in 1927, supported the theory of wave function collapse, positing that at the point when observation occurs, the superposed quantum system undergoes a collapse from the many into the one, and that this collapse *must* happen because the reality of the macroscopic world demands it.[165] The problem is that nobody has been able to come up with the math to support this.

The many-worlds interpretation, proposed by the American physicist Hugh Everett in 1957, challenges this theory of wave function collapse, positing instead that the superposed quantum system persists and branches.

At every juncture—in every Zen moment when possibilities arise—a schism occurs, worlds branch, and multiplicity ensues.

Every instance of *either/or* is replaced by an *and*. And an *and*, and an *and*, and an *and*, and another *and* . . . adding up to an infinitely all-inclusive, and yet mutually unknowable, web of many worlds.

The astrophysicist Adam Frank told me that what's important to remember about quantum mechanics is that while there are many interpretations, including the Copenhagen and many-worlds hypotheses,

---

165. Schrödinger proposed his enigmatic cat as a challenge to this idea of observer-induced collapse. He maintained that physicists hung on to the notion of collapse because without it, all possibilities, physical and otherwise, would begin to propagate, and before long, "we should find our surroundings rapidly turning into a quagmire, or sort of featureless jelly or plasma, all contours becoming blurred, we ourselves probably becoming jellyfish."

quantum mechanics itself is a calculus. It's a machine for predicting experimental results. It's a finger, pointing at the moon.

Professor Frank was refering to an old Zen koan about the Sixth Patriarch of Zen, who was illiterate. When asked how he could understand the truth of the Buddhist texts if he couldn't read the words, the Sixth Patriarch raised his arm and pointed to the moon. Truth is like the moon in the sky. Words are like a finger. A finger can point to the moon's location, but it is not the moon. To see the moon, you must look past the finger. To look for the truth in books, the Sixth Patriarch was saying, is like mistaking the finger for the moon. The moon and the finger are not the same thing.

"Not same," old Jiko would have said. "Not different, either."

# Appendix F: Hugh Everett

Hugh Everett published what came to be called his "many worlds" interpretation of quantum mechanics in 1957, in *Reviews of Modern Physics*, when he was twenty-seven years old. It was his doctoral thesis at Princeton. It was not well received. The leading physicists of his day called him crazy. They called him stupid. Everett, disheartened, gave up on quantum physics and went into weapons development. He worked for the Pentagon's Weapons System Evaluation Group. He wrote a paper on military game theory, entitled "Recursive Games," which is a classic in the field. He wrote war games software that would simulate nuclear war, and he was involved in the Cuban Missile Crisis. He advised the White House on nuclear warfare development and strategy during the Cold War, and he wrote the original software for targeting cities and civilian population centers with atomic weapons, should the nuclear Cold War turn hot. He'd already written the mathematical proof of his many-worlds interpretation, and he believed that anything he could imagine would occur, or already had. It's not surprising that he drank heavily.

His family life was a mess. He had a remote and troubled relationship with his kids. His daughter, Liz, who suffered from manic depression and addiction, tried to commit suicide by taking sleeping pills. Her brother, Mark, found her on the bathroom floor and rushed her to the hospital, where the doctors were able to restart her heart. When Mark returned home from the hospital, Everett looked up from his *Newsweek* and remarked, "I didn't know she was so sad."

Two months later, Everett himself died of a heart attack at the age of fifty-one. In this world, he was dead, but he believed that in many worlds he was immortal. His wife kept his cremated remains in a filing cabinet in their dining room before eventually complying with his wish and throwing them in the garbage. Mark went on to have a successful career as a rock musician, but Liz's life spiraled downward. When she finally succeeded in killing herself with an overdose of sleeping pills in 1996, she wrote a suicide note that said:

> Please burn me and DON'T FILE ME ☺. Please sprinkle me in some nice body of water . . . or the garbage, maybe that way I'll end up in the correct parallel universe to meet up w/ Daddy.

# Bibliography

Arai, Paula Kane Robinson. *Women Living Zen: Japanese Soto Buddhist Nuns.* Oxford: Oxford University Press, 1999.

Bardsley, Jan. *The Bluestockings of Japan: New Woman Essays and Fiction from Seitō, 1911–16.* Ann Arbor: Michigan Monograph Series in Japanese Studies, Number 60. Center for Japanese Studies, University of Michigan, 2007.

Byrne, Peter. *The Many Worlds of Hugh Everett III: Multiple Universes, Mutual Assured Destruction, and the Meltdown of a Nuclear Family.* Oxford: Oxford University Press, 2010.

Daumal, René. *Mount Analogue: A Novel of Symbolically Authentic Non-Euclidean Adventures in Mountain Climbing.* Boston: Shambhala Publications, 1992.

Dōgen, Eihei. *Shōbōgenzō.* Translated by Gudo Wafu Nishijima and Chodo Cross. Berkeley: Numata Center for Buddhist Translation and Research, dBET PDF Version, 2008.

———. *Treasury of the True Dharma Eye: Zen Master Dogen's Shobo Genzo.* Edited by Kazuaki Tanahashi. Translated by Kazuaki Tanahashi, Peter Levett, and others. Boston: Shambhala Publications, 2011.

Ebbesmeyer, Curtis, and Eric Scigliano. *Flotsametrics and the Floating Word: How One Man's Obsession with Runaway Sneakers and Rubber Ducks Revolutionized Ocean Science.* New York: Smithsonian Books/HarperCollins, 2009.

Fowler, Edward. *The Rhetoric of Confession: Shishōsetsu in Early Twentieth-Century Japanese Fiction.* Berkeley and Los Angeles: University of California Press, 1988.

Galchen, Rivka. "Dream Machine: The mind-expanding world of quantum computing." *The New Yorker* May 2, 2011: 34–43.

Hane, Mikiso, ed. *Reflections on the Way to the Gallows*. Translated by Mikiso Hane. Berkeley and Los Angeles: University of California Press, 1988.

Hirastuka Raichō. *In the Beginning, Woman Was the Sun*. Translated by Teruko Craig. New York: Columbia University Press, 2006.

Hohn, Donovan. *Moby-Duck: The True Story of 28,800 Bath Toys Lost at Sea and of the Beachcombers, Oceanographers, Environmentalits, and Fools, Including the Author, Who Went in Search of Them*. New York: Viking, 2011.

Kundera, Milan. *The Book of Laughter and Forgetting*. Translated by Michael Henry Heim. New York: Alfred A. Knopf, 1980.

Leighton, Dan. *Visions of Awakening Time and Space: Dōgen and the Lotus Sutra*. Oxford: Oxford University Press, 2007.

Levy, David M. *Scrolling Forward: Making Sense of Documents in the Digital Age*. New York: Arcade Publishing, 2001.

Noma, Hiroshi. *Zone of Emptiness*. Cleveland and New York: World Publishing Company, 1956.

Ohnuki-Tierney, Emiko. *Kamikaze Diaries: Reflections of Japanese Student Soldiers*. Chicago: University of Chicago Press, 2006.

———. *Kamikaze, Cherry Blossoms, and Nationalisms: The Militarization of Aesthetics in Japanese History*. Chicago: University of Chicago Press, 2002.

Proust, Marcel. *In Search of Lost Time*. Translated by C. K. Scott-Moncrieff, Terence Kilmartin, and Andreas Mayor. London and New York: Penguin Books, 1989. Copyright: Editions Gallimard, 1954. Translation copyright: Chatto & Windus and Random House, 1981. Based on the French "La Pléiade" text (1954).

———. *Swann's Way*. Translated by Lydia Davis. New York: Viking, 2003.

Suzuki, Tomi. *Narrating the Self: Fictions of Japanese Modernity*. Stanford: Stanford University Press, 1996.

Yamanouchi, Midori, and Joseph L. Quinn, trans. *Listen to the Voices*

453

*from the Sea: Writings of the Fallen Japanese Soldiers*. Compiled by the Japan Memorial Society for the Students Killed in the War— Wadatsumi Society. Scranton: University of Scranton Press, 2000. Originally published as *Shinpan Kike Wadatsumi no Koe* (Tokyo: Iwanami Shoten, 1995).

# *Acknowledgments*

First, I offer thanks to my teachers: to my Zen teacher, Norman Fischer, whose wise words entered my ears, excited my mind, and spilled back out, willy-nilly, onto these pages; to Teah Strozer and Paula Arai, who guided me on matters pertaining to Zen practice and custom; to the kind scientists Adam Frank, Bill Moninger, and Tom White, who answered my questions about quantum physics and never once laughed; to Tim King, for his beautiful French translations, and Taku Nishimae, for his nuanced Japanese; to Karen Joy Fowler, who gave me courage at a critical moment in time; to John Dower, who many years ago encouraged me to write about the kamikaze diaries; and to Missy Cummings, for sharing her insights into creating moral buffers in human/computer interface design over high tea at the Empress Hotel . . . I thank you all for your generosity, expertise, and guidance, while hastening to add that any mistakes and omissions in this book are entirely my own.

Second, I offer thanks to my sangha of readers and friends: to Tim Burnett, Paul Cirone, Harry Hantel, Shannon Jonasson, Kate McCandless, Olwyn Morinski, Monica Nawrocki, Michael Newton, Rahna Reiko Rizzuto, Greg Snyder, Linda Solomon, Susan Squier, and Marina Zurkow, for taking precious time from their busy lives to read early drafts and offer priceless feedback; to Larry Lane, for sage counsel on matters of dharma and plot; to David Palumbo-Liu, John Stauber and Laura Berger, and to the Friends of the Pleistocene, who generously agreed to let me put them in this fictional world; and to Kwee Downey, who once said she'd like to read a novel with Zen in it, and then suggested I might write one.

Third, I offer thanks to the institutions and temples of learning that have supported me: to the Canada Council for the Arts, for professional writers' grants in 2009 and 2011, which enabled me to live and write; to the Massachusetts Institute of Technology and to Stanford University, for fellowships that supported research and conversations that inspired key elements of this story; and to beloved Hedgebrook, for the precious gift of solitude, sisterhood, and *time*.

Fourth, I offer my deepest thanks to my treasured publishing sangha: to Molly Friedrich, Lucy Carson, and Molly Schulman, who represent me with such wit, grace, and enthusiasm; to my wise and wonderful benefactors at Viking Penguin, Susan Petersen Kennedy, Clare Ferraro, and Paul Slovak, for their guidance and unflagging support over the years, and also to Beena Kamlani, Paul Buckley, Francesca Belanger, and the many dedicated others who have worked so hard to make this book a thing of beauty; to Jamie Byng, Ailah Ahmed, and all my new friends at Canongate, U.K., and around the world; and, most of all, my eternal gratitude to Carole DeSanti, my dear friend, editor, colleague, classmate, and the reader who calls me into being on the page.

Fifth, I offer thanks to the island and the islanders, for imbuing my fictional fantastical isle with your very real beauty, tenacity, humor, expertise, and willingness to help.

And finally, I offer my abiding thanks to Oliver, for his love and companionship—thank you for your generous collaboration on this book and for being my partner and my inspiration in this and all our many worlds.

I bow to you all.